Seat 7a

Also by Sebastian Fitzek

The Package
Passenger 23

SEBASTIAN
FITZEK

Seat 7a

translated from the German by

Steve Anderson

HEAD
of ZEUS

First published in Germany as *Flugangst 7A* in 2017 by Droemer Knaur
First published in the UK in 2021 by Head of Zeus Ltd

Flugangst 7A copyright © 2017 Verlagsgruppe Droemer Knaur
GmbH & Co. KG, Munich, Germany
Translation © 2021 Steve Anderson

9 7 5 3 1 2 4 6 8

A catalogue record for this book is available from
the British Library.

ISBN (HB): 9781838935818
ISBN (XTPB): 9781838935825
ISBN (E): 9781838934545

Typeset by Divaddict Publishing Solutions Ltd

Printed and bound in Great Britain by
CPI Group (UK) Ltd, Croydon CRO 4YY

Head of Zeus Ltd
First Floor East
5–8 Hardwick Street
London ECIR 4RG

WWW.HEADOFZEUS.COM

For Manuela
Seventeen years long distance and no end in sight.
What luck!

EU Recommends Mental Health Checks for Pilots
Drug testing and psychological support: an EU working
group calls for more stringent monitoring of pilots after
the Germanwings airliner crash.
Die Zeit
17 July 2015

Prologue

'When can we interrogate the suspect?'

Dr Martin Roth, on his way to the intensive care unit of the Park Clinic, turned to the homicide detective who'd actually had the gall to ask him such a ridiculous question.

'Interrogate?'

'Yes. When's he going to wake up?' The squat policeman downed the last drop of coffee he'd got from the machine, suppressed a burp and jutted out his chin defiantly. 'We've got two corpses and one severely injured man whose eyes will be bleeding for the rest of his life. That scumbag needs a good talking to.'

'Talking to... hmm.'

The head physician, his face smooth and far too youthful-looking for his age, scratched at his balding hairline that was receding more by the year. He didn't know what was worse: the policeman's cheap Bruce Willis imitation or his flagrant stupidity.

'You were there when they brought the man in, right?'

'Of course I was.'

'Didn't anything occur to you?'

'He's half dead, I know, I know.' The detective pointed

to the frosted-glass door behind Roth, which separated the hospital corridor from the intensive care wing. 'But I'm sure your medicine men in there can patch the bastard up using their bag of tricks. And the moment he wakes up, I'd like a few answers.'

Roth took a deep breath, counted silently down from three and, when he'd reached zero, said, 'All right, I'll give you a few answers, Detective…?'

'Hirsch. Chief Detective Hirsch.'

'It's still far too early for a reliable diagnosis, but we strongly suspect that the patient is suffering from locked-in syndrome. In layman's terms this means that his brain is no longer in contact with the rest of his body. He's locked inside himself. He can't talk, can't see anything and can't communicate with us.'

'How long's he going to be like this?'

'Thirty-six hours at most, I'd say.'

The policeman rolled his eyes. 'So I won't be able to interrogate him till then?'

'*Then*,' Roth said, 'he'll be dead.'

A click sounded behind the doctor and the automatic double doors with frosted panes swung open.

'Herr Dr Roth, come quickly… The patient…'

Roth turned to his assistant doctor, who'd come rushing from intensive care, her face bright red.

'What about him?'

'He's blinking!'

Thank God!

'He is? That's fantastic,' he said in delight, nodding goodbye to the detective.

'He's *blinking*?' Hirsch stared at the head physician as

if Roth was the sort of man pleased to find chewing gum stuck to the sole of his shoe. 'You call *that* good news?'

'The best we can expect,' Roth replied, then added as he set off to see the dying man, 'and maybe the only chance we have of finding those missing people.'

Even though he harboured little hope in this regard.

1

'There are two types of mistakes. Those that make your life worse. And those that end it.'

Nele could hear the lunatic's words.

Mumbled, muffled. Panting.

She couldn't see his lips. The man was wearing a training mask over his face. A black, elastic neoprene skin with a white resistance valve over the mouth. Athletes used them to improve performance. And psychopaths to heighten pleasure.

'I'm not really up for this right now,' Nele said out loud as if that would change anything. And when the masked man opened up the bolt cutters, she changed the channel.

The Golden Autumn of Folk Music.

Out of the frying pan into the fire. Nothing but crap on the tube, which was hardly a surprise. Who actually chose to sit in front of the TV before the sun had even come up?

Clicking her tongue against her front teeth with

impatience, Nele kept zapping until she came to a shopping channel.

Ronny's Household Aids.

New kitchen gadgets, presented by a man made-up to the eyeballs: vermillion skin, cyan lips and titanium-white teeth. Right now he was screaming to his customers that there were only 223 of the super-duper water carbonators left. Nele really could have used one of those in the last few months. Then she wouldn't have had to heave the deposit bottles up the stairs on her own. Fourth floor, rear courtyard, Hansastrasse Weissensee. Forty-eight shiny steps. She counted them every day.

Better than a water carbonator, of course, would have been a strong man. Especially now in her 'condition' – a full forty pounds heavier than nine months ago.

But she'd already kicked out the man responsible.

'*Whose is it?*' David had asked as soon as she brought up the test result. Not exactly the words you wanted to hear when you came back from the gynaecologist seeking refuge from your raging hormones.

'*I never touched you without a condom. You think I'm suicidal? Fuck, now I'll have to go get tested too.*'

A resounding slap finished off the relationship. Only it wasn't her who'd struck out in anger, but him. Nele's head had jerked to the side and she'd lost her balance, toppling to the floor along with her CD tower and giving her boyfriend an easy target.

'Have you gone nuts?' he'd asked as he kicked her.

Again and again, in the back, in the head and of course in the tummy, which she'd desperately tried to protect with her elbows, arms and hands.

Successfully. David hadn't achieved his goal – the embryo wasn't harmed.

'You're not foisting a sick child on me that I'll have to support for the rest of my life,' he'd screamed, but then he'd left her alone. 'I'll make sure of that.'

Nele felt the spot on her cheekbone where the tip of David's shoe had narrowly missed her eye and which still throbbed whenever she thought back to the day they separated.

It wasn't the first time her boyfriend had lost his temper, but it was the first time he'd laid a finger on her.

David was the proverbial wolf in sheep's clothing, who in public radiated an irresistible charm. Even Nele's best friend couldn't imagine that this witty man acting like such a good catch had another, brutal side to him, which he was careful to display only when he was in private and felt sure of himself.

Nele railed at herself for always getting mixed up with these types. There had been violent outbursts in previous relationships too. Maybe her sassy yet childish ways made men think of her as a girl more than a woman, someone to be possessed rather than just desired. And no doubt her illness was also part of the reason that many regarded her as a victim.

Well, David Kupferfeld is history, Nele thought with satisfaction. *And inside me the future's growing.*

Thankfully she'd never given that shithead a key.

After she'd given him the boot, David spent a long time stalking her. He bombarded her with calls and letters urging her to get an abortion, sometimes appealing to reason (*'You barely earn enough as a singer to support yourself!'*),

7

sometimes issuing threats (*'Wouldn't it be a shame if you tripped on the escalator?'*).

He kept at it for three months, finally breaking off contact when the legal time limit for abortion had expired. Apart from the wicker basket she'd found outside her front door on Easter Monday. Decorated like a crib. With a pink pillow, and a fluffy blanket covering the dead rat.

As she recalled the sight, Nele shuddered and stuck both hands between the seat cushions of her sofa even though it was anything but cold in the apartment.

Her best friend had advised her to call the police, but what could they do? They were already powerless against the nutjob who'd been slashing the tyres of every third car out on the street for weeks. They were hardly going to post an officer outside her building just because of a dead rat.

What Nele did do was ask building management to have new locks fitted at her own expense, in case David had got a duplicate key made.

Deep down she was grateful to him. Not for the beatings or the dead rodent, but for his horrific insults.

If he'd stayed quiet, she might have listened to the voice of reason. To the argument that it was far too dangerous to give birth to the baby. On the other hand, thanks to early treatment with antiviral drugs, HIV wasn't even traceable in her blood any more and so the risk of infection was negligible. But it wasn't zero.

Was it right to run the risk? Could she, at the age of twenty-two and with her illness, shoulder this responsibility? A baby? Without financial security? With a mother who'd died far too young and a father who'd fled abroad?

All good reasons to say no to the child and yes to her

singing career. No to swollen feet, fat legs and a ballooning belly and yes to continuing a relationship with an artiste who was as good-looking as he was testy and who earned his living performing magic tricks at children's birthday parties and corporate functions. (Of course, David Kupferfeld wasn't his real name, but a pathetic, Germanised homage to his great role model, David Copperfield.)

She checked the time.

Twenty-five minutes till the taxi arrived.

At this time of the morning she'd be at the hospital in less than thirty minutes. One hour too early. Her admission time was seven o'clock, the operation scheduled for three hours later.

It's not the sensible decision, Nele thought with a smile, stroking her round belly with both hands. *But the right one.*

She felt this not just because her family doctor, Dr Klopstock, had encouraged her to keep the child. Even without treatment, fewer than one in five foetuses would become infected by HIV. With her good blood levels and all the precautionary measures they'd taken with closely monitored treatment, there was a greater probability of the delivery room being struck by lightning during her caesarean section.

Though that's probably happened before too.

Nele hadn't yet come up with a name for the miracle growing inside her. She didn't even know if it was a boy or a girl. But she couldn't care less; she was just looking forward to a new person in her life, whatever sex it might be.

She switched to another channel, and suddenly felt hot again. Hot flashes: here was another thing she couldn't wait to finally end once she got her body back after the birth. As she pulled her hands out from between the cushions, the fingers of her right hand felt something hard.

Huh?

Was it those earrings she hadn't seen forever?

When she leaned to the side and felt for the object caught down there, a short, sharp pain hit her.

'Ow!'

Pulling her index finger back out, Nele was astonished to see the tip bleeding. Her finger throbbed as if she'd been stung by an insect. Shocked, she put it in her mouth and licked off the blood before inspecting the wound. A fine cut, as if made by a sharp knife.

What the hell...?

She stood up to waddle over to the desk, where she kept a first aid box in the top drawer. As she opened it a brochure for vacation homes on Rügen fell out. David had wanted them to go there for Valentine's Day. Back in another age.

The one thing for which Nele still gave her ex credit for was that, unlike most men, David hadn't abandoned her on her first date when she told him that she took a cocktail of drugs three times a day to avoid developing AIDS. Nele was sure he'd believed she wasn't a slut or a junkie. That she hadn't become infected from a needle or indiscriminate sex with a stranger. But from a butterfly.

It looked beautiful and it was always with her. On the inside of her right upper arm.

The rainbow-coloured butterfly was supposed to be a lifelong souvenir of her wonderful holiday in Thailand. Now, whenever she showered, she couldn't help thinking of the filthy, unsterilised needle her tattoo had been inked with, and how harshly God sometimes punished youthful recklessness. He was more displeased, apparently, with tipsy teenagers visiting sketchy tattoo parlours in the bar district of Phuket than with ISIS thugs tossing homosexuals from roofs.

Nele wrapped the bandage around her finger and went back to the sofa, where she lifted the cushion.

When she spotted the silvery, shiny object, she groaned in disbelief.

'How the hell did *that* get there?' she whispered. She cautiously pulled the razor blade away from the cushion, stuck there as if by chewing gum. In fact it had been fastened with double-sided tape, *deliberately!*

Horrified, Nele slumped back onto the sofa. The blade in her hand felt as if she'd just plucked it white-hot from a blazing fire. She trembled and the blade slipped out of her hand, falling onto the cushion.

Nele checked the time again, her heart now racing, and calculated how long till the taxi came.

Another fifteen minutes!

She didn't want to spend another fifteen seconds alone in her apartment.

She stared at the razor blade, which changed colour as different images flickered across her TV screen.

How the fuck did that get down my sofa? Positioned with precision, as if somebody wanted her to cut her finger.

And what the hell was written on it?

The blade was smeared with her blood but had flipped onto the other side as it landed and now she could make out some very fine handwriting, as if scrawled on with the thinnest of marker pens.

Nele reluctantly picked up the blade again and stroked the letters with her throbbing index finger.

Your blood kills!

Her lips moved subconsciously and mechanically, like a schoolchild reading for the first time.

My blood kills?

She screamed.

Not because she'd realised that David must have got into her apartment somehow.

But because something tore inside her. She felt as if she'd been stung by a scorpion's tail. In her most delicate spot. It felt like someone had ripped the fibres of thin and sensitive skin with their bare hands.

The brief, but intense pain stopped and she felt wet.

Then came the fear.

It spread like the stain between her legs. The dark sofa cover became darker and... *it's not stopping.*

That was her first thought, which she repeated over and over again.

It's not stopping.

My water broke and I'm leaking.

Her second thought was even worse, because there was every reason to believe it.

Too early.

The baby was coming too early.

2

Is it going to survive? Can it survive something like this?

She'd forgotten the razor blade; it was no longer relevant. In her panic Nele could only formulate a single thought, a question: *But didn't my doctor tell me weeks ago that the baby was capable of living from that point on?*

The due date was fourteen days from now.

With a C-section the baby's risk of infection was even lower, which was why they'd moved up the date of the operation. To avoid precisely what was happening now: Nele going into natural labour.

Can they operate once your water has broken?

Nele didn't know. She just kept hoping that her munchkin (as she called the thing inside her) would enter the world healthy.

Christ, when's the taxi coming?

Eight minutes.

She'd need every one of those.

Nele stood and felt all the liquid running out of her.

Is this going to harm the child? A horrific image flashed through her mind: the baby inside her womb gasping in vain for air, like a fish out of water.

She teetered to the door of her apartment and grabbed her maternity bag sitting there packed and ready.

Changes of clothes, loose-fitting trousers, nighties, stockings, toothbrush and cosmetics. Plus, of course, the pouch with the antiviral medicines. She'd even packed some size 1 diapers, though they'd surely have those in the hospital. But Juliana, her midwife, had said you could never be over-prepared since nothing ever turned out as expected. Just like now.

My God.

Fear.

She opened the door.

Nele had never felt so worried for someone other than herself. And never felt so alone.

Without the father. Without her best friend, who was on tour with a band in Finland.

Out in the hallway, she paused briefly.

Should she get changed? Her wet tracksuit bottoms felt like cold flannel between her legs. She should've checked the colour of her amniotic fluid. If it was green she shouldn't be moving around, *or was it yellow?*

But if it was the wrong colour and she had moved, would she now be making it worse by going back and putting on dry clothes? *Or wouldn't she?*

Nele pulled her door shut. As she made her way down the stairs she held on tight to the banister, relieved not to see anyone so early in the morning.

Why did she feel ashamed? Giving birth was the most natural thing in the world. But in her experience, very few people sought any direct involvement in the process. And she didn't want any hypocritical or embarrassed offers of help from neighbours who she'd barely exchanged a word with otherwise.

Once downstairs Nele opened the front door and stepped out into the autumn air that smelled of leaves and earth. It must have just stopped raining.

The pavement on the broad Hansastrasse gleamed in the bright light of the streetlamps. A puddle had formed by the kerb and in it – thank God – the taxi was already waiting. Four minutes before the scheduled time. But not a second too early.

The driver, who was leaning against his Mercedes, buried in a book, tossed the thick volume through the open window onto the passenger seat and ran a hand through his dark, shoulder-length hair. Once he realised that something wasn't quite right with the way she was shuffling along, he hurried over to her. He probably thought she was injured or the bag so heavy that she was forced to hunch forward. But maybe he was just being polite.

'Morning,' he said tersely, and took her bag. 'Airport?'

He had a faint Berlin accent and his breath smelled of coffee. His V-neck sweater was a size too big, as were his cords that threatened to slide off his narrow hips with each step. His half-open Birkenstock sandals and his Steve Jobs glasses completed the cliché of the sociology student moonlighting as a cab driver.

'No. The Virchow Clinic. It's in Wedding.'

Eyeing her belly, he gave a knowing smile.

'Sure. No problem.'

He opened the door for her. If he'd noticed her soaked

trousers he was too polite to mention it. Nele imagined he'd seen far more disgusting things on his night-time tours and probably fitted his rear seats with a plastic cover.

'Well, here we go.'

Nele climbed into the car, worried that she'd forgotten something important even though she was clutching her bag containing her phone, charger and purse.

My dad!

As the car headed off she calculated the time difference and decided on a text message. Not that she was afraid of calling her father in Buenos Aires at this time of day. But she didn't want him to hear the anxiety in her voice.

Nele wondered whether she should tell him that her water had broken, but what would be the point of worrying him unnecessarily? Besides, it was none of his business. He was her father, not her close friend. The reasons for having him come to Germany were purely practical rather than emotional.

He'd abandoned Mom. Now he could make up for that by supporting Nele with her munchkin, even if his fatherly assistance would be limited to running errands, shopping and helping out financially. She certainly wouldn't trust him to look after the baby. After all, she hadn't wanted to see him before the birth and she'd virtually ordered him to stay put until the day of her operation at the earliest.

'It's starting!' she tapped into her phone and sent the message. Short and sweet. She knew he'd be hurt by the lack of a greeting. And she felt slightly ashamed by her cold manner. But she only had to recall her mother's eyes – open, empty, virtually engraved with the fear of that death she'd had to suffer all on her own – and she knew she'd been far too nice to him already. He should count himself lucky that she'd listened to her therapist and re-established contact with him after all these years.

Looking towards the front, Nele discovered the green tome that the young man had been leafing through, now wedged between the handbrake and the driver's seat.

Pschyrembel Clinical Dictionary.

Not a sociology student, but a medical one.

Then she noticed: 'Hey! You forgot to start the meter.'

'What? Oh… crap!'

When they sat at a red light, the student gave his meter a good tap. It seemed to be broken.

'That's the third time now…' he moaned.

A motorbike approached from behind.

When it stopped right beside her window, Nele turned to the side. The driver was wearing a mirrored helmet, which is why she only saw herself when he lowered his head to peer in. His bike was gurgling like a seething lava lake.

Confused and apprehensive, Nele faced forwards again.

'It's green!' she squeaked.

Looking up from his meter, the student apologised.

Nele's eyes wandered to the side again.

Rather than taking off, the motorbike rider tapped his helmet as if in greeting, and Nele could imagine the diabolical smile this man must be wearing beneath his helmet.

David, Nele thought.

'The ride's on me.'

'I'm sorry?'

The student winked at her in the rear-view mirror and put the car into gear. 'Your lucky day. The meter's had it; you won't have to pay a penny, Nele.'

The driver's last word sliced through the very fabric of her sanity. 'How…?'

How does he know my name?

Nele realised that they were coasting slowly into a driveway, a right turn just after the lights.

'Where are we going?'

She saw a frayed wire fence, beyond which two industrial brick chimneys towered into the dark sky like stiff fingers.

The taxi rolled across bumps into the entrance of a long-abandoned factory complex. Nele grabbed the door and shook the handle.

'Stop! I want to get out.'

The driver turned around and stared at her swollen breasts.

'Don't worry,' he said with a smile that looked so incongruously shy and harmless.

The five words that followed unnerved Nele more than anything she'd heard in her life: 'I just want your milk.'

An inner fist unleashed all its fury on the most sensitive spot in her womb.

'Aaagh!' she screamed at the student, who eyed her in the rear-view mirror as the headlights brushed across a rusty sign.

To the Milking Parlour, Nele read.

Then her contractions reached their first peak.

3

Mats
Buenos Aires
11:31 p.m. local time

It's starting!

Mats Krüger put his briefcase down in the aisle and took out his phone again to take a look at the text his daughter had sent as if a secret message were hidden in the two words, which he hadn't decrypted on the first reading.

Wiping the sweat from his brow with a handkerchief, he wondered why there was no movement after row 14. They were already delayed by half an hour. White light from the ceiling flooded the interior of the brand-new aircraft with its lilac-upholstered seats, and Mats could smell air freshener and carpet cleaner. The high-pitched hum of the auxiliary power in his ears, he stood in the right-hand aisle of the gargantuan aircraft with his back to the cockpit. Twenty-four metres tall, taller than an eight-story office building – or 'five giraffes', as a newspaper once commented.

The journalist with a love for animal comparisons had also calculated that the plane was as long as two blue whales.

It's starting!

The text that Mats received four minutes prior to boarding had both excited and troubled him.

He was looking forward to seeing his first grandchild, to maybe even being permitted to hold it in his arms. At the same time he was afraid of encountering in Nele's eyes the same coldness with which she composed her brusque messages.

Only a fool would entertain the hope that she'd forgive him. And although Mats felt old, he was certainly no fool. He knew what he'd destroyed when he'd abandoned her mother, and he was still unsure why Nele had asked him to come back to Germany for the birth of her first child. Was she reaching out for a cautious new beginning? Or to give him a slap?

'Finally,' muttered the man in front of him with the rucksack, and the line started moving again.

Finally?

Mats would've preferred to wait a while longer in the aisle, as long as the 550-ton colossus remained on the ground. Four years ago he'd emigrated to Argentina on a freighter, to settle in Buenos Aires as a psychiatrist. He was terrified of flying, and had even attended an aviophobia seminar, but that hadn't helped much. He himself had often used phrases such as *'Accept your fear; don't try to fight it'* or *'Try to take longer breathing in than breathing out'* on his phobia patients and knew that such advice helped many of them. But it didn't in the slightest alter his view that human beings were not made to be propelled ten thousand metres into the troposphere in an over-pressurised metal tube with wings. *Homo erectus* simply didn't belong in this hostile environment; with outside temperatures at negative fifty-five degrees, the smallest error could lead to disaster.

Mats was less worried by any technical details, however, than by the principal cause of error responsible for most fatalities, not just in the air, but on the ground and in the water too: mankind. And there was scarcely another flight on which mankind would have so many opportunities to showcase his imperfections as the one Mats was about to make.

Mats hadn't just chosen the largest passenger aeroplane currently in operation for his first flight in over twenty years, his was also one of the longest non-stop flights in civilian air travel. It would take the flying colossus a little over thirteen hours to complete the 11,987 kilometres from Buenos Aires to Berlin. Not counting the hour it took for the 608 passengers to occupy their seats in the double-decker. Mats would've much rather travelled by ship again – he had, after all, known about Nele's pregnancy for months – but at this time of year there were no convenient transatlantic connections.

It's starting!

Mats was shuffling along with his briefcase past an on-board kitchen smelling of coffee, situated on the same level as the central emergency exits directly above the wings, when a distraught-sounding woman stopped him in his tracks.

'*You're not understanding me.*'

Key words for a psychiatrist.

Turning to his left, Mats peered into the kitchen and saw a tall male flight attendant with a dark-blue uniform that looked tailor-made. He was standing beside the coffee machine talking to a young, red-haired woman holding a baby in her arms.

Outside it was dry and twenty-eight degrees, but the

steward's freshly gelled blond hair looked as if it had just escaped a stormy drizzle. Only upon closer examination was it clear that he must've spent considerable time in front of the mirror to make his hairstyle look so skilfully unstyled.

'I'm really sorry.'

The steward managed to pull off the feat of nodding sympathetically while stealing a glance at his chunky wristwatch while the mother dexterously balanced her cooing baby on her hip.

'My online booking was for a family seat,' the woman said wearily. She had her back to Mats, but from her wavering voice he guessed that she was on the verge of tears.

'I think this old guy in front of me has fallen asleep,' Mats heard a teenager grumble behind him. Now he was the one blocking the aisle, but he was riveted by the emotional conflict playing out in the on-board kitchen so he stepped aside to allow the other passengers through.

'Honestly, I really do understand your problem,' the steward attempted to comfort the mother. His firm poise exuded experience and competence; his voice betrayed impatience. 'But there's nothing I can do. Unfortunately they gave us the wrong baby beds in Chile. They don't fit in the brackets in the partition in front of your seat.'

'So now I've got to sit with my baby on my lap for thirteen hours?'

Rocking her hips to keep the gurgling baby quiet, she said, 'Suza suffers from colic. I'm really worried that if she can't lie down she'll scream all night long.'

Another sympathetic nod, another glance at the watch. 'I wish things were different, ma'am, but I'm afraid I can't help you.'

'Maybe I can,' Mats heard himself say, immediately annoyed at himself for having opened his mouth.

Two astonished pairs of eyes turned to him.

'I'm sorry, what did you just say?' asked the mother.

The light in the on-board kitchen that Mats believed was officially called the 'galley' was harsh and unfriendly, emphasising every blemish and wrinkle in the young woman's face. Her eyes were as red as her hair and she looked as tired as he felt. She was wearing subtle lipstick that matched her freckles, and both her jewellery and clothes suggested that, despite the helpless little thing on her hip, she still wanted to be regarded as a woman, not just as a mother.

'You can have my seat.'

His first German words in a long time tumbled awkwardly from his mouth, and no sooner had they been uttered than Mats wished they'd stuck in his throat.

'Your seat?' the mother asked.

His trained eye detected a minuscule contraction of the musculus orbicularis oculi. However exhausted the young woman might be, her eye muscles moved involuntarily, indicating to Mats an unmistakable sign of genuine delight.

'I could offer you seat 7A,' Mats said.

'But that's in business class,' the steward said, baffled. The silver badge on his lapel shone with the name 'Valentino'. Mats didn't know whether this was the pretty boy's first name or surname.

Two questions were probably running through Valentino's mind: why would a man voluntarily give up his comfortable bed seat to a complete stranger on such a long flight? And what was he doing down here in cattle class when they were meant to be boarding?

'I'm afraid there won't be a basket for your baby in business class, either,' the steward said.

'But the seats are so wide that Suza could lie beside you comfortably,' Mats interrupted, pointing to the baby. 'According to your ads, the seats turn into flat beds.'

'And you're really willing to swap seats with me?' the mother asked in disbelief.

No, Mats thought, wondering again what on earth had got into him. Agitation heightens fear. It was a perfectly simple formula. He'd resolved to go to his seat, learn the safety instructions on the laminated sheet by heart and, once he'd watched the on-board demonstration, begin his autogenic training exercises to calm himself. Yet now, within the first few minutes of boarding, he was already straying from this plan.

How damn counterproductive could he be?

There was no rational explanation for why he'd given up seat 7A to a mother and baby.

And yet he often behaved like this. With his patients, Dr Mats Krüger was calmness and sobriety personified. In his private life he'd often struggled with the irritants that triggered his emotional ups and downs.

Mats could hardly withdraw his impulsive offer now, so he asked, 'Would you like the seat?'

As a shadow wandered across the mother's face, no expertise in the interpretation of mimic micro-expressions was required this time to read the frustration in her eyes.

'Listen, Herr...?'

'Krüger.'

'Pleased to meet you, Herr Krüger. My name is Salina

Piehl.' She pointed to the wall separating the galley from the passenger cabin, in the vague direction of where her seat must be. 'My seat is in the middle of a loud group of slightly drunk men. Do you really want to do that to yourself?'

Shit.

Had Salina politely declined, he could've given her a friendly nod and moved on. But now that he knew she was doubly in need of help, there was no way he could leave her in the lurch.

'My offer isn't quite as generous as you think. You see, I don't mean to swap with you; I have another seat on board.'

'But... why?' She looked at him wide-eyed.

'I suffer from an acute fear of flying. In preparation for this flight I evaluated all the available statistics relating to aeroplane crashes. According to the data there are seats in which passengers have a greater chance of survival following a disaster than in others.'

Valentino the steward raised an eyebrow. 'And?'

'I booked all of them.'

'Are you being serious?' the mother asked.

'As far as was possible, at least.'

'Oh, that was *you*,' Valentino said. Mats wasn't surprised that he was already known to the cabin crew. His peculiar booking activity must've become quite the topic of conversation.

'How many seats did you book?' the mother said.

'Four. Besides 7A in business class, there's 19F, 23D and 47F.'

The mother's eyes widened even further in amazement. 'Four?' she asked in disbelief.

In actual fact he'd wanted to book seven seats, but the

others were already taken. And Mats had encountered considerable problems reserving multiple seats. Although the airline had an online booking option for overweight passengers who needed two seats, these of course were next to each other, not dotted throughout the aircraft. It had taken him numerous telephone calls and emails to explain to the airline what he wanted and to convince those responsible that he was neither a lunatic nor a terrorist. Finally there were problems with his credit card limit, as his fear of flying had cost him a small fortune. Luckily he earned enough and for the last few years had been leading a fairly frugal life as a single man.

'But why? I mean, couldn't you decide on one seat?' the mother asked.

'I plan on changing seats during the flight,' Mats explained, making the bewilderment complete. 'You see, the relative safety of the individual seats depends on whether we're taking off or landing, or flying over land or water.'

The young mother grabbed her hair nervously. 'So for what part of the flight would you want your business class seat back?'

'I won't.'

She could hardly have looked more perplexed if he'd undressed in front of her and started dancing around naked.

Mats sighed. He'd already been marked out as an oddball, so he stuck to the truth. 'In 2013, scientists wired up a passenger aeroplane and deliberately made it come down on the US–Mexico border. A sort of crash test for civil aviation.'

'And they concluded that seat 7A is the safest?' Salina said.

Valentino had clearly lost his tongue. His jaw dropped even further when Mats gave his answer: 'The way the crash test dummies were deformed revealed that, in the case of an accident, being in the first seven rows would mean almost certain death. Seat 7A was even catapulted from the Boeing – the only one.'

The baby gave a dry cough then started whining quietly as Mats concluded: '7A is the most dangerous seat on an aeroplane. I only booked it out of superstition. Because I wanted to be absolutely sure it was empty on this flight.'

4

A ninety-five per cent chance of survival.

Mats knew the statistic before the seminar leader announced it to the aviophobia group with a self-assured smile.

'Even if an incident does occur, you still have a ninety-five per cent chance of survival in an air accident. Flying on a plane is roughly as dangerous as using an elevator.'

The seminar's Argentinian pilot couldn't have known that he'd come up with the worst comparison imaginable to prepare his most difficult participant for this night flight. Two years ago, in the period apartment building in Recoleta where Mats had his psychiatric practice, the caretaker had been squashed to death by an elevator cabin while undertaking some unofficial maintenance work inside its shaft. That day Mats had gone home earlier than usual, and as he waited in vain on the fourth floor, he'd been the one who'd had to listen to the man's last gurgled screams.

But Mats didn't want to be unfair. With his facts and statistics, the seminar leader had surely been of help to the other participants. Mats, however, was a hopeless case.

He'd prepared himself for this flight for weeks, sifting through all the crash reports, even studying construction plans of numerous aircraft, and now he was throwing all his resolutions overboard right at the start. Offering complete strangers a very carefully selected seat, idling away important time during boarding, and now this happened: in the most important seat of all – the one he'd chosen for take-off – sat a corpse!

The comparison was remarkably apt, looking at the sleeping man occupying seat 47F, his body turned to the window. He wore a straw hat that reminded Mats of the one his wife had bought for him from a street trader on their honeymoon in Spain. The way it was angled over the head made it impossible to see the face. And Mats couldn't detect any movement of the chest beneath the grey woollen blanket the man had wrapped around him.

Either the man was exhausted or he had the enviable ability to maintain a deep sleep even when surrounded by such commotion.

Mats again looked at his boarding pass, verified that he was in the correct row, and mulled over what to do.

Was it a bad omen that he'd given up his business class seat to the young mother?

For a brief moment he'd felt good, like a minor hero, when she shook his hand effusively with tears in her eyes and said, *'Google Salina Piehl. Piehl Photos, I'm a photographer. If you ever need a portrait or family photo or something along those lines, call me. You're a really good person.'*

Well, suddenly his decision didn't feel quite so good. Had he tempted fate by offering Salina the most dangerous seat on the plane? And was his punishment having 47F occupied by this comatose patient who reacted neither to words nor a gentle shake of the shoulder?

What now?

The centre and aisle seats next to the sleeping man were both free, and with any luck would remain so. The 'boarding completed' announcement had just come through.

What the hell, Mats sighed to himself.

Placing his briefcase in the middle, he dropped into the aisle seat.

In truth, he wasn't one hundred per cent sure that his calculations were correct.

As part of his meticulous preparation for the flight, Mats had got hold of the seating plan of LANSA flight 508 – the Lockheed Electra that flew from Lima to Pucallpa on 24 December 1971. After being struck by lightning during a storm, the aeroplane was torn apart and plummeted into the Peruvian rainforest. Everyone on board perished.

Everyone apart from Juliane Koepcke. The Christmas miracle. The seventeen-year-old girl was flung out of the aeroplane. Still strapped into her seat, she fell around three thousand metres. And was the sole survivor of the catastrophe, suffering just a broken collar bone, a gashed arm and a swollen eye.

Her seat? 19F.

The Lockheed was a very different, much smaller type of plane, of course. Basically, however, the tubular shape and seating had barely changed over the decades. Mats had compared the take-off weights, lengths, breadths, heights and volumes of the two aircraft and, if his calculations were correct, Juliane Koepcke's seat corresponded approximately to 47F on this flight.

To this day her survival cannot be explained scientifically.
But if she was able to survive a fall of three kilometres then at the very least it couldn't hurt to sit there in the case of an accident during the one of the most dangerous phases of the flight: the take-off.

'Scared of flying?' he heard a smoky voice say behind him. Looking to his left at the aisle seat in the middle row, Mats saw a man with a friendly smile who'd boarded shortly after him and had just sat down. At first glance he reminded Mats of a famous British actor, but as Mats had a terrible memory for names he couldn't immediately say who the man resembled with his grey-white hair, clipped beard and weather-beaten sailor's face.

'Sorry?' he asked, and the man smiled again with a wink. Around his neck, like a whiplash victim's collar, he had an inflatable violet-coloured neck cushion.

'You do speak German, don't you?'

Mats nodded.

'Excuse me for being so frank, but you should take a look in the mirror. Honestly, you really look like a guy I saw in a documentary once. He wasn't in an aeroplane, but in Texas – in the electric chair.' He laughed and spoke with the unmistakable Berlin dialect that reminded Mats of so many wonderful things: the take-away spot on Mehringdamm where he'd always gone with his fiancée Katharina after a night's dancing; the taxi driver loudly cursing as he got lost driving them to the registry office; the lady caretaker in their first apartment who burst into tears when she first set eyes on Nele in her buggy. But the dialect also reminded him of the pastor of the Peace Church who only spoke *Berlinerisch* when he was annoyed. Such as on the day of Katharina's funeral. Which Mats hadn't attended.

'Rüdiger Trautmann.'

The passenger offered his hand across the aisle, and Mats had to wipe his fingers on his trousers before shaking it.

Fear, as Mats liked to tell his patients, was like a boa constrictor you keep as a pet. You think you've tamed the wild animal and happily place it round your neck. But every so often, without warning, the snake suddenly tightens. Winds its way around your chest, cuts off your breathing, sets your pulse racing. Mats hadn't reached that stage yet.

He could feel the serpentine movements, sense the noose getting tighter, but he wasn't yet on the verge of leaping up, screaming and thrashing about uncontrollably in an attempt to wrench the invisible, softly hissing author of his fear from his body.

'Mats Krüger,' he said to his neighbour, leaving out the 'Doctor'.

Unlike many of colleagues, Mats attached no importance to academic titles; his wasn't even in his passport. Even though his PhD was still cited in the standard works on post-traumatic stress disorders.

'I'm sorry. My girlfriend says I talk too much,' Trautmann said, probably having misinterpreted the nervousness in Mats' eyes. 'But don't worry that I'm going to ramble on at you the whole flight. You see, I'm about to take my twelve-thousand-dollar pill.'

Trautmann shifted awkwardly to one side, to slide a small white pack of pills from the back pocket of his jeans.

'A twelve-thousand-dollar pill?' Mats asked, realising the distraction was helping him. Although the snake hadn't loosened its grip, at least it wasn't pulling tighter while he chatted to this rather odd but friendly passenger.

'Have you got a selfie stick?'

'What?'

'Then I assume you don't. But you must know those horrible stick things that people clamp to their phones and then grin like idiots while they take photos of themselves?'

'Yes, sure.'

'Well, that's me. I invested early on in a company that manufactures these moronic gadgets.'

'Must have been worth it.'

Trautmann laughed. 'You could say that.'

He leaned over the armrest and into the aisle, as if about to whisper something into Mats' ear. But he was talking so loudly that they'd be able to hear him as far away as the next set of emergency exits.

'I could be sitting right up at the front,' he said, pointing to the cockpit. 'First class. Twelve thousand dollars one way, quaffing champagne, eating off china and admiring the firm asses of the trolley dollies from the comfort of my flat bed. But am I a fool?'

'I imagine that's a rhetorical question.'

Trautmann laughed even louder. 'Exactly. I'm not. I swallow these pills instead.'

He'd squeezed a pill from the foil and now rolled it between his thumb and index finger.

Lorazepam, Mats reckoned.

'I take this appalling stuff and five minutes later I'm knocked out, as if my wife has bashed me over the head with a mallet. I'm no longer aware of anything. And I spare the cash for a first class flight. Even selfie sticks couldn't earn me money more quickly or simply. So what do you say? Would you like a twelve-thousand-dollar pill too? I'll let you have it half price.'

He laughed as if he'd cracked a brilliant joke.

'No, thanks,' Mats said, however enticing the offer sounded. He had initially toyed with the idea of taking a benzodiazepine to retreat to the Land of Nod during the flight. But in the event of a disaster it would mean certain death as he wouldn't be able to find his way to the emergency exit in the burning aircraft.

'I'd rather stay awake,' he said.

'Suit yourself.' Trautmann shrugged and slipped on a pair of tassel slippers. Then he washed down the pill with the last gulp from a water bottle he'd got from the vending machine at the gate.

The big man was holding onto both armrests with his powerful forearms as if this were his personal chair, and at that moment Mats realised who Trautmann reminded him of. He looked like Sean Connery, only considerably portlier.

'Have a good flight, pal,' Trautmann said before laying his head to one side of his neck pillow, folding his hands where the seatbelt crossed his voluminous belly and closing his eyes. 'It'll be okay.'

Yes, of course. It will.

Mats turned to glance at the passenger by the window, who'd been asleep for some time.

Then he tapped the touchscreen monitor in the seat in front of him and searched for the safety video, which should inform him about what to do in the event of an accident.

A female flight attendant came from behind, glancing

at the rows to check that all passengers had their seatbelts fastened.

She gave Mats a grateful smile when he showed her his belt but made no attempt to wake the sleeping man in 47F, even though she couldn't see if he was buckled in beneath the blanket.

'*Excuse me, but you've forgotten something,*' Mats wanted to call out after her; he hated any instance of carelessness where safety was concerned. But the snake tightened its grip, cutting off not just his breathing, but his voice too.

What the hell...?

He looked to his right again. Sweating. With a terrible pressure on his chest.

Did I really hear that?

Mats couldn't be sure, but he thought that the man in the straw hat occupying his window seat had just talked in his sleep. And even though it was just one word, it had completely unnerved him.

Because the word was 'Nele'.

His daughter's name.

5

Nele

The barn with its peaked roof was as long as a football field and so tall that a double-decker bus could fit inside.

It stank of excrement, old hay and damp ashes. And although the corrugated iron roof and the thin, prefabricated walls provided poor isolation for the building, it was already unpleasantly muggy inside at this early hour. But that was mainly due to the cold sweat running down the back of Nele's neck.

'Where are we?' she asked the taxi driver, who'd bound her arms and legs with cable ties.

To a hospital stretcher!

The man with the slightly long hair and round nickel glasses didn't answer.

He hadn't said a word since he'd taken advantage of the first wave of contractions and dragged her defenceless out of the taxi. Now he was pushing her, strapped to a rickety mattress frame, through this blood-curdling, empty torture chamber.

Nele had experienced Braxton Hicks contractions, but whatever her body was trying to test in her thirtieth week of pregnancy, it hadn't remotely begun to prepare her for the unbearable pains that suddenly overwhelmed her in the back seat of the taxi. It was as if a fist dipped in acid had tried to yank her womb from her body but was undecided about which way to pull, since she felt the spasms in her vagina as well as her back.

'WHERE ARE WE?'

Her voice echoed in the bare, windowless barn. The light came from several construction lamps that hung at irregular gaps from wooden rafters in the ceiling.

'They used to keep cattle here.'

Nele, who hadn't expected an answer, raised her head as the taxi driver pulled her across the bumpy slatted floor, past bent poles and rusty tubing that formed a sort of metal fence on either side of the gangway.

Nele remembered the sign to the milking parlour she'd seen at the entrance, and a smell of livestock hung in the air, although the dirt and state of the barn suggested no livestock farming had taken place here for some years.

She saw animal stalls. Unlike in stables, these weren't made from wood or stone but resembled cages enclosed by metal tubing, partitions that let in air and light, each smaller than a parking space.

'I'm in prison!' was Nele's first thought.

She felt as if she were being dragged down a prison corridor, past the cells where chained-up animals must have led a miserable existence.

And now one of these cells is for me.

'Almost there,' said her abductor, who was probably neither a taxi driver nor a student, but just a madman.

Where were they heading in this gruesome hall?

Things took an even more sinister turn when the madman started talking to himself, in a whisper, as if trying to give himself courage.

'It's a good thing I didn't have to use the needle. I'm sure I would've been able to, I mean I practised, but it's better this way. Yes, much better.'

'What the hell are you talking about?' Nele said.

'I imagine you view it differently at the moment, but it's a good thing your contractions have already started. I would've had to inject you with oxytocin otherwise, to bring them on artificially.' All of a sudden it got brighter and Nele raised her head again. Her brain was struggling desperately to comprehend the full extent of this horror.

The pen to her side differed from all the others in a terrifying way: next to the caged partition stood a professional video camera mounted on a tripod. And on the hastily swept concrete floor full of cracks lay a heavy metal chain, attached to a waist-high, empty plastic crate. The crate had a hinged viewing grate and reminded her of the boxes used to transport animals on planes.

'No!' Nele screamed, tearing at her shackles.

NOOOOOOOOO!

The worst thing about this scene wasn't that the fencing was bent in a way that meant the madman could force Nele to stick her head through it from behind – like a cow ripe for slaughter! Nor that the purpose of the chain was to shackle her to the frame like a helpless beast and keep her immobilised.

Nele screamed because of what was written there.

On the strip of wood immediately above the stall.

'NELE', it said above the area obviously reserved for

her and the stretcher. And above the plastic crate it said, 'NELE'S BABY'.

'What are you going to do with us?'

Fear had stripped all expression from her voice. She heard herself speak like a robot.

To her surprise, her abductor offered an apology.

'I'm sorry,' he said, pulling the bent metal bars to one side and stepping behind the stretcher.

'I'm sorry, but there's no other way.'

He pushed her stretcher into the stall that reeked of cow dung.

And if Nele hadn't seen the tears with her own eyes she would've doubted her own sanity. For she could hear it quite clearly in his brittle, faltering voice. Despite her fear. Despite the hopelessness that for some reason her abductor appeared to share with her.

He was crying.

Bitterly.

6

Mats
Thirteen hours and five minutes till
scheduled landing in Berlin

As they commenced take-off, Mats could not get the voice out of his head.

'*What are a thousand deaths?*' it asked, the voice of reason, which sounded very faintly like the aviophobia seminar leader. It was however slightly hoarse and difficult to understand amid the din of the aeroplane accelerating into the sky. Mats' fingers clenched the armrests and he lowered his head.

'*Nothing. Statistically, a thousand air accident deaths per year are of no consequence.*'

He knew all this, but it left him cold.

The statistics didn't help. On the contrary.

The moment the cabin light had briefly flickered and the engines had roared into life, Mats was convinced that all studies and forecasts declaring aeroplanes to be the safest means of transport in the world – with 'only' a thousand deaths per year on sixty million flights – were bogus.

'*This equates to 0.003 deaths per billion passenger kilometres,*' the leader had announced with a laugh. Because this figure was so low that the German Statistical Office had rounded it down to zero. Statistically, there was absolutely no risk of a fatal accident when flying.

'*Tell that to the relatives of the passengers whose plane disappeared from radar over the Indian Ocean recently,*' the snake snickered, having coiled itself around Mats' neck as well as his chest. As it pulled ever tighter, the snake hissed, '*Can you hear the rattling? Do you think that's okay? I didn't know the Argentinian runways had recently been paved.*'

Mats glanced to his right, looking over the head of the sleeping man to the window. He saw the lights of the terminal race past and felt the nose of the aircraft climb as the noise of the engines grew louder.

They must've reached the speed of 280 kilometres an hour required for take-off, which was just below that of his blood shooting its way through his throbbing jugular.

It's starting.

Mats wanted to swallow but his mouth was too dry. His hand moved up to his neck and loosened an invisible tie. When the rattling stopped and the giant became airborne, he felt like thrashing around.

He looked up at the ceiling, where the creaking of the creamy-white overhead lockers imparted little confidence. Mats could hear the glasses clinking in the galley. On the screen in front of him he saw a map of the world and an aeroplane symbol the size of an insect setting its course for the Atlantic. Its flight route was marked with a dotted semi ellipse.

Flight time: 13 hours and 3 minutes

Wind: 50 km/h

Height above sea level: 360 metres

Distance to destination: 11,900 kilometres

Good God. So high already?
And so far to go?
The angle at which he was sitting reminded him of being hauled up to the top of a rollercoaster. Just before you plunge back down.

Crash.

Mats shook his head and reached for the paper bag in the pocket of the seat in front of him. Not to throw up, but to have something he could breathe into if things got worse. Which he was bound to need if he couldn't banish the image of a burning plane wreck in the ocean from his mind.

Mats peered again at the window.

A mistake.

The densely woven carpet of the lights of Buenos Aires lay below them.

Below me!

He looked back at the monitor, saw the reflection of his haunted, haggard face hovering above the ocean to the west of the South American coastline and tried a trick.

Acupressure often helped when he had a migraine. Counter-pain.

Mats had realised long ago that this technique worked for acute psychological pain too. To relieve the thrust of his fear of flying he needed a mental counter-pressure.

Which is why he thought of Katharina.

Her hair on the floor. And the blood she'd vomited into the toilet along with her food.

Back then.

He recalled those last, frayed signs of life he'd witnessed from her. The death rattle through the closed bedroom door. Which he could still hear outside the front door as he left, never to return. *'I've got to get out of here,'* he heard the snake hiss. It had appeared back then too, uttering the same words when he'd abandoned his wife.

'Out of here!' it now repeated, four years later, and Mats heard the hissing, accompanied by a hydraulic humming beneath his seat. The sound of that freely spinning, gigantic drill they'd prepared him for in the aviophobia seminar.

The retraction of the undercarriage and landing flaps.

That's done! Mats thought, without feeling any better.

The angle at which they were sitting levelled out and the snake loosened its grip a little, allowing Mats more air, but still it lay heavily on his chest.

Better than nothing.

The take-off, the second most dangerous phase of the flight (after the landing), during which 12 per cent of all accidents occurred, was almost over. The engines were practically at cruising speed. It became quieter.

'Now we're one of ten thousand,' Mats thought. Swiss researchers had discovered that at any point in time at least ten thousand aircraft were in the air simultaneously. With more than a million passengers on board.

A city of people with no ground beneath their feet.

Mats looked to either side of him and envied the two

sleeping passengers. The guy who'd nabbed his window seat had pulled the hat further down his head. And Trautmann was snoring lightly with his mouth open.

Mats couldn't imagine finding peace in these cramped seats. Just for the hell of it he tried closing his eyes briefly and repeating in his mind the mantra of the aviophobia seminar leader: *'It's unpleasant, but not dangerous.'*

He managed to keep it up for a while: about five minutes that felt like five hours, at the end of which he was hardly any calmer. The fact that he no longer felt like jumping up screaming and running to the emergency exits he considered a minor triumph. Mats wouldn't be able to hold out for long, however, so again he tried to conjure the image of his dying wife. Without success, or at least not in the way he'd expected.

Because all of a sudden – with his eyes still closed – a heady, aromatic oriental ladies' scent filled his nose.

That perfume...

The memory associated with it was so intense that it triggered a number of physical reactions all at once. He shuddered, the right corner of his mouth began to twitch. And his eyes were so itchy that he wrenched them open. Full of both fear and hope.

It's not possible, he thought – the only conceivable thought – and when he saw the woman hurrying away down the aisle he tried to convince himself that his eyes were fashioning images his brain wanted to see: a medium-height woman with shoulder-length brown hair, a slim back and ample hips, who occasionally grabbed onto the head rests of the seats as if she were struggling up a hill even though the plane was no longer climbing so steeply.

She'd pulled down the hem of a black rollneck sweater to the top of her thighs.

Because she thinks her bum's too fat.

Mats watched the woman with the familiar gait: small steps with the tips of her feet facing slightly inwards. '*As if you were dribbling an invisible soccer ball,*' he'd once jokingly described it to her.

'*You should talk. You stomp around like a pirate with a wooden leg,*' had come her reply and that put him in his place.

He undid his belt with tears in his eyes. He wanted to slip out of his seat, even though the seatbelt sign was still lit. Wanted to go after the woman who couldn't be who she reminded him of. With her scent, which only on her skin reminded him of dark hollyhocks.

With her clothes, her gait, the slightly curly hair. And not least her way of pulling up the curtain dividing cattle class from business class.

With her left hand.

She's left-handed!

Like Katharina.

His wife who died four years ago.

7

'Would you please remain seated with your seatbelt on for a while longer, sir?'

Valentino, the flight attendant from earlier, had appeared beside Mats out of nowhere and was pushing him back into his seat with a professionally joyless smile.

'It's urgent,' Mats said, without success.

'You can go to the restroom in a few minutes, as soon as the captain gives the go-ahead. It's for your own safety.'

Mats craned his head and shoulders to peer down the aisle past the gelled upstart, but the woman with the perfume that was as familiar as it was rare – it was no longer being made – had already vanished into business class.

'Okay?' Valentino asked, as if addressing a child in kindergarten, expecting them to understand the reprimand.

Mats didn't reply, in part because he was distracted by a vibration that he alone could feel on this flight. Because it came from the inside pocket of his jacket: his phone.

Christ, did I actually forget to switch it off?

He couldn't believe it. He, the aviophobia patient, hadn't stuck to the simplest, most basic of safety rules. He was like someone terrified of dogs putting on a mailman's uniform by mistake.

'Okay,' he mumbled eventually, to be rid of Valentino who was of course standing beside him like a guard dog.

Must be an appointment reminder or the alarm clock, Mats thought, taking out his phone.

Unknown number.

For a moment Mats was so bemused that he didn't bother covering the screen with his hand.

'How's that possible?' he wondered, before remembering the video ad on LegendAir's website. Didn't it mention something about mobile and wireless reception being available on all flights since 2009?

Yes, of course.

The wireless was even free, though calls were meant to be restricted to three minutes out of consideration for the other passengers.

And there it was: to the right of the five dots that indicated full reception, it said 'LC- FlightNet'.

Mats looked around, but his immediate neighbours were still asleep, and none of the other passengers were taking notice of him.

He remembered the tiny earplugs he'd brought with him to listen to music on his iPod.

To avoid losing the call, which might be from the hospital or even Nele directly, he hastily fished the earphones from his trouser pocket and plugged them into his phone, which he replaced in his jacket pocket.

Pressing the switch on the slightly tangled wire, he took the call.

'Hello?' he whispered, his hand in front of his mouth. 'Nele?'

'Herr Krüger? Is this Mats Krüger?'

Mats recognised the voice at once. He might have a poor recall for names but his memory for voices was excellent, and he'd listened to this one for several hours at a time. Even though – and right now this was most unsettling – he'd never met or even seen the man in his life. Like millions of others, Mats only knew the faces of the world-famous stars the caller had loaned his voice to. To Johnny Depp, for example, or Christian Bale. Actors who were dubbed by this voice.

'Who is this?' Mats asked.

'Call me what you like,' the unmistakably melancholic, faintly smoky baritone said. The voice was clipped, slightly apathetic and accompanied by a breathing and hissing that must belong to someone else. The person who was actually calling. Because Mats obviously wasn't really talking to the man who dubbed Johnny Depp. It sounded as if the caller was using a voice changer, speaking into a device that replaced his own voice with that of a celebrity. No doubt he could have just as easily chosen Tom Hanks, Matt Damon or Brad Pitt.

'It's about Nele,' the voice said, again accompanied by the breathing of the actual caller. 'Listen carefully and she won't suffer any more.'

Mats blinked intensely. 'Suffer? Is there something wrong with the baby?'

His knees trembled and his tongue lay like a dead fish in his mouth that now felt far too small. All of a sudden the caller's voice seemed to come from a great distance, which was due to the tinnitus that had started buzzing in his ear. The sound of dying synapses, growing louder with every word the caller uttered:

'You're going to go straight to the nearest restroom and wait for further instructions. If I can't get hold of you in two minutes, Nele is dead.'

Dead?

'Who are you?' Mats was going to shout, but the man didn't let him speak. He fired his words like arrows, all striking their target with the greatest accuracy.

'You will receive new instructions in three minutes. If you don't answer, Dr Krüger, Nele is dead. If you alert anyone on board, Nele is dead. Especially if you inform the police or air traffic control. I have eyes and ears everywhere. If I get even the slightest hint that you're notifying the authorities – for example, if the captain changes course or sends a radio message – or the police start asking questions, your daughter and the baby will meet an agonising death.'

There was a crackling, as if the stranger was hanging up, and immediately afterwards Mats heard the ping announcing a text message.

'Nele... suffer? An agonising death?'

Had this conversation really taken place? Had the stranger with the famous voice really said that?

'Hello? Are you still there?'

The effort Mats required to inch his phone from his pocket – just enough to check the call had disconnected – was almost painful. A pop-up window signalled the arrival of a new message.

This is a joke, he tried to persuade himself.

Nobody knew that he was on his way to Berlin. Not even Nils, his elder brother who'd emigrated to Argentina over a decade ago and with whom he'd initially lived following the tragedy with Katharina.

Up till the very last moment, Mats had been unsure whether he'd be able to summon the courage and strength to board this plane. So who could be calling him if not...
Nele!

One horrific thought gave way to the next.

Was this his daughter's way of paying him back? Was this morbid phone call her attempt to frighten the wits out of him, as punishment for having abandoned his family at the worst possible moment?

Mats' hands were trembling so badly that he was barely able to unlock the screen. When he finally succeeded he wanted to scream. But no sooner did he see the photo than the snake choked his neck.

A photo of Nele.

With an enormous swollen belly.

Her face contorted with pain.

A dirty gag in her mouth.

Tied up.

To a hospital stretcher.

Please, no, Mats implored a God he'd stopped believing in since Katharina's first unsuccessful course of chemotherapy. He looked for signs that the picture wasn't genuine. Photoshopped or deliberately staged, but he knew Nele's expression. That slight skew of her pupils and the tiny reddish blood vessels standing out against the white – a look of utter despair he'd seen in her only rarely. But on the few occasions he had, they were moments of intense mental pain, such as when she'd been unhappy in love or when her best friend from kindergarten had died in a road accident. Mats knew that the agony in this picture was real. And Nele's life in danger.

Which is why he believed the blackmailer, who reminded him with another anonymous message:

Two more minutes. Or your daughter dies.

8

Mats was staggering more than walking.

On his way to the nearest lavatory he could scarcely keep his balance even though the plane had been gliding through the night sky as if on rails ever since the seatbelt signs had turned off. He passed a family of five, whose children had no intention of behaving or leaving the seats in front alone as their exhausted parents kept urging vociferously.

Further ahead, a couple had screened themselves from the general noise with sound-absorbing headphones and were snuggled up watching the same comedy on separate screens. As Mats made his way slowly forwards, step by step as if through syrup, he saw small children, retirees, men, women, South Americans, Germans, Russians and citizens of various Asian countries; he heard them snoring, laughing, chatting, leafing through newspapers and rustling packaging containing the sweets or sandwiches they'd brought on board. One hundred and twelve passengers in the lower-rear third of the aircraft alone. All their sounds of life served as accompaniment to the monotonous, hoover-like drone of the engines, which grew louder the closer Mats got to the wings. But the cacophony sounded feeble against the echo of the caller's final words, which wanted to haunt his mind like some ghost train on an endless loop:

'... *if you inform the police or air traffic control... your daughter and the baby will meet an agonising death...*'

Mats tripped over a foot that an elderly man had stuck out into the centre aisle.

... meet an agonising death...

'I'm sorry,' he apologised, both to the passenger he'd kicked as well as to the woman in front, whose headrest he'd made a clumsy grab for.

He sensed the shaking of heads of his fellow passengers as he moved on. Everything was turning black, but luckily he'd made it to the restrooms by row 33 and there was no line.

Jerking open the folding door, he stumbled into the tiny cabin. When he locked the door the ceiling lights turned on.

Mats' eyes flooded with tears and he felt a vague headache that he attributed to the shock, even though he'd never had a migraine right behind the eyes as a symptom of a panic attack.

Just a joke, he repeated the absurd thought, because it was the only one that offered a harmless explanation, however distasteful.

For one crazy moment he even wondered whether the call might've been part of his aviophobia seminar. To develop the worst possible variant of mental counter-pressure possible. But the caller had managed to put him under so much stress that the plane crashing was the least of his worries right now. Mats wiped the sweat from his brow and looked in the mirror, at his face that had aged years and then flinched when the phone vibrated.

The anonymous caller was sticking to his ultimatum. Mats answered and forced out his words as firmly but also as quietly as possible: 'Who are you and what—'

'Shut up and listen,' interrupted the blackmailer. 'No matter how shocking the information I'm about to give you might be.'

'But...'

'What part of "shut up" don't you understand?'

Mats swallowed hard. The drone of the engines, which in the restroom was somewhat muffled, now sounded like a maelstrom pulling him under.

'Nele's water has broken. The contractions have started and there's going to be no caesarean. If you don't listen to me carefully I'll hang up and let your daughter bleed to death. Do you understand?'

'Yes,' Mats replied after a short pause.

'I'm only going to say this once, and it's essential that you understand.'

There was another crackling, then the bizarrely familiar yet strange voice informed him, 'Your daughter has been abducted. She's still all right, but she's without medical care. The chances of Nele giving birth to a live baby while in captivity are very slim. And even if she does, I can't guarantee that the madman who's got his hands on her will even allow her to live. Unless...'

Mats closed his eyes and grabbed at the sink for support.

'Unless you do exactly as I tell you.'

Okay, whatever you want. I'll do whatever you demand.

Mats knew he wasn't a hero. Nele thought of him as a

coward, and in some respects she was right. Four years ago, he wasn't able to support Katharina at her most difficult time. He wasn't able to watch her die, as he couldn't bear losing the love of his life to the dark conveyor belt of death, powerless to do anything about it. Yet now it was different. If anything could save Nele's life, he would attempt it. Immediately. Without prolonged discussion.

Mats was convinced of this – right now at least.

'On board this plane is someone you know very well,' the voice said.

Katharina, Mats thought, despite all reason, and it dismayed him as always. His wife had died of lung cancer four years ago. Alone, without him. Because he'd abandoned her. There was little doubt that this dubbed Johnny Depp, whom Mats was now calling 'Johnny' in his head, possessed no powers to grant life, but only to destroy it.

'It's a former patient,' the voice said. 'You successfully cured her of her psychological suffering.'

'There are no cures in psychotherapy. Just relief,' Mats wanted to scream at him, but the fear of losing any connection to his daughter if this call ended was constricting his throat.

'Your task, Dr Krüger, if you wish to save Nele's life, is to activate the psychological bomb on board.'

'What?' Mats gasped.

'Find your former patient on board. And reverse your therapy.'

'I, I don't understand...'

Johnny interrupted him once more: 'This patient of yours I'm talking about suffered from massive post-traumatic embitterment disorder for a very long time. Characterised by aggressive phases with explicitly violent fantasies. The patient didn't just want to kill herself, but as many other people as possible. As revenge for what was once done to her.'

Mats jumped when the door rattled. Either a passenger hadn't seen the red 'occupied' bar on the lock or it was their way of signalling that the person inside should hurry up and finish.

'I still don't understand what...'

'Several years ago your therapy successfully liberated this patient from her murderous thoughts and allowed her to lead a normal life.'

And?

'I want you to reverse this therapy. Reactivate your patient's violent fantasies. Unleash the murderous thoughts within her again. And make her crash the plane.'

Thunk!

The last sentence came hurtling down like a guillotine. Severing Mats' head and depriving his brain of control over his body.

Mats collapsed onto the closed toilet seat and stared at the flip-down ashtray in the door beside the No Smoking sign. That seemed to make little sense but, unlike his situation, it had a simple explanation. Ashtrays were in fact mandatory in aeroplane restrooms. To prevent any passenger who defied the smoking ban from starting a fire by discarding a cigarette butt into the wastepaper bin. Mats wished there was a similar logical solution for the schizophrenic state the caller had placed him in.

'Have you lost your mind?' he whispered. 'Are you

asking me to kill six hundred passengers?'

Including myself.

'Six hundred and twenty-six to be precise if you, quite rightly, include the eighteen crew members,' the voice said, its peculiar monotone still without emotion, which had to be because of the voice changer.

'But I don't understand. Why…?'

'My motive is none of your business. You just need to know the following, Dr Krüger: as soon as flight LEA 23 vanishes from the monitor, Nele will be set free and will receive medical care. But if the Airbus lands in Berlin unscathed, your daughter and the baby are dead.'

The door rattled again and this time Mats thought he could hear a man's voice cursing outside, but right now there was nothing he cared about less than a fellow passenger with a weak bladder.

'Please listen to me. Whatever it is you want, let's talk about it. There must be another way we can do this than by…'

Mass murder.

'You're wasting your time, Dr Krüger. Don't bother looking for a way out. Go look for your patient. You're going to need every minute of this flight to reactivate the mental explosives inside her.'

'My patient…?'

'It's a she, don't forget. I think you might already have an idea who I'm talking about.'

Mats gave an involuntary nod.

There was only one female matching the patient history Johnny had described. Only one woman among his many patients who in theory might actually be able to cause a plane crash.

'Yes,' Mats rasped, and then the voice uttered the very name he'd been fearing:

'Kaja Claussen.'

9

Mats
Ten years before

'There's a reason why they offer the food so cheap here, you know.'

Nele shrugged at Mats. Clearly his twelve-year-old daughter was far less interested in another popular science lecture than in the strawberry yogurt in the display case that had been mesmerising her for some time now.

'I'm serious,' Mats said, grabbing her dessert and pushing her tray down the line that slowly but purposefully moved towards the main course counter.

'Köttbullar with potatoes, apple juice and a hot drink for €4.95. They're not making anything on that.'

'Can I have a cola?' Nele asked and took a quick look around. Katharina had disappeared into the restroom for a moment.

'Cola?' he said with raised eyebrows. 'Did you ask Mom?'

'Yes.'

'And what did she say?'

Nele rolled her eyes. 'Dad, honestly. Can't you ever make up your own mind?'

Mats had to laugh, and he stroked her mop of frizzy hair. 'We get the soft drinks after the cashier. Even if I wanted to, I'm afraid you wouldn't be able to keep that brown gunk secret from your mom.'

The metal tray rail took a sharp left, and they shuffled on. Lunchtime on a weekday wasn't very busy so they made good progress. Nele should actually still be at school, but classes had been cancelled due to a broken water line.

'Enjoy your meal!' A plump cook with white cap and her face splotchy from heat smiled and winked at the people in front of them as she gave their plates dollops of lingonberry jam.

Mats picked up where he'd left off. 'What I wanted to say was: IKEA is always advertising how cheap everything is. That's often true, but sometimes not. To get you thinking that all the furniture here is super cheap, they first offer you the food.'

'Dad,' Nele said, clearly annoyed by her father's constant need to explain everything and everyone psychologically, so Mats tried getting to the point.

'It's the reason the very first stop on our tour here is up in the restaurant. It smells yummy, and you think, *Wow, a schnitzel's only 1.99*, and you transfer that to everything in the store. That's what they call conditioning. You understand?'

'Dad!'

'All right, fine. I'll shut up.'

Nele shook her head to tell him this wasn't what she meant. 'Dad, your phone.'

'What?'

He felt at his trouser pocket.

Sure enough. He hadn't even heard it ringing.

'You know if you want fries or mashed potatoes?' he asked Nele before taking the call.

'Hello?'

'It's me, Feli.'

Right then the cook asked for his order. Mats didn't want to be rude so he said, 'Hey, I'm at IKEA right now, could we—'

'No, we can't. I'm sorry. It's an emergency.'

Mats squinted and held up his finger to tell the still-smiling cook he'd order in a second.

'Who's it about?' he asked, glancing at his watch. 12:34 p.m. He now remembered that Feli – Felicitas – only manned the mental health emergency hotline on weekends, and always after 10 p.m. at night, when dark thoughts crept out of the recesses of people's souls.

'Her name is Kaja Claussen, eighteen years old,' the psychiatrist told him. 'She's just called me from the bathrooms at her school.'

'Does she want to kill herself?' Mats asked as quietly as he could, yet the cook still heard. She wasn't smiling now.

'She does,' Feli replied, sounding stressed. 'Herself and everyone else on the school grounds.'

10

Mats
Present day
Still twelve hours and thirty minutes till scheduled
landing in Berlin

'Are you doing all right?'

Valentino took a peek past Mats into the restroom compartment as soon as Mats started pushing the door open.

'Yes,' Mats lied and tried pushing by the flight attendant, who resorted to pressing his hand to the restroom door. 'Why do you ask?'

'Passengers who've been watching you are concerned about your health.'

Valentino nodded towards where Mats had tripped over the man's leg. Though Mats' view was blocked by two female flight attendants and a service trolley.

Mats looked at his watch.

It was half past midnight and food was being served?

Then he remembered they'd been delayed. When he booked, he'd been told about a midnight snack, which they were obviously now trying to get out to people.

'I'm doing great, thanks.'

Valentino didn't look convinced and he sniffed like a bunny, which produced an exasperated sigh from Mats.

Expecting to be blamed for smoking in the restroom, he said, 'Maybe the smoking signs aren't working right?'

He realised he hadn't tried the flushing alibi, which surely didn't escape Valentino right outside the door. That explained his scepticism, especially since the sink hadn't been used – easily confirmed with a glance.

'You do know I suffer from a fear of flying,' Mats said, deciding to give the sceptical flight attendant at least some of the truth. 'I had a panic attack.'

'Hmm.' Valentino's face already showed somewhat more understanding. Only his narrow-lipped smile still annoyed Mats. 'That last seat you finally decided on not so great after all?'

Mats raised both hands and forced out a smile. He'd now attracted this pretty boy's ire for the second time in a row. And no matter what he devised to stop this madness – it definitely would not help to be eyed by a wary flight attendant in the process.

'I needed a moment to myself,' he explained, as friendly as he could be. 'Alone, in a secluded room. It helps me.'

'That so?'

Two words. Yet such a curt reply carried so much sarcasm and mockery. A rage flared up in Mats, scorching all his good intentions.

He didn't hold back now, even though he knew he was making a mistake and that what he was about to say would only bring the briefest satisfaction. 'I don't know what you want from me,' he said, just loud enough for only Valentino to hear. 'I booked several seats and I was using the restroom. Neither is a crime, the last I heard. It's not my fault you'd rather be working on the ground, doing air traffic control, I'm guessing, since you love having control so much. Am I right? Your shirts are wrinkle-free, meaning you buy them yourself instead of letting the airline order them for you. You've just polished your shoes, otherwise the carpet wouldn't be showing so much static, and you keep unconsciously touching your hairline every twenty seconds even though that cement you slathered on your head wouldn't budge even in a hurricane. But you're too unrestrained, too impatient, want answers right now and never later. Really would've liked to kick that door in, wouldn't you? Not the best tendency to have when working in a flight tower requires calm and a clear-headed view of things, what with twenty of those dots moving around the monitor all at the same time. Don't you think?'

Mats knew he had got to him for a second. Maybe not with every word, but his theory had caused a tiny crack in the flight attendant's mask. The giveaway was Valentino's quivering lower lip, which he, true to his nature, quickly got back under control.

He bent down to Mats, smiling.

'You don't know shit about me,' he said without losing the put-on smile.

Oh, but I do, Mats thought and cursed, as he so often had in life, his lack of self-control. *I know for example that you are now my greatest enemy on this plane.*

Essentially, Mats hated himself for using cheap psychological tricks even though he could excuse them as required by extenuating circumstances. His pregnant daughter was fighting for her life, and a madman was blackmailing him to commit mass murder. It was only logical that he'd target a weak person as an outlet for his powerless rage.

'Listen, I'm sorry, I...'

Mats broke off his half-hearted apology, having noticed Valentino taking a step back in near revulsion.

'What's the matter?' Mats asked, yet he could already tell. A second later he could even taste it.

The blood.

Trickling out of his own nose.

Oh, damn, not that too.

When he was excited he sometimes got a bloody nose. Harmless, but not pleasant.

Mats grabbed his face and was about to disappear back into the restroom when he got a sneaky idea.

'How dare you?' he hissed at Valentino, who understandably wrinkled his brow in confusion.

'Come again?'

'Why'd you just do that?'

'Do what?' His eyes showed even more anger.

'Hit me!'

Mats displayed his blood-smeared fingers, letting the blood drip right on the carpet.

'I, I... didn't do any such thing—'

'Oh yeah, then why am I bleeding?'

Mats had raised his voice. The curtain to his left didn't let him see if anyone noticed on that side, but up the aisle to the right a young woman turned around in her seat.

'Go get Kaja Claussen right now,' Mats whispered,

11

Nele

Fuuuhhh!

Her contractions exposed her to a new dimension of pain that compared to nothing she'd ever experienced. And it made Nele fear this was just the start. On a scale of one to ten, maybe a two, yet this level already felt like a soldering iron live in her belly.

Breathe out? Or take deep breaths?

But don't they always pant in all those crappy movies? Damn it.

She'd never taken a birthing course, and why should she? A caesarean section didn't exactly require breathing technique, especially with the full anaesthesia they'd use on her so as not to endanger the baby from haemorrhaging during birth.

Oh God… Her abduction, the horror, this pain… all that had completely suppressed the dangers of a natural birth for her munchkin.

But this is far from anything natural.

Tied up in a cow stall. Ogled at by some lunatic with puppy dog eyes and hair like a hobo.

'Fuuu...' she uttered again.

She had no idea what to scream in this empty barn. There was no foetal monitor, no heart rate monitor, not even any towels. Only this psychopath behind his camera who hadn't stopped crying while he filmed her suffering.

What she'd really like to do is kick that lens right off its stand, but that wasn't going to happen with her legs all tied up.

At least this madman still hadn't felt the need to pull down her tracksuit bottoms. As a medical student, if that's what he even was, it had to be clear to him that there wasn't much to see there yet anyway.

She dreaded the thought that no one would find her or save her and that her abductor would go ahead and do it at some point anyway.

'Fuuuhhhaaahhh...!' Her scream faded. She got some relief as the last contraction waned, hopefully signalling a longer phase without pain before the next round drove all the sweat out of her pores.

'Why?' she shouted at him once she could breathe right again. 'What do you want from me?'

And why are you blubbering like a little child? You going to keep wiping away tears and the snot from your nose this whole time?

'I'm sorry,' her abductor said with surprising care.

'Then untie me.'

'I can't do that.'

'Please, it's really easy. Just cut through these plastic ties...'

'Then they'll never learn.'

'Learn what? Who?'

'Them. Everyone. The population.' He stepped behind

the camera. 'I don't actually want this. I don't have anything against you. Or your baby.'

'Her name is Viktoria.' Saying the name surprised Nele. *The victorious one. A survivor.* The name hadn't been on her list, but it fit, at least for a girl. For a boy she'd change it to Viktor. It was good for her to give the future a name. It felt better knowing her abductor understood that this creature inside her wasn't just an object but a human being with a name and feelings.

'She'll die if I don't deliver her in a hospital.'

'You're lying.'

'No, I'm not. I have AIDS. I can give it to Viktoria. Without a caesarean, she'll die.'

Her abductor lowered his wire-framed glasses. 'I... I didn't know that.'

He wiped his glasses on the hem of his sweater and set them back on. 'But even so. I can't turn back now.'

Nele really would've liked to scream but she forced herself to keep this absurd conversation going as calmly as possible so as not to sever whatever loose bond she had with her abductor.

'Can you tell me your name?'

'Franz.'

'Franz, good. I won't narc on you. I swear. Me and the authorities don't get along so great anyway. Just let me go. Please...'

'No.' Franz forced fingers through his hair. 'I can't do that. This isn't about us. Not about you, about me or about your baby. It's about opening people's eyes, first yours and then the world's.'

'Mine? What did I do?'

'I went through your garbage.'

'And?'

He briefly left the stall and came back with a yellow garbage bag.

'I found this,' he said and reached inside. He brandished an empty milk carton as if it were the most crucial evidence in a trial.

'Don't worry. I just want your milk.'

Wasn't that what he'd said before?

'What about it?'

'You drank it.'

Nele couldn't take it anymore. Her voice rose. 'Sustainable organic whole milk, 3.5 per cent? Right! My God, is that somehow a crime?'

The corners of his mouth turned down with contempt. 'The fact that you even have to ask shows just how necessary all this is.'

'*All this* what?' she asked him. 'What are you planning to do with us, Franz?'

'You'll feel it soon,' her abductor said, grabbed the garbage bag and left her alone in the stall.

12

Mats

Mats could not resist the temptation to turn in a full circle.

He'd never seen anything like it, not even on YouTube or in travel brochures. He knew that LegendAir had the world's most luxurious first class cabins and had heard their slogan: *Sky Suite: Your Private Residence in the Clouds.*

Still, considering this world that had just been revealed to him, even that assertion was a modest understatement.

What they called the Sky Suite was almost as big as his apartment in the Calle Guido. It stretched over twelve windows in length on the upper deck, and in stark contrast to his plain apartment an interior designer had clearly been given free rein to indulge in the most expensive woods, carpets, and select leather upholsteries. Everything was maintained in soft, brownish cream tones. The dark mahogany grain of the wall panelling pleasantly juxtaposed with the light dining table, where four people could quite comfortably take a seat in cappuccino-toned leather chairs.

'Impressive, isn't it?' Kaja Claussen said once she'd brought him up here.

After Mats had got louder and passengers started

growing uneasy, Valentino had reluctantly given in and notified his superior. And despite the circumstances, Kaja was sincerely happy to see her former therapist again after such a long time.

It was her suggestion to discuss his incident with Valentino one on one and undisturbed. Yet Mats couldn't have imagined her mention of a 'safe haven' would mean *all this here.*

His feet actually sank in the mossy-thick carpet of the three-room suite, which was located directly over the cockpit. To reach it, they had walked up a spiral staircase at the front of the aeroplane and had to pass through what resembled an expensive London cocktail bar. Up here at an altitude of 9,750 metres, passengers in first class actually had their own bartender offering cocktails, specialty coffees and the largest selection of gin in the skies, all from a semicircular bar polished to glossy perfection. Shielding the Sky Suite from the lounge was a thick, sound-absorbing door.

Its location in the nose made it the most dangerous place on the plane in the event of a crash or collision, but that mattered less to Mats considering the crisis he now found himself in.

'Is that a double bed back there?' he asked, though there could be no doubt. In a rear area, shielded by another sliding door currently open, he spotted a full bed. An armada of pillows took up nearly the whole mattress.

'French down and Egyptian linen.' Kaja smiled and handed Mats a fresh hand towel.

For a moment he'd actually forgotten he was still holding his nose, though it had luckily stopped bleeding.

'Sorry,' he muttered, looking around for a garbage can. In doing so he discovered another door between the living and sleeping areas.

She led him to what he'd assumed was a bathroom, which could easily fit four of the restroom compartments he'd just been in. It even had a glass shower, level with the floor. Mats disposed of his bloody hand towel in a garbage can, stepped up to the double sinks and washed his face and hands.

'Why didn't you try contacting me before the flight?' he heard Kaja say behind him, keeping a respectful distance.

'I didn't want to bother you.' The truth was, he hadn't thought of her at all when booking. He had known that his former patient was a senior flight attendant with a large airline but had figured her for a German carrier. Only when the blackmailer mentioned her name had he put two and two together.

'That quadruple booking of yours caused a minor sensation,' Kaja said.

'I can imagine.'

Mats took a second to get a better first impression of her in the mirror now that she wasn't looking directly at him and thought no one was watching. It was amazing – Kaja Claussen had actually turned into a beauty. Her long hair with its blondish strands looked as good on her as the twenty-odd pounds she must have put on. She naturally had to cover the piercing holes on her chin and right upper lip with make-up, yet she had learned that too. Just as she had her straight and self-confident posture complete with broad shoulders, which couldn't all be due to her form-fitting uniform.

Kaja the senior flight attendant gestured at the suite living room and invited him to sit with her at the table there. The automatic window blinds resembling real silk curtains had been lowered, and the silver lamp on the broad sill between window and table gave off a warm and soft light.

'I would just like to apologise for the incident, Dr Krüger. Ken can sometimes lose self-control but I never thought he'd resort to violence. On you of all people. I truly am sorry.'

'Ken?' Mats asked, glancing at her name tag. 'So is Valentino his last name?'

She laughed. 'No, no. We just call him that. Because of his looks, and because his girlfriend looks a little like Barbie.'

Barbie.

It sounded enough like 'baby' to remind him of the pain that Nele now had to endure. If only he was the victim of some sick joke.

'Everything okay?' Kaja asked, his anxiety obviously not escaping her.

'I'm not feeling so great. I suffer from a fear of flying.'

'You?' Kaja started to smile but immediately corrected herself.

'Optometrists wear glasses too,' Mats offered as justification.

The senior flight attendant didn't say anything for a moment. She just looked at him with her large bright-blue eyes and then nodded. 'I see, okay. That does make more sense.'

'In what way?'

'Well, I mean, back then you were able to put yourself inside my head like no one else. Maybe a person has to know psychological problems themselves to understand them so well.'

Mats was now the one nodding, even though he didn't believe the theory. You didn't need to hit your shin with an axe to be able to imagine the pain.

'What I wanted to say was: I was having a little panic attack down there in the restroom. I might have overreacted. Now I'm not even sure if Ken, if Valentino, that is, actually hit me.'

Kaja squinted in confusion. 'How else could it happen?'

Mats was about to say something about the dry air on board and the fact that he tended to get nosebleeds when he suddenly needed to grab at his head – not for show, but because a dull pain had just hit him, this time at his temple.

Kaja stood and pointed towards the bedroom. 'Let's get you some rest before anything.'

'No, no.' Mats shook his head and only made the pain worse. He felt at his nose and was relieved to find it had stopped bleeding for good.

'It almost looks like I'm trying to finagle an upgrade out of you.'

His former patient laughed. 'You booked four seats, for a vast sum. You even gave away your seat in business class. No one on board thinks you're looking to finagle anything.'

Kaja glanced at her watch. 'I have to go check on first class. But, don't worry about a thing. The Sky Suite is actually almost never used – the airline only keeps it running for the image. No one up here actually pays the thirty-two thousand euros per person. You could get a private jet for that.'

'But you won't get into trouble, Frau Claussen?'

'My position gives me the authority to make executive decisions about transferring passengers to other seating.'

She smoothed out her skirt. 'I had good reason to write you back then, Dr Krüger.'

Mats nodded, recalling the card with an image of the clouds that had hung on his fridge a good while until it fell off at some point and was likely discarded by the cleaning staff.

Dear Dr Krüger, I'm now a senior flight attendant. Not exactly my dream, but close. It's thanks to you alone. Just let me know if there's ever anything I can do for you.

Kaja had actually wanted to become a pilot, but that was no longer possible after those incidents back in school. She never went to college either.

'I'm happy that you're on board.' Kaja smiled, her expression almost motherly. 'Maybe I can still show my gratitude somehow. For everything that you've done for me.'

Mats waved away the notion. 'Please. I was doing my job.'

'No, I'm serious. Without you, I wouldn't even be alive. I know that. I wouldn't have this job, wouldn't have my wonderful fiancé. We're trying to have a child, can you believe that?'

She showed him the diamond ring on her finger.

No.

Not when he thought back to her condition. Ten years ago now. Her transformation was breathtaking – from that girl with black-dyed hair on his psychiatrist's sofa, zombie-like, outwardly dead, her skin itself the only thing holding her together, to this practically Amazonian, curvaceous beauty. It was a true before-and-after image like those usually seen only in deceiving teleshopping promos.

'I'm happy you're doing so well,' Mats said, and he spoke

the truth. Kaja Claussen was probably the biggest success story of his career. A patient he even dared speak of as being healed.

And now he was supposed to destroy her again.

No. I can't do it.

Mats took a deep breath as he watched her go.

No.

Of course he wouldn't sacrifice her. Complying with the blackmailer's absurd demands was simply not possible. Under no conditions would he destroy his former patient psychologically, all in order to make her his tool for mass murder.

Then he was forced to think about Nele again.

'Frau Claussen?' he asked right as she opened the door to leave the suite.

She turned around. Smiled. 'Yes?'

Just what am I doing? he asked himself.

It couldn't be coincidence he was on board the same flight as her. Someone must've been planning this long beforehand, and that in itself could be his starting point for coming up with some kind of plan to prevent this catastrophe after all, without anyone getting hurt. Neither here on board, nor, even more importantly, in Berlin.

But to save Nele and the baby in Berlin, he needed time and a room where he could make a phone call undisturbed. He'd already found the latter right here in the Sky Suite.

There is a solution, he told himself, to give himself the courage. *And I still have over eleven hours' time to find it.*

He'd keep Kaja's previous mental illness as his plan B, just in case.

Only if necessary.

In case his plan A fell apart, and he had to consider the unthinkable.

At the very latest, on their approach to landing in Berlin.

And so Mats felt like vomiting from disgust and self-loathing, because he knew what the words he was about to say would unleash within Kaja. His words would be long fingernails dragging across that well-healed scab of her psychological wounds, exposing those first connecting scars.

He said: 'Fortunately, I was able to overcome any suspicions I had about your version of the story back then, Kaja.'

13

Feli

Considering the fact that she was a late sleeper, she'd got into the shower fairly early today. Given what awaited her, it wasn't exactly a surprise.

Oh God, Feli thought and put a hand to her mouth. *Did I really just think 'what awaited me'?*

Her best friend Jasmina would bust right in with Sigmund Freud himself if she knew. And Jasmina wasn't even a psychiatrist, unlike her. Though Jasmina's teacher–parent evenings where she had to grapple with the parents and legal guardians of her primary school students often demanded even greater finesse than Feli's shifts working the mental health hotline.

'I'm delighted. I really am delighted!' Feli said and put on a wide smile that she held while she shampooed and rinsed her hair.

After a minute and a half at the most, the brain could be duped into actually making you feel happy, even when the smile was fake. The method was called facial feedback, which worked even when patients simply held a pen in their teeth crossways.

But that's not something I actually need.

I really am happy.

Feli turned off the faucet and stepped out of the shower.

'Today is my lucky day!'

She wrapped a towel around her wet hair and dried it off before slipping into her bathrobe.

Janek tended to just stagger across the bathroom dripping all over and pull his grey terry robe over his wet skin, but Feli hated it when fabric got damp on her body.

She liked it warm, dry and cosy.

But it was the differences that bound people.

Still smiling, yet still not feeling any endorphin release, she stepped up to the sink and used a make-up tissue to wipe off the rest of the toothpaste that had miraculously made it from Janek's toothbrush to the tip of the faucet once again.

'Roll?' she heard him shout from the bedroom.

'Prefer toast,' she shouted back and added a 'I'll be right there, honey.'

Right then her phone buzzed. She grabbed it off the edge of the bathroom counter, where the vibrating alert made it travel in a circle, and tried making sense of the number.

It seemed familiar to her but wasn't saved as a contact.

She answered, not feeling great about it. And the feeling got even worse when she heard the voice on the other end. Noisy signal, far away, echoing a little. It was as if the man were standing in a wind tunnel.

That always pointless round of phone-greeting Jeopardy ensued.

'Feli?'

'Mats?'

Her colleague and once closest friend. He wasted no time, got right to the point.

'I... I need your help.'

'What's happened?' Feli asked, falling automatically into her emergency hotline routine. She would've preferred to hang up. Or at least screamed:

'*You need my help? What are you thinking? Four years of radio silence and suddenly you call. Just like that? And TODAY, of all days?*'

But she held back her anger along with all justified criticism. For now.

'Nele, she's... I think she's in danger.'

'In what way?'

'I just spoke to Charité Hospital in Virchow. She was supposed to deliver there today.'

Feli nervously scratched at her neck, which was starting to itch. She hated getting blotchy from stress, and she definitely didn't need it on a day like today.

'Nele's pregnant?'

'Yes.'

'Congratulations.'

'She was scheduled for a caesarean this morning. But she never made it to the location in Virchow. Someone there who I went to school with confirmed it for me.'

'I don't understand.' Feli's itch got worse, but she managed to keep her hands off her neck this time.

'I tried the number I have of hers by the way. She didn't pick up.'

'Okay, that does sound weird. But maybe she decided to go to another hospital.'

'You can't just switch to a new operating room, Feli, as

you know. There's something else…'

'Something *else*?'

Mats paused a moment, and Feli thought she faintly heard what sounded like an announcement over a speaker.

'Are you on a train?' she guessed, since the noise on the line kept getting louder in between speaking.

'On an aeroplane.'

'You?'

Didn't he once tell her that he'd rather spend ten hours at the dentist than a single hour up in the air?

'What are *you* doing on a plane?'

He sighed. 'Nele didn't want to be alone after the birth. So I'm on my way to Berlin from Buenos Aires right now. But…'

'What?'

'Right after take-off, I got a phone call. Someone has kidnapped Nele and is threatening to kill her.'

'Oh, God…' She put her hand to her mouth again, like she had in the shower. She turned away from the mirror and whispered, 'Is this, I mean… is this true?'

'This is what I'm trying to find out. I don't see any reason so far to doubt the threat, unfortunately.'

'Fine, I'll call the police.'

'No. Under no circumstances.'

Feli laughed nervously. 'But how am I supposed to help you?'

'Please drive over to Nele's apartment.'

'To do *what*?'

'I'm not sure. Look around. Go through her stuff.'

'Hold on. How am I supposed to get in?'

'That's true. Sorry. I'm not exactly thinking clearly, being so worked up. But, maybe by going over there you'll find some kind of clue as to who's behind this. Speak to the neighbours or the building caretaker. I know it sounds desperate, but you're my only hope.'

'What do the kidnappers want from her?'

A pause. The hissing grew worse, reminding her of an old kitchen blender. It broke off when Mats said, 'That's... what I can't tell you.'

'You're such an asshole.'

'I know. I know.'

Her lower lip quivered, and Feli hated how shaky her voice sounded. 'It's been four years since you just, just vanished out of thin air. Okay, it was only one night, and maybe it was a mistake, but that does not give you the right to abandon me like some whore.'

'True.' Mats could only agree again.

'So that gives you no right to ask me for a favour.'

'You're right. I... I just don't know who I can turn to. I don't know anyone in Berlin I can trust like you.'

'You bastard,' Feli snapped. Then she hung up. Shut her eyes in exhaustion.

She found it hard to breathe, her chest trembling.

'Was that him?'

She turned around, startled.

His dark eyes were a shade more melancholic than usual. It had been a mistake telling Janek about Mats. But she'd sworn to enter into their relationship with honesty and no baggage, and Mats had been the biggest piece of baggage she'd been schlepping around. Even though they'd never been a couple and he had never reciprocated her passion. *Except for that one night...*

'Yes, that was Mats.'

Feli added an apologetic nod and took a step towards Janek. Their foot-and-a-half difference in height made her look up to him.

If he wasn't holding that tray she would've pressed right up against his hairy chest, closing her eyes, breathing in his warm body scent of cedar and musk.

'What did he want?'

'To congratulate us,' she said after a suspiciously long pause. 'I told him he could take his hypocrisy somewhere else.'

Janek tilted his head. 'Huh,' he said. Not enough to tell if she'd managed to curtail his mistrust at least a little.

'Come on, let's eat.' She smiled at Janek and pinched him on the hip as she squeezed by.

'But no more than one slice for you,' she teased even though he had almost no fat on his muscular body.

He forced out a smile after all. It looked far more natural than the ones she'd managed.

'Look who's talking,' he joked back. 'Planned on taking off ten pounds by today and only managed, what, six?'

'Jerk.' She laughed and threw a little pillow in his direction.

'Now you've done it...'

He placed the tray on the night table and threw himself onto her.

'Help,' she panted. 'Help, I give up.'

As always when she lay in his arms, Feli marvelled how strong his body felt. Like a young man's, not exactly what you'd expect from a fifty-year-old lawyer.

'I love you,' Janek said. 'Dieting or not, doesn't matter to me. And there's one thing I know for sure.'

She let him kiss her, and with her eyes closed she heard him say:

'You're going to look so amazing today in your wedding dress.'

14

Mats

My body's reaction to panic is changing.

Mats, amazed he was still capable of self-analysis, perceived a burning in his stomach that he wasn't familiar with. When under stress he tended to get dry skin, blisters on his lips, heat splotches, and – the only positive – a loss of appetite and weight.

He'd luckily been spared the acid reflux and stomach cramps, until now.

Yet extraordinary circumstances call for extraordinary symptoms.

It was as if an inflamed stomach ulcer had suddenly hit him. The stinging cramps began the second he'd seen part of Kaja's eyes darken a little – the briefest dimming, matched with a fleeting twitch of her upper lip.

That was when Mats knew his words had affected her, that he'd got the first ball rolling. She would wonder what he'd meant by that and whether he really had considered her experiences to have been her 'version' of events and her 'story' and not what they were: grim reality. Kaja Claussen's horrible fate.

Considering the sort of mental issues he was preparing her for, his stomach ache truly was justified.

Mats swallowed hard, and after his ears popped that hissing of the turbine engines sounded somewhat clearer again. He raised a hand, stretched it out flat and observed his fingers trembling, like feathers in wind. He had trouble getting the flush-mounted remote to detach from this table he'd been sitting at for a good hour, facing against the direction they were flying. After three attempts he found the button for the blinds, which rose silently and disappeared into the side of the plane.

In the now transparent window pane, a dark hole was widening. Light from rear rows of windows sloshed around like a gleaming liquid in the dark abyss and was swallowed up by it. Mats fixed his gaze on the signal lights at the tip of the wing, which punctuated the darkness with their steady rhythm. They were blinking at such regular intervals, *yet were also ready to send out an SOS.*

Save our souls.

Over six hundred souls had to be saved.

From an insane blackmailer... no, no – Mats corrected himself:

From me!

Me right here, I'm the greatest danger on board.

He grabbed his face in despair and sighed.

He had considered so many dangers in advance. The possibility of being rammed on the runway by a plane landing, of bursting into flames on take-off, of being hijacked by a terrorist. Of explosives in luggage.

But not of that most homicidal weapon, the only bomb that every person could actually bring on board without being detected by any detector on earth. He hadn't considered that perfect weapon of mass destruction: the human mind.

As his mentor always said: '*Every human being carries the ability to kill inside them. Everyone has a point at which they snap. Luckily there are only a few who possess the immorality to uncover this mental absolute zero in others.*'

I'm such an idiot, thought Mats.

He was a professional psychiatrist with a PhD, one wall of his office patterned with certificates and diplomas. Yet he'd never given a single thought to the fact that every person had a time bomb ticking inside them that could be detonated under the right circumstances, using the right trigger.

Mats could feel the pressure increasing on his body. The pilot was clearly changing altitude. A single glance up at the fifty-five-inch flat-screen showing the flight's progress that they were now at 10,200 metres.

The cramping in his stomach was getting worse. He pulled off his blazer and set it next to him on the sofa.

He decided, with a shrug, to ignore the seat belts lying there ready. They were no match for the turbulence he found himself in.

Mats stood and looked around the Sky Suite for something to write with. Along the row of windows opposite was actually a small walnut writing desk with a swivel armchair. He opened the drawer and took out a pencil and notepad with the LegendAir logo. To his left he discovered a small glass refrigerator and helped himself to a bottle of mineral water.

The water was so cold it almost hurt, and Mats felt the slight hope that gulping it might help lessen his constant headache a little.

He'd left his medications in his carry-on, back at his seat in economy.

'Now, let's try approaching this logically,' he told himself after taking another look at his watch to confirm the time remaining.

Ten hours and sixteen minutes left.

He sat down.

Not even half a day left to solve the biggest and possibly last conundrum of his whole life.

The less time you have, the more carefully you need to prepare, he recalled, something else his mentor always said. That was about medical emergencies, not averting an air disaster, but Mats had always believed that criminology and psychology were closely related. If you wanted to get to the bottom of things for either, you had to know the cause of the problem.

I. The Motive

he thus wrote on the notepad.

If he only knew why the blackmailer was demanding he commit such insanity, he'd be a huge step closer to the man's identity. Next he wrote, below and indented a little:

a) Consequences

What were the consequences if he did what this Johnny

was demanding. And who might benefit from it?

– Death

There would be hundreds of deaths. So, a terror attack? That would be a tough one, because a political motive usually meant the participants were hopelessly blind. On the other hand, such attackers often had overriding goals, such as the release of certain prisoners, so there might be room for negotiation.

Mats put a big question mark in the margin. The methods being used didn't feel like an act of politically motivated violence, but he didn't see any strong argument for excluding it either.

– Money

LegendAir was owned by shareholders. Someone always profited from accidents, wars, catastrophes. So many, unfortunately, that it was impossible to limit the possibilities within reason.

From speculators who bet against insurers in the event of a crash, to competitors who aim to drive their rivals into bankruptcy. Anything was conceivable.

Mats unconsciously shook his head.

Or it might not be about the people on board at all, but rather a specific piece of cargo that was supposed to be destroyed.

He told himself to ask Kaja about any conspicuous items being transported she might have been told about, though he wasn't getting his hopes up.

It was also possible, however, that the one or several offenders were not aiming for some bigger picture but rather a single person.

Which just as well might be...

– Revenge

Someone who, in the blackmailer's eyes, deserved it so much that it was worth sacrificing six hundred people.

Or they were after a prisoner, guarded by a sky marshal, being handed over incognito.

Or it was a spy? Someone who had access to secret information or a principal witness with knowledge that threatened someone in business or politics?

'Gah!'

Mats gave a shout, slammed down the tip of the pencil so hard it snapped on the desk.

Shit!

He tore the page from the notepad in anger and crumpled it up.

There were simply too many possibilities.

And too little time. Far too—

His phone chimed, halting his thoughts from spiralling ever downward.

He'd received a text.

URGENT!!!

read the preview notification. Of course he couldn't see the number – it had been sent via anonymous email using a webmail service.

Mats clicked on the image, a photo of a page of standard A4-size letter paper. On it, written in black type:

Turn your monitor on immediately.

Movie channel 13/10

15

SkyCinemaDeluxe was what LegendAir called its digital on demand service, and the selection rivalled that of a big-city video store. Most of the films were brand new, some still running in theatres, and two hadn't even come out yet – they were celebrating their 'Premier in the Clouds' on the plane's exclusive movie channel.

Mats had no idea if the offerings were only this wide-ranging up here in first class or if every passenger had access to them.

All he knew was that there was no channel 13/10.

From drama and comedies, to thrillers and documentaries – every genre had their own channel, and every one sported at least fifty different films.

Using a wireless controller he had to aim at the flat-screen like a laser pointer, he was only able to scroll until reaching the horror-comedy *Tucker & Dale vs Evil*. There was nothing else after that on channel 10, movie 49.

At least not officially.

Mats looked at the controller, which was shaped like a computer mouse, and pressed on the right arrow button.

Nothing.

He stood up from his seat and pressed again. And again.

The cursor suddenly jumped to a new screen. It was empty.

White.

Channel 11/1

he read on the otherwise blank display.

He pressed to the right again, and the screen still offered no content.

Only the number up in the right corner of the screen had changed.

12/1

Ten mouse clicks later, he'd done it. According to the display, he had reached channel 13/10. And the screen wasn't white any more. Now it was grey.

It stayed like that a while, with nothing to see apart from a bright, blinking dot in the middle of the screen, its steady flicker reminding Mats of those red signal lights on the wings.

Then it crackled, and what looked like a flash of light cut off the image that was obviously about to appear.

'What the...'

Mats took a step up to the monitor, which had such high resolution that the image he saw didn't change even with him standing right before the screen.

It resembled a saturated and faded video from the 80s that had been copied too much. Too many pale browns, which ironically matched the Sky Suite's lavish interior perfectly.

Eleven years ago, was Mats' first thought, since he'd instantly recognised what he saw.

It's been that long.

Yet it had still lost none of its horror.

The quality of the original video was terrible, yet the jerking, fuzziness and bad focus had little to do with the reproduction but rather the cheap camera that had captured the horror. On top of that, the camera was much too far away, standing or hanging or placed somewhere. At least ten metres from the woman who right at that moment was fighting for her life.

He jumped as his phone buzzed again.

'Enjoying the on-board entertainment?' asked that Johnny Depp voice, accompanied by that now-familiar breathing of the person actually speaking.

'Where did you get this?' asked Mats. He'd stopped the recording.

'Doesn't matter. Just use it.'

Mats shook his head. 'Kaja knows this video by heart. It won't trigger anything in her any more. She's worked through that ordeal from school.'

Johnny laughed robotically. 'No, she hasn't. No one can ever completely work through a trauma like the one Kaja suffered.'

Mats sighed in despair. 'Even so, your plan won't work. I spent years stabilising my patient mentally and emotionally. In dozens of sessions. That's not something I can just change back in a few hours.' He added a snap of his fingers. 'I'm sorry but the mind isn't some device you can turn on and off. Even if I wanted to, it's simply not possible for me to manipulate Kaja Claussen into acting out her violent fantasies and becoming a mass murderer within just a few hours.'

'Don't give me that,' Johnny barked. 'Think about September eleventh. Constructing the north tower of the World Trade Center took seven years. Making it collapse, just one hour and forty-two minutes. It's always faster to tear something down than it is to repair it. That's especially true for someone's mind. Isn't that right, Dr Krüger?'

Mats released a groan, imagining the fireball of an exploding aircraft. The image was not only so ghastly because he himself was sitting in a craft doomed to crash. It was because he also knew that Johnny was speaking the truth.

'All you need is one hard shove, make contact, a hit, something to shake the foundation of Kaja Claussen's psyche so severely that her self-control collapses like the house of cards that it is. And you can do it, Dr Krüger, I know so. The video gives you that extra tool, for speeding things up.'

'Is there something else on there that I don't know about?'

'Wait until minute nine. From eight seconds on.'

'What happens then?' Mats asked, but the connection was dead. The blackmailer had delivered his message and was sticking to his rule of never saying more than absolutely necessary. Mats felt a mix of revulsion and curiosity. Rubberneckers at the scene of an accident must feel similar when wondering what horrors were hidden beyond the police barriers. He also wasn't sure what exactly in the video could make it possible for him to transform Kaja back into a psychological wreck. Into someone who wished for the death of herself and of others.

Like she was back then, with her first phone call.

As she sat on the school restroom toilet.

With a gun in her hand.

Mats tried fast-forwarding to the minute indicated in the video but had trouble getting it right. He skipped all the way to the end on his first try.

Okay, take it easy.

He was sweating. His fingers left damp marks on the remote, but he at least managed to find the slower fast forward.

Right when he reached minute eight, he heard a click behind him.

'Dr Krüger?'

He turned to face the female voice, managing to turn off the monitor at the same time.

Too late.

'Is that TV you're watching?' the flight attendant asked him. Holding a tight smile, she set a basket of fruit on the buffet counter next to the sliding door she'd just come through.

'What were you just watching?' she said.

And Mats had no idea what he was supposed to tell Kaja Claussen.

16

Feli

Something just wasn't right here.

Feli could practically smell it. No, you didn't have to be a profiler with clairvoyant tendencies to get suspicious on account of a front door ajar in Berlin. The Weissensee neighbourhood wasn't exactly the Bronx, but people in these apartment buildings didn't usually leave their doors open either.

'Nele?' she tried, for the second time after first ringing and then knocking. But no one answered.

As expected.

God, what am I doing here?

Feli went down the hallway, and a feeling of melancholy crept up on her when she saw a small, freshly wallpapered children's room. The restored baby cradle looked ancient and likely came from a flea market, in contrast to the changing table with warming lamp.

She kept going and entered the living room. The creative chaos that reigned between the sofa, TV and desk in front of the window reminded her of a time when she herself was still living alone and often felt lonely, but also free.

The wall behind the old tube TV must have been painted with magnetic paint, since a sea of postcards, party photos, flyers promoting bands and various concerts were stuck there with magnets, a cheerful and colourful collage from Mats' artistically gifted daughter that suited the delightfully unconventional mix of furniture. No pieces matched. Viewed individually, the low coffee table, the fringe rug and the batik curtains were even ugly, but together they formed a stylish, creative ensemble.

I wouldn't mind living like this again, she thought.

It wasn't so sterile, unlike the designer furniture and modern art that her fiancé Janek had picked out.

She again considered doing the only reasonable thing: ignoring Mats' call and his request and leaving this apartment right away. Yet then she spotted the cordless landline phone in its charger on Nele's desk. It was blinking like her own did when she had a message.

Curious about it, she lifted the handset from the cradle and pressed the green envelope symbol under the call button.

'You have ONE new message,' reported the bored-sounding and interchangeable female voice in her ear. Feli had expected considerably more messages, at least a half dozen, especially some from Nele's father. Then it occurred to her that Mats probably didn't have the number to her landline and had been trying Nele on her mobile phone.

The one message Feli heard came from a short-winded man in a broad Berlin dialect:

'Frau Krüger? So, now it's... er... five minutes past time. I'm standin' down here, the ride you ordered through Med-Call. Your cab. And now I'm, uh, confused, see, 'cause I'm

ringin' up a storm and no one's comin'. Switchboard's tellin' me the ride got pushed back an hour. Can that be right? Or did it get changed again or what? Man, oh man...'

Feli stopped the message and checked the display for when the taxi driver made the call.

12:33 p.m. on 2 May 1999.

Great, just great.

Apparently Nele avoided programming her devices even more than Feli did and had left the thing in factory mode.

Feli stuck the phone back in the charger and wiped a thin film of sweat from her forehead.

Man, it sure is hot.

The temperature in here was almost like summer despite it being September. It was expected to reach twenty-five degrees with sunshine – a perfect day to get married.

The only thing it was clearly too hot for was detective work.

Plus it was completely nutso to let herself be told what to do, and on today of all days, and by Mats at that.

If Janek found out what she was doing here (*and for who!*), he'd call off the wedding outright. That said, she'd be back home again soon.

Luckily she still lived over on Greifswalder and not on the west side that Janek loved so much, unlike her. If it were up to him, she would've moved her practice on Oranienburger over to Dahlem, Grunewald or at least Lichterfelde a long time ago. But then it would've taken her an hour to get here by car easily instead of just fifteen minutes by bike. Though it was pretty stupid of her to rush over here so fast. Now she'd have to take another shower when she got home.

Feli grabbed her phone and dialled the number Mats called from earlier.

'Hello?' she blurted, misinterpreting the pause between rings as her former lover picking up.

As it rang and rang, Feli observed a dark spot on the grey and slightly worn-out sofa.

Apparently calling someone up in the skies wasn't quite all it was cracked up to be.

Just when she went to hang up, the connection crackled.

'Mats?'

There was a slight pause before he answered – all she heard at first was the usual hissing sound inside an aeroplane, and then: 'I'm sorry, I was under some stress and couldn't pick up. Where are you?'

'In Nele's apartment.'

'And?'

She shrugged. 'What can I say? She's not here, and all signs point to her leaving the place in a hurry.'

'Any sign of violence?' Mats asked.

'The door was ajar, but not forced open. No lamps or chairs tipped over if that's what you mean. Just stains on the sofa—'

'Blood?'

'No.'

Feli felt at the seat fabric. The liquid was colourless and left nothing on her fingers. 'The stain is fresh. Like she'd spilled water.'

'*Her* water?' she heard Mats blurt. 'Amniotic fluid.'

'No idea. It's possible, sure. Maybe her water broke.'

Mats moaned. 'Then that goddamn blackmailer was telling the truth.'

Feli glanced at the clock. Luckily Janek had set the ceremony for 4 p.m., the latest possible time slot.

'Mats, I'm sorry, but you really should get the police in on this. In six hours I'm having a civil ceremony and—'

'You're getting married? I'm sorry, uh, I mean, congrats. But, you're my only chance. Please, Feli. Nele's going to die if you don't help me. I need to know who's behind it, and locate Nele. I only have a little over ten hours left – until landing.'

'The kidnapper gave you an ultimatum?'

'Yes.'

'So what happens when time runs out and we haven't found Nele?'

'Please, Feli, don't ask me any more questions. It's in your best interests. You don't want to know. And I can't tell you.'

Feli shook her head, horrified. 'But what am I supposed to do now?'

She searched for the bathroom door down the hall. She really needed a drink of water.

'Think logically,' Mats insisted. 'We know that one or several of these offenders had knowledge of my daughter being pregnant. Plus they have the capability, the means and the manpower to kidnap Nele as well as to change the flight attendants' shift schedules in a way that matches my seat booking.'

'Which means what?'

She had found Nele's bathroom. The creative hodgepodge of furnishings continued as expected. The mirror over the ancient sink was bordered with a baroque picture frame, a leather chair stood next to the bathtub, and a guitar stand served as a towel rack.

'It means you'll need to search for some kind of connection. Somewhere there's someone who had access to Nele's medical records as well as to my flight schedule. A doctor or a nurse with contacts at the airline maybe.'

Somewhere, someone... some day this is, thought Feli.

'She was supposed to deliver at Virchow, right?'

'Yes.'

'Just great. Charité Hospital only has about 13,000 staff overall.'

'Too many. I know.'

Her eye caught the thick, old-fashioned safe used for stacking magazines next to the toilet.

Parents, My Baby & Me, Family & Co...

Feli slid the magazines and periodicals back a little to open the door to the cabinet. She was expecting Nele to keep toilet paper, soap or towels inside.

But the contents she saw left her astonished, at first. Then she got sad.

'I didn't know,' she said, down on one knee before the cabinet.

'What?' Mats sounded distressed. 'What didn't you know?'

'That she was so sick.'

How could she have? They'd had no contact.

'Sick how? What are you talking about?'

She lifted a paper bag with a red-and-white logo from the safe and pulled out one package of meds after the other. 'Tenofovir, emtricitabin, efavirenz.'

'She had that just lying around?'

'In the bathroom, yes.'

A pause. The hissing surged.

'No, that can't... I didn't know either,' Mats said after a while, confessing his ignorance. Nele – infected with HIV! His voice sounded lost all of a sudden, weak. As if the air pressurisation had stopped working on his plane and he could hardly get any air. 'This is one stressful birth, for God's sake. The baby, it can't get infected.'

'The bag is from the pharmacy on Seestrasse,' Feli said, mainly because she didn't know how else to fill the depressing silence. A diagnosis of AIDS might no longer be a death sentence, and they couldn't even know for sure if Nele had had a breakout of the disease, yet simply living with the threat of HIV was a constant physical and mental burden.

'The one in Wedding?' Mats asked to confirm the pharmacy's location.

'The same.'

'Then Nele normally goes to the Wedding Medical Centre.'

'That's what I meant, yes.'

The medical centre as well as the pharmacy specialised in HIV and cancer patients and shared an almost identical red-and-white logo. Both facilities were located in the same building and were regarded as the most advanced in Berlin. Oncology and infectious diseases had their own state-of-the-art laboratory and even employed psychologists and psychiatrists to support HIV patients.

'I'm afraid that doesn't get us much further,' she heard Mats say, his voice sounding firmer again.

Right then Feli heard a click. In the hallway. Behind the door.

Behind her door.

'Mats?' she whispered, whipping around.

'What?'

'I think...'

'*Someone is here,*' she wanted to say, but she couldn't get it out.

Instead she had to scream, as the lights went out in the windowless bathroom.

All she could see now were outlines, shadows, silhouettes.

'For God's sake, Feli, what's happening?' she heard Mats shout while she slowly moved towards the crack of the door, where sparse light was coming in. From the hall.

She stretched a hand towards the crack, feeling her way forward.

And she screamed again.

Higher, louder, longer.

Not from fright this time.

But from the excruciating pain.

17

Mats

'Feli? Hello? What's wrong? You still on the line?' The connection had died. And he got no more response. With that echo of Feli's tortured scream still in his ears, cutting off abruptly when the connection ended, Mats finally hung up and desperately wished for something to drink.

Not water, but something higher-proof. Something to lessen the shock. Because his own psychological crash was starting to look even more imminent than that of this aircraft. Addiction patients had often told him about that fog of obliviousness falling over them when the rush kicks in. Up here, with the altitude, he'd need a lot less alcohol in the blood to create such a condition.

Yet he needed to keep a clear head, of course he did.

Just what was going on?

He tried reaching Feli once again, but the phone only rang.

Meanwhile the cruel realisation mounted inside him that he had no options. The kidnappers were deadly serious. They were holding Nele, and now Feli appeared to be in danger as well. His first desperate attempt to gain a sense of the perpetrators, and thus their motive, had led him nowhere. Whoever was planning this madness was several steps ahead of him. Within the few hours left, it was completely impossible for him to accomplish anything else from this aeroplane than exactly what the blackmailer wanted from him: destroying a patient mentally, all in order to send himself and hundreds of innocent people to their deaths.

'Gah!'

Mats pressed his hands over his mouth and screamed in despair. Then he rubbed at his throbbing temples and recalled that he'd meant to grab his carry-on from economy so he could finally take something for his headache.

Or, first watch the video to the end?

On channel 13/10, from the ninth minute. He still didn't know what could be so volatile that it would put Kaja Claussen into September-eleventh mode.

No, first the drugs.

As much as Mats needed to know more, his head was also ready to explode, and he knew that if he didn't take something right away, soon he wouldn't be capable of a single clear thought. His stomach had calmed down, at least. His fear of flying had dialled back its symptoms.

Apparently there was evolution for psychological stress. Darwinism for agony. The most severe pains asserted themselves and gobbled up the weaker ones.

So Mats didn't need to combat his fear of flying for the moment. Quite the opposite: the fear of losing his daughter was driving his mind to perform at its maximum, spurred on as well by his concern for Feli and his bad conscience about dragging her into this madness.

18

'I'm sorry,' they said at the same time, equally startled.

Mats hadn't been counting on Kaja returning to see him once she could get free, not after she'd caught him watching the video.

'Just some boring documentary,' he had lied to her when she asked what it was. Then he had acted as if he were getting a phone call, whereupon Kaja left again without a word.

'May I...' She pointed at the serving trolley behind her.

It took a moment for Mats to get it.

'Thanks, but I'm afraid I'm not hungry,' he said, but let her enter.

'That's too bad,' she said without sounding very sorry. Kaja appeared to be exerting herself pushing the food trolley, as if the thick carpet were giving her trouble. She parked it between two chairs facing each other along the right-side windows.

Deploying its clever handles, she transformed the trolley into a dining table that she decked out with a white tablecloth, napkins, silverware, a salt shaker, and a vase of orchids before pulling out a plate of food from the compartment below.

SEBASTIAN FITZEK

She lifted the stainless-steel dome covering the china. 'Grilled winter cod with a roasted onion stock atop green beans and shiitake mushrooms. Normally you'd have more to choose from, but it's also true that people aren't supposed to eat heavily late at night, so...'

She looked at her watch and imitated a smile. 'If you'd like, I could get you a menu and the caviar cart sent up instead?'

'No, no, thank you. Not necessary,' Mats said and grabbed her by the hand when she unswervingly switched back to serving him.

His headache had balled up like a fist behind his forehead, and he felt awful. He didn't want to harm anyone, goddamnit. He didn't want to *die!* On the other hand, he was now being offered an opportunity, and almost literally on a silver platter.

'You didn't come back up here just because of the meal, am I right?'

He gestured for her to take a seat.

Kaja dodged him half-heartedly. 'I need to get back to business class.'

'And yet you went to the trouble of providing me with a nice meal. Though not much is supposed to be served at this hour. And even then you could've sent someone else, no problem. So, Frau Claussen, what's going on? What is it you wish to tell me?'

She swallowed hard, smoothing out her skirt.

'That video you had on,' she began haltingly.

He sat down and waited for Kaja to do the same.

The senior flight attendant's voice had turned a shade deeper than before. Typical for people at the onset of depression. The voice was often a better reflection of the soul than the eyes, since negative feelings made the voice box's capacity increase. He had learned that from Feli, who often only had speech and tone of voice to work from when assessing an emergency on her hotline calls.

'Yes?' he said.

'I thought I saw myself. Ten years ago. The gym video, I'm talking about. Of course that's ridiculous. I mean, my little drama could hardly have made it onto in-flight programming.' She forced out a laugh.

Mats opened his mouth but she raised a hand in her defence and continued: 'But there's also a reason why my imagination's running away with me. Our conversation before. When you told me that you hadn't believed me back then either—'

'I didn't mean it like it sounded,' fibbed Mats.

Kaja shrugged. 'Anyhow, when you said that you were happy to, eventually, believe my version of events, it brought me back to my chamber for a moment.'

'You felt the walls moving?' he asked, reviving a subject of their old therapy conversations. The 'chamber' was a metaphor that helped Kaja describe her feelings of powerlessness and isolation. By her final year of school she had transformed into a kind of trash compactor, with hydraulic walls that kept closing in, inch by inch. Thick and hard walls of reinforced concrete, threatening to crush Kaja inside.

'It wasn't as intense as before. But I could feel it. How the walls kept pressing at me again. I was standing in the galley and could feel the cabin getting smaller and smaller all around me...' Kaja grabbed at her neck and let her words trail off.

'I'm sorry about that. I didn't mean for my thoughtless comment to cause that,' lied Mats, since this was exactly what he had intended. And it now made him feel like a miserable pig.

'I'm tired and working too much,' he added. 'That should not have happened. I have to apologise to you.'

Kaja nodded, but he saw in her eyes that an apology was not enough. Every painful comment struck like a nail in that mask people wore to protect themselves from psychological abuse. With unstable personalities, it was quicker to crumble, and quickest with those whose defences had to be reconstructed in painstaking detail with psychotherapy.

'I'm going to speak frankly, Frau Claussen. I shouldn't have told you that I thought your experiences were made up.'

That I thought the horrible rumours about you at the time weren't completely unfounded.

Kaja leaned her head a little towards the window, like she used to do in her sessions, when she couldn't fall back on her memories, only her fantasies.

Mats followed her eyes into the darkness and thought he could sense her doubt.

'Do you want to talk about it?' he asked, not sure which answer was better.

A 'no', which would cease all this talk and save the hundreds of lives on this plane, him included.

Or a 'yes', which would put him in the position of becoming possibly the worst psychological mass murderer of all time.

Even if he wasn't sure how Kaja was technically supposed to pull off making a plane crash, he was nevertheless certain that he could fulfil his mission and revert her to a mental state where she would *want* to do just that.

'What am I supposed to tell you?' she asked.

Mats just wished he could break off this discussion right here and now. So he forced himself to think of his daughter instead, of that image of Nele being held by her kidnapper. Then he got to work chiselling away, adding another breaking point to Kaja's psychological armour with the following question:

'How many of your fellow students did you want to shoot?'

She shook her head, but said quietly, 'All of them.'

Mats gave her a moment's pause, then continued: 'But who especially?'

She avoided his gaze. 'I'm not sure, I—'

'You know. Who was first to die on your wish list?'

Silence. Then, after a while, she said with noticeable reluctance, 'Johannes.'

'Johannes Faber,' Mats expounded. 'Eighteen years old, just like you were then. What had he done to you?'

She stood up abruptly and nearly stumbled on the wheels of the service trolley.

'I think this conversation is a mistake, Dr Krüger, I, I don't see how it could make me feel any better.'

Mats stood too and tried to put on a trusting expression, which his headache made extremely difficult.

'Frau Claussen, please give me a chance. I hurt you with that thoughtless comment of mine. I have to make it up to you.'

Gentle beeping sounded above their heads. The seatbelt sign lit up.

'But right now our conversation is only making me feel worse,' Kaja protested feebly. 'I haven't felt this bad in years.'

That's something we have in common.

Mats tried giving his voice as much of a calming and ingratiating tone as possible. 'Tell me, how were you feeling that very first time we had a therapy session?'

She had come voluntarily yet was sent by her parents, who at the time were just glad that the worst had been prevented. This was mostly because of Feli, who'd taken Kaja's desperate call to the mental health hotline and connected the potential school shooter to Mats.

'Similar to now,' admitted Kaja. 'Awful. Tired. Not feeling very hopeful.'

Mats nodded. 'You do know that a therapy session is like a fever, Frau Claussen. At the beginning you feel terrible, but the truth is that you're sweating out the illness.'

Kaja shrugged and gave him an exhausted 'if you say so' look, and Mats continued his inquisition.

'All right. Then let me formulate it another way: ten years ago, you entered your school with a gun. You stole the pistol from your father, a member of a shooting club.'

'I didn't steal it. He gave it to me so I could defend myself in case such a thing ever happened to me again at school.'

Such a thing.

Kaja still didn't possess the courage to express concretely and openly what had been done to her, exactly one year before she locked herself inside the school restroom while armed. Despondent, with the firm intention of killing.

'I replaced the gas cartridges with real bullets. My father had only loaded the gun with tear gas.'

'Which, however, was not sufficient for your purposes.' She blinked, and Mats continued: 'Because you wanted to kill Johannes Faber.'

She nodded.

'He had done something to you.'

'Yes.'

Mats pointed at the monitor on the wall. 'He made that video that you believed you saw just now.'

'Yes, yes, yes. You know all that. Why are you trying to torment me, Dr Krüger?'

'I'm not tormenting you. I'm getting the sense that you still haven't fully worked through what happened. I want to help you, you see.'

'It doesn't feel like that, though.'

'That's the fever,' Mats repeated. 'It needs to get out. Just like the truth.'

'But all I've ever told you was the truth.'

'You're certain?'

'Yes, of course.'

'About the video, too?'

'Of course I did.'

He gave her a second to collect herself, then he said: 'Fine, Frau Claussen. Then please describe it all once again for me.' He forced out a smile. And while the aeroplane gently shook as a result of slight turbulence, he asked: 'What did Johannes Faber record on that video back then that was so bad it made you want to kill him a whole year later?'

Him and everyone who'd watched it.

19

Nele

The intervals were getting shorter. The pain, stronger.

After five hours (Nele knew it couldn't have been that long, but the pain had made the time stretch on, thirty seconds of contractions feeling like thirty minutes) the madman had finally untied her. He sure could've done that a lot sooner. After the third contraction, the breaks had left her able to do little more than stare in exhaustion at the vast ceiling and hope that this was all only a bad dream from which she'd soon awaken.

She couldn't escape. She could probably manage to get up from the stretcher, maybe even drag herself all the way to the entrance to the stalls, but by then he would've caught up with her.

This life inside her, wanting to force its way out, was stronger than anything tying down her hands or feet.

Nele felt at her stomach in despair.

For my munchkin.

'Everything will be okay,' she said and cried. 'Everything is going to be fine again.'

Then she screamed at the lunatic behind the camera:

'Let us out! Let us out at once.'

'I can't do that, unfortunately.'

From behind his tripod, he checked another setting on the device that looked like an analogue single-lens reflex camera but presumably had video mode turned on. After he made sure that the little red light stayed lit, he stepped up to her stretcher, holding a bottle of water.

'Hey, I noticed your *Pschyrembel Clinical Dictionary*,' Nele said and took the water after hesitating initially. He wasn't going to poison her, not after going to all this trouble. No, she was facing some other demise.

A worse one.

'You're studying medicine?' she asked after taking a gulp. God, she was thirsty. And tired. Her whole body was trembling from exhaustion. Her tracksuit was drenched with sweat. There was no other way around it now. She needed to take her trousers off.

'I was before. I have more important work now.'

Torturing pregnant women?

The thought nearly escaped from her lips but Nele was able to curb her anger, and take another drink.

She didn't know if it was always so stuffy in here or if the sun outside was beating down on the metal roof and turning these stalls below into one big heat reservoir. She could just imagine how bad it must be in the middle of the summer.

'Look at me,' she said as they guy tried turning his back to her. Despite his transformation into a gruesome kidnapper, he still looked like a cab-driving student.

She sat up a little on the stretcher and tugged at her waistband. His eyes got bigger. But she couldn't detect anything voyeuristic from him. It was more like, and it surprised her, shame.

'Do you really want to do this? Throw your life away? You know that all this is going to get out. I mean, I'm carrying a high-risk birth. Even in a normal hospital there's a good chance that my child and I could die. You want to go to prison as a double murderer?'

She pulled off her trousers and tossed them onto the slatted flooring along with her panties.

Animals used to stand here, to be fattened up, she thought. *Today I'm going to bleed to death here.*

'I'm not going to prison,' Franz said. He shook his head firmly and turned away. There was nothing sexual about this for him, no question. He didn't want to see her naked, at least.

Again Nele noticed how thin he was, practically emaciated.

If I wasn't lying here having contractions, he'd be no match for me at all.

'I'm not throwing my life away,' he said, and his voice hardened. 'And I *want* it to get out. Everyone should know about my mission.' He pointed at the tripod. 'That's exactly why I'm filming you.'

'What sort of mission are you on?' Nele asked and prayed that it wasn't a religious one.

'Milk.'

Here he goes with that again.

It made her angry, and she welcomed her rage, because it was the only thing that let her combat her fear of dying.

'That's a pretty crappy fetish, isn't it?' she said and tapped at her forehead to show just how nuts he was. 'Are you some kind of pervert? You're all into mother's milk, that it?'

Franz shook his head and turned to her again, rubbing at his nose. The reaction was one of shame, just like her father had once explained to her.

She sighed, emptied the water bottle and flung it at the floor in rage. 'Then why don't you try enlightening me, because I'm not understanding at all.'

He nodded, his eyes directed only at her upper body. She was also ashamed, lying here before him so exposed and vulnerable, still only wearing a T-shirt and socks. But her motherly instincts were stronger. She would do anything to bring her baby into the world.

Anything.

'I know that you don't understand this,' Franz said, and his voice got lost in this vast hall he'd carried her off to. He gazed over her head, then above, turning in a circle as if seeing this stall for the first time.

'And you are not alone in your ignorance,' he explained. 'Millions of people don't understand it. Very few know of it at all, and it's time that someone started opening their eyes.'

'Franz, please...'

He placed a finger on her lips. She briefly considered grabbing his hand and trying to break his wrist, but then what, what happened next?

'I didn't want to be the one,' he whispered while she frantically tried coming up with a plan. 'But apart from me, there is no one who will do it. You understand?'

'No.'

She did not understand. And there was no way out.

Instead she sensed that storm brewing again inside her.

How that stinging sphere was pushing forwards inside.

She grimaced and turned sideways because it let her endure the pain in her sacrum a little better.

'What do you know about milk production?' he asked abruptly.

'What?' she said, convinced it was a trick question.

'Just tell me: what do you know about how our milk is obtained?'

'Not much, just what everyone knows, I'm guessing – Fuuuh…'

Here it comes again. Goddamn. Here it comes…

'Cows get milked,' she panted, one hand clamped to the edge of the cot. 'It's preserved somehow—'

'Stop.'

'What?'

For a moment she was so thrown off by Franz barking the word that she swallowed her own words. Then the contractions forged on, and she could only hear the psychopath as if from afar while she tried not to drown in a sea of pain.

'Your knowledge is so untenably incomprehensible I can hardly believe it.'

As she tried planting her feet on the stretcher, so she could heave herself up and take some pressure off her pelvis, she heard him shout: 'You said cows get milked?'

'Yes,' she grunted through clenched teeth.

'Why do you all say that? Why does the story always start there?'

'How else?' she barked at him. She screamed all her pain, all her suffering out into this horrible stable, right at this lunatic's face.

Who, if she wasn't mistaken, now had tears in his eyes again.

'I will show you,' she heard him say. His voice was nearly all sobs. 'I'm so sorry,' he cried. 'But you'll have to experience it in your own body, and the whole world will be able to see. Then you will definitely understand why all this here is so necessary.'

20

Mats

After some brief turbulence, the plane returned to gliding as quietly through the night as a limousine on freshly paved autobahn. The seatbelt sign over the door to the Sky Suite still hadn't gone off though.

Mats felt an itch in his throat, as if from speaking too much. He pressed a button in the table showing a champagne glass symbol. This opened a long compartment he hadn't noticed before, recessed in the cabin wall as part of a wide shelf between the table and window. It contained pleasantly cooled juices and waters with a range of carbonation.

He grabbed a still water and wished he had a Maxalt painkiller. Kaja declined with a thanks when he offered her something. She sat on the very edge of her seat, as if about to jump. She folded her hands, only to undo her fingers right away, yet interlaced them again.

'Dr Krüger, do you remember that time we spent the whole session just talking about horror movies?' she asked.

Mats nodded.

Most people thought of a psychotherapeutic session as targeted, analytical questioning. The truth was, the route a therapy session took was never predictable. Casual observers were sometimes left with the impression that the patient and doctor were drifting into small talk and chatting about trivial things. This was also the case every now and then. Yet a good therapist never interrupted a patient's voluntary flow of speech because deep insights often were revealed in an apparently randomly chosen topic of conversation that could be beneficial for later treatment. For example, Kaja's penchant for gruesome, unbelievably violent movies had shown him that she'd long been seeking an outlet for her worries and fears, disappointments and anger.

'You'd explained to me how in American teen horror films the first to die were always the ones who'd had sex with one another,' Mats said.

Kaja nodded. 'And you explained that as a manifestation of American prudery. A punishment for immoral behaviour.'

'And?'

'I think there's something true in that. As you know, the first shots sounded when I was sitting in physics class. The topic was the Schrödinger equation. But I wasn't paying attention.'

'You were whispering to Tina Delchow,' Mats said, 'your best friend.'

'I was gossiping with Tina, yes.'

'About the night before?'

'She was angry with me.'

'How come?'

'Do we need to go through all this again?'

Mats reached for her trembling hands. 'I don't have my files with me, and it's been a long time. I don't remember it all anymore. Please, trust me. Right now it's upsetting, but afterwards this despair that's gnawing at you will all be forgotten again.'

She pulled her fingers away, looking anything but convinced. She eventually said, sighing, 'Tina was angry with me because I didn't sleep with Johannes.'

'Johannes Faber, your boyfriend at the time?'

Mats took a big gulp. The water tasted bitter, but that was likely all in his mind. A projection.

'Almost-boyfriend. He wanted something from me. But I didn't from him. I didn't feel I was ready yet. Tina and Amelie kept telling me I was going to screw up the relationship. You couldn't keep putting off great catches like that forever.'

'Who was Amelie again?'

'The third Painted Chicky.'

Mats nodded. 'Right, your coloured toenail gang, I remember. You three made a pact to always wear the same polish to school, that right?'

'Embarrassing now, but true. That day it was a green camo-pattern polish. Of all things.'

Mats waited for Kaja to take a deep breath before continuing.

'Tina was the most experienced in our little gang. I can still remember her telling me, "You want to die an old virgin?" When...'

'When what?'

The aeroplane gently vibrated, as if intending to tremble along with Kaja.

'I heard a bang out in the hallway,' she said softly. 'At first I was thinking someone brought firecrackers to school. But then it kept going bang, again and again, and people started screaming. Our teacher Frau Nader-Rosinsky was still telling us: *"Remain calm everyone. I'll go take a look at what's going on."* But she didn't even make it to the door. It flew open and suddenly he was standing there in the room. Army outfit, combat boots, ski mask.'

'His name was Peer?'

'Right.'

'Was he shouting?'

'No, he was real calm. That's why I could hear what he was saying despite the mask.'

'What did Peer say?'

A tear rolled down Kaja's cheek. 'Fritz the fisher fishes fresh fish.'

'Why did he say that?'

She sighed. 'Because he was Peer Unsell. Everyone called him "Lisping Unsell". We had all teased him about how he spoke.' Kaja took the tissue Mats had taken from his trouser pocket and offered her. She blew her nose. 'Peer just looked at us all at first. He said: "So, why isn't anyone laughing now?" Then he raised his pistol and shot Frau Nader-Rosinsky first and then—'

'Then Tina,' Mats said, naming her best friend for her.

The precocious one.

The one who's first to die in the horror movie.

'Kaja, do you know why Peer picked you as a hostage over everyone else?'

Mats was purposely calling her by her first name to break down the distance between them.

'I don't know. I think it was just chance. I was sitting next to Tina, who was suddenly lying there dead on the floor. Closest to the door. I was weak. Easy prey. That was probably the reason why he grabbed me, pulled me out by my hair.'

'Just chance?' Mats repeated, though he'd figured the same. That was in contrast to her schoolmates, who over the course of the coming months had spread one conspiracy theory after another.

'You don't believe me?' Kaja asked.

Mats didn't answer the question on purpose.

'So, Peer dragged you outside, across the schoolyard to the gym.'

Where the video was shot.

'Yes.'

'Was anyone in the gym?'

'At first there was. Tenth grade was having class there. He fired into the air and they ran for their lives. It was chaos. Frantic. I didn't know what was going on.'

Mats could still remember the news on the radio. Some students had fled the locker room naked.

'But, he didn't kill anyone else on the way over?'

'No.'

Mats recalled the investigation report.

In physics class Peer had fired indiscriminately at first, then deliberately selected victims (Tina was the girl who'd teased him most often, and his liaison teacher Frau Nader-Rosinsky had never been able to do much for him), but when the fire alarm sounded throughout the school he switched into flight mode and chose Kaja as a hostage for his exit strategy.

'So, let me ask you again: at the end of his shooting spree, you really have no idea why he went for you, out of everyone?'

'I don't know. I have no idea why Peer did that to me, before he...'

Her voice broke.

Before he put his gun in his mouth and shot himself dead.

Mats gave her time, even though he was running out of it himself. Not that he assumed he could do enough damage in a single conversation – that wasn't his intention yet. He still wanted to keep all options open in the event that he couldn't find any other way to save Nele.

To do so he would need to take things a step further with Kaja. But she couldn't just keep sitting here forever. She had to work after all and her team was surely missing her already.

He finally picked up where he'd left off. 'So, he took you into the gym?'

'He made me go into the girls' locker room.'

'Was it empty?'

'That's what he probably thought.'

'But?'

'But it wasn't. Two girls were still hiding in the showers.'

'What did Peer do?'

Kaja closed her eyes. Her eyeballs trembled under their eyelids, as if electrified. 'He stopped dragging me by the hair and pointed his gun at them. Kim and Trisha. I knew them from theatre group.'

'Did he shoot them?'

'No.'

'But he wanted to?'

'Yes.' She opened her eyes again.

'So why didn't he kill them?'

'Because. Because... goddamnit, you know what I did!'

Kaja abruptly stood. 'Listen, I've been here too long already. I have to work, I—'

'Kaja.'

She went to the door, keeping her back to him.

'Kaja, please. You'll have to come back. We can't just stop here...'

She didn't respond. His last words hadn't reached her – she'd already marched out of the Sky Suite. Angry, worked up, hurt.

Good God, what am I doing?

Mats stood up, shaking, still holding the empty water bottle, when his phone rang.

He checked the name of the incoming caller.

'Feli? Are you all right?' he asked in a panic. He felt hot and cold at the same time, and was expecting the worst, that someone had found her phone next to her body and called the last number she'd dialled. Only when he heard her voice did he realise what a weight he'd been carrying and how much better he could breathe now that it was gone.

'Yes, Mats. I'm okay. Someone broke into Nele's apartment. He slammed the bathroom door on my fingers.'

Thus the screaming.

'Good. I mean...'

Mats unconsciously paced the whole Sky Suite on the phone, wandering from the door to the restrooms and back again.

'I meant, good nothing worse happened. Did you see who it was?'

'No. But I have something better.'

Mats stopped abruptly. 'What?'

'I think I know who kidnapped your daughter.'

21

Feli

'You have a photo of her kidnapper?'

Mats had shouted so loud into the phone that Feli worried her taxi driver had heard every word.

'Yes,' she said tersely and hoped she could pay for her trip with a card. She'd spent her last cash buying Ibuprofen for the pain and Kytta natural ointment for the swelling. Just her luck to grasp at the door frame in the dark the very moment the bathroom door slammed shut.

Not true.

Someone had slammed it shut.

On purpose!

Someone who'd switched off the light to make sure he could harm her. On one of the most sensitive spots of the body, there where all the nerve endings ran together.

There was good reason why the world's most brutal henchmen concentrated on the extremities when performing torture during interrogation.

At first, when the pain rushed up her arm with the force of a heavily loaded freight train, she was certain her fingers had not only been smashed but severed. She had expected to see her ring, middle and index fingers lying on the floorboards in Nele's hallway. But once she finally managed to turn the light back on, she saw her hand was not a bloody stump, and the bones of her fingers were all still connected. They apparently weren't broken, either, even though she could hardly move them because of all the bruising under the skin.

'Say that again: you have a photo of Nele's kidnapper?' asked Mats, who still couldn't believe it. 'How did you get it?'

Feli couldn't hold her phone with her uninjured hand that great either. Meanwhile, all those burst blood vessels in her injured one felt like they were swelling to the size of a bowling ball. *Of course it had to be the left!* She and Janek had their wedding rings fitted for their left hands, intending to wear them on the same side as their hearts. Her ring finger now looked like it had been worked over with a sledgehammer. How was she going to tell her husband-to-be?

It was easier explaining to Mats how she thought she'd seen the kidnapper's face.

'In Nele's building, there's a pharmacy on the ground floor. When the pharmacist was helping me bandage my hand, I noticed the cameras over the front door.'

'Are you saying you recognised the kidnapper on a surveillance video?' Mats asked.

'I am.'

The taxi, an old Volvo smelling like sweat and wet dog, stopped behind a big, tall truck, either in a traffic jam or at a stoplight. There was also noise on the line, and for a moment Mats' voice sounded like an alien's before the metallic reverberation faded.

'I still don't understand. Wasn't the intruder trying to break in?'

'Screw that. One of the cameras caught the street along with the sidewalk.'

They drove on again.

'It's actually illegal, but recently the cars parked on the street were getting their tyres slashed. The residents got together and started filming the sidewalk and parts of the road. I told the pharmacist that a friend of mine had a similar issue just this morning and suspected the culprit was a taxi driver who picked up customers around here. So he let me look at the video.'

'I see. Clever. So on the video, you saw Nele getting into a taxi?'

'At 5:26 a.m. It stopped right in front of Nele's building. And, yes, your daughter got in. Heavily pregnant. Waddling too, like her water had just broken.'

'My God. But how do you know this was the kidnapper for sure? I mean, maybe they took her right to the clinic?'

'Not likely.' Feli spoke even lower. 'Because there was a second taxi, too,' she whispered with a glance at the driver, who didn't seem to take any notice of her or show any reaction in the rear-view mirror.

'Say again?' Mats asked in confusion. 'A second taxi? What's that supposed to mean?'

'It came over an hour later. At 6:30 exactly. Listen to this, Mats. This second cab was the real one. Ordered through Med-Call, a service specialising in patient rides. I'd listened to a message from the driver on Nele's answering machine beforehand so I just called him back. Bingo! Nele's ride to the clinic had been ordered weeks ago, for 5:30. But yesterday someone called, wanting to cancel. The service told the caller this wasn't possible – on such short notice he'd still have to pay. They wanted a credit card, but the caller decided to keep the ride instead and asked to reschedule it for later.'

'I don't quite understand,' Mats said. 'How did the kidnappers know which cab company Nele was using?'

'Probably didn't. But there's only a handful of dispatchers in the city, actually only three big ones. I'm guessing they called all of them on the off chance they could cancel Nele's order. That's how they found out about the scheduled time.'

They were crossing Prenzlauer Allee at the spot where Ostseestrasse turned into Wisbyer Strasse heading west.

'What for?' Mats asked, a little slow on the uptake apparently from so much stress.

'Makes sense; think about it. To push back the pick-up time so that the kidnappers could get there before the ride service.'

'You mean with that first taxi?'

About time, Feli thought with a sigh. 'That's right.'

'Nele was abducted by a cab driver?' Mats nearly screamed it.

And now Feli was getting another call.

She moved the phone away from her ear to see who was calling.

Crap.

Janek. What was she supposed to tell him?

'Sorry, honey, but I'm in the middle of hunting down criminals for my ex-lover right now, so you might have to get started on your own down at the registry office.'

If she had any sense left at all, she would hang up on Mats and tell the driver to turn around as fast as possible and take her home. But 'sensible' wasn't exactly the first word her friends used to describe her, unlike 'impulsive' or 'gullible'. She might well be deceiving herself right now, convincing herself she needed to save Mats' daughter from a grave emergency, but the reality was (and as a psychiatrist she was more than qualified to analyse herself) she was really doing this for herself, first and foremost. Her feelings for Mats were nothing like they used to be, having faded and yellowed after all these years of radio silence. But they hadn't disappeared, only gathered dust like forgotten furniture in an abandoned home. And despite the sorry circumstances, she nevertheless liked the feeling of this man finally needing her again, a man she thought she would never get over.

'A cab driver!' Mats shouted again, and her call-waiting stopped. Janek had hung up.

'At least someone pretending to be one,' Feli said. 'I can't make out the licence plate on the video.'

'But you have an image of the kidnapper?'

'Yes, he looks like a typical student. Tall and skinny, gangly. Messy hair, open sandals.'

'Can you make out his face?'

'Even better...'

The driver of the taxi abruptly hit the brakes and apologised for seeing the light on Bornholmer too late. Feli loosened her belt again.

'What's that mean, you have something better? Tell me. My daughter's life is at stake.'

She nodded. 'When he got out to wait at his double-parked

taxi, he was holding a bag. He put it in the trunk. The logo on the bag—'

'Was what?' Mats interrupted, losing all patience.

'It's the same as the bag in Nele's bathroom. The one with her meds in it.'

She was about to spell it out but Mats beat her to it: 'The Wedding Medical Centre.'

'Exactly,' Feli said, and glanced at the taxi's navigation screen.

They would be there in about fifteen minutes.

22

Mats

Most of them were sleeping. Women, men, children. Exhausted from all the ticket and passport and baggage checks, weary from the long wait before boarding. Lulled by the engine purring, full from warmed-over prepared meals, the cabin lights already dimmed. Only a few passengers had switched on reading lights and many, their faces glowing from their monitors changing colours with every scene, had their eyes closed. They'd fallen asleep during the movie.

Sleep. Such a merciful state of unconsciousness.

Mats felt his way along the aisle of the lower passenger area, his eyes stinging from tears, and his inner unease swelled the closer he got to the wings.

One of the passengers had pulled down their shade despite the darkness, which was smart if you didn't want to be woken by the sunrise in a few hours.

As long as they were all still alive.

Mats prayed that Feli really had found out something that could save Nele's life without endangering the innocent.

He saw a few unoccupied seats on his way back through the plane, now orphaned place holders for the lucky ones who'd changed or missed their flight or hadn't flown for some other reason and because of that would still be able to enjoy their lives tomorrow.

Apart from the seats he'd booked himself, though, almost all taken. A young couple in row 31 had made themselves comfortable across four seats and by the time the plane took off must have been feeling pretty lucky about having so much room. And an older man with thick-framed glasses used the empty spot between him and a sleeping woman as his shelf for the various documents he apparently needed to work on, tapping away at his laptop. Otherwise the rows hardly showed any open spaces.

If this lunatic somehow managed to make his goal a reality, 626 people would die. Murdered, insidiously.

By me.

The aeroplane glided along straight as a board, yet it felt to Mats like he was having to climb a mountain. It seemed to take forever for him to finally reach row 47. He first glanced at Trautmann. That twelve-thousand-dollar pill of his was working perfectly – the businessman slept with his mouth open, snoring, and the strings of drool hanging on the stubble at the corners of his mouth reminded Mats of a bulldog. Trautmann must have woken briefly, since his seat was all the way back. The slight incline could hardly be bringing him much comfort, and the way Trautmann was stuck all crooked in his seat was sure to make itself known in every joint once they landed.

That is, if they hadn't smashed into the concrete-hard water of the Atlantic by then.

Mats carefully opened the baggage compartment over his seat, slowly and deliberately so that his bag didn't fall out after possibly shifting on take-off. But his concern was unfounded. He took it out and set it on the outside seat. His Maxalt painkillers were in the outside pocket for easy grabbing. He hastily placed one on his tongue and waited for it to dissolve. He briefly imagined the kink in his neck already loosening its grip somewhat, then opened his eyes again.

Only now had he noticed it.

47F.

A window seat.

It was empty.

In theory there was no cause for alarm or even concern, since the passenger who'd been occupying his seat might have simply woken up and gone to the restroom. Yet Mats had just been on the lookout for empty spots on his way back here, and he was certain that he hadn't seen *this one*.

It was dark, sure. And from far off a person might mistake the crumpled blanket for a person and possibly the pillow squashed between the headrest and cabin wall for its head.

Or, maybe not.

Mats looked around. Among the restroom signs, only a single red showed anywhere near. All the other restrooms were free. With the exception of the one he himself visited earlier.

To call his blackmailer.

He considered what to do, asking himself what exactly was troubling him. Considering the clear threat he was currently facing, it was absurd to lose control all because of a passenger who'd earlier been sleeping and was now presumably taking a moment to relieve himself. And yet Mats could feel his aviophobia symptoms flaring up again.

Heart racing, sweating, trouble breathing. That snake of fear was tightening its grip and Mats needed to sit down, also to make way for a young father dragging his groggy son in tow, presumably to the restrooms by the end rows.

Trembling, he stroked at his suit trousers restlessly, in an attempt to wipe the sweat from his hands, yet his eyes found seat 47F.

Nothing.

No handbag, at least not under the front seat. No personal objects in the storage net on the back of the front passenger's seat.

Nothing, apart from a tiny glass ampule. So small that Mats had nearly overlooked it. It was lying under the sky-blue airline blanket, along the depression from the seam of the fabric seat. Mats turned it in his fingers, unsure what he was holding and whether it had any significance. He turned on the reading light and inspected it. The little vial held a gleaming brownish liquid similar to whisky, though it was also possible it was just the coloured glass. He looked around. The restroom 'occupied' light that had been on was now out, but there was no one in the aisle. No one finding his way back to row 47.

Well then.

He held the ampule up to his nose. When he didn't smell anything, he took the next step and opened it, doing so with even more care than he had the baggage compartment, yet that did not prevent its enormous, breathtaking, and wholly transformative power.

Mats shut his eyes and so wished he could scream. With rage, happiness, sadness, pain, despair and delight all at once.

Yet this unsettling scent stimulating all his senses, this unmistakable smell that he thought he'd recognised shortly after take-off, it literally jolted him out of his seat. It wasn't his body, but his very soul taking a journey back through time. Four years back, to Berlin. To the bedroom of his apartment on Savignyplatz, where he'd once been so happy. Back to then, that last time he had smelled that rare perfume on her.

Back to Katharina, his dying wife.

23

Berlin
Four years before

'Do you remember?'

She sounded as if her lungs were filled with rice, rattling with every breath in her bronchial tubes. She turned the old cocktail glass in her hands. It had dulled over the years.

Mats sat with his wife at the side of the bed, stroked her underarm and gave a sad smile.

Of course he remembered. How could he ever forget that day he'd stolen that glass from the bar on Hindenburgdamm? It had been a mild summer night, the seventh of July, the most important day in his life, even more important than Nele's birth, seeing how she wouldn't even have entered the world without the seventh of July.

'You were so embarrassed.' Katharina laughed, and her normally contagious laugh resembled just a faint echo of her former outbursts of joy before descending into a coughing fit.

The story was like 'Yesterday' by the Beatles – he'd heard it a thousand times and was still not tired of it. At this moment he'd give anything to listen to Katharina over and over again too, hearing her just how she was when they'd met: back then in the Bluebird Bar, he at the piano during his Humphrey Bogart phase with trench coat and cigarette hanging from his mouth, treating them all to what was arguably the world's worst version of 'As Time Goes By'.

In front of Katharina and her friends, who, between their amusement and embarrassment for him, couldn't turn their eyes away.

'At least you gave me your number,' he said, smiling, and she corrected him as always.

'No, I gave you a fake number.' It was the landline of her boyfriend at the time.

Her lipstick smeared on that very cocktail glass that she still owned, years later.

'If you really hadn't wanted to see me you would've just made up any old number,' Mats continued, in a conversation replayed a thousand times. 'That way I was able to track you down.'

Of course the inscription had long disappeared, like Katharina's hair from the chemotherapy. The glass was only a reminder of things that didn't exist anymore: hope, a will to live, a future.

To that end, it had been filled for the first time in years, with a hundred millilitres of a clear, gin-like liquid, its smell reminiscent of almonds.

'Give me the straw,' Katharina said and squeezed his hand, hers only as firm as a feather pressing against rock.

'I can't do it,' Mats said, who'd come up with thousands of things to say but now couldn't prevent the truth from blurting out of him. 'Please, how about we just—'

'No.' Her objection was weak, but decisive. Katharina had everything prepared. Contacted the Swiss assisted suicide organisation. Obtained the means. Set the day. Today.

How laughable his attempt had been to delay the inevitable. What kind of argument could ever negate a tumour and its unbearable pain?

'Just for the winter, my sweet. There's still something I wanted to show you. Do you know what it looks like when a soap bubble freezes? It's wonderful. The most fragile Christmas tree ornament in the world – at minus sixteen degrees it freezes over with these little twinkling stars, all within seconds. You will love it, Katharina. Let's just wait until winter, only six more months, then—'

'I don't want to die in the cold,' she countered and shut her eyes.

He didn't respond. Helpless, tired, sadder than ever. In his powerlessness he remained sitting on the edge of the bed, staring at the glass she held with her hands clamped tightly, even though she – as he noticed after a while – had fallen asleep.

Mats considered whether to remove the glass from her hands. Pour out the poison, thwart the attempt. Or at least delay it.

But he was even too cowardly for that.

'I'm so sorry, my love,' he said finally and stood. The final words he was to say to his wife. Before he kissed her, stuck the straw into the glass, and left the house. Full of rage, pain and exhaustion after that long battle he'd wanted to fight with Katharina until the very end. The truth was, though, he had abandoned her in her final hours. And set out to do the lowest and vilest thing in his life, and...

★ ★ ★

'Excuse me?'

Mats' eyes popped open.

The scent that had suddenly taken him back into his past had vanished. The window seat next to him was still unoccupied. A female flight attendant now stood in the aisle, leaning down to him.

'Would it be all right if you put your phone on silent?' she asked, and only then did Mats notice that his consciousness had been blocking out his ring tone.

'It's been ringing the whole time, and other passengers would like to sleep.'

24

'Where were you, Dr Krüger?'

Mats had let the first two calls ring and only picked up the third once he was back in the top-level Sky Suite. He'd been hounded by the illogical yet inescapable need to speak to his blackmailer inside a secluded room, as if this could provide him with even the slightest scintilla of control. It was why he was now standing before the bed in the sleeping compartment and trying not to yell.

'I've followed your psychotic instructions.'

'Did you? Or were you trying to spy on me?' the Johnny voice asked.

Mats closed his eyes.

The assault. Her fingers jammed in the door.

They, whoever *they* were, must've been watching Nele's apartment and surprised Feli.

'I don't know what you're talking about.'

'You don't? That's fine. You won't be able to get anything going anyway, no matter what you try. Better not to waste your time, otherwise Nele will—'

Mats stopped Johnny there:

'How is she?'

'Not good.'

'You son of a bitch, I want to speak to her—'

'Not going to happen. Her contractions are killing her right now.'

Please, dear God...

'Is she... has she... I mean, is she getting care?'

'She's not alone, if that's what you want to know. But the guy who's looking after her isn't exactly a trained obstetrician. Rather the opposite, if you know what I mean. He won't hesitate to kill your daughter and her baby should you fail in your task, Dr Krüger.'

Mats swallowed hard. 'Why are you doing this? Why make me torment my former patient?'

'Who's making you? You don't have to do anything as long as you feel that 625 strangers, plus yourself, are worth more than your daughter. And the baby of course. I don't think it'll take much longer for the baby to arrive.'

Mats anxiously grasped at his face. He could nearly feel the splotches of heat stretching from his neck up to his cheeks. 'Listen, can't we talk reasonably about all this?'

'I think that's what we're doing.'

'No. This is all insane. Reactivating Kaja's trauma is one thing. But how do you know she'll transform her violent fantasies into reality? It's not exactly easy to seize control of an aircraft, not even by a flight attendant.'

Johnny giggled. 'You let that be my concern.'

'But—'

'You'll see soon enough. All you need to do is stick to my instructions. Have you seen that video from the gym, Dr Krüger?'

He sighed, exasperated. 'I already know it; it's from the day of the school shooting.'

'Have you watched it all the way to the end?' Johnny asked him.

'No, Kaja interrupted me.'

His blackmailer now sounded quite elated, which annoyed Mats. 'Did Frau Claussen see what's playing on channel 13/10?'

'She might have in passing—'

'Good. Very good. She should watch the whole thing.'

'What good will that do?'

Mats now stood at the door to the sleeping compartment, cooling his forehead on the metal frame.

'You'll see once you get to the end. Trust me.'

His blackmailer sounded as if he were about to hang up so Mats quickly added: 'I have another question.'

'What?'

'All this here, does it have anything to do with my wife?'

A pause.

For a moment he smelled Katharina's scent again, but his olfactory reprieve was only the wishful thinking of an overstrained mind of course.

'What makes you think that?'

'I... I'm not sure. Right before the plane took off, I had a feeling that I saw her.'

And the guy who stole my seat, he left her perfume lying there.

'No, Dr Krüger,' his blackmailer said. 'Your wife has nothing to do with this. I promise you. I'm very sorry, by the way, that she had to die so alone like that. It would be such a shame if Nele were to go the same way.'

Mats had the feeling he was plummeting hundreds of metres down even though the aeroplane remained stable. He heard the words that came next with a hissing in his ears, as if he were sitting back below in row 47 and breathing the stale recycled air of economy class.

'You have a remaining flight time of eight hours and seventeen minutes. Use every second. Watch the gym video all the way through from beginning to end. Then you'll know just what levers to pull with Kaja.'

'And once I've done that, then what?'

'Then you don't need to do anything more. Simply wait.'

'For what?'

'Well, what do you think? For the crash, of course.' Johnny sounded truly amused now. 'Take Kaja Claussen to the brink of her deepest mental abyss. The rest will come naturally.'

25

Feli

Sunken faces, bloodshot eyes, scrawny and nearly emaciated bodies belonging to people who could only raise their heads wearily, their hands folded in their laps.

As Feli passed through the waiting room of the Wedding Medical Centre, she couldn't help thinking that all the people who worked here owed their livelihoods to personal tragedy. Tumours that embedded themselves in the lungs and spread metastases, radiation-resistant growths, autoimmune diseases whose treatment cost as much as a small car. This was obviously cynical and unfair. It was like saying that policemen profited from criminals. And yet Feli remained wary of that discreet luxury she'd encountered after opening the sliding glass doors so cleverly integrated into the former industrial building that they didn't look strange in the old-fashioned walls. On the way to the reception, black-and-white photos on those walls recalled the past labours of this erstwhile printing house, now the medical centre run by Doctor Professor André Klopstock for treating the chronically and the terminally ill.

Then there was the patient who'd shamelessly jostled in front of Feli at the reception counter. He had more than enough energy. 'Take heart, Solveig,' he said to the doctor's assistant behind the counter. 'I mean, just look at me.'

The lean, roughly twenty-five-year-old dark-haired man took a step back towards Feli and in doing so shortened that distance requested for patient privacy. She was now the involuntary witness to a stage-worthy performance.

He grasped his chest with his feigned theatrics that had already elicited a smile from the motherly-looking assistant. 'I'm at the end of my rope.'

'I'm so sorry, Herr Kress.'

'Livio. Please call me Livio.'

Feli rolled her eyes at the obvious flirting tactic.

'I can't fit you in anywhere, Herr Kress. And you know that.'

'But I need my vitamin cocktail. Please, Solveig. Look into these brown eyes. At this part-Italian and entirely honest face.'

The man dropped to one knee and extended his hands in prayer to the assistant, beseeching her. She shook her broad head and pinned-up hair with regret.

'You just had an infusion the day before yesterday.'

'Which did me soo much good.'

Solveig placed a finger to her lips and appeared to consider something. 'Would you take me out dancing tonight?'

'Are you being serious?' Livio asked, taken aback that his ploy might actually have success. He pulled himself up and patted the dust off his black cargo trousers.

The doctor's assistant thwarted him with a smile. 'No, I'm not. It was just a joke. You know insurance won't accept that on a whim. If you want another infusion this early, then you pay out of pocket.'

Livio sighed, pretending to wipe tears from the corners of his eyes.

'Then this might be the last time that we ever see each other again, Solveig. Please remember me when you read the headline: "He died all alone under a bridge. From a lack of vitamins."'

Feli felt her whole body wince as the man abruptly turned around and ran right into her. She staggered, had to grab at the counter so as not to fall. That sent another jolt of pain through her squashed hand and it was all she could do not to scream out.

'Oh, my bad, I'm sorry,' the man said like he meant it, staring at her with his wide, dark-brown eyes. He held her firmly by both arms and asked, 'Did I hurt you? I didn't mean to.'

His facial features comprised a peculiar combination not easy to classify. Angular on the one hand, which gave him a roguish, even slightly shifty aura. On the other hand, his eyes were so large and his mouth so full that Feli could've understood if Solveig really had been receptive to Livio's attempt at flirting.

'No, no, it's fine.' She shook off his hands, one of which held her shoulder and the other her hip as if he'd wanted to dance with her.

'You sure?'

'I'll be all right.'

'I really am sorry.'

He took his leave with a sweeping gesture, not forgetting to wink at the doctor's assistant one last time.

'Such a scammer.' Solveig kept smiling at him, then greeted Feli. 'How can I help you?'

Good question.

She wanted to find out any connection between the supposed cab driver and this clinic – if there was any. Just five minutes ago, this had seemed like an audacious and yet reasonable idea to her. Now she wasn't sure how to tackle it.

She was a psychiatrist, not an investigative reporter, let alone a detective. The only investigations she was supposed tackle today were whether her wedding dress fitted correctly and how she was going to keep her hairdo looking good in this drizzle all the way to the registry office. Instead she was playing Miss Marple for a former lover. And, strictly speaking, by searching for Mats' daughter she was also helping him rediscover the main cause for their estrangement.

He never would've taken off to Buenos Aires if it wasn't for Nele.

'Is Dr Klopstock here?'

'Do you have an appointment?'

Feli shook her head. 'It's personal. We're colleagues.'

She didn't need to tell Solveig that they didn't know each other personally. Klopstock was known all over town, at least in professional circles. This wasn't so much due to his – admittedly – respectable success with treatment as to his amazing business sense. He wasn't just an oncologist but a psychiatrist as well, which gave him the advantage of being able to treat, as well as invoice, both the biological as well as mental impairments of his often terminally ill patients. He also operated one of the city's largest blood laboratories and wrote popular non-fiction bestsellers with titles like: *The Klopstock Method: Beat the Cancer of Your Soul So Your Soul Can Fight the Cancer.*

'Sorry,' said the doctor's assistant, 'but he's over in the clinic on Ku'damm today.'

Klopstock, seeing himself as more of an entrepreneur than a doctor, had several branches spread out over the city. He gave them the pretentious title of 'clinic' even when they were only one storey in a renovated old building.

'Can I give him a message for you?'

'No, but thank you.' Feli moved to leave, but she thought otherwise when she searched her jacket pocket for her phone and felt the folded piece of paper.

Well, why the heck not...

Now that she was here, she might as well give it a shot.

'Do you know this man?' Feli asked and showed Solveig the photo the pharmacist had printed out for her.

'Hmm...'

The assistant reached for reading glasses and scrutinised the zoomed-in, black-and-white video still. It wasn't the best quality but better than many of those manhunt photos the police used to find subway thugs and other criminals from public surveillance cameras.

The assistant pointed at the lanky man with the gaunt face, whom Feli was calling a student. 'You mean the taxi driver?'

'Yes.'

She thought she'd spotted a brief flash of recognition on Solveig's face, yet the assistant only shook her head and was about to say something when Livio suddenly barged in.

'Look, my dear Solveig, what I just plucked for you!'

Adding a charming smile, Livio squeezed in next to Feli, leaned across the counter and handed the doctor's assistant a bouquet of long-stemmed chrysanthemums.

'Put those back now,' Solveig demanded, no smile on her face this time. 'In that vase by the doorway.'

Feli couldn't tell whether Solveig's sudden change of mood had anything to do with the Livio's brashness or with the photo she handed back to Feli as soon as Livio pushed off again.

'I don't know him, sorry. I have to go see to something in the lab now.'

Solveig stood an On Break sign on the counter and said good day.

'Very well, if you say so.'

Feli heard the front door close, Livio presumably having just left. When she turned back to the counter she saw Solveig had withdrawn to a back room, leaving her alone in the reception area.

All right, fine. I was high time she rushed back home to start changing anyway.

She put the photo back in her pocket and planned to call a taxi but found her other pocket empty. Irritated, she patted all her the pockets, in vain. Her phone was gone.

Could I have left it lying in the taxi?

No. She remembered she was still holding it when she stepped out of the taxi, then put it away.

In her trench coat.

That she had on the whole time.

Without taking it off.

Nothing had fallen out of it – she would've heard especially here on the clinic's hard parquet floor. And even then it would've been lying right at her feet. Which meant it could only have happened *when Livio had bumped into me, and held onto me...*

LIVIO!

Her heart started racing, and she felt her hand throb with pain again.

'That lousy bastard,' he hissed, looking around, and rushed over to the door the patient had vanished through, into the stairwell.

26

Mats

'Just like cobblestones.'

Another phrase from Mats' aviophobia seminar leader entered his head now that the plane was passing through an area of 'heavier wind shear' over the Atlantic, as the captain had called it a few minutes ago in an announcement.

'The wings can sway up and down a whole tall storey high without a thing happening.'

Mats sat buckled up in the Sky Suite armchair, fighting an internal battle against the shock waves hitting the Airbus. His fear of flying wasn't hitting him as hard as he'd feared. Though it wasn't exactly calming to know that the two wings, which also happened to hold nearly 400,000 litres of explosive fuel, could bend a good few metres without harm. And yet, his fear for his daughter would prevent him from running screaming through the aeroplane or hyperventilating down on the floor of the Sky Suite, gasping for air. Even so...

Cobblestones?

It felt to him more like a fishing boat being grabbed by monster waves before plummeting down from high breakers into a deep ocean trough. He knew of course that the brain perceived height differences to be stronger when the body was moving faster – passing over a pothole felt different at ten kilometres per hour than at a hundred. And the plane's speed was currently showing about a thousand!

Focus. You need to focus.

Mats scribbled 'perpetrator not acting alone' on the notepad before him. The voice had mentioned at least one other lunatic holding Nele. The whole thing involved a broader operation that demanded planning. This ruled out a lone perpetrator acting on an impulse such as jealousy or revenge, a former patient, for example, who felt they'd been mistreated. The more complicit, the greater the risk. This 'Johnny' was striving for a goal that had to hold extreme importance for him.

The plane was dumped into another air pocket, an 'unstable stratification', as it was correctly called, because of course there were no pockets in the air. Even though it felt like that.

EXPENSE

was the next item Mats wrote down.

They had a vehicle for transporting her, a place where someone giving birth couldn't be heard screaming, and her abductor.

THE TAXI DRIVER!!!

Dear God, please let Feli find out something.

When was she going to call? She'd been at the clinic for a while now.

RESEARCH!

Extremely important. They knew all about him, about Kaja, and Nele. About their worries, troubles, fears, and traumas. They even had knowledge of his wife dying alone.

ACCESS!

This could be the crucial part.

The kidnappers had access to Nele's apartment, but also to this aeroplane. They hadn't needed to place a physical weapon on board – that was the most treacherous part of their plan. A psychological bomb could pass through even the most meticulous ground checks unnoticed. It couldn't be coincidence that Kaja had ended up on the same plane with him. How had they managed that? And how had they fed the video into in-flight programming?

The video!

Mats turned in his chair so he could see the monitor built into the restroom wall, and flipped back to channel 13/10.

The video began with those same shaky images that Mats must've watched a thousand times already while preparing for their therapy sessions.

Kaja called them the 'gym tapes' though it was just a single recording, and he'd officially referred to it as the 'Faber video'. Named after its creator, Johannes Faber.

Kaja had thought they were alone when the school shooter led her into that locker room aiming his pistol.

Mats saw the bright blur that suddenly gained contours.

Heard two girls crying, Trish and Kim, who'd stayed hidden in the showers and were now fleeing the locker room. Half naked, barefoot in track pants, running for their lives that they owed to Kaja. Because she had sacrificed herself.

'Do *what you want with me,*' she said, and to this day Mats was still amazed by how utterly fearless she was. '*You already have me. Let those two go.*'

The same capacity for self-sacrifice was now being demanded of him.

As if the circle were now closing...

Mats fast-forwarded through the minutes to follow. He knew them already. Peer shoving his pistol into Kaja's mouth. Forcing her to remove her clothes and kneel down before him.

'*Like a dog in heat,*' he'd ordered her. And she'd obeyed. She had to present herself to him down on all fours. The gun to the back of her head by now. Seven minutes long. She was at his mercy, without pause. His thrusting continued until he came inside her, her scream like an animal wounded in the belly.

In the medical report of the rape there was mention of severe tearing in the vaginal tract but also of bite wounds in the shoulder and upper arm. Pressure from the gun barrel had left a bruise on her head. Worse, however, as is so often the case, was the psychological damage. Kaja wetted the bed at night for two months, haunted by nightmares where Peer took her hostage. Night after night she was raped by him, over and over. And even though the school celebrated her as a heroine (Kim and Trisha had even given *Bild-Zeitung* an interview attesting that they'd had no chance of escaping the killer without Kaja's selflessness), she was plagued by enormous feelings of guilt.

'Why didn't I defend myself, Dr Krüger? Why did I simply let that happen to me like some cheap slut?'

She might have managed to climb out of her deep hole without permanent psychological damage. The self-help group she'd attended (though not regularly) after a period of more intensive support from a school psychologist might well have proved enough.

Yet the video immediately changed everything.

Filmed by Johannes Faber of all people, the boy Kaja hadn't allowed to 'do it' with her the day before the school shooting because she didn't feel she was ready. When the first shots rang out, Johannes had fled to the girls in the locker room during the ensuing panic. He'd stayed hidden from Peer in the showers there together with Kim and Trisha. Neither Kaja nor the school shooter had seen him and neither were they aware that he was secretly filming the rape with his phone. Only to, right as Kaja was slowly regaining a daily routine nine months later, make the video public in a group email to his sports performance class.

Subject: Here's how our heroine really got off!

From that point on, everyone's opinion of her plummeted.

Kaja wasn't the brave one anymore. She was the whore.

No longer sacrificing herself. Ultra horny instead.

No more the heroine. The nymphomaniac accomplice of a school shooter instead.

Of course, there were many who remained on her side. Many had condemned sending around the abominable video, pointing out that it was all too clear how brutally Kaja was abused. That she'd screamed in pain and not lust like the haters' comments in the student forums tried to claim. That he kicked her off him like a piece of dirt after he'd finished with her. Shortly before the recording turned black, and Kaja could only be heard whimpering.

That was how it had always looked, judging from the tape Mats had seen before.

The video on channel 13/10, however, continued to play.

What the hell…

Mats practically had to rub his eyes. He undid his seatbelt to get closer to the screen. He focused on the display, and could not believe what he was seeing.

No, it can't be.

He reversed. To minute nine. And it was just like Johnny had said.

If Kaja's psyche was the north tower of the World Trade Center, then this video was the aeroplane that steered right into its heart. She only needed to be shown it.

Goddamn.

His blackmailer was right.

It would destroy her.

And change everything.

Everything.

27

Feli

The soles of her high-heeled ankle boots clacked like spanking down the clinic stairs.

Feli ran outside, nearly stumbling over a woman trying to enter in her wheelchair, and in her excitement forgot to excuse herself.

Right, left. Straight ahead. She peered in all directions, pivoted around, and saw a half dozen Livios.

One was crossing Seestrasse, another was waiting at the bus stop smoking, two more were walking into a pharmacy one corner away.

In this drizzle, every third guy looked like a slim half-Italian with dark hair from afar.

Damn it. She didn't get the best look at him, and dark trousers and a grey parka weren't exactly distinguishing characteristics.

Crap, crap, crap.

Smashed fingers, stolen phone. There was more and more she'd have to confess to Janek. And less and less time until the ceremony.

Feli checked her watch and looked for the next taxi

stand, then it occurred to her that she needed to block her phone immediately. Banking info, account access – it was all on there, though encrypted, but who knew what criminal talents pickpockets were capable of these days?

Angry now, she wanted to head right back to that doctor's assistant and lodge a complaint with her, since Solveig knew the thief and had his info in their records.

On the other hand... She hesitated.

She probably wouldn't learn much more from Solveig than that the guy was named Livio Kress. It wasn't as if the woman could testify to his stealing her phone from her trench coat. Solveig would've said something right when it happened.

Hell, she hadn't even noticed herself.

And all other information fell under patient privacy.

But Solveig did have a telephone.

Feli turned back for the clinic entrance and was about to open the door when her eyes landed on the display window of the pharmacy housed among the ground floor retail shops.

Bright, nearly white light streamed out between the window displays onto the wet rainy pavement. She saw a cardboard cut-out of a laughing woman happy about the effects of an athlete's foot ointment, next to a rack of stomach drops. And in between, further inside the store: Livio.

That really takes some nerve!

He was leaning over the sales counter to a young female pharmacist with a short haircut, showing her a phone.

My phone.

Presenting it to her like a street vendor his goods. Grinning, with sweeping gestures.

The pharmacist was sympathetically shaking her head, which made him put the phone away. He'd obviously just tried converting it into cash on the spot. All Feli heard as she sprinted through the sliding front doors inside was: 'Without a receipt, you're not going to be able to anyway.'

'Call the police!' Feli shouted.

'What?'

'Say again?'

The pharmacist and Livio stared at her. The other customers did too, a man with a runny nose and an elderly couple, the woman leaning on a walker – all turned to Feli and eyed her in bewilderment.

'That man just stole my phone,' she said to the short-haired pharmacist and pointed at Livio.

'He stole it?'

Livio blew up his cheeks like a puffer fish. 'That's a lie.'

'Then what did you just stick in your pocket?'

'You mean this?' Livio pulled out her phone.

'Oh, please. Now you're even admitting it.'

'No, I'm not at all. I found it in the gutter.'

The pharmacist couldn't help rumpling her forehead, and Feli just shook her head.

'You don't even believe it yourself. You're trying to pawn it off.'

'Listen to me, please...' Livio held out his hands to the pharmacist who, her eyebrows rising, said, 'Should I really call the police?'

'No!' Livio shot back, then he said to Feli, 'Please, think about it. If I was the one who stole it, wouldn't I have headed for the hills? Would I be in this pharmacy? I didn't know it belongs to you. I swear.'

'Was he trying to sell it to you?' Feli asked the pharmacist.

'Not directly...' She wasn't sure what to say. 'He only asked if I knew someone who might be interested.'

Livio clapped his hands, laughing. 'A misunderstanding. All I was trying to find out was if any customers had reported it missing.' He smiled his charming smile but Feli was anything but convinced.

'I am certain that if I call the police they'll have something on you. That right?'

Livio's smile vanished, and Feli nodded in triumph.

'Oh, did I hit a nerve? Explain all you want. You know what, I'm going to dial 110 now, and we'll see what the authorities have to say about your lost-and-found story.'

'Please, don't do that.'

Livio stepped close to her and looked around. Once he seemed certain no one was listening, he whispered to her in desperation: 'You're right. I'm in enough trouble. Please. You have your telephone back. Let me go.'

'Why should I do that?' Feli snarled in anger. 'You'll just rip off the next person around the next corner.'

She punched 110 into her phone, turned away from him.

'I can help you, that's why,' she heard him whisper behind her right before she pressed the green dial button.

She side-eyed him over her shoulder. 'Help how?'

'That photo, the one you were just showing Solveig.' Livio pointed at her phone. 'Please, leave the police out of this, and I'll tell you who that is and where you can find the cab driver.'

28

Mats

Mats found Kaja in the 'lobby', the lower-level reception area for first class passengers – the first thing those well-heeled travellers saw when they entered the aircraft on a separate gangway reserved just for them. Apart from the curving cabin walls, hardly anything here resembled an aeroplane. It certainly did look like the reception desk of an ultramodern boutique hotel with its semicircular leather lounge chairs that harmonised perfectly with the cream-coloured carpet, illuminated by an arc lamp of the sort usually seen in a nice living room.

The lobby was situated between the cockpit and the fully reclining chairs of first class and wasn't being used by the passengers at the moment. When Mats came down the spiral stairs, Kaja was alone at a pearlescent sideboard, filling a champagne flute on a mirrored silver tray.

He could've used the glass elevator next to the restrooms, presumably reserved for handicapped passengers. Surely some who could afford that three-room villa above would be even older and less fit than he was.

'Kaja?' Mats asked gently, and she jumped so violently

the liquid she was pouring missed the glass. 'I'm sorry, I didn't mean to frighten you.'

Not yet.

The truth was he wanted, no, *needed* to talk to her about the Faber video.

The video was so explosive it had shaken even him to the core. Everything he thought he'd known about Kaja now appeared in a wholly new and mysterious light to him as well.

'It's no problem.' Kaja gave a fake smile and looked around. Mats got the sense that she wasn't checking to see if anyone had noticed her little mishap.

She was scared of being alone with him.

'Should I have someone clear your plate and get your bed ready?' she asked as she dried the tray with a cloth napkin.

'That's not why I'm here.'

She topped off the glass and shook her head. 'I'm afraid I'm unable to see to you personally at the moment, Dr Krüger. But you don't have to go to the trouble of coming all the way down here when you need something. There's a call button on every remote. Just push it and a flight attendant will be there immediately.'

'I don't want *a* flight attendant. I want to talk to *you*.'

Kaja lifted the tray and all her body trembled as she, in the span of a second, dropped any and all professional courtesy: 'And I do *not* want to talk to you,' she snarled at him. 'Our conversation, it has to end. Leave me in peace.'

'I can't do that,' Mats answered, as calmly as was possible for him.

He glanced to the right, down the aisle to first class, but could only make out a velvety curtain fluttering as if in the wind. The aeroplane kept gliding along through this rough sea that was the night sky, still shaking slightly, and the seatbelt signs had stayed on.

'In addition, I have to insist that you return to your seat at once. This turbulence could get worse at any time.'

Mats gave her a harsh stare. 'Are you talking about the flight? Or yourself?'

Kaja's eyes searched his. Frightened, nearly speechless. He could see in her eyes that she was questioning whether he was still the reasonable man she'd confided in before.

No. I'm not.

In the dim light of the arc lamp, her face looked nearly white now as if deliberately made up pale. As she held the tray, he could see some polish was lacking on one of her fingernails.

'I'm not doing great. I don't understand, Dr Krüger. I get the feeling that you're trying to open my old wounds on purpose. I haven't had to think about everything as much in the last few years. There are days when it doesn't even enter my head. But now, a few minutes with you and I keep seeing all these images.'

The champagne glass quivered on the tray, nearly in sync with her lower lip.

'Which images?' Mats asked maliciously, but she didn't take the bait.

'No, don't. Please stop.'

He took a deep breath and acted as if he'd respect her wishes. 'Okay, all right. I understand. And, yes, I'm sorry. Please listen to me a moment, though. I won't ask you any more questions – it's not you I want to talk about at all.'

'Then what?' she said warily.

'Let me tell you something about me. Because I know exactly how you feel.'

'Dr Krüger, please I...'

He pointed at the seating area, but she didn't follow him.

'You might know that I lost my wife four years ago.'

'I read the obituary in *Tagesspiegel*. I'm very sorry. She had cancer, right?'

'Yes. But she died from the poison that she drank.'

'So, suicide?'

He nodded.

'Katharina couldn't take the pain anymore. She contacted organisations abroad that support people in cases of assisted suicide, obtained the appropriate means. All against my will.'

'Why are you telling me this right now?' Kaja asked with a timid glance towards the curtain. In the few hours since their first conversation, she had shrunk a couple of centimetres. She was letting her shoulders slump, and the burden weighing on her was making her spine curve. 'I have a passenger waiting for his order.'

She tried passing by Mats.

'Just one minute, Kaja. That's all I need. Katharina, she didn't want any more than that from me herself. One final minute, with me by her side. The final minute of her life. Yet I couldn't do it. I couldn't stand it, that all that I once loved, that light of my life, showing me the way, was supposed to die right there before my eyes and fade away.'

'I understand that.'

Mats could feel the tears coming, and no wonder, having never opened up to anyone like this up until now. Everything he said matched reality. Sadly.

'I haven't forgiven myself to this day. It was selfish, egotistical. Just like what I did afterwards. The lowest thing I've ever done.'

'What was that?' Kaja had to know, and Mats could tell that it was working. By exposing a little of himself, he'd won back a little of their lost trust.

Hopefully.

He was also realising that confiding in someone really did have a cleansing effect. He'd been dragging his feelings of guilt around with him for too long, incapable of healing himself. But his professor always used to put it like this: '*Psychology is doomed to fail because we're making the absurd attempt of hoping to understand our minds using our minds.*'

'I drove over to a colleague's. Felicitas Heilmann. You met her, briefly. She's the psychiatrist you talked to when you called the mental health hotline. A good friend of mine. I felt horrible, hopeless, and alone. Well, she trusted me.'

Kaja placed the tray back on the sideboard. 'What are you trying to tell me, Dr Krüger?'

'That was four years ago, Kaja, and I've been running away from it ever since. I ran from the bedroom of my dying wife and into the bedroom of my younger colleague, who I knew loved me. Although I didn't reciprocate her feelings. I was fleeing from myself, into a low and egotistical form of self-pity. I slept with her.'

Mats swallowed hard.

'I ran from a highly sober state into that of a senseless drunk and was barely able to form a sentence when my daughter Nele called me on my phone. I was still lying in that bed, and Feli picked up for me. To hear the message that Nele had found my wife dead in *her own* bed.'

The time had come. Mats couldn't fight it anymore. The tears flowed yet didn't keep him from vividly describing to Kaja everything weighing on his chest:

'And then I kept fleeing. From Nele, who's hated me with no end ever since that day. *"You miserable, cowardly piece of shit,"* she screamed at me when I came home. *"You cheat on Mom while she's dying?"*

'And she was right. With every single one of her furious accusations. Nele forbade me to come to the funeral, which she planned all by herself. And me? I didn't want it to become a scandal. I was even so weak I packed up my things and kept on running, as far away as I could this time, to my brother in Buenos Aires. I eventually found my feet there. Or at least, so I thought.'

'But what does that have to do with me?' Kaja said. 'I'm not running away.'

'Oh, yes you are. I didn't want to make it so explicit at first. But you haven't really faced the truth either. You fled. Not physically, but certainly mentally. Otherwise you wouldn't be reacting so strongly right now, especially since I've only presented you with fragments of the actual truth.'

Kaja cleared her throat. The splotches on her neck were darker. 'What is that supposed to mean? What *actual* truth? There's nothing that we haven't spoken about in full detail.'

Mats grimaced with remorse. 'Not true, Kaja. There is. Please, just give me a brief moment, and I will prove it to you.'

As he spoke that last sentence, the curtain was pulled to the side and Valentino, the attendant she apparently called Ken, stepped into the lobby.

'So this is where you're hiding,' he said, and his expression darkened once he saw who was here with her.

He pointed at the tray on the sideboard. '3G is annoyed enough already.'

'I'm coming right now,' Kaja promised and picked up the tray again, pushing hair out of her eyes with her free hand.

'Please,' Mats whispered into her ear as she passed. 'I have to show you something. It will change your life.'

She shook her head and kept going, yet turned around again right before the curtain Valentino was holding open for her. 'I'll see to it, Dr Krüger. Just give me five minutes.'

Then she disappeared into first class with her fellow flight attendant.

29

Nele

How nice. A moment with no pain. The most divine form of pure bliss.

Nele's breathing slowed. She let her muscles relax a little and, as best as she could on the cot, tried stretching her arms and legs.

Her abdomen, still basically one single cramp, now relaxed noticeably and it was a blessing after the last set of contractions.

'I have to go to the bathroom,' she moaned, which was a lie. During the last contractions she hadn't been able to hold out any more and had relieved herself. She could smell the faeces and urine between her legs, and it didn't bother her. Or her kidnapper, strangely. He handed her a damp cloth from a bucket he'd stood next to the camera. It's light kept blinking the whole time, so Nele assumed he was recording everything. That included the monologue he annoyed her with between those contractions coming faster and faster, getting more and more severe, *which seemed to indicate that the first stage of pregnancy was passing into the final expulsive phase – wasn't that how it worked?* Nele couldn't remember, neither from that one section in the birthing guide she'd only skimmed over nor what her gynaecologist had told her.

'Did you know that animals don't have any pain when delivering?'

'Please, just leave me alone,' Nele said and cleaned herself off better than nothing.

'Elephants might, though they're an exception,' Franz continued. 'The Bible says, God punished Eve. *I will greatly multiply your hardship in childbirth. You shall give birth to children in great pain,*' he recited, apparently from a Bible verse. 'But that's all nonsense of course. The truth is, it has to do with our upright gait.'

Upright?

Nele wondered whether she should use her break from the pain to stand up from the stretcher. How much time was there until the next contraction? And how close was it until the baby came out?

'Thanks to an upright gait, we humans have our hands free, allowing us to do many intelligent things at the same time, such as walking and carrying a tool. The upright gait requires a narrower pelvis. But we're also more intelligent, thus our brains are getting larger and larger yet have to pass through an increasingly narrow birth canal.'

'Apparently your mom's pelvis was like the eye of a needle,' she snarled and was even able to manage a cynical laugh. 'That at least explains why you're such an imbecile, you perverted lunatic – your brain got smashed. Now let me go.'

Franz didn't get a chance to respond, because a freight train suddenly rolled through the industrial hall. At least it sounded that way, like some decrepit rail car attempting to brake on a poorly oiled track.

Nele screamed but was drowned out by the screeching echo filling the stalls. She looked at Franz and saw the same fear in his eyes.

'What the hell...' he whispered. Then Nele felt a draft on her face and she realised what had caused this racket, which had meanwhile ceased. Earlier Franz had pushed her through a small, busted-open entrance door set inside a huge rolling gate. Someone must've just opened this same gate electronically, someone who obviously had the necessary means on them, using a remote control or a key. With a booming bass voice.

'Hello? Someone in here?'

Nele's eyes widened. A vague feeling of hope swelled inside her. But Franz placed a finger to his lips while imitating a knife running across a throat with his other hand. She heard footsteps, then another shout: 'Identify yourself or I'll call the police.'

One peep and you're dead, said the look Franz gave her.

Yet Nele had no clue how she was going follow his silent command.

She was feeling that first tug in her abdomen. That surge of labour pain was about to flood her any moment, at which point she wouldn't be able to stop from screaming out loud in pain, into the open barn. Even if Franz did follow up on the threat he whispered to her:

'If you don't keep still, I'll have to suffocate you.'

30

Franz

'Just a sec, I'm coming, I'm coming,' Franz yelled at the stranger who already had his phone to his ear.

The newcomer stood at the exit where the cows used to be driven from trucks and down the ramp into the stalls. Or from them, when the emaciated and by that point worthless milk cows, having been pumped dry, had to go to the slaughterhouse.

'Sorry, my mistake, I didn't hear you.'

Franz rushed over, having no idea what to tell the massive figure in the blue-grey uniform. His research had told him that the private security firm only came once on Tuesdays and never today. Something must have broken the routine. *Shit.*

'What the hell you doin' here?' demanded the security guard.

He stood with his legs planted apart, which he had to do or he'd probably fall forwards on account of his well-rounded belly. He didn't give a very athletic impression in general, what with those burst veins on his cheeks and all his panting and wheezing despite not having moved a centimetre more than necessary. In one hand he held a phone that looked like a business card in his big paw, while his other hand held a flashlight that reminded him of a truncheon and for good reason.

'There a problem?' Franz held a box cutter in his right hand, hidden in the long sleeve of his sweater, and his fingers grasped tighter around it the closer he got to the man.

'You bet there's a problem.'

The man from M&V Security pointed his switched-off flashlight at the broken padlock on the dairy floor. 'You broke in here.'

'No, no. The lock was already like that when we came in. I thought this was just some industrial ruin, didn't belong to anyone.'

'Right, sure. That's why there's only about thirty No Trespassing signs around here, you kook.' The security guard tapped at his temple with the flashlight.

'Listen, we don't want any trouble.'

'We?'

It was time to improvise. At least long enough to get closer, so that he could reach the guard's throat with one swipe.

'College buddies. We're studying photography,' Franz rambled on. 'We're using this morbid setting here for our thesis project.'

What a cliché. But it seemed to be working. Still. The more tourist types that poured in, the more people attempting to capture the 'charm' of the busted capital in photos. Franz certainly couldn't be the first one the security guard had caught here.

'Do you have permission?' he demanded.

'No, like I told you, I didn't know we needed any.' Franz

took a step closer, extending the box cutter blade a little further.

'But if you'd give us about five minutes, we'll break it all down and...'

A muffled scream sounded from the rear stalls and made the security guard step back.

'Thesis project?' he said warily as more of the screams rang out through the open barn, not as loud now yet still clear.

Nele screamed: 'Good God. Ohhhh...'

Shit. What now?

To Franz's amazement, the fleshy security guard's face contorted with a lusty grin. 'I see what kind of film you're making here.'

'You do?'

'There a part for me?'

'No, uh, I'm afraid—'

'Come on, buddy, at least gimme a look. I always wanted to be around for one of these.'

Franz wondered which of them was luckier – he or this super horny security guard. Maybe he didn't need to use this box cutter on him after all.

'Okay. Okay, fine. I'll go have a chat with the others. But I need time. Give me five minutes?'

'Ohhh, please, please, please, fuuuhhh!'

'That girl, she hot?'

Fritz nodded emphatically. 'Yes. Real hot. Totally. She's gonna really dig you.' *You idiot.*

'Really?'

'Yes, but I have to get her ready. That means changing the shot. We can't just surprise her.'

'Right, okay. Understood.'

No, you haven't understood a thing, not since the blood started leaving your brain and dumping into your crotch.

'What's your name?'

'Helmuth.'

Franz wondered how long he'd need to get Nele to his second hiding place.

'So, Helmuth, I suggest you go get a little fresh air for now, and then, in about an hour—'

'Oh, shit.'

'What?'

The security guard glared at his phone. 'Alarm at the old lake warehouses, break-in. At the very end of my route. Crap. How long you all still here?'

'Two, three hours for sure.'

'Okay, keep an eye out. I'll be back later. I first need to go see what's up.'

'Great, okay. That works.'

Franz watched the security guard leave, waddling off to his car in no great hurry for a burglary, into a decrepit Golf with a suspension that creaked as Helmuth squeezed himself into it.

'And you better not be playing with me,' he shouted out the open window before steering around the taxi Franz had driven here, making a large squeaking arc towards the exit.

Fucking hell, what were the chances?

Franz turned back for the stall where Nele was still screaming her lungs out.

He checked his watch and on the way back considered whether he should first call his contact or just drive right over to the fallback location before that meathead came back again.

'Fuuu...' Nele screamed, strangely high-pitched. When he reached her stall she was pressing so hard that ruptured red veins appeared in her eyes that were too wide open, like someone with Graves' disease.

She was squatting on the stretcher panting, on all fours like she'd switched to during the last contractions, apparently more able to endure the pain this way.

'Fuuu... ckkk!!' Nele spat out into the room. So loudly and clearly, and Franz now started shouting too. Because Nele was not squatting, screaming and pressing in reality.

It was only on the camera display.

From the recording.

She had disappeared.

Her stretcher was empty.

The only thing in the stall was the camera, which Nele must have rewound and switched to playback.

31

Mats

Mats longed for a sink. A toilet bowl would work – he just needed some way to spew out all the revulsion he felt for himself. But he couldn't exactly get up and leave Kaja alone with the video here in the living room while he threw up in the Sky Suite bathroom.

She had kept her word and had come. Now she sat in one of the armchairs placed together and watched the monitor Mats had turned to channel 13/10.

'That's not me,' Kaja whispered, her eyes fixed on the screen in the cabin wall, slipping into that phase of self-denial typical of trauma patients attempting to distance themselves from the nightmares of their past.

Kaja was actually right in one respect. She wasn't that person in the video any longer. Not that rebelling, writhing woman. First lying under her torturer, then squatting before the rapist. So brutally at his mercy. Exposed to such raw violence.

Back then, twelve years ago, Kaja was not simply a completely different person than she was now; she'd also found herself in a nearly insane state that was definitely driven by instinct. She had unthinkingly and wholly reflexively switched into survival mode and blindly did anything she deemed necessary.

She had endured his blows to her behind. And sucked on the gun barrel as well, just like the boy had apparently ordered her to.

Mats stopped watching Kaja, who kept staring at the monitor as if in a trance, and took another look at his phone. At the most horrific of the photos, the one showing Nele's eyes with all their horror and complete hopelessness. And he recalled something the blackmailer had said: '... *the guy who's looking after her isn't exactly a trained obstetrician. Rather the opposite, if you know what I mean. He will not hesitate to kill your daughter and the baby should you not fulfil your task, Dr Krüger.'*

Task.

Such a trivial description of the mental contamination he was practising right at this moment.

On the video the school shooter clawed at Kaja's right breast, practically tearing her nipple right off. The video had almost no sound at this part, yet Mats heard his panting and her screaming. It was nearly as unbearable as the question Kaja now so agonisingly whispered: 'Do I really have to watch this?'

The correct answer would've been: 'No, *of course not. It's highly damaging to reactivate your trauma, Frau Claussen. No reasonable person would expect that of you. Only I would, me, Dr Mats Krüger.'*

The plane was gliding along comfortably again. Mats still expected a jolt at any moment as the tension inside him was swelling by the second. His skin suddenly felt stretched too tight on his body, and he felt feverish, as if suffering from a sunburn all over.

'It'll be over in a second,' he fibbed to Kaja, since he well knew what was to come: the worst of it. *It* had completely thrown even him off. The images she'd seen so far would already haunt her permanently. For years, Kaja had kept them mothballed inside a crate where she could forget them, yet now they lay back out on a platter for her to see all too clearly. Ready to grab at her, there to remind her, anytime she wanted to suffer. Seeing the rape video again now after all this time was like going back on hard drugs after years of abstinence. They always said: the longer a person stayed clean, the deeper the fall.

'You swear to it?' he heard Kaja ask. Her voice trembled. Tears sparkled like dewdrops in the corners of her eyes. 'You swear it's all going to be all right?'

In his panic he nearly burst out laughing.

Swear to it?

Mats couldn't help but recall the Declaration of Geneva, that modern version of the Hippocratic oath which guided present-day doctors.

He had given his solemn vow. *Of my own free will and upon my honour. Never to harm the patient. Never to violate human rights. Not even under threat.* Those were the words verbatim.

And now this!

Now, at this moment, the school shooter let go of Kaja. Pushed her away. And turned from her.

He left her in the middle of the locker room, distraught, trembling, and was pivoting, his face directed at the hidden camera, his eyes, however, lowered pensively towards the floor.

Kaja ran off. She fled for the locker room door and down the gym hallway. Only on the video, however.

Here, in reality, Kaja remained sitting in the armchair, unmoving. Her eyes wide open, barely blinking. Her fingers clawing at the folds of her uniform skirt. She had to be waiting for that surge of memory in her head to stop. This poorly oiled, squeaking conveyor belt dragging all the horror past her eyes once again.

'Now what?' she asked softly, then she winced, similar to the way Mats too had winced before. When the video didn't stop as expected but a floor tile was suddenly visible onscreen instead. The focus changed, a blurry pan of the camera. The secret cameraman must've taken a step out of the shower to better capture the scene.

The images shook and all looked washed out and far too dark, but after observing Kaja and the school shooter together for nine agonising minutes, it was instantly clear what the camera was now capturing. What was unclear was *why*.

'Where did you get that?' Kaja asked. The horror in her voice was so great, the shock in her eyes so intense, that Mats was certain she was seeing the evidence here for the very first time.

'The real question is: why did you do it?' Mats replied ruthlessly. Now, seeing it in flashback, he even suddenly understood why Johannes Faber, Kaja's ex-boyfriend of all people, had made the video public. Nevertheless, and surprisingly, Johannes had left out the final seconds of video. 'Peer Unsell threatened you with a gun, took you hostage. You let him rape and abuse you to save your life and those of your schoolmates. So why in heaven's name did you go back after he let go of you?' While Mats spoke, he stepped around her to remain in her line of sight. 'Were you trying to stop him from shooting himself?'

Kaja stared right through him, her cheeks sunken and her jaw slightly forward, which lent her ashen face a dim-witted, somewhat moronic expression.

Her lips formed a 'no', but no sound came out of her mouth.

'Were you friends?'

Another vague shake of the head.

'So why did you return to the locker room? First you took his hand, then you hugged him?'

Mats was relentless. He pointed to the now black screen as if that final disturbing scene he was describing were still playing. 'Christ, you even ran your fingers through his hair as if you'd just fallen in love – and gave him a long, deep French kiss while you were at it.'

32

Feli

The shock hit him abruptly, like the impact of a car wreck. Feli could see it. Could practically hear the man scream inside, despite Doctor André Klopstock quickly regaining control of himself.

Only the dark shadows under his eyes remained. And now that xenon-smile he had showed her when receiving her in his office wasn't exactly shining with a thousand watts.

'Frau Heilmann, how nice to see you again,' Klopstock had said in welcoming her to his clinic, though she couldn't ever remember exchanging more than a cursory nod with the psychiatrist whenever they'd happened to cross paths at various conventions.

He'd been waiting in the doorway for her, at his corner office with its view of the modern glass buildings of Kranzler Eck, and had shook her hand so warmly a person would think they'd once been the closest of friends who'd unfortunately lost touch with one another.

'What brings you here?'

'I just have a quick question and don't want to take up

too much of your time,' she had promised while honouring Klopstock's gesture to sit in a chair with an absurdly tall backrest as he took a seat at his desk directly facing her, a custom-made piece, Feli was convinced of it, just like his suit, a simple but perfectly tailored pale-blue single-breasted with vest.

'You're not taking up my time, my dear colleague,' the psychiatrist told her in a low and lulling voice while realigning a picture frame on his desk. It contained a portrait of a quite young, dark-haired beauty. Feli vaguely recalled an article in the tabloid press a few months back about the 'scandal' that Klopstock had exchanged his very pregnant wife for a Romanian model some twenty years younger.

'I'm happy to help, Frau Heilmann.' The mood of the conversation had been surprisingly relaxed at first, possibly because Klopstock had misinterpreted Feli's smile. As she sat across from him and saw him up close for the first time, one of her mother's worldly maxims had entered her head: *'Beware of men with faces like dogs. They only wag their tails long enough to pounce on you.'*

Professor André Klopstock certainly did bear the prototype of that very facial expression Feli had been warned of: corners of the mouth drooping like a basset hound's, a dachshund's furrows on his brow, and sad, dark beagle eyes he could use to talk a patient into any additional treatment he wanted. One thing she could say for Klopstock was that his athletic figure was in no way inferior to that of a trained Doberman.

'So what's this about?' he had added, and she had got right to the point and shown him the printout of the surveillance camera freeze-frame.

'It's about this man here.'

'Bono?'

'So you know him?'

'Not the best image, but sure, there's no mistake it's him.'

'A patient?'

'You yourself know I'm not allowed to tell you that.'

Yeah. She knew. Yet she also hadn't expected that he'd make this easy for her. To be honest, she hadn't even expected to get in to see Klopstock at all when the elevator dumped her out onto the third floor of his clinic.

The reception area looked more like a five-star hotel lobby than a medical establishment. Waiting behind the reception desk was a doctor's assistant in a page's uniform, who offered Feli a cappuccino and a glass of water while she filled out the necessary registration form on an iPad in the lounge area. Luckily Feli was quickly able to make her understand she wasn't a patient but a fellow doctor, and it really had only taken a moment as promised to be seen by the director.

'I was told he's your chauffeur.'

She'd got the information from Livio, the scammer who dropped her off here on the Ku'damm as part of making amends for trying to steal her cell phone.

'*I think that student drives him from clinic to clinic,*' he'd told her. '*I get treatment once a week. Every time I've seen Klopstock at the clinic, the guy was always waiting downstairs in a car.*'

'May I ask what you want with Bono?' the psychiatrist had asked Feli.

'Bono, you said? Is that his first or last name?'

'Neither, I just call him that. To be honest, I don't even know his real name.'

'Then he could hardly be a patient of yours,' Feli had concluded. 'Unless...'

Bono.

A thought had formed in her head and she voiced it: 'He drives around town, and you treat him for free, is that right?'

No money flow, no records.

Many successful doctors maintained pro bono cases, patients they treated free of charge. Most of the time it was to give them a good conscience. Klopstock had obviously cut some kind of favourable deal with the gaunt taxi driver. In a profile of him in one of the popular doctors' magazines, he'd responded to the question *'What's your greatest strength?'* with the following: *'The ability to recognise opportunities for profit where others see only problems.'*

He generated more profit from his lab than by treating people. He analysed the blood, hair and other DNA carriers for disease-causing pathogens, but also for drugs and alcohol misuse. Klopstock even owned patents for several controversial home tests, for HIV, hepatitis and even paternity checks.

'Have you been doing some kind of barter with this Bono?'

'I'd rather not comment on that either, my dear colleague. But what does this have to do with you? Why your interest in the fellow?'

'It's about Mats Krüger.'

Klopstock had nodded in appreciation. 'Brilliant mind.

Haven't heard from him in a long while. Doesn't he practice in Brazil now?'

'Argentina. At the moment he's on a plane to Berlin from Buenos Aires.'

And that was when it happened. The about-face. That turning point in the conversation where Klopstock lost all self-confidence.

'His daughter is in great danger,' Feli said, and Klopstock blinked quickly twice.

'What's happened?'

'*I too* can't say. But I think this man has something to do with it.'

Feli tapped at the printout. Klopstock had pushed it away. He stood and stepped up to his window. He nervously played with the cord to the blinds. His face as white as the white stucco ceiling. Those deep shadows suddenly showed under his eyes.

'Where do I find Bono?' Feli demanded.

'I don't know.'

'But there's something else you know, am I right?'

He turned to her. His mouth opened. He gave a barely perceptible nod, another micro-expression only, yet Feli had spotted it.

'What is it? Herr Klopstock, please. I don't tend to overly dramatise things, but if I'm hearing Mats correctly, this might concern life and death.'

Feli also heard her stomach rumbling although she didn't feel the least bit hungry. She wasn't any less on edge than the psychiatrist, that much was certain.

Klopstock stepped back to his desk and leaned over his phone system, and for a moment Feli was hoping that he actually was going to have his assistant at reception bring him all available patient records. Instead he said: 'Frau List? Could you please send in the next appointment? Unfortunately, Frau Dr Heilmann has to leave now.'

33

'Just one moment...' Feli stood and tried protesting.

But Klopstock kept pressing the button for the intercom and said with fake kindness: 'Can I call you a taxi, Frau Heilmann?'

Feli nearly choked on her words and had to cough from anger. 'You know something? I couldn't stand you before I met you. Thank you for now giving me even more reason not to.'

She strode resolutely out of the office and tried to slam the door behind her but was prevented from doing so by a mechanism that made sure the door closed softly.

What now?

Feli took a deep breath, gave a friendly parting nod to the reception lady, who wasn't at fault for her boss's impossible behaviour, after all, and stomped back to the elevator without knowing where to turn next.

Not true.

She basically knew exactly what she needed to do, but she was afraid of doing it. How would Mats react to her news that there was a possible connection between Klopstock and a taxi driver with the nickname Bono but that she couldn't tell how that would help him get Nele free?

Her phone rang right as she pushed the button for the elevator.

Janek!

She wanted to dismiss the call but did it wrong and got him on the line.

'Darling, where in the heck you been hiding this whole time?'

Using a term of affection didn't hide the tension in his question. Her fiancé was clearly irritated, which Feli understood quite well. He'd probably been searching long and hard for some rational explanation why he'd been unable to reach his soon-to-be wife either on her mobile phone or landline with just a few hours before the ceremony. She should've been at home, freshening up, blow-drying and doing her hair, possibly with a glass of champagne in her hand, yet another manifestation of all the anticipation filling her every breath.

Instead she'd let his texts and calls go unanswered and had now picked up at possibly the most inconvenient time of all.

All worked up, confused, and without a plan.

'I'm at a colleague's on the Ku'damm,' she said more or less truthfully and pressed the elevator button again since she wasn't getting any signs that the elevator was moving anywhere.

'*Where* are you?' Janek sounded so dumbfounded, she might as well have confessed that she'd spontaneously emigrated to Australia. 'You're not still *working*, are you?'

'No,' she said, forcing herself not to get short with him.

It would've been easy for her to launch a counterattack, simply by asking why certain privileges only applied to the male in the marriage. *He* was the one who'd gone into the office today and not her. But paying him back with such a comeback was only projecting her anger on him when it was really about herself and the situation she was in. An impulsive surge of goodwill had let her be taken in by a person whose concerns she'd wanted nothing more to do with. He'd already used her once after the death of his wife. Even though he knew that she loved him and wanted far more from him than only one night, he had misused her as temporary consolation. And he dropped her again as soon as Nele had found out and never wanted to see him again. A stronger man wouldn't have only stayed with his wife for the final minutes of her death – he would've given the future a chance and attempted to create a new life for himself, one in which Feli might have had a chance too. But Mats had fled and left her behind.

'Something bad has happened to Mats Krüger's daughter,' Feli told her fiancé after deciding not to taint her big day today with a lie. 'I'll see you at home in a bit, okay? Then I'll tell you everything.'

As much as I can.

'Huh,' Janek grunted over the phone, and Feli wasn't even sure whether he'd heard the name *Mats Krüger*.

'A half hour more, then I'm home,' she promised and included an 'I love you' when Janek had nothing to add.

Well, that's not exactly setting the best mood for the big celebration, she thought and looked at her watch. She had exactly three hours and twenty minutes until the registry office.

Ugh.

Now she was mad at herself for sending Livio away after he'd dropped her off in his banged-up Renault here at the corner of the Ku'damm and Meineckestrasse. Now she had to figure out how to make it home on time without a car. The streetcar was probably faster than a taxi.

Ping!

The elevator opened, but Feli didn't get in. At the very second the chime sounded, she'd realised the mistake she'd made.

Just now, in Klopstock's office.

She turned around and hurried back to the reception desk.

'You know, I was thinking,' she said to the beauty behind the reception desk.

Klopstock!

He had put out his hand for a shake but she'd rebuffed him. Feeling slighted, angry about her apparent dismissal.

'The thing is,' she told Klopstock's reception lady, 'I'm getting married today and still have to run all over town.'

His hadn't been a dismissal at all, but rather an offer: *'Can I call you a taxi?'*

'And, the good doctor was saying he could recommend a dependable driver.'

'Dependable?' The reception lady crinkled her nose. 'He was supposed to pick the doctor up from home this morning, but he never showed up.'

'That so?' Feli could feel her cheeks flushing from the excitement. This meant that she wasn't far off. The only question was why Klopstock had just prevaricated so much. And which one of her findings made him so visibly nervous, possibly even scared.

'Could you try the driver again anyway?' Feli asked.

Without saying a word, the reception lady fished a tattered business card from a note box and hooked her phone headset behind an ear.

'We'll see. Maybe Franz will pick up now.'

34

Franz

The phone in his trousers was vibrating but he didn't have time to answer. Worst case it was his contact, checking in about how things were going, and what was he supposed to tell the man?

'I'm sorry, things suddenly got a little hectic here. I was only trying to get rid of some horny drooling security guard when the pregnant girl flat took off during contractions.'

'Shit!'

Franz's scream echoed through the far-too-empty hall of stalls.

Why had he gone and untied her? Many cows themselves had to spend their whole lives tethered these days. But he'd gone soft again. Wanted to make her delivery easier on her.

Now he had a mess on his hands. What was he supposed to do first? Run out and search the surroundings? There had to be gaps somewhere in the walls of these stalls – she might have squeezed through one outside.

Maybe she was only squatting in a nearby stall? Under straw and biting her hand bloody to prevent her screaming from giving her away?

Franz had once read that the Church of Scientology forbade women from uttering the slightest sound in childbirth. So a silent delivery was indeed possible, and with Nele so scared to death she could probably manage the unimaginable. The human body was a mystery and capable of far more than most could even begin to imagine.

This sucks.

'Nele?'

Franz didn't want to keep calling her name. He'd rather cry again, like earlier when he'd suddenly realised the implications of his undertaking. And he wouldn't be able to suppress his tears for long. He was already close to tearing up again anyway; this was all getting to be too much. He had demanded far too much of himself, even if it had to be done and no one else could be found for such an important task. Yet he might simply be the wrong man for this.

Yep, damn it, he was definitely the wrong man.

Who but he was capable of such a feat – losing a hostage who was naked and so limited physically, who now seemed to have vanished into thin air?

That said, it wasn't completely true. There were a few clues to follow. The only thing was, he wasn't exactly a tracker and also wasn't sure which prints he'd made in the dirt himself.

After all, he'd already been inside this old industrial building multiple times before today. First when reconning the place, then when setting up Nele's birthing spot.

What about this footprint here...

Franz knelt on the dirty concrete floor and the odour made his nose tingle, of hay and dung, still festering here years later.

Yep, these were prints of naked toes. And the ball of a foot. He saw it quite clearly.

And there, about twenty centimetres further, the next footprint. Plus he discovered a thin, damp trail. Blood, or urine?

Maybe I truly am a pathfinder in disguise, thought Franz.

At least he now knew the general direction in which Nele must have disappeared.

He stood up and tried to recall if there was another exit at the other end of the hall. But he held the sketch up to his eyes that he'd made when planning all this and found nothing on it.

Nothing but a ramp leading directly down to an old cadaver room in the basement. The place where those poor expired animals had been deposited temporarily.

And the exact place, Franz decided, that he was going to go check out first.

35

Livio

Ninety-three euros and twenty-four cents.

Not bad, Livio thought, though he'd definitely had better hauls.

He couldn't do much with Feli's credit cards. He might get something for her ID at health and social services – people-smugglers were always hanging around there trying to score new identities for refugees.

Felicitas Heilmann looked really German in the photo on her biometric passport, though, which made it tough.

Livio went through all the compartments of her wallet again. He'd taken it off her in his car, once she'd started getting out, pretty easy to pull out of her pocket. Much easier than stealing her phone, which demanded all his skill and powers of distraction. It'd been a long time since he'd killed time pickpocketing, but it was nice to know he still had it.

Livio smoothed out the bills and shoved them into his trouser pockets.

Nearly a hundred euros wasn't bad side earnings when you took into account that he wasn't even expecting it.

Definitely better than that mobile phone he was never going to get much for.

He shook the wallet and dumped all the credit, rewards and insurance cards onto the passenger seat of his car. Lastly, he unfolded a white piece of paper he'd figured was a receipt.

It was an invitation, in fact. For a city registry office wedding.

He looked at the date.

Damn.

That was today!

'Old lady's getting hitched after this,' he muttered to himself, and his eyes found the rear-view mirror for a relatively good view of the clinic building. He grabbed Feli's ID card. First he compared that photo with the one on the invitation, then with her face in the rear-view mirror, but she was too far away to see fully. Felicitas Heilmann was stepping out the front entrance and onto the pavement at this very second, her phone at her ear, and seemed to look around puzzled for a moment. Then she disappeared from his view, heading down the Ku'damm in the direction of Memorial Church.

Having no clue that she and that stuck-up-looking guy on the invitation were in for a nasty surprise in a couple hours tops.

Livio wasn't sure, but he highly doubted that a person could marry in Germany without proper ID.

36

Mats

'That's it, I'm done,' Mats heard Feli say. She was breathing harder, probably from crossing an intersection judging from the traffic sounds in the background. 'I'm ending this now.'

After Kaja, this made her the second woman wanting to cut him off in the span of a few minutes. His last lifeline was about to break.

Kaja, for her part, had simply stopped speaking to him. His former patient had stood silently and switched into tunnel mode when leaving the Sky Suite. No eye contact, frozen expression, robot-like movements. A typical symptom of severe psychological trauma, and entirely comprehensible considering the fact that Mats had just tossed her a mental hand grenade with that video. The images had bothered him enough – he could only imagine what they were doing to Kaja.

That kiss, her deep embrace of the shooter, such an intimate bond – why would she ever return to her tormentor? Could Kaja have been suffering from perceptual distortion so soon?

Unlikely.

Her predicament had actually been too brief to establish the type of emotional captor – captive bond known by the term Stockholm Syndrome. Mats would probably never know the answer, because even if he did survive this night he'd lose his medical licence for trying to manipulate the situation and would never be allowed to work as a therapist again. Certainly not with Kaja Claussen.

'I'm hanging up now,' he heard Feli say.

'No, please, don't!' Mats turned on the faucet in the bathroom he was inside now because he thought he might throw up any second. Silken lampshades softly filtered the light from the two lamps mounted to the mirror, making him look less beaten-down than he felt.

'Please, Mats,' Feli groaned. 'I've managed to get the number and even the address of the man who's most likely involved in your daughter disappearance. Klopstock's driver, Franz Uhlandt. The doctor's assistant who gave me his business card said he never showed up for work today. So what more do you want? Call the police and let the pros worry about it.'

'I can't do that. Not until I'm one hundred per cent certain where Nele is.'

'Why?'

Mats held his left wrist under the stream of water, to cool his pulse. Then he tore a bunch of tissues from the stainless-steel dispenser next to the mirror, wiped the sweat from his face, and dragged himself back into the Sky Suite living room.

'You remember Kaja Claussen? The schoolgirl you prevented from committing suicide?'

'*You* were the one who did it, Mats – I only put you in

contact with her. What about her?'

'She's a flight attendant on board this plane I'm in right now.'

'No way.'

'It's true. And, no, it's no coincidence. The one or more perpetrators – I'm assuming it's several – have uploaded the Faber video into in-flight programming.'

'The Faber video?' asked Feli, confused.

'The one showing Kaja getting raped by the school shooter. Making the video public was the trigger that made her plan her own shooting spree.'

'Right, okay. I remember, just didn't know the name of the tape.'

Mats grabbed the remote and turned on channel 13/10. He only had to press the arrow button three times to jump to the final minute. A few seconds before that unexplainable kiss.

'For the first nine months, Kaja was the school hero. She'd sacrificed herself so that others could live. Until her spurned ex-boyfriend, Johannes Faber, sent the video out to his friends. Then Kaja obtained a gun and went into the school intent on killing him. And everyone else who'd seen it and ridiculed it.'

'Right, right, I know all this,' Feli said, losing patience. 'But I don't understand what that has to do with Nele.'

'I'm supposed to confront Kaja with the Faber video,' Mats confessed, not revealing to her that he'd already done so.

'What for?'

'I'm supposed to trigger her. Reactivate Kaja's auto-aggressive feelings. Get her to kill herself and everyone on board.'

Feli gasped. 'This is some kind of joke!'

'No, it's not.'

'This can't be, it's—'

'It's true,' Mats interrupted. 'Those are the blackmailer's conditions. Nele dies if I don't make this aeroplane crash. Now you see why you're my only hope? The name of the person alone doesn't do me any good. I need to know where Nele was taken!'

Mats had thought it through every which way:

If the police were involved beforehand, he'd be revealed as the victim of a blackmail attempt to endanger a passenger aircraft. From that moment on, the crew would take no risks. They'd immediately isolate him, even put him in preventative detention on board if possible. The prospect of the blackmailer getting wind of that and killing Nele before the authorities located her was just too great a risk at this point.

He froze the video at the exact moment the camera panned over the floor tiles where Johannes Faber had been hiding.

'Feli?' he said since she hadn't responded. Only the background noise told him he still had a connection.

'You're an asshole,' she growled finally.

'True,' he said.

'You have any idea what you're doing to me?'

He'd thought she'd only been talking about Kaja, but it was just as unreasonable of him to be demanding so much from her. 'I know it's your wedding day. But, Feli, please—'

'Screw the wedding day!' she screamed into the phone. 'Human lives are at stake. Hundreds, my God. And you've made me an accessory. Now I can't just act as if I didn't know anything. I now *have to* call in the police.'

Mats groaned and was tempted to bash in the plasma screen with his fist, remote and all.

'No, for God's sake, don't do that. You'll kill Nele.'

'Oh, Mats. Your daughter is worth more than anything in the world to you, of course she is. I understand that. But to me? What if I *don't* find Nele? I can't just try to help you save one single life all so that you end up sacrificing a whole plane full of people if we don't find her.'

Mats was getting dizzy. Nothing he could say seemed to be working.

'But that's not what you're doing, Feli. Listen to me. I'll keep away from Kaja, I swear to you. I'm not giving in to the blackmailer's demands. No one on this plane will come to any harm.'

'I'm supposed to believe that?'

'Yes.' He continued lying. 'Trust me. I'm no mass murderer.'

But he was. And a malicious, cunning one at that.

Feli hesitated. The background traffic noise was gone. She might be sitting in a taxi or have stepped into a building entrance. My God, what he'd give to be standing right before her, holding her hand and making it personally clear to her all that was at stake.

'I'm not sure,' she said. 'If you're lying and I don't inform anyone soon, I'll have to live with the guilt of a hundreds of souls on my conscience.'

'I'm not lying, Feli. Look. We're still in the air for over six hours. If you notify the authorities now, the crew will be warned and the perpetrators will find out their plan's been blown. And they'll kill Nele at once. Her, and her baby.'

'We don't need to tell them anything about you or the plane. Only that a pregnant woman's gone missing. And I did give you that tip about Uhlandt.'

'Yes, I thought about that too. But how can you guarantee that the blackmailer won't hear about the cops investigating?'

'Maybe he already knows about me,' Feli argued.

'Maybe, yes. But you're not an official threat. Whatever these lunatics want from me, it has to be something really, really big. Something that cannot be taken public. Which it will be as soon as I call in the police. I'm scared it's still too early for that. Please, Feli, I'm begging you. Just gain me a little time. Find out where this Franz Uhlandt took my daughter, and then, I swear, we'll notify the police and this nightmare comes to an end. Okay?'

Feli fell silent a while, and on the phone their pause seemed to echo that monotonous white noise of the plane. Mats felt like he was in a wind tunnel. Everything was rushing all around him. Finally Feli said: 'Like I said: you're an asshole, Mats.'

Then she hung up without telling him whether she was going to listen to him or dial 110.

Mats dropped the phone, buried his face in his hands.

Oh, God, what should I do? What can I do?

He wiped the tears from his eyes, then searched for the remote to banish this miserable image from the screen. That was when he saw it, from the corner of his eye.

Because of the headache still seething behind his eyes, and his nausea, and that leaden exhaustion weighing him down, it took a while for him to be cognizant of what was being presented to him.

On the monitor.

In freeze-frame.

In the lower corner, in the shower of the girls' locker room.

On the blurred tile.

A tiny detail, barely recognisable. Captured only because he'd happened to pause the video at that exact second.

Is that what I think it is? Mats asked himself and wished he could zoom the image or at least print it out. He stepped closer to the monitor – and made a fatal error. Hoping to make that frozen detail more visible, reversing and fast-forwarding a little using the monitor's touchscreen function, he lost the exact frame.

The airline's playback software was far too clumsy, kept jumping five seconds. What he really needed was a fucking slow motion button.

For fuck's sake.

No matter how hard he tried. The video simply wouldn't pause on that exact spot he needed to confirm his suspicions. Yet he was certain that his eyes hadn't deceived him.

He had seen it, even though it was less than a couple of centimetres long. The very thing that put Kaja's trauma in a whole new light.

And, even though Mats couldn't verify why he was so certain at the moment, he did trust his gut, which was telling him that his daughter's kidnappers had made one huge goddamn mistake.

37

Nele

'Like crapping a bowling ball.'

Such a stupid comparison could only come from a man. It was far too mild.

To Nele it felt more like trying to press a car battery spiked with nails out her vagina.

And yet she didn't scream. At least not as loud as she wanted. Not any louder than an aeroplane taking off.

Still, her panting wail sufficed to transform the basement corridor where she lay into a droning cathedral. Her reverberating anguish drifted dully down the corridor, swallowed up by the half-light surrounding her. She'd only made it a few metres away, though it was down metal-grate steps descending from one end of the stalls and into darkness. Then she literally collapsed. Another contraction had seized her, ripping her legs out from under her, sending her to the floor.

Once the contraction ended, she thought she'd been blinded for a moment. But then the shadows returned, of a metal drum in the middle of the corridor, and of wooden doors askew, lining the hallway like so many livestock blinders.

A dungeon, she thought. *I've fled into a dilapidated dungeon.*

Down here she could hardly see more than silhouettes. On the other hand, she could hear and smell that much better.

She smelled faeces, urine, her sweat, and the effluvia of her fear. Heard the wall mortar crumble when she tried pulling herself up using a protruding copper rod (maybe once a water pipe?). To keep running, despite all her pain, down the dark and seemingly tiled corridor, on into the darkness stinking of mud and mould. Away from the footsteps behind her. On the stairs.

The footsteps were getting closer, along with that voice turning her despair into naked panic.

'Nele?' she heard her kidnapper yell. This lunatic whose real name was apparently Franz, who'd revealed his actual name to her. Because he never dreamed of ever letting her free again.

'Nele, come back. Please. I can explain it all to you.'

Another contraction kicked in. The third in only a few minutes.

Please, dear God, don't let it last another hour, Nele prayed. It was clear to her, of course, that her sense of time was turning as hopelessly dire as this situation she found herself in.

Alone, naked, at his mercy.

'It's my fault. I'm not mad at you for running away. I should've explained things better.'

His voice had a sad tone to it, completely different than in those movies where the serial killer either sounded quite refined or talked in some sing-song crazy voice. Franz on the other hand sounded so... *honest*. As if he really were sorry about what he was doing. That didn't mean he wasn't crazy.

His next question only confirmed it: 'Do you know what makes humans radically different from the other mammals?'

Killing others for no good reason? Nele wanted to scream at him but was far too busy trying to breathe from her diaphragm.

She'd discovered it was the best way to manage the impact of these bodily tremors that kept erupting inside her every second.

'We're the only mammal in the world that still drinks milk as adults,' she heard Franz in response to his own question. His voice still sounded like it was coming from the foot of the basement stairs. He'd stopped moving.

'And no one, truly no one, ever bothers to imagine what that means. What the consequences are of our misguided consumption of milk!'

Nele meanwhile managed the impossible and pulled herself up by the copper rod. Inch by inch, until she was back on her feet, even if squatting.

She felt something damp running down her bare thighs and leaned forward.

And went onto all fours, with her most sensitive parts pointing in her kidnapper's direction, and she was hoping he couldn't see any more than she could.

'I'm not talking about diarrhoea, from lactose intolerance. Or prostate cancer, even though milk causes that as much as it does osteoporosis and diabetes.'

Nele shuddered at the thought that Franz might have some kind of night-vision device. Or that his voice was taped and he'd already crept right up to her.

Only a second more before she felt his fingers on her. Breathing down her neck.

'I'm talking about an unbearable suffering of a far greater magnitude!'

Nele staggered, couldn't help toppling forward. And rolling on her side, not meaning to, but she couldn't avoid it. She simply didn't have the strength.

'Please, Nele. Come back. Let me explain it to you. You're a smart woman, you'll understand.'

She propped herself up off the floor, which had changed in texture. What up until now had felt like cold and crumbling tiles and rough concrete now gave her a splinter, from her hand running over wood.

Wood? On the floor?

She kept feeling the ground until she found a narrow gap. Traced the wooden groove with her fingers.

Hope surged through her with the same intensity as the labour pains gathering force inside her.

'You'll see why this is necessary. That we all need to make sacrifices if anything's going to change. Nele, you hear me?'

Yes, I hear you, you sick psycho!

Nele heard him along with the footsteps that were getting closer again. But she heard the clanking most of all. Metal on metal. She clawed at a chain ring mounted to the wood. Pulled on it with all her might.

'Nele? What are you doing there?'

She couldn't have told Franz even if she wanted to. She had no idea what she was opening. Didn't know why there was a wooden door here in the basement floor below the old livestock hall or if it was letting her flee to freedom or descend into more doom.

'Let's be reasonable about this,' she heard Franz call out right when she was finally able to move the wooden slab.

She plunged her hands into the dark void, now crouching at its edge. Had no idea how deep it dropped below her. If this stench of carrion rising out of the hole like the breath of some dying animal descended several metres or just a foot.

'There's no way out of here. I checked it all. I really don't want to resort to force. At least not any more than is necessary to finally open everyone's eyes.'

And I don't want to die, Nele thought and, against all reason and yet barring any alternative, lumbered down into the hole. And as she fell she screamed so loudly that her voice broke, leaving her shriek far weaker than the contraction that hit her while freefalling deserved.

38

Mats

Mats reacted to the soft doorbell chime like a cold finger creeping up his spine once he realised who'd just opened the door to the Sky Suite.

'Augusto Pereya,' said the roughly forty-year-old pilot, removing his hat in introduction. The man had olive skin and dark hair thinning a little on the back of his head. His nose was crooked and misshapen, reminding Mats of a poorly squeezed toothpaste tube. He wore a white shirt and dark tie with his anthracite-coloured jacket that had four golden stripes on the cuffs. 'I'm the captain of this plane.'

'Is there a problem?' Mats asked the Argentinian, speaking to him in Spanish.

'May I come in?'

'Yes, yes, of course.' Mats moved out of the way of the door, and the relatively short yet rather strong-looking pilot followed him inside. Pereya scanned the Sky Suite and his eyes stopped on Mats' untouched meal cart right as Mats' phone rang in his trouser pocket.

'What's this about?' Mats asked undeterred, but Pereya said: 'Go ahead, Dr Krüger. Have at it.'

'Come again?'

'Our ad.' The captain bared a row of coffee-stained teeth. 'Incoming calls are free on LegendAir all month. So, you'd better take it. Calling back will only cost you. Those cutthroats are currently charging ten dollars a minute.'

Mats pulled out his phone. 'Aren't they expecting you back in the cockpit?'

'I'm on a break; first officer took over.' He wagged a hand at Mats' phone. 'Go ahead, I can wait.'

Mats smiled at him helplessly and took the call from an unknown caller. 'Yes?'

'How far have you got?' asked the fake Johnny Depp voice. Again Mats could hear the actual speaker's breathing in the background. He still had no clue who he was dealing with.

'Okay, sure. Thanks for your call,' Mats said and intentionally exaggerated feigned happiness. 'This all sounds great, but I'll need a little more time to get the documents together.'

'There's someone with you?' the voice said.

'Uh, yes, exactly.'

'Is Kaja with you?'

Mats smiled at the pilot and shrugged as if to say, *Sorry, I'll be with you in a sec.*

Pereya only nodded casually, not bothering to sit down. 'No.'

'Another passenger?' Johnny asked.

'No, *I'm* sorry.'

'So someone from the crew?'

Mats sighed. 'Uh-huh, but I'd first need to discuss it with him. He is the boss, as you know.'

'The captain? The captain is with you?' The voice turned even more menacing. 'One false word to him and your daughter is dead. Understand?'

'Yes.'

'All right, fine. I'll keep it brief, and you're simply going to have to listen.'

Mats glanced at Pereya again, who now seemed interested in the monitor on the wall even though it was only showing the flight path he already knew along with data for altitude, wind speed, outside temperature. Negative sixty Fahrenheit.

About as cold as my soul feels.

'Are you ready for further instructions?'

Mats kept prevaricating. 'Um, yes, sure. I can remember.'

'Good, Dr Krüger. Then pay good attention: once Kaja is at that point, and I hope for Nele and your baby that it's soon, she'll need a weapon. It's advisable for you to keep this weapon on you in case things get serious and you need to act quickly.'

'Fine. So where should I send the documents?'

'We have placed the weapon under your seat.'

Mats' mouth turned dry. It was all he could do not to sigh out loud. 'Oh... uh. Yes. Okay, but...'

A weapon? Where? Under which of my seats, goddamnit?

He cleared his throat. 'Uh, there are several offices in the building. I'd need the exact one.'

'Ah, right. You booked several seats, you scaredy-cat. We chose the finest one. 7A. In business class.'

It had to be that one.

'Very well.'

'You'll find the weapon with the life vest.'

Mats closed his eyes, and felt nauseous as he said into the

215

phone: 'Wonderful, thanks a lot. Got it. Yes, best regards too.' He hung up.

'Everything all right?' he heard the pilot ask. Mats had turned his back to him near the end.

'Yep, everything's great.' Mats smiled and pointed at the armchairs. 'Please, take a seat.'

'Thanks. I'm fine standing.'

Mats nodded nervously. 'So what's this about?'

'I was just speaking with Frau Claussen about you.'

'You were?'

'And I'm concerned.'

Aha. So that's what this was about. The captain must've got word she wasn't doing so well.

'That's not something I can talk about it,' Mats said, hoping to rely on doctor–patient confidentiality.

Pereya nodded. 'I understand. Very well actually.' His cap moved from one hand to the other. 'Nevertheless. Is there something I need to know?'

Mats unwittingly reached for his throat. 'How do you mean?'

'Well, I want to be completely honest with you. Frau Claussen doesn't quite seem to be her usual self.'

'In what way?'

'She dropped a tray full of glasses in the galley.'

'What does that have to do with me?'

The pilot's stare hardened. 'That's what I'm asking you, Dr Krüger. When I asked Frau Claussen if she needed a break, she said, and I quote, *"I'm doing fine; I just had an intense discussion with Dr Krüger is all."*'

'Aha.' Mats pretended to be unmoved.

The captain abruptly changed the subject. 'As a psychiatrist, you've probably heard about the proposed PPT law?'

Mats nodded. 'Uh, sure.'

The PPT, or pre-psych test, was the name for a dubious procedure that supposedly provided fast-track testing for identifying certain patterns of psychopathological behaviour. Mats considered it charlatanism and scare tactics. Yet after the Germanwings catastrophe, in which a mentally ill co-pilot killed hundreds of people by locking himself in the cockpit and crashing his plane in the Alps, demand had multiplied for early psychopathological detection. Mandatory participation in standardised multiple-choice psych evaluations as well as blood tests were becoming the favoured methods of regularly examining an entire crew for the use of psychotropic drugs.

'I consider PPT to be completely useless,' Mats added. 'Just as you can't tell a perpetrator by their hair colour, you can't see into their mind with the help of some questionnaire. And not everyone taking antidepressants is unable to work, let alone a danger. There's good reason why most figured the law wouldn't get a majority in the European Parliament.'

Pereya nodded. 'Nevertheless, we at LegendAir are contemplating voluntary tests that well exceed the legal minimum.'

Mats tried to endure the pilot's intense stare. 'That's interesting, but I'm guessing you didn't take the trouble of coming here just to tell me that?'

The pilot took a step closer. 'I want be completely honest with you, Dr Krüger. I'm not worried about Frau Claussen. She's a capable, if somewhat overworked, crewmember. For me, it's about you.'

'Me?'

'I only wish we'd already adopted a PPT procedure so we

could do a series of tests on you right here on board. Because I have an extremely bad feeling in my gut and would like to know just what's going on with you. Someone like you would be just the person for preventative examination.'

He laughed joylessly.

'I mean, you first attracted our attention when you booked several seats at once, and then you suffer a panic attack right after take-off. Later, you start causing havoc with my crew. You actually accuse one flight attendant of assault, and then you go harass Frau Claussen.'

'I didn't harass anyone,' Mats said. A thought had occurred to him. If he remembered correctly, one of his colleagues had been heavily involved in PPT research. A doctor, whose name he'd heard for the first time today after a long, long time: Klopstock!

That cannot be a coincidence.

Mats told himself to Google it as soon as he had an opportunity.

'Let's not waste words. All I want is for you to stay clear of Frau Claussen. Okay?'

Mats showed no reaction.

Pereya, on the other hand, smiled in an apparently conciliatory manner and gazed around the Sky Suite. 'You'll make do somehow up here without her, I take it?'

He put his pilot's cap back on, and suddenly his voice superbly matched his cold-steel eyes that he now fixed on Mats: 'I do not want to hear about any more incidents. Do we understand each other? That way I won't have to consider taking further action.'

39

Nele

Packaging, boxes, trash... Nele only had a vague sense of what she'd landed on. In any case it was soft and brittle, luckily, otherwise she would've broken her back – and not just sprained her foot.

'Fuuuuh...' She screamed her birth battle war cry into this pit, sewer, drainage or whatever it was.

She sat with her legs bent atop the garbage, on some kind of slatted frame that had been dumped here at some point. On the leaves and old blankets wedged between the one box that must have split open on landing. Her left foot and tailbone had nasty bruises, but that didn't exactly matter considering all her other pain.

Nele smelled blood and excrement and heard herself screaming and couldn't think of anything but—

'Fuuuuh!!!'

The word didn't mean anything, wasn't cursing or pleading, was simply just a scream. Forcing out that long drawn-out vowel provided her with some relief, however fleeting.

The intensity of her contractions had changed again. She

propped her elbows on the metal slats, no longer fighting the waves of cramps running through her body. It was likely instinct that kept her trying all she could to somehow prevent the birth from happening up there in those stalls, in the presence of that madman. Now she accepted it, breathing along with and not against the cramps anymore. She could feel it. Her munchkin didn't want to stay inside her any longer. Wanted out of the safety of her stomach and into this world that had never shown itself to be as grim as it did to Nele right at this moment.

'Fuuuuuhuhuu!' Her scream tore into the darkness, and then it was over. For the moment. The flood had reached its peak. The contractions pulled back. For now. Left Nele trembling and panting and whimpering, all alone with her wounded body. For the moment.

'Are you doing all right?'

Nele looked up, to the edge of the pit.

She couldn't see Franz. Just a shadow, leaning over the opening. 'Just what have you done?'

Exactly. Just have I done to deserve this?

'My God. Do you know where you are? You've jumped into the latrine. They used to dispose of the cadavers down there. Those poor cows, after they'd been milked to death and weren't even good enough for the slaughterhouse. Stillbirths. Scraps of meat.'

That's exactly where I'm at, thought Nele with a tinge of infinite sorrow.

She was lost. Abducted by a pervert, she had reached the very spot that matched her current emotional state. She was just a scrap of meat. Capable of little more than producing a stillborn baby. Even if she was able to get it out somehow down here, now injured, her crotch torn open and body bruised, she was sure to have infected her child with her own blood.

'Listen, this won't do, this wasn't the plan,' the psycho explained to her in all seriousness.

'You think? You sick motherfucker?' Nele couldn't hold back anymore. She screamed out all her built-up rage at him. 'So sorry to make things unpleasant for you.'

'You don't understand. I already told you, this isn't against you or your baby. I don't want anything to happen to you.'

'Then let me go,' Nele screamed back, well knowing how even more impossible her demand was now. The pit was narrow; there was, as far as she could make out in the darkness, no ladder or other way of climbing up. And even so, she'd hardly be able to use it in her condition.

'I can't leave you down there like that. That won't do. I can't document it like that!'

'Document what, for fuck's sake? This get you off, filming women having birth?'

'No, no, no,' echoed down on her. 'It does not. Please, don't say things like that.'

Again such sincerity in his voice. Attempting to make himself understood.

'I'm only doing this to demonstrate to the world how cruel milk production is.'

'You've lost your mind!'

'I have?' His voice squeaked. 'People have lost theirs. I'm the only one who appears to be in full possession of their mental faculties.'

Yeah, right.

'I ask you, Nele. Have you ever given thought to the fact that milk is the only product that isn't produced in a species-appropriate manner?'

No. And there's nothing I could care less about at the moment, Nele thought.

'You can let animals run free in the wild and kill them at the end of a long life. You can give chickens and cattle full access to pasture grasses. It's more than possible for us humans to provide our livestock with a happy life. I myself don't eat meat, but I do acknowledge those few farmers who do strive to provide animals with a meaningful existence before they die. No one, and I mean truly NO ONE in this country gives any thought to the fact that milk can only be produced with such unbelievable lifelong suffering.'

Death. Lifelong suffering.

Those were the only two possibilities Nele was seeing for herself at the moment.

She pushed a plastic bag and an empty beer can to the side and lay on her back as flat as she could so she could better relax her pelvis. The baby had slid further down, she was sure of it, the contractions having shifted it into a new position, yet it wasn't feeling right somehow. Not right at all.

Though she definitely couldn't say whether this was just her imagination, never having given birth before and with an insane animal rights activist for a midwife.

'Cows are highly sensitive and intelligent creatures,' Franz said. 'Equipped with the same motherly instincts that you're now feeling, Nele. So. What do you think has to happen for these emotional animals to produce milk?'

They have to have children, Nele thought and stroked

her belly, which she'd been rubbing with marigold oil daily over the last few weeks to fight the stretch marks.

'Exactly,' Franz yelled as if Nele had said something. 'Cows have to become pregnant. And then, so that they'll give milk all the time, we have to take their calves away from them. It's double the crime, you see what I'm saying? We snatch the baby from this highly sensitive mammal right after birth! And we steal the baby's milk, which we shouldn't even be drinking because our bodies can't tolerate it.'

'But what does that have to do with me?' Nele yelled back, though she didn't want an answer. Or any conversation. She only wanted this madness to finally stop. 'You want to punish me because I drink milk?'

'No. I want to show you what it means when a mother loses their child after a birth. It's drastic, I know. But I don't see any other way. I've tried it all. Petitions, protests, spoken up on YouTube and Facebook. But in this loud world of ours you only hear the one who yells the loudest. You know how many videos I've uploaded already? Of cows crying for the calves, for days on end? Those poor little creatures, crying for their mothers, tied up inside a tiny box. Only so that their mother can eke out a wretched existence clamped to milking machines her whole life before that final miserable shadow of herself is driven into the livestock truck with stun guns. That is, unless her open wounds and ruptured intestines are so obvious that not even the most money-hungry meat baron would want to convert this still-breathing cadaver into discount sausage. In which case the animal gets dumped into this pit.'

During Franz's outburst, Nele had nearly forgotten about

the pain in her stomach. Her fear that his underlying threat had unleashed now dominated all her worries.

'You want to take away my baby?'

After the birth?

'I have to,' he yelled, sounding as sad as he was committed. 'A video of your pain when experiencing such a loss would bring a million times more attention than the millions of videos that PETA and other animal rights organisations have already put out about the wretched conditions of milk production. You need to understand! Hardly anyone knows how the milk is made that we dump in our coffee and pour over our corn flakes. Many even believe the advertised lie that calves are allowed to stay in their mothers' stables. But that's not possible. A nursing cow would never let anyone get close to milking her, not with her little one next to her. She'd protect it, start kicking around. That's why it's taken away from her. Which is why I'm doing all this. After this video, everyone will know what it means for a mother to be separated from her baby, all for a drink of milk. All for our enjoyment.'

At the start of his speech, Nele was still burying her face in her hands in shock and assuming that reason could never appeal to this lunatic. But an idea came to her during his monologue. She let Franz's words hang in the air for a while, without comment. Only when he asked whether she'd understood it all did she, now true to her newly adopted survival strategy, softly tell him: 'I've never actually thought about it like that. But I think—'

'What?'

'Yes, I think I do understand you,' Nele said, and it wasn't even a lie.

In his delusion, and this was a good thing, Franz was still following his own inner logic. This meant he was acting rationally and not unpredictably. Plus he actually did seem to loathe what he was doing to her, even if he did consider it necessary and unavoidable. That made him the opposite of a psychopath. He experienced feelings, not only for those animals he loved so much, but also for her, the victim. The fact that he'd cried was evidence of empathy, and thus a certain accessibility – which might just be something she could exploit.

'I still don't quite understand fully,' she said, opening up to him, her words bouncing dully off the walls of the pit as she raised her voice. 'But we can definitely talk about it once you get me out of here.'

'Good, right. Happy to.'

Franz sounded truly thrilled. His reaction was like a toddler that had been crying because it had fallen but the next second was back up running around laughing after the father had promised him ice cream. 'I need to see if there's a hardware store somewhere around here. I'll get a little cable winch and a carrying strap or something so I can pull you out. Okay?'

He'd apparently stood up from the edge of the abyss, as his voice sounded more distant.

'Yes, that's fine. But please hurry,' Nele said, already panting again. It wasn't quite there yet but it might only be a matter of minutes before the flood returned to try pressing something far too big out of something far too narrow.

Her little munchkin, who was hopefully now in the right position. Even if this nearly literal gut feeling growing inside her was saying the exact opposite.

40

Mats

Dr André Klopstock, PhD

Among the hundreds of pages and articles on the net, Mats picked the Wikipedia entry for the infamous doctor. The internet connection up here in the clouds was stable enough but clearly slower than on the ground, which might have had something to do with Mats using the browser on the monitor and not his phone to go online. His eyes were watering from his lingering headache and he had barely been able to make out the little screen on his phone.

Klopstock is a German oncologist and psychiatrist, read the first sentence of the article. Mats only scanned it from there.

He used the arrows on the remote to scroll from paragraph to paragraph. Keywords like *married, several clinics in Berlin, socially engaged, Rotarian* and *laboratory* caught his eye.

It wasn't anything he didn't already know about his shady colleague. They'd both been students at the Free University of Berlin in Dahlem and Mats had even stood next to him at the dissecting table in a group taking their exams. André's cockiness had rubbed him the wrong way even then, as did his need for recognition (including the profile he'd written of himself for the med school magazine). His 'business savvy' was nothing more than flagrant greed as far as Mats could tell. In just one example, Klopstock had maintained a lucrative and possibly copyright-infringing trade in old exam papers.

The man was conceited, arrogant and most certainly corruptible.

But a criminal?

Mats shook his head. Even if he did think André Klopstock capable of plenty, it didn't include kidnapping and certainly not mass murder.

Or maybe it could?

Klopstock Home Testing

A new phrase caught his attention. It was blue and underlined, a hyperlink, but it still didn't get him where he needed to be.

Fine, so Klopstock didn't just make a mint from HIV – or from cancer patients, by using his expensive lab procedures before treating patients. He'd also tapped into the lucrative self-diagnosis market and held patents for sinfully expensive HIV tests sent to patients worried about going through a regular doctor, mostly out of shame.

If you followed Klopstock's career, it was all very consistent.

Mats scrolled on and then, *finally*, the three letters he was looking for jumped off the screen at him.

He stood up. He stepped closer to the monitor, electrified.

PPT

I knew it!

Pre-psych test

Mats felt an urgent need to sit back down. He was swaying, only his lack of equilibrium wasn't from the plane moving. He was swaying inside and, since he knew his internal unease wasn't about to subside just by dropping into a chair, he remained standing and propped himself on the table.

Under a news photo of Klopstock, the editor of the PPT entry had quoted part of a marketing brochure:

> *Klopstock Medical (KM) is already known as a leader in urine and hair analysis for pilots, drivers and soldiers – individuals carrying great responsibility. Hundreds of human lives often depend on the reliable performance of their duties, for which we regularly carry out drug and alcohol tests with the consent of all parties involved and according to current legal guidelines. In addition to these tests, which are designed to assess physical well-being, KM has also been working on the early detection of psychological abnormalities for some years now. Depression, suicidal thoughts, delusions, psychoses. All these disorders are no less dangerous than physical illness and intoxication. Only they haven't yet been identified in tests. KM, however, has achieved a breakthrough in this regard with the first pre-psych test procedure.*

The PPT procedure will make it possible to detect suicidal intentions among pilots of passenger aircraft at an early and timely stage. This is a highly sophisticated test questionnaire that allows crew members and even passengers to be assessed for abnormalities while waiting for departure. The psychological quizzes are accompanied by blood tests of the on-board crew. PPT is still in the trial stage, but there is already a legislative initiative to standardise psychological screening once clinical studies prove positive.

Mats looked out the left-side window into the darkness, which seemed even denser to him than before. Not even the ocean floor could be this black.

It gave him the feeling of possessing a mirror that was inscribed with the truth and the answer to all his questions, only it now lay shattered on the carpet before him and he had to piece all the shards back together into a whole that made sense.

– **Feli believes that Klopstock's driver has something to do with Nele's kidnapping.**
– **Klopstock himself is active in PPT research.**
– **The pilot talked about PPT.**

The connection was practically shouting at him.

Yet what did Nele's disappearance have to do with psychological screening tests?

The motive! That had been his very first question, still

unresolved. *Who profits from my making this aeroplane crash?*

Mats grabbed at his temples, massaging them. He felt he was getting closer to the big picture. More precisely, he sensed that the question of motive was too limited.

'PPT!' he blurted. 'That's the connection. The blackmailer doesn't care *that* I make the aeroplane crash.' *For that he could've planted a bomb or provided me with a weapon.*

Instead, the blackmailer was taking the trouble to spy on him, to match his flight to Kaja's, and to slip the secret video into in-flight viewing.

'The question is more a case of *why* I'm supposed to cause an aeroplane to crash in *exactly this way?*'

For me to manipulate an individual.

For me to ignite a psychological bomb.

Mats trembled from the buzz of excitement. Again the answer led to Klopstock: PPT.

Klopstock wants PPT to be licensed.

The law doesn't have the votes.

He needs a precedent.

All at once, everything made sense.

Klopstock wants to cause the aeroplane to crash in order to prove there's a need for psychological checks. Not only for pilots. Rather for the crew. And for passengers like me. To amass millions once his tests suddenly need to be deployed in dozens of airports across Europe.

Mats felt a chill, deeply frightened from his conclusions. He turned off the monitor and stared at his hand, still holding the remote, not wanting to stop trembling.

He was so worked up, so excited, that it seemed he could feel every single hair on the skin of his scalp.

Yes, it does make sense, he thought again, and yet – something didn't quite fit.

And that was a certain six foot one vain peacock by the name of Klopstock.

Would he really sell out so many lives all to simply pile up more money in bank accounts already threatening to overflow?

To find out, Mats made his way down to seat 7A.

41

Feli

Back courtyard, fourth floor. Grey graffiti-smeared concrete, indestructible bike racks in the lot and a stench like cat piss in the stairwell.

Feli never would've thought such desolate living conditions existed in such close proximity to the Paris Bar, which was consistently frequented by people who figured they counted among Berlin high society simply because they'd once had a drink there.

Poor yet ugly, some joker had written with a sharpie on a brown door that looked bulletproof, borrowing from the city's famous 'poor yet sexy' quote from former mayor Wowereit.

Feli couldn't argue with its creator.

The cramped 1970s building where Franz Uhlandt supposedly lived was a spawn of architectural barbarism. Low ceilings, pimpled sprayed concrete walls and slit pillbox windows, at least from what could be seen of it from Kantstrasse.

Feli made her way up the stairs, passing baby buggies, dirty shoes, yellow sacks and bags full of empty returnable bottles until finally reaching the fourth floor. She didn't feel she could trust the claustrophobic elevator.

She was now a little out of breath from the stairs, standing before a door with a nameplate inscribed with F.U.

Franz Uhlandt?

If the info under 'company headquarters' on his business card was correct, this had to be it.

Taxi, Patient Transportation & Chauffeur Services, read the plain, small rectangle of cardstock Feli had got from Klopstock's reception lady. Fourth floor, left.

She rang the bell but couldn't hear whether it actually sounded inside the apartment, so she knocked on the door with a flat hand.

Ow.

For a second she'd forgotten her fingers had been squashed. Not too smart using them as a percussion instrument.

So she tried again with her other hand, calling Uhlandt's name at the same time.

Suddenly the door opened. But not the one before her, the one behind her.

'All right, all right... just don't shout like that!' droned the hoarse voice from the apartment opposite. It seemed the laws of nature didn't apply in this building so that sound travelled faster than light – she first heard the old man's voice before his haggard frame stepped from the half shadows of his apartment into the hallway.

'Hold on, just hold on...'

His bathrobe rustled like dry paper as the easily eighty-year-old man in brown slippers shuffled up to Feli. He had unwashed, severely parted grey hair and a face that seemed to curve inward, which might have had something to do with the lack of teeth in his mouth. Which in turn explained his hoarse muttering.

'Are you the new one?' he said.

'Excuse me?'

'Why else didn't you ring my bell?'

Feli didn't respond, for the simple reason that she had no idea who this man was and what he wanted from her. She could explain even less why he was pulling a set of keys much too large for his liver-spotted hands from the depths of his robe and opened up the door to Uhlandt's apartment.

'He said you'd check in with me when you came.'

'Franz?' Feli said, completely confused.

'Brad Pitt, who you think?' countered the old man in typical Berlin manner. When a true Berliner was offered the chance to bust someone's balls, he was sure to seize it. 'Brad Pitt lives quite the life of luxury here. Sold off his mansion in Malibu just to get it.'

He pushed the door open with a smoker's cough-worthy laugh. 'Just pull it shut again when you've finished the ass-wiping,' he squawked. 'Okay?'

'The what?' she blurted.

'Oh. Apologies. Didn't mean to hurt your feelings. So, how about it, you want in?'

'Yes,' Feli said having no clue whom the old retired guy was confusing her with. She eagerly waited for him to disappear back inside his apartment. But he kept standing there, staring at her like a bellboy expecting a tip. Since the man made no effort to go, it now fell upon her, it seemed, to her to wrap up this bizarre encounter.

The most reasonable option was doing an about-face

and leaving this building as fast as possible. But what was she supposed to tell Mats?

Sorry, I was actually standing at the open front door of your daughter's possible kidnapper, but I didn't dare go inside?

The unreasonable alternative was to go inside for a start and take a look around the apparently deserted apartment while she had Mats on the phone.

'Thanks so much again,' Feli said, deciding on her second choice.

She entered Uhlandt's apartment and shut the door behind her. In the peephole she saw the weird old geezer remove himself and disappear inside his own four walls.

Feli waited a little while longer, then she opened Uhlandt's front door again and left it cracked open so she'd able to flee faster in case it was a trap.

What now?

She took a step into the hallway and was startled by the ceiling spots that lit up by a motion detector. They bathed the hall in a warm, soft light.

'Hello? Herr Uhlandt?'

Feli waited in vain for a response and looked around. The apartment was neat and orderly, almost painstakingly tidy. Rubber boots were positioned perfectly aligned on a drying mat, keys labelled with stickers hung on hooks next to the door, and a precisely aligned doily garnished a chest of drawers.

Franz had likely made a mistake matching the air freshener to the season. It was only fall yet already smelled Christmassy, of cinnamon and sugared almonds.

'Hello? Is anyone home?' Feli asked of the darkness

stretching out beyond the hall. This was the second time inside a few hours that she was creeping around in a stranger's apartment. It was painful enough at Nele's. And this time she had a much worse feeling.

She reached for her phone and waited for an eternity for the call to go through.

'Mats?'

There was the usual delay before he answered.

'Where are you?'

'In Franz Uhlandt's apartment. I think. It looks strange in here.'

'How do you mean?'

'Not sure. I have really bad feeling doing this. What am I supposed to be doing here?'

'Are you alone?'

'I hope so.'

'Okay, look for a laptop, any kind of documents, an office.'

'Sounds good.'

Feli opened the first door to her right and saw herself – the bathroom mirror was mounted on the far end of a rectangular, windowless room. Here too all was kept squeaky clean. No water stains on the mirror, just the essentials on the sink washstand. Toothpaste, soap dispenser, razor.

'Have you found anything?'

'No.'

Feli opened the mirror cabinet over the sink.

Over-the-counter medications in packages and tubes presented themselves, all lined up with equal spacing. A total contrast to Nele's chaotic bathroom arrangement.

Ibuprofen, zinc pills, aspirin, vitamin B, Voltaren.

Nothing that caught Feli's attention. Except...

What the heck...

'What you got?' Mats asked. He must have heard her clicking her tongue.

'I think this Franz is altering the way he looks.'

'How do you mean?'...

'Here's a tube of adhesive cream. And an empty denture container.'

Pause.

'Okay, what about his office?'

'I haven't got there yet.'

'Good, call me when you have something new. I'm on the trail of something here too.'

'Sounds good.'

Feli hung up, closed the cabinet, and tossed her phone screaming when she spotted the figure in the mirror that had crept into the bathroom wielding an axe. And Feli screamed even louder when she realised that her attacker was not alone.

42

Just like Mom's flashed through her mind absurdly. The axe had a dual-coloured blade – a bright graphite edge and a black top mounted to the grip. It looked like the cleaver her mom always used to employ in the kitchen when dealing with meat or something frozen. Not very big, though much too hefty for the weak person now clutching it with both hands.

Especially for swinging the thing down on Feli, something this person was not remotely capable of in her position. Maybe for throwing it. The woman in the wheelchair had no other choice if she really wanted to wound Feli.

That was exactly what she seemed to have in mind. Her face looked rapt and practically glowing with anger as she swung back to throw.

Feli heard the woman scream 'INTRUDER!' as the axe left her hands. She thought she felt a slight draft before the whirring metal was able to penetrate her skull, split it open and find her brain. She screamed expecting pain and death though not as loudly as the old woman was howling – not from anger now but fear.

Just like Feli.

The woman in the wheelchair, who didn't look so old and angry anymore as much as ill, whipped her head around and glanced up with the whites of her eyes right into the face of the man who'd just wrested the weapon from her.

'HELP!' she screamed, and Feli slapped a hand over her mouth.

Immensely relieved and glad that she'd left the door open.

Through which Livio had obviously followed her.

43

'HELP! INTRUD—'

The wheelchair lady's scream expired as choking gagging sounds as Livio pressed his hand over her mouth. She was far too weak to fight him off. Altogether she didn't appear to weigh much more than the lilac-coloured silk pyjamas she wore.

'Calm down, calm down,' said Feli's saviour and went on one knee to get eye level with the woman. 'We're not going to do anything to you, do you understand? We're not intruders, and we don't mean you any harm.'

The woman's eyes widened, and she stopped screaming.

'What are you doing here, Livio?' In her excitement, Feli called him by his name as if they were somehow friends.

'I'm wondering the same of you,' Livio said and briefly turned to her. 'I only wanted to bring you your wallet – you left it in my car.'

Feli felt her jacket pocket, confirming it was empty.

Meanwhile the wheelchair lady had stopped screaming for good, and Livio dared to remove his hand. 'Good thing I caught up with you.'

The old woman coughed and wiped a string of saliva from her lower lip. 'Who in the hell are you?'

Feli went down on one knee next to her too. 'My name is Dr Felicitas Heilmann,' she said, hoping to gain respect by mentioning her title, and some trust along with it. It seemed to work.

'You're a doctor?' asked the old woman.

'Yes.'

'So what are you doing here in my apartment? What were you looking for in my bathroom?'

'We're looking for Franz Uhlandt. Does he live here?'

'That the guy's name?' Feli heard Livio ask. He'd stepped back behind the wheelchair. He stood with one foot in the bathroom, the other in the hall. Feli recalled that he'd already left Klopstock's clinic by the time she talking to the doctor.

'My Franz?' the wheelchair lady asked.

Only now did Feli have the composure to take a closer look at her face. She was thin in that way only a person suffering from a severe illness could be. Hardly any fatty tissue showed under her skin, which stretched so tightly over the bones of her skull that Feli was scared she could burst like a balloon if someone so much as scratched her with a fingernail. Her hair had fallen out except for a few ashen-coloured tufts. If she'd once been attractive, as evidenced by her symmetrical facial features, high forehead, and smooth cheekbones, she was sure to suffer all the more whenever she looked in the mirror. The old woman had been robbed of all her beauty by whatever it was she suffered from.

'We believe Franz is in trouble,' Feli said, filled with a sudden sympathy.

The old woman gave a hollow laugh. 'You don't need to be psychic to tell that. Trouble is our middle name.'

'You always charge strangers with a cleaver?' Livio asked behind her.

'You usually break into disabled people's homes?'

Feli saw the old woman's wrinkly neck twisting around to get a look at Livio and couldn't help think of a turtle.

'Consider yourself lucky that I don't have a shotgun in the house. How did you get in anyway?'

'Your neighbour let me in,' Feli explained. 'You didn't open up and he apparently thought I was your caregiver.'

The old woman slapped at her forehead. 'That idiot, swear he's got dementia. She already came yesterday. Such a moron. I asked him to open up because sometimes I don't hear the bell on account of my meds. But not today. My son told me not to answer the door today like I usually do. He warned me that someone could break in.'

'Franz is your son?' Livio asked.

'I'm only fifty-five. Yes, I know. Look double that. Goddamn osteoporosis.' Uhlandt's mother wagged a hand in resignation. 'My Franz says it's because of milk.'

'Come again?'

She looked at Feli with her cloudy eyes and added a feeble shrug. 'He's vegan, you see. Got carried away with this obsession that animal products are making us all sick. Milk above all. Good Lord, can't have cheese, no yogurt, not even a chocolate bar here in the house ever since he's been living with me. Says humans are the only mammals that keep drinking milk after breastfeeding, and that's the cause of my illness. I'm more inclined to think it's bad genes. But my Franz will hear none of it.'

She reached for her spokes to roll herself out of the bathroom, but Livio held her there.

'Why weren't you supposed to answer the door and expect intruders instead?' Livio asked her.

'What does it matter? What am I doing talking to you anyway? Get lost or I'll call the police.'

'You're talking to us because we want to help your son,' said Feli, who noticed that Livio was listening to her just as attentively as Uhlandt's mother. 'And I guarantee Franz doesn't want you involving the police. A woman is missing. A pregnant woman. She's the daughter of a friend, and I'm afraid that your son might have something to do with it.'

'He might?' Uhlandt's mother slumped noticeably. Hunched her back in her wheelchair and stared at her hands folded in her lap. 'A pregnant girl, you said?'

'Yes.'

Her lips moved, but it took a while before Feli heard her say anything, almost as if she had to exercise her mouth before attempting to pronounce the words. 'I don't know what's going on. Franz is up to something, that's for sure. I don't mean to talk bad about him, I don't. He is a loving boy, and he takes good care of me. But ever since he's had this new friend of his—'

'What friend?' Feli asked.

'I've never seen him. Don't even know if it's a guy, but Franz has never had a proper girlfriend. He only ever talked about having a soulmate. "Someone who finally understands me, Mom," he said. And that the two of them were planning something that the whole world would be talking about. He even got money for it.'

'To do what?'

'How should I know? I think it was for some video equipment. Been working on it day and night, scoping things out somewhere. But I have no idea what.'

She turned to Livio and looked past him to the door opposite the bathroom, on the other side of the hall.

'I'm never allowed in his room.'

44

Mats

Row 7, seat A.

The most dangerous seat in the aeroplane if the results of crash tests in the New Mexico desert were to be believed. The seat with a one hundred per cent chance of death in a frontal collision.

And it wasn't like an aeroplane was ever going to fly backwards into a mountain.

It was a window seat on top of that.

Which significantly raised the threat of skin cancer.

Mats, nearly at seat 7A, knew how stupid it was be thinking about such a statistic right now, and in the middle of night besides; but those facts about flight risks that he'd researched over the last few weeks were like some tune he couldn't get out of his head. They buzzed around his brain and there was nothing he could do to turn them off.

Aeroplane windows barely absorb UV rays, and as the plane's altitude rises any protection from the atmosphere decreases, which is why pilots are twice as likely to get skin cancer as the rest of the population.

Some said a long-distance flight was worse than

twenty minutes in a tanning bed. Mats currently felt as if he'd already been tanning for several hours unprotected. Feverish, overheated, dehydrated, and he was nauseous as if from sunstroke.

All symptoms of fear and stress. Manifestations of his despair about having no idea what to do to avoid this catastrophe.

Once he reached his destination, he looked around.

Three quarters of the seats were occupied down here in business class, and all the passengers were sleeping. The lights had been dimmed to only the safety lighting, and the shades were pulled down. The symbols for the restrooms were illuminated green, the toilets unoccupied. No one stood in the aisles stretching their legs. No one to observe him as he halted at seat 7A and looked down on that red-haired woman he'd offered his seat to.

I'm all alone, thought Mats. *More alone than ever before in my life.*

The uneven rows of business class had what they called 1-2-1 seating – a window seat, two middle seats, and another window seat on the other side.

7A was thus a single seat, which was the good news, since Mats wouldn't have to climb over neighbouring passengers to make contact with Salina Piehl.

The bad news was, she was a mother and sleeping like all of them were, as soundly as her baby slumbering peacefully on her stomach. Only that little hairless head was poking out of the blanket, its tiny little eyes firmly shut. It kept twitching involuntarily and sucking on a pink pacifier.

To be able to rest so easily, Salina had lowered the seat into a flat bed.

Mats knelt down in the aisle alongside them and raised the overhanging blanket a little to see under the reclined seat.

It was as dark as he'd feared, meaning he wasn't able to tell where the life vest was.

He also feared that he wouldn't even be able to get at it unless the seat was in the upright position required in an emergency situation.

Then again, what if such an emergency caught you sleeping?

No, that wasn't possible. Even then a person had to be able to reach the life vest, so Mats tried again, this time using his phone as a flashlight. Again with no success.

The phone's weak light only let him see dropped newspapers, a straw and other travel garbage. Nowhere did he see a pocket or a pouch that might hold a life vest.

'Can I help you?'

Mats banged his head on the outside armrest as he shot up, alarmed by the familiar and uncivil voice above him.

Valentino!

The idiot was just what he needed now. The captain had asked him to keep away from Kaja as well as to avoid causing any more 'incidents'. And now here he lay at the feet of that very flight attendant he'd accused of nothing less than assaulting him a few hours ago.

'No, no, it's all fine,' Mats whispered, pulling himself up. The flight attendant seemed unable to decide whether to view him with amusement, derision or disapproval, which was why he did all three in that exact order.

'Looking for something?'

'Uh, yes. This was my seat originally.'

'So?'

Mats was trying not to wake the mother and child, but the snotty flight attendant was speaking at normal volume.

'I think I lost something here.'

'What might that be?'

Mats switched into confrontation mode, still whispering. 'I don't believe that it concerns you.'

'And I don't believe that you were ever sitting here.'

'That may be, but...'

... a madman did call me to say that he's placed a weapon down here. And if you don't clear out at once, you'll be the first person I try it out on.

'Is there a problem?'

The seat reading light came on next to him, and Mats was looking into Salina's tired eyes. She kept blinking with concern.

'Do you want to have your seat back?' she said.

Mats turned to Valentino. 'Great. Now look what you've done.' He knelt down to Salina. 'No, no. I'm sorry. I was hoping not to disturb you.'

He gave Valentino a scathing look, but he only grinned as he moved on and left Mats with the mess.

'Damn it, now we've woken the baby.'

The baby girl had spat out her pacifier and was stretching out across her mother's chest like a cat just waking from her nap. Mats unavoidably thought of Nele, who as a baby had always slept like an angel but then, after a short period of waking up, frequently lapsed into screaming for minutes on end. He hoped this baby was different from Nele in that regard, even though Salina had said it suffered from colic. For now it just chuckled.

'I'm terribly sorry,' he added.

'No problem,' Salina said, her facial expression saying the opposite.

She pressed a button on her armrest and the seat rose to its upright position. As it did, she pressed her baby to her chest and gently rocked it back and forth.

'Suza needs to be fed anyway.'

She unbuttoned the breast pocket of her blouse, and Mats glanced away in respect. His eyes landed on a little sign directly under the monitor in the backrest of the seat before her.

LIFE VEST.

'Excuse me, may I?'

Now that the seat wasn't down, Mats could open the compartment below the monitor no problem.

'Everything all right?' Salina asked in amazement when he pulled out a red-and-yellow life preserver and loosened the tape keeping it in a little packet.

'Yeah, yeah. I think I dropped something inside this compartment earlier,' Mats lied, and as he spoke he saw a little object no bigger than a lighter come loose from the vest.

He stuffed the life vest back in, closed the compartment and felt around the floor for the missing object.

'Dental floss?' Salina asked in more amazement right when he saw what he'd picked up off the floor.

It was. A sky-blue, see-through plastic case with the inscription: *Super Floss*.

'Yes. It wasn't very polite of me to disturb you for this.'

He hastily stuffed the case in his pocket and felt as if his trousers were being pulled down by a weight of ten pounds or more.

Dental floss? What perverse genius.

He could just imagine what the tear-proof material wound up in the inconspicuous dispenser was really made of. Razor-sharp plastic fibre that could be used to garrotte a person yet didn't attract the attention of any security check. Who'd ever been forced to clean the gaps between their teeth while airport security watched?

'Please excuse me,' Mats told Salina when leaving, glad that the baby still had not cried. 'I don't want to disturb you any longer.'

Just kill you possibly.

Salina pointed at the baggage compartment about her seat. 'Could you please get me my diaper bag?' she asked, and Mats did her the favour, of course.

When pulling it down, he noticed a silver metal case right next to her linen bag that was stuffed full of diapers, wet wipes and oilcloth. A thought was forming in his head, just a loose idea.

'That a camera in there?' he asked – more excitedly than he'd meant.

'Yes.'

'Looks professional.'

'Well, I did say I'm a photographer.' She fished out a new pacifier from the outside pocket.

'Is it digital?'

The idea was now taking concrete form.

'Yes. But I have analogue models too. You ever want to come by my studio some time and check them out?'

Mats shook his head.

'No, I mean, yes, I'd love to. I only wanted to know if this digital camera...' He pointed at the metal case up in the compartment. 'Does it have a slow motion function?'

Salina looked at him just as confused as when he'd first offered her his seat.

'It does,' she said hesitantly, and Mats nearly clapped with excitement.

'Do you think I could borrow it?'

'Now?' She laughed as if expecting to hear the punchline of the joke.

'Yes, now. I really need it.'

Mats wasn't counting on Salina's curt response.

'No,' she said, stroking her baby's head.

'No?'

His pulse raced like a sports car passing an autobahn sign for no speed limit.

'My camera is sacred to me,' she explained to him. 'But I'll make you a proposal. You tell me what you have planned, and I'll help you with it. Okay?'

45

'Wow...'

Salina pivoted around and gently whispered her admiration, likely so as not to wake her baby just now dozing again in her arms. It was also possible that seeing it all really had taken her breath away.

Mats had briefly been worried that a crew member might block their way since he wasn't allowed to take other passengers upstairs with him, but they hadn't encountered anyone on their short trip up.

'This is unbelievable!'

Mats looked around the Sky Suite with her. All this luxury was simply obscene to him, especially considering the fact that he'd transformed this flying hotel suite into the command centre for his nightmare of planning psychological warfare against Kaja and all the passengers. Unsuspecting people like Salina Piehl, on the other hand, couldn't help getting completely blown away by the sight of the swivelling leather chairs, its own bathroom with shower, and a bedroom with king bed.

'Now I get why you let me have 7A. I'd rather be flying up here too,' she whispered in amazement and immediately shook her head. 'Sorry, I didn't mean to sound presumptuous. I'm just happy that you were so generous.'

'Don't worry,' Mats said to appease her. 'I'm the one who should be thanking you.'

He rolled the still-unused serving cart aside and moved one of the two chairs into its 180-degree flat position. Salina understood the gesture and lay her baby down there along with its blankie. The aircraft was gliding along through the night yet she still chose to strap in her sleeping baby by gently stretching the belt across its chest before stepping over to Mats, who was just turning the monitor on.

'What's this about?'

'An emergency, if I may say so,' Mats began and reiterated the story that he'd cooked up on the way to the upper level and could now feed her.

'I'm a psychiatrist and on the way to Berlin for a highly complicated case. I've received the patient's treatment video but I'm not able to review it up here as precisely as I'd like.'

'I see,' Salina said but didn't look like she did.

'It's complicated, and I can't show you the video because of doctor–patient confidentiality of course.' At this point Mats made things purposely vague, blurry. 'It's of utmost importance that I get a better look at a certain portion of the video. A patient's micro-expression.'

'Like in slow motion?' Salina asked.

'Exactly. The software here on board doesn't allow that, unfortunately. But with the help of your camera…'

Salina nodded. 'You want to film the screen and then watch the result in slow motion?'

'Better yet, frame by frame.'

'Okay, no problem.'

Mats looked her firmly in the eyes and noticed that more of Salina's freckles were showing on her pale skin than a little while ago. It wasn't only because she'd stopped applying much make-up – she was agitated. He had jolted her from sleep, practically abducted her up to this luxury wonderland of a flying two-room residence, and asked for unusual assistance with the therapy of a disturbing patient. It was a miracle she was even going to tell him how her camera worked and not simply how nuts he was.

The device she removed from her the flight case along with a tripod was not difficult to understand, but Mats wrote down the most important instructions step by step. Once he was sure he understood, he asked her to leave the living room.

'You're joking.'

'I'm sorry. I have to insist. Doctor–patient confidentiality.'

Salina nervously rubbed her hands together as if cold. She obviously didn't feel comfortable leaving him alone with her camera.

'It's safe and secure on the tripod,' Mats promised. 'I will not move it from this spot.'

'Very well,' Salina said after more hesitation, though not looking at all happy about moving into the bedroom with the baby.

He waited until she shut the door, then immediately fast-forwarded channel 13/10 to the ninth minute. To the moment right before Kaja returned to kiss the shooter.

He let the video run from 552 seconds on and started the digital camera, which was pointed at the wall monitor. Seeing it this second time, he was even more certain of how explosive his discovery was.

He first stopped playback, then the recording, and let his newly taped footage replay on the camera's folding beermat-sized display. He waited about thirty seconds before pressing pause. From there he skipped forwards second by second, and soon he reached the part he wanted to see.

He didn't even need to switch to single-frame mode. The still image on the display was perfect.

And tragic.

This can't be.

Mats felt a thumping inside his chest, as if he had no heart there but a wild troll desperately wanting to escape from his body instead.

Salina had shown him how to connect her digital camera to the monitor using the HDMI cable from her case. That worked easily, which meant the fifty-five-inch monitor was now exhibiting the disturbing image and in surprisingly good resolution.

His hands wet with sweat, he pulled out his phone and clicked a photo of the still image on the monitor.

The feet.

On the blurred tile.

On which the cameraman had stood while filming Kaja's rape, down to the bitter end.

And who was not named Johannes Faber and wasn't even a male. It was a female, with green camo-patterned nail polish on her toes.

Just like all three friends in her special gang had worn that day, as their very own sign.

Of all people.

'Can I come back out now?' he heard Salina say from behind the bedroom door.

Mats swallowed hard, but the bitter taste in his mouth only got stronger. All the truths, all that he thought he'd known about Kaja and her therapy, was turned on its head with this one image.

Even worse: the photo he now had on his phone, this one single image, was possibly the most lethal weapon on board this aeroplane.

'Yes, of course,' he told Salina, deleting the video from her camera, and turning off the monitor at the very moment he felt a gentle waft of air behind him.

Mats turned around and only saw the door to the Sky Suite closing with a soft click.

He froze a moment in a state of shock, and far too long, because once he'd pulled himself back together, once he'd run to the exit and thrown the door open and peered down the hall to the Sky Bar to see who'd been watching him, to see who'd been looking over his shoulder – they were long gone.

46

Feli

'So where we going?' Livio asked Feli as she entered the address in his navigation device. The thing looked even older than his completely filthy Renault.

'This piece of junk even work?' she said and tried entering the info for a third time.

'Not with your stubby fingers,' Livio shot back and steered into the outer lane of the traffic circle at Ernst Reuter Platz.

'You didn't have to drive,' Feli said. The display now said it was searching for a satellite.

'Right. 'Cause you're doing so well on your own. Turn here?'

She nodded, and they headed towards the Victory Column on Strasse des 17 Juni.

'Listen, maybe I do have skeletons in my closet. But I'm no idiot. I can tell when someone's in trouble.'

Feli laughed out loud. 'It doesn't exactly take a genius. I literally told the woman: the daughter of a friend is missing. And her son might've kidnapped her.'

'Kidnapped?'

Shit. Feli bit her lip. She'd just spilled the beans.

Livio gave her a wary look from the corner of his eye. 'So in that mommy's boy's room you think you found—'

'His plans. Exactly.'

The navigation had found the satellite and was calculating the route. Still twenty-three minutes to Weissensee.

Still two-and-a-half hours until the wedding.

Good Lord, how am I going to explain this to Janek?

At least she was now heading in the right direction with Livio.

She started typing a response to her fiancé's countless texts but couldn't find the right words.

She was far too worked up about all she'd discovered in Franz Uhlandt's apartment, and calling Mats first was more important.

'Hello?'

It rang and hissed static, but he didn't pick up. When voice mail came on, she hung up.

Shit.

Why wasn't he picking up? She needed to make a decision. What she'd just experienced was telling her – at the very least – to now call the police.

Ten minutes ago, Feli had gained access to Franz Uhlandt's combination bedroom and office, against his mother's will, using a screwdriver that Livio found in a kitchen drawer. They'd only needed to give the lock a hard jerk, without damaging it. It was so easy that Feli had been certain Franz would leave nothing revealing simply lying around.

She'd been wrong.

In contrast to the rest of the apartment, Franz's room was an utter mess. The bed wasn't made, laundry lay strewn all over the floor between medical journals and crumpled tissues. At a window covered with plastic sheet was a school desk with an *Atomkraft? Nein, Danke!* sticker on the desktop along with Panini collector cards of Germany's 2006 World Cup team.

There was no computer, no camera, nothing electronic in the room, not even a TV. The ingrain wallpaper held no pictures or photos, though Feli did spot holes from tacks and nails and scotch tape, as well as dirty borders from items that must have been recently taken down.

Against the protests of his bickering mother, Feli had first opened the drawer of the desk and then the wardrobe, and eventually made the classic under-the-mattress discovery.

Satellite photos, printouts of a building from a bird's-eye view. City maps, always of the same area. An address circled in red.

And, finally, the interior shots. Photos. Clearly a milking facility.

What would a vegan want with that? Feli was wondering. Then, when she'd realised why, she had grabbed the printouts now lying on Livio's back seat and run out of the apartment as if on fire. Not even saying goodbye, Livio running after her.

The question now wasn't where Franz had taken Nele. It was whether they should finally be calling in the police.

Yet Mats, who still hadn't answered twice now, was making her have to decide.

What if Nele was being held prisoner and tortured in those old cow stalls? Then every second counted.

But what if she was wrong and sent the police down the wrong track?

If it was the former, Nele might just be saved by the police acting quickly.

If the latter, Nele could die. Mats had left no doubt of that. She was useless as leverage once the blackmailer lost contact with Mats. And they were sure to lose it just as soon as the authorities found out about the kidnapping. To thwart any possible crash attempt and protect the lives of the passengers, Mats and Kaja would be seized immediately on board the plane.

In her anger, Feli again made the mistake of balling her injured fingers into a fist.

She screamed out all her frustration. 'Fuck!'

Livio, driving towards Brandenburg Gate, asked what he could do to help.

Feli vented her rage at him. 'Just what is it with you? You don't look like much of a Good Samaritan to me. What's in it for you?'

'A C-note wouldn't hurt,' he admitted openly, and his chutzpah stole some of her anger.

'A hundred euros?'

'That's the Livio taxi fee.' He grinned, and although this reckless wannabe wasn't her type at all, Feli could see how some women fell for his swashbuckling charm, usually those victim types who kept seeking the same fake machismo. She'd heard it often enough in her therapy sessions.

'That include a ride to my husband's too?' she asked, not quite serious.

'To your wedding, you mean?'

Her head whipped around in surprise. 'How do you know that?' she asked warily.

'I went through your wallet looking for an ID or an

address. That's when I saw the invitation. Shouldn't you be home by now?'

'Shouldn't you have taken my billfold to my house instead of following me?'

'Oh, sorry for just happening to see you come out of Klopstock's clinic. Man, you were running fast, and I lost sight of you. Just be happy I ended up spotting you again on Kantstrasse. You're so paranoid!'

'And you, you're—'

She wasn't able to get the insult out.

Her phone was ringing.

'Mats, thank God!'

47

Nele

Every person has a breaking point. Where they confess to all under torture, even to murder, if only to make the pain finally stop.

Nele had reached this point. At least she thought.

Her munchkin was threatening to tear apart her insides. She screamed, begged for a hand to squeeze or even crush, but of course there wasn't one in this garbage pit that barely had any light and stunk of blood, sweat and pungent trash.

She'd even reached the point of wishing for her kidnapper to return.

What was that saying? Everyone dies alone in the end. Which, in her case, was actually a lie.

She was dying together with her baby that wanted to get out of her but couldn't. For a reason that she'd probably never know, not unless they had an information desk in the afterlife.

'Fuuuuhh!' Nele screamed. She felt like she wouldn't be able to see after this, even if a stream of light did come down out of nowhere all of a sudden. She had pushed so hard while forgetting to close her eyes that all her veins were guaranteed to have burst. She'd seen images of women after delivery who looked like they'd had chlorine sprayed in their eyes.

'Fuuuuhuhuuh!'

She was choking on her own battle cry. It had stopped giving her any relief and was now just a scream, hacking its way up her dry throat.

Seized by another contraction, she clawed at the filth under her. Didn't feel the splinter digging in under her fingernails yet did feel a cold, smooth surface.

A mirror?

At the peak of her pain the contraction ebbed again, and for a moment Nele was able to touch the piece with both hands.

It really was. It felt like it, and even reflected what little light pooled here below in this pit.

The shard of a mirror.

Pointy, sharp, and portable, nearly like that razor blade between her sofa cushions earlier.

Inside her head, she imagined herself dragging the shard across the skin of her wrists.

And that was the first happy thought she'd had in long time.

48

Mats

'Feli? Where are you?'

The aircraft's monotonous drone drowned out any of that telling background noise that a person normally heard on a phone call.

He had no idea if she was heading somewhere or at home changing for her wedding or maybe already on the way to the registry office, which he hoped was not true.

'I'm driving to that former East German meat processing plant.'

'Where's that?'

'An abandoned industrial complex, right near Nele's neighbourhood.'

Mats heard his low battery warning and pulled his phone from his ear real quick.

Only 15 per cent left.

'Is she there?' he asked, agitated now.

'I plan on finding out. But, Mats, wouldn't it be better to call the police?'

Mats took a deep breath and halted in the middle bend of the circular staircase leading down to the first class lobby. 'Not until you're certain that Nele's really there,' he implored.

'I don't think you know how big this property is. There's a derelict children's hospital, meat factory, old livestock stalls.'

The perfect playground for a psychopath.

'Keep an eye out for a taxi,' Mats said and continued down the stairs.

'All right, that's one idea. But what if I don't find anything—'

'Call me before you try anything else. When will you be there?'

'About twenty minutes.'

Mats prayed that he could still be reached by then and ended the call.

It didn't matter what the captain had demanded of him – he simply *needed* to speak to Kaja. And what was Captain Pereya supposed to do about it? It wasn't as if the man could have him locked up just for having suspicions.

'Kaja!'

Mats nodded at a black-haired, extremely slender female flight attendant who was luckily already on her way to first class with a cart holding a selection of magazines, presumably to gratify those passengers suffering from lack of sleep with new reading material. Once she disappeared beyond the curtain, he stepped up to Kaja. She hadn't responded to him yet.

She was standing at the glass elevator next to the bar and acting as if she hadn't heard him coming.

'I need to talk to you,' Mats said fairly brusquely – he didn't have a second to lose.

Kaja pointed at the elevator. 'Unfortunately I have no time for you, Dr Krüger. I have to get back to the crew's cabin.'

'Where?'

'An area not open to passengers, below near the cargo area. A real step forward. We used to only have a curtain we could pull shut. Now we have these small but lockable cabins available to us, with a bed and TV.'

Kaja was trying to sound as normal as possible, but her smile looked about as real as an abused wife scared of her husband hitting her again.

'Are you doing all right?'

'No, I'm not, Dr Krüger. Which you very well know.'

He had no plan, hadn't thought up anything to say, so he spat out his most burning question: 'Were you just upstairs?'

She pressed the button again even though they could already hear the elevator moving.

'Please, I'm on a break. I was just going to the bathroom really quickly and would now like to go and lie back down again.'

Mats shook his head. He wasn't going to let her go this easily.

'The video. Those final scenes. I have to know what that was all about.'

'Why?'

Good question.

The deciding question.

'Could it be you were being blackmailed? Even back then?'

Kaja's eyes turned cold. 'You haven't understood a thing, Dr Krüger,' she said softly, nearly imperceptibly.

He grabbed her shoulder and felt her go cold from his touch.

'Which is exactly why I need to talk to you. Look. At the time, Johannes Faber was sentenced to a hundred hours' community service. But kept asserting, over and over again, that he'd never made that video. And now I know that he was telling the truth.'

'How so?'

'Because it was a female holding the camera.'

He pointed at his phone, at the image he'd taken from the monitor.

'You see the female foot? With the camo toenail polish? The same kind you were wearing that day, Kaja. Just like the other girls in your special gang. Tina was killed. So it was Amelie who took the video and released it. Isn't that right?'

The elevator opened.

'No,' Kaja stated firmly. Her expression didn't show she was certain, only her desire that this could not possibly correspond to the truth.

'Then tell me who it was.'

Kaja stepped inside, but Mats held his hand over the sensor so the door couldn't close.

'Why should I?'

'Because I am certain that this person, whoever it is, is still making your life hell, even today.'

And wants to turn it into an inferno. For you, for me, and for all here on board.

'Why did you kiss the shooter? And who was filming you? What's this really about?'

Mats posed the question in the agonising hope that the

answer might somehow bring him closer to the blackmailer or at least to his motive.

'Like I said: you don't understand this in the slightest.' Kaja held a chip card to another sensor. 'Even then you didn't.'

Mats' phone rang again and he made the mistake of checking the screen. In the process he removed his hand from the door, which shut immediately.

'You never understood me before either,' he heard Kaja saying.

And as she looked right through him with her fixed stare, as if he too were made of glass, the voice on his phone asked: 'Did you find the weapon?'

Mats felt for the floss dispenser in his suit pocket. 'Yes.'

'Give it to her.'

He looked down. Saw only the dusty grey roof of the elevator cabin and the metal cable suspending it. Kaja had disappeared from view.

'That's not going to work any more,' Mats protested. 'She won't talk to me any more. She's reported sick and is now spending the rest of the flight in a part of the plane that passengers can't access.'

'Good, good. So she's unstable again.'

'Yes. But you have to understand. I can't get at her any more!'

All he wanted to do was hit himself on the head, in anger, and despair.

'That's your problem. Overcome it. Otherwise all this is just a stroll in the park compared to what your daughter will have to endure.'

In the background Mats heard a horrible sound. A scream

from deep in someone's throat, long drawn-out and so loud and agonising and unrestrained that it was tough to tell if a man or a woman was being tortured.

'Fuuuuhuuuh!' the victim shrieked, and the scream kept echoing in Mats' ears, louder than the droning ring of a giant church bell, following him the whole way back, up the circular stairs and into the suite, where he shut the door behind him, weeping.

49

Feli

On the internet the East German state-owned meat processing plant ranked among the 'Top Ten Berlin-area Ruins for Photographers', right behind the Beelitz sanatorium and the decaying US intelligence listening station atop Teufelsberg.

Already run down during East German times, this central livestock and slaughterhouse facility was dubbed 'Lotsa Misery' by the people and still lived up to the name today.

Some parts – the slaughterhouses among them – had been torn down while others were renovated, such as the cattle auction hall, and new residential buildings had been erected along with a streetcar stop, pedestrian tunnel, and shopping. Yet vast stretches of the premises lay undeveloped and movie directors loved to use them for end times movies or big-city slum scenes.

These were the very parts of the grounds where Feli concentrated her search.

As Livio's car lurched through the north entrance and headed into this land of ruins, the ground well muddied from the drizzle, Feli couldn't help but think about death.

She couldn't understand why people spent their free time here, voluntarily, hunting through the junk and garbage for morbid photos or broken reminders of a bygone age. Last year one young tourist fell off a chimney taking a selfie and was now a paraplegic. Apparently God was all about teaching strict lessons.

'What are we searching for now?'

'For a taxi,' Feli said. They drove past a sign reading 'To the Milking Parlour', which only increased Feli's unease.

In less than two hours, she was supposed to be leaving the registry office dressed all in white, a ring on her finger.

She couldn't think of a bigger contrast to right now.

They were passing red-brick factory buildings. The mighty jaw of time had sunk all its teeth into the abandoned buildings, ripping out plaster and brick, scattering roof shingles, shattering windows.

As if those butchers who decades ago killed, hacked up and disembowelled the animals here had resorted to pouncing on inorganic matter for lack of any fresh new meat.

'If the kidnapper was smart,' Livio said, 'he'd have hidden his car somewhere.'

'Then we'll never find him,' Feli replied.

They stopped at a fork in the road, exchanging indecisive glances.

'Looks like the slaughterhouses are to the right,' Livio said. The signs were decaying and hardly legible anymore.

'What's that say below? Pairy?'

'Dairy, I think. That's the way to the milking yards.' The world 'milking' made Feli wince.

'Remember what Uhlandt's mother said?'

'That he's vegan. He must hate every inch of this place.'

'But especially the milking facility, right? She said she wasn't even allowed to eat yogurt at home any more because of that anti-milk kink of his.'

Even though it was to blame for her osteoporosis.

'Then we've decided where to look first,' Livio said and put it in gear.

One minute and two turn-offs later, he hit the brakes again.

'Why are we stopping? There's no car here.'

'But there was one.'

Livio pointed through the windshield at the courtyard before a barn with a pitched roof. The tracks in the mud clearly came from one or more vehicles that had driven up, backed out, turned around. Most of the tracks had to be fresh since it hadn't been raining very long.

He turned off the engine, and they climbed out. The two of them walked up to the door in the shed's corrugated metal wall and were surprised to find it unlocked.

'What is all this?' Feli asked after venturing a few steps into the musty, stinking hall and taking a look around.

'Looks like the former milking parlour. The animals were tied up here for milking. Electrical equipment looks like it was dismantled long ago. Just the stalls are left.'

Feli looked at her watch, and at her white sneakers, already covered with mud.

Doesn't even matter now.

'All right. We're running out of time. Let's split up. You search the other end of the barn. I'll look around here up front.'

'Whatever you want, but, hey…' Livio gave her his Three

Musketeers smile. 'Watch out for yourself. I don't want to have to save you again.'

She returned the smile and her self-confidence surprised her. Of course she was scared and felt guilty about Janek, but her work on the hotline had rarely given her challenges like these. And rarely ever a direct result. She was noticing that, despite the danger and tragedy of the situation, it was doing her good to have something real and tangible to tackle. Not just talk.

'I'm a big girl,' she said.

She turned around and made her way to the steps.

She thought she'd spotted something like stairs about twenty metres away, possibly leading to a basement level.

50

Nele

First her mind, now her voice. Here below in the pit she had lost both, not necessarily in that order. More like at the same time.

Her momentarily waning pains had carried her along the crests of waves and washed her onto a shore where she no longer had control of her senses.

Nele had opened her eyes, but couldn't see. Her mouth moved, but no sound crossed her lips. Yet she was overcome by hallucinations of sound.

She even thought she heard someone calling her name, but this was only wishful thinking. A Fata Morgana, like that of the man in the desert dying of thirst who suddenly believes he's kneeling before an oasis.

Even so, it was surprisingly loud for a delusion.

'Nele?' She heard the voice again, one she'd heard before, a long, long time ago, in another life, before she was carried off here two hundred years ago (even longer if agony and not hours had been the deciding factor).

The fact alone that she knew the voice was further proof that she was already near death. Wasn't it said that in your final moments you'd encounter people you'd trusted?

Nele closed her eyes and felt herself drifting into merciful sleep. Which was sure to only last a few minutes until the next contraction, which would prove even more merciless and yet still futile. Her munchkin wasn't coming out right, she could tell, just like she could tell that she wouldn't be able to deliver her baby alive without outside help.

Could my baby have shifted somehow when I fell?

That made her at fault, she thought. Since she was the one who ran away and jumped and was left all alone, with all this trash and a splinter in her leg and the shard in her hand that she hadn't yet used, and that voice that had stopped calling her name but now sounded as if it were talking with someone on the phone.

51

Feli

'What is it?'

Feli had been calling Nele's name the whole time but wasn't getting any response down here in this disgusting basement corridor with rooms lining both sides like medieval dungeons.

Luckily her phone had a good flashlight, but now that Livio was calling her she had to stop using it for the moment.

'Did you find her?' Feli asked, excited.

'No,' she heard him say. 'But something's not right here.'

'What?'

'There's a camera tripod in a stall. Standing at what looks like someone's sickbed.'

'Say that again?'

'Just like I said. The whole deal looks like some real perverted filming. Like someone's shooting sodomy porn. It's even got an animal cage.'

'Oh, God.'

She heard Livio cough, his voice becoming muffled. He was apparently moving.

'Where are you heading?' she said.

'I'm gonna keep taking a look around.'

'No, wait,' Feli told him. 'I'm coming your way.'

'Okay, meet you back at the stalls.'

She took a deep breath and had to cough. No wonder, with all the dust down here.

'Sounds good. Give me a couple minutes. There's something I need to check out here too.'

Feli hung up and directed her phone's flashlight back at the ground.

At that round wooden slab she'd discovered right before Livio called.

It looked like the cover for a well.

52

Nele

There were only two possibilities. Either her delusions were getting worse. Or Franz had come back from the hardware store with the winch and the belt he needed and right at this moment was pulling the lid back off the opening to the cadaver pit. It was getting brighter in any case. Much too bright for Nele's eyes so used to the dark.

Blinded from it, she shut her eyes, and nevertheless it seemed that the beam of light was stabbing at her pupils right through her eyelids.

'Who's there?' she croaked. Not much louder than a fish behind thick aquarium glass. Then she heard the voice again, now much too clear and distraught to be just a dream.

'Nele, is that you down there?' it asked.

Nele popped her eyes back open. Blinked the tears away, and along with them the halo above the person who'd arrived to save her, the last person on earth she'd expected.

'Thank God. Help me, please, save me!'

Her inability to remember the woman's name proved she still wasn't thinking clearly, but it had also been a really long time since she'd had anything to do with the person.

Like two hundred years, if not more.

And now she'd just showed up. How was that even possible?

'Did my father send you?' she asked, since he was probably the only one who was concerned about her now and was hopefully moving heaven and earth to find her.

Though she wasn't sure how much time had gone by, or whether he'd even landed yet.

'Help me!'

Her voice stuck to her throat like sandpaper. Yet she tried again, whispering 'please' and sounding just as hopeless as her attempt to raise her hand. She even smiled, or meant to anyway, at least until the moment the impossible happened and the dread inside her reached a whole new dimension.

It was the moment she heard this one final phrase:

'Just die!'

Then the light was gone again, and the lid to the pit shut over her head again with a loud rasp. Moved by someone who had been her one final hope.

'Just die!'

Never before had she heard such rage and hate in two small words.

Never before felt such darkness, smothering her like the watery masses of the deep sea.

Never before had Nele been so close to death.

53

Feli

'What happened?' Livio said.

He was waiting back at the stalls as planned, and his smile was long gone. He stared at her with either mistrust or concern, she wasn't sure which. Then he pointed at her filthy hands that she'd wiped clean on her jeans little better than not at all.

'I was in this basement corridor,' she told him. 'Thought I'd found some kind of hatch, but it was apparently just a board. Got myself all dirty in the process, and on the way back I slipped on the stairs.'

She stepped by him and took a look at his find – the cameraless tripod and a stretcher bed.

The bed was smeared with blood and faeces, and something turned in Feli's stomach. 'Looks like Nele was having contractions.'

Livio agreed.

'And then someone must've taken her away.' He pointed at the phone in her hand. 'Are you finally going to call the police?'

Feli nodded but said: 'I'm not sure. Probably. I'll need to ask Mats first.'

'All right, but if you're gonna call the cops...' Livio didn't finish, but she knew what he was asking.

'Fine, take off!'

Livio looked like he wanted to explain, then added: 'I mean, there's not much more the both of us can do here together. And you know the police and I aren't exactly best buddies.'

'Fine. Just go!' She pointed at the exit.

'Really?'

'Just one more thing.'

'What?'

He'd already turned to leave, but pivoted back around.

'My wallet.'

'What? Oh, right.'

He pulled it out of his trouser pocket, grinning, and joked, 'A guy's gotta try.'

Feli fished out two fifty-euro bills, intending to give him his promised fee, but he declined. 'You can take me out to dinner,' he said, blew her a kiss, and headed off for the exit.

Feli waited until he'd disappeared into the rain outside the corrugated walls and heard the sound of his car starting. Only then did she take a deep breath and dial Mats' number, her heart pounding wildly.

54

Franz

Shit, shit, shit.

He knew he wasn't supposed to curse, his mother had always told him that, but she also didn't listen to him and still kept secretly drinking her milk, that deadly juice. So he too could secretly use the S-word, and for good reason.

Where had they come from all of a sudden?

He'd been worried the security guard would show up before him. That he'd wasted far too much time at the hardware store because he hadn't wanted to ask anyone working there and tried finding what he needed instead. But what in the hell was this scruffy, dark-haired pretty boy doing here?

And where was he driving to now?

He'd had a rare piece of good luck by choosing to park his taxi a little further off in an empty auction hall this time. He'd walked the last few metres over and was now soaked from the rain, but the caution he'd taken to check the situation out first had paid off.

In doing so he hadn't passed the Renault driving off but

instead had been able to observe the intruder from the cover of a burned-out construction trailer some distance away.

Well, the black-haired guy was gone, but the way it looked, *damn it*, was that he hadn't come alone and had left someone here.

A woman.

To get a look at her, Franz had left the cover of the trailer and crept over to the open entrance door. He first only spotted her movements, a shadow at the other end of the hall. Yet the shadow was speaking, apparently with someone on the phone, and that made him move in closer.

'Hello, Mats? I'm going outside, might get better reception out there,' he heard. The woman sounded distressed, as if she'd discovered something.

Franz looked around, considering whether to go back to his car and take off.

But then all would be over, all lost. Everything he'd planned for so long.

'No, this is about a higher goal,' he whispered to himself.

And bent down.

Picked up one of the many rusty iron rods lying all over here.

And was glad to see that the very rod he'd use to lie in wait for the woman even had a hook on the end.

55

Mats

The risk of dying in a car was 104 times higher than in an aeroplane.

And the possibility of throwing up after hearing his kidnapped daughter screaming into the telephone was 100 per cent.

Statistics, Mats thought as he stared into that aluminium sink that all aeroplanes had and always reminded him of a prison toilet, even here in the highest luxury class.

Statistics only help calm a person as long as a person is not affected themselves.

'What's that mean, Nele's not there anymore?' he asked, kneeling on the restroom floor, the phone lying next to the toilet on speaker since his hands were shaking so badly he couldn't hold it to his ear anymore.

'There's a tripod and a stretcher here in the livestock hall,' Feli replied, sounding agitated. 'But no sign of Nele. She could be anywhere. The place is far too big. It has one basement and possibly more.'

Feli's last words were accompanied by a peep indicating that Mats' battery was now only running at 10 per cent. He knew he needed to get up and plug his phone in, but even that seemed like an unbelievable exertion at the moment.

'Then keep looking around,' Mats said, seized by heavy nausea.

'These grounds are huge. Aren't you listening to me? I can't do it.'

'You don't want to, you mean.'

Mats knew he was being unfair but at the moment all he had were his powerlessness and his anger, and Feli was the only lightning rod available to him.

'You don't even want to help me.'

'How can you say that?' she said, incensed now.

Mats ripped a bunch of tissues from their dispenser and wiped the rest of his vomit from his face, then finally managed to pull himself up by a toilet handle. 'You never did like Nele. You see her as the reason I left you. You hate her.'

And I hate myself.

'Mats,' Feli protested, and Mats really would've liked to rewind his violent outburst or at least channel his anger in the right direction, but he couldn't stop insulting the only person who'd been helping him.

'You know what I think? Even if you did find Nele, you'd probably just abandon her there.'

'Mats!' Feli shouted again but this time it didn't sound like a protest. The truth was, it hadn't sounded that way the first time either. It sounded more like a scream for—

Help?

'What's wrong?' he panted.

'Mats, I think someone's here, someone...'

He never did get to find out. The last thing Mats heard

from Feli was a scream and then a sound like something fragile shattering.

Then his display went black.

56

No, no, no...

Mats flung open the sliding bathroom door and staggered into the Sky Suite living room. With a droning in his ears, as if the craft were already plummeting down to crash, he pulled his briefcase open, ripped out the charging cable and plugged it into one of the sockets installed in the armrest of every seat.

The depleted battery symbol showed on the display and a lightning bolt signalled recharging, but Mats knew from experience that it would be an eternity before he could make another call. And that was at home, with a stable network. How long would it take for his phone to reconnect to the airline's network up here at ten thousand metres?

In the end it only took sixty seconds.

A full minute where Mats took turns staring at his phone, at the table lamp along the windows, at the darkness beyond, at the signal light blinking red on the end of the massive wing, then back at his phone.

Now with two screams echoing inside his head. One of his daughter and the other of the only person he'd found who could save her.

The phone started buzzing back to life, and Mats entered his passcode wrong but eventually got it right and opened the notification showing three calls while he was gone.

'Feli?' he said when the fourth call came through. He was trying so hard not to shout that his voice ended up sounding like only whispers.

'Who's Feli?' the voice asked him.

Mats closed his eyes and sank into the leather chair he didn't even know he was sitting in until this second. He still only sensed most of his surroundings as if through fogged-up glasses. His world had shrunk, had been reduced to a tiny extract involving only Nele, her baby, and this person on the other end of the line, for whom an acid bath would be far too kind treatment.

'I want to speak to Nele,' Mats said, somewhat louder now.

'Did you give Kaja the weapon?'

'I'll do so as soon as you release my daughter.'

The voice sounded amused. 'Do you take me for an idiot?'

No. Someone who could think all this up might be a psychopath but was guaranteed not to be a fool who would give up his only leverage.

Mats posed the question of all questions: 'This is about establishing precedence, that right? You're working for Klopstock! You want me to make the plane crash so that the bill passes and he makes millions from tests.'

Like before, Mats didn't get an answer, but he could hear that something had changed in the character of the voice. He couldn't say with certainty, but it now sounded even more mechanical and somewhat staccato, though the breathing in the background had intensified, making the blackmailer sound tenser, more nervous.

'I've been sitting here for over eight hours watching the flight tracker on the internet, and so far your flight seems to be going according to plan,' he said. 'Altitude, route, air speed, all perfect. That's good on the one hand, since it shows me you haven't involved the authorities. Otherwise interceptor jets would probably be soaring up there to escort you, in which case you can be sure you wouldn't be talking with me any more. What's bad, however, is that you now only have a few hours left to make that plane steer into the ocean. Or do you want to risk harming even more people once you've reached the continent and Kaja makes it crash into, say, some residential area?'

When the voice paused, Mats seized the opportunity to beg: 'Please, let me speak to Nele.'

'You're not in a position to make demands any more, you...'

The voice suddenly got drowned out by an in-flight announcement:

'Ladies and gentlemen, please note that the seatbelt signs are on again. We're nearing a poor weather zone over the Atlantic and...'

The captain enriched his Spanish-language warning with more details and Mats suddenly had the unreal, nearly tipsy feeling of hearing it all double. And with a lag, as if the craft's curved walls were creating a slight echo. It took a moment for him to realise the cause of this unsettling effect – and another moment for him to comprehend what it meant.

The announcement, or at least the captain's initial words, hadn't come through speakers in the ceiling. But instead though the phone he was still holding to his ear. The blackmailer had now hung up. At the exact moment that he too must have recognised his phone was not only transmitting his artificially altered voice but also the captain's announcement.

Which in turn meant...

The force of his realisation pressed Mats even harder against his seat.

He looked to the side, touched the window, felt the night's cold creeping through the pane, through his fingers, up his underarm and directly into his heart.

That's impossible, he thought, and yet there couldn't be any other explanation:

The blackmailer was so close to him.

Here on board this aeroplane.

57

Think!

Mats was already on the way to leave but turned back. He needed to force himself to proceed methodically, calming his storm of thoughts and not running mindlessly through the world's largest aeroplane on some panicked manhunt for a suicidal assassin. There was only one single person he thought capable of wanting to sacrifice herself, but this very person was also the only one he could rule out: Kaja.

She'd even been standing in the elevator when the voice called him. Without moving her lips, without a phone to her ear. It couldn't have been a recording either because he'd had a conversation with the blackmailer.

Who was a suicide case?

Mats sat down, wrote: 'What I know for certain', and tried writing down notes such as:

- Nele is kidnapped and suffering.
- The video wasn't filmed by Johannes Faber.
- Klopstock makes money off the plane crashing because of his psychological tests.

But he wasn't capable of much self-control or reasoning.

There was only one certainty clamouring inside his head, and it said: 'THE VOICE IS ON BOARD!'

And it was precisely this realisation that propelled him out of the suite, past the deserted Sky Bar and into the rear end of the upper level.

First into upper business class, thirty seats, occupied by passengers sleeping, reading or watching movies. The closed windows made everything as dark as the nocturnal animal building in a zoo. The subsequent area, premium economy, was only slightly brighter since the cabin lighting was switched off here too, but there were more seats and so more monitors fluorescing in the dark.

What am I looking for?

Mats saw old men, young women and sleeping children. Yet how could you recognise a suicidal blackmailer with motives that weren't clear?

He didn't have the slightest clue, knowing that it was completely pointless scouring all 550 square metres of regular passenger areas, especially since the perpetrator might also be sitting in the cockpit or freight area and certainly wasn't making calls out in the open with a voice changer over his mouth.

And yet he couldn't just sit there idle, doing nothing. He was like a goalkeeper who knew he didn't have much chance of stopping a penalty kick yet still had to decide which side to leap because standing there with his feet planted was just not an option.

The further back Mats went, striding through the whole seventy-five metres of the plane, the fuller it became. In the far rear of economy, around twenty passengers were housed in the same area solely available to him alone in the Sky Suite. A total of two hundred passengers, the vast majority of whom would've been more than able to go into the restroom and make a phone call holding a vocoder to their mouth. Anyone and everyone would have to be considered.

- Nervousness
- Excessive sweating
- Erratic movements
- Trembling hands

Mats recalled the symptoms that suicide bombers occasionally displayed, though not always. If they had blocked out their fears using drugs or hypnosis, they could act completely normal until triggering the detonator of their suicide belt.

It was nonsense anyway trying to identify a quite probably mentally disturbed person using traits that didn't even always apply to politically motivated attackers.

He'd reached the end of the plane and switched to the other aisle by the rear restrooms. Now he marched in the direction of the cockpit. Scrutinised the backs of heads, tops of thighs, smelled stale socks, flatulence, and moist towelettes and knew: this was all completely pointless.

Just as pointless as his blackmailer's behaviour.

If the voice really was on board and actually taking its own life, why would it need such a complicated scheme? Why not use its clearly existing intellectual and logistic talents to make the plane crash itself?

Why Nele? Kaja?

Why me?

He answered his own question: *'Because it doesn't need a bomb or an act, but a psychological incident instead.'*

A 'conventional' crash, such as one involving hostages, would only have implications for the physical and mechanical security measures performed during check-in.

In this case a psychological explosive was to be ignited, one which no scanner in the world could detect. Which was exactly what they needed him for.

The only thing he still didn't know was how the world was supposed to learn that he'd been successful in activating the psychological bomb. Though he also feared this was soon going to be made clear to him.

Mats had reached the stairs, near row 33, near the beginning of the front third.

The stairs led down to the galley between premium economy and economy. Two flight attendants sat conversing quietly between the emergency doors and the restrooms. They took no notice of Mats.

They couldn't be ruled out either.

Neither could Valentino, whom Mats also had to consider as he pressed on with his illogical routine and took a good long look at the passengers while standing in the aisle.

It didn't take long for his eyes to start screwing up.

Despite the fact that there wasn't anything unusual to see, not at first. But his mental seismograph had obviously started registering the vibrations of a quake that was still forthcoming, one that less sensitive people presumably could not detect.

Vibrations that had their epicentre in row 47.

The whole window row was now empty, all three seats including 47F, which Mats had reserved for himself and the sleeping man had blocked upon boarding. He still hadn't got back to his seat, but that wasn't what drew his attention.

It was the middle row instead, seat 47J. The aisle seat.

Mats advanced slowly, creeping up like a predator trying not to startle its sleeping prey, when it happened: the passenger who lay motionless with his chin directed at the cabin ceiling, his mouth half open and eyes closed, pulled a phone out from under his blanket, took a look at the screen and put it back before acting just as he had been, as if he were still sleeping.

Trautmann. The name pierced Mats' thoughts like a war cry. The man who was supposedly intending to sleep through the whole flight thanks to his 'twelve-thousand-dollar pill' sure had amazingly lucid waking periods.

'Trautmann,' Mats heard himself scream after he'd first passed by him and now closed in on him from behind. Alarmed by how loud he was but also by the consequences implicit in his actions. His whole life he'd been conditioned either to resolve conflicts verbally or dodge them. Now he felt his hand automatically find its way into his trouser pocket. Pull out the little plastic box that dispensed 'dental floss', and then things reached that very point his patients often described in their near-death experiences: he seemed to leave his own body and, floating above himself, observed himself pulling the noose around the neck of the supposedly sleeping man from behind. And as he did he screamed: 'Where's Nele? What have you done with my daughter?'

Not even a second later, Mats lay on the floor of the aisle with his nose broken and a pistol to his temple. Then all went dark.

58

Livio

The itching wasn't just from the side effects.

Livio knew he was supposed to take his pills much earlier in the day but he'd still forgotten to this morning, and then things didn't exactly turn out like he expected.

He scratched at the crook of his arm and looked over his skin in the mirror of the gas station restroom.

At twenty-nine he was far too young for age spots and yet disease was still so new, only a few weeks since that test result had steamrolled him.

Considering his way of life, he had to have figured he could have caught the virus at any point and ended up in a place like the Wedding Medical Centre.

Pretty astounding that Feli never even asked why I was being treated there.

For a moment Livio wondered if he should be angry that the bride-to-be took so little interest in his private life. But he probably wouldn't have either in her position. Between the kidnapping and her wedding coming any minute, God knows she had enough in her head already.

But still.

He turned the faucet on, held his mouth under it and then swallowed the pill cocktail he'd gathered inside his cupped hand. So that the disease didn't break out. So that the symptoms stayed away.

A little more interest would've been nice. With my helping her out so much and all.

'Hey, you fall in the toilet or what?' he heard an old man yell from outside the door.

Now Livio took even longer.

He pulled his phone out of his back pocket and scrolled through the dialled numbers.

Right at the top was the one from Felicitas.

What was that last name of hers again?

'Man, you must be attracting flies by now,' griped the old man outside the door. He pounded on the door pretty feebly.

Livio didn't even bat an eye. Getting all pushy wasn't about to fluster him.

The only person who'd ever managed to do that to him was himself, and he hated himself for that.

Why even waste a single thought on that dumb psychiatrist? Ever since they'd said goodbye, he'd been feeling a steady, dull droning in the back of his head.

Like some cryptic warning signal.

'You shouldn't have left her there alone,' he said, reciting the whispering inside his head, somewhat louder than he meant.

'What, you talking to yourself now too?' asked that pushy old man outside. 'Or you calling Mommy? Can't find your little peter again?'

Livio heard people laughing – pushy old man now had an audience apparently – but he could tune that out.

Better than that humming inside his head, that little demon whispering in his ear, telling him to press Call Back.

'*Everything's okay with the lady*,' continued Livio in his inner dialogue with himself.

He then repeated the sentence three more times out loud. First when leaving the restroom (after stealing all the toilet paper, just to piss off the pushy old man), then when starting his car that he'd just now filled up.

And, finally, when Feli didn't pick up for the second time and again let his call go to voice mail.

'Don't worry your head, let it go,' he said one last time, already following the navigation directions leading him back to the abandoned stalls.

59

Mats
*One hour and thirty-eight minutes until regularly
scheduled landing in Berlin*

Iron.

Most crime stories talked about how blood was supposed to taste like copper, but the element actually wasn't contained in the body's fluids at all. That was typical know-it-all crap and it did Mats little good as he slowly regained consciousness.

Of course it was iron that he was tasting and smelling and making him nauseous. The man sitting across from him, who apparently was responsible for Mats coming to wear plastic cable-tie handcuffs, now stood up from his seat and shone a flashlight in his left eye.

Mats saw dancing flames and explosions of light.

He felt like a boxer who never even heard that redeeming ding after the last blow and now found himself sitting back in his corner of the ring.

Except Trautmann definitely wasn't there to get him back into shape for the next round.

'I figured you were making trouble, boy.'

He scratched at his grey Sean Connery beard, put his flashlight away and took a step back.

'Who are you?' Mats slurred, wondering how long he'd been unconscious.

The opaque blinds had been pulled; he couldn't tell if it was light out yet. And he also didn't know if it was a Taser or a shot of anaesthetic that had put him out of action.

It had all happened so fast that he had no recollection of being carried upstairs, back to the Sky Suite, where they'd placed him out cold in an armchair at the window, facing away from the direction they were flying.

'You work for Klopstock?' Mats asked and was able to steal a glance at Trautmann's watch.

Provided he hadn't changed the time zone, it was still showing Buenos Aires time.

He swallowed down all the spit tasting of blood in his mouth. His headache and his lingering grogginess made it hard for him to calculate remaining flight time, but if he wasn't mistaken... *Good God...*

He'd slept nearly three and a half hours!

'Who you say I'm working for again?' Trautmann said.

He shook Mats' cuffs, which were wrapped around his wrists and table leg so tightly that standing up was impossible. His legs were tied at his ankles too, so that he couldn't step or kick.

'That company of yours – you didn't invest in selfie sticks. You were financing Klopstock's psych tests, weren't you?'

Trautmann squinted and cocked his head to one side.

The thought crossed Mats' mind that this was how a mouse must feel to have a cat watching over it.

Trautmann even looked equal parts curious and merciless.

He would certainly want to find out how much his opponent knew about him, but there was no doubt he'd also do away with him as soon as he grew tired of their little game.

How much flight time do we still have? An hour and a half?

'You don't want to make the plane crash at all,' Mats said, his brain running at half capacity tops. 'You only need an incident. A crazy flight attendant. A psychiatrist on board going nuts. The cliché that serves its purpose. Am I right?'

That would bring that very law that Klopstock so desperately needed. All airlines would be required to subject all pilots, the entire crew and perhaps even passengers to a psychopathological screening test. A worldwide business worth millions, if not billions.

'They were already talking about psych tests after the Germanwings crash. But passing the law was touch and go. With a second incident, there'd be no way around it. Right?'

Trautmann eyed him as if he were a madman escaped from the mental hospital. 'Man, I have no idea what you're talking about. I knew something wasn't right about you. No normal person reserves so many seats. So I waited to see which seat you chose, then found the seat closest to you.'

Trautmann paused and held up the pack of floss Mats had found in the life vest at seat 7A.

'Dental floss?' he said. 'You really believed that would work?'

'It's not dental floss,' Mats said, 'it's a weapon.'

Trautmann flipped open the dispenser lid and pulled out a long string of the stuff. He tore it off, smelled it, and smiled.

'This *is* dental floss, buddy. I think we can spare ourselves the talk. You got a screw loose.'

He turned to leave.

'What do you want?' Mats said to him.

Trautmann stopped, glancing over his shoulder. 'Security.'

'For who?'

'For everyone on board.'

Trautmann lifted his shirt away from his trousers and revealed a gun holster on his belt. Next to it, a silver star, like a sheriff badge.

Mats shut his eyes.

Of course.

'You're the sky marshal?' he asked.

When Trautmann nodded, Mats knew that all was lost.

Nele hadn't been found.

His connection to Feli gone.

Kaja not even close to sufficiently triggered.

And he'd put himself out of action with his ridiculous attack on Trautmann.

'I'd rather have kept an eye on you the whole flight, buddy,' the marshal said, 'but I'm responsible for the entire plane and can't just sit here with you in the Sky Suite.'

Mats shut his eyes again.

Extremely tired and extremely exhausted, he wished he were somewhere else. Somewhere where his thoughts faded and all he felt could be switched off with a lever.

'He's finally awake. Make sure he doesn't try anything stupid,' Mats heard Trautmann say, and he suddenly had the fear the marshal was going to leave Valentino with him as his watchdog. The man did still have a score to settle with him.

'I'm going to take a look at his bags and will be right back.'

'Okay,' Mats heard, and then he knew that it wasn't Valentino whom Trautmann had assigned as his minder. Instead it was the very person who'd been observing him this whole time.

Mats' eyes popped open and he found his suspicions confirmed. Kaja said, 'You can rely on me,' and the door closed behind Trautmann.

60

She smiled.

Of all the emotions her face had shown in the last few hours – confusion, uncertainty, distress all the way to naked despair – this expression was the most disturbing.

Even more disturbing than that flicker in her eyes, that psychotic background noise that kept finding its way into Kaja's gaze even in the times of intense emotional isolation. A clear sign of her misery and of the pain gnawing at her sanity. It had even been present when she'd looked right through him from the elevator. But now?

Kaja came closer to Mats with this smile of hers forming at the corners of her mouth, and it was real. Not feigned, not acting, not put on. She didn't look very happy, but she did resemble someone who was at peace with herself.

If Mats didn't know better, he might've interpreted it as an expression of mental healing.

Instead he got a chill when Kaja stepped up to the table and said in a calm voice: 'You're simply too good, Dr Krüger. I should have known. But I'd probably repressed just how well you understand your profession.'

'I don't understand.'

'No, you do not, but I already told you that. You've never comprehended a thing. But that doesn't matter now.'

Kaja opened the minibar and helped herself to a bottle of still water and a chilled glass. She poured it halfway full and took a tiny glass bottle from the inside pocket of her uniform top.

The vial looked like the nose drops that, whenever Mats got a cold, his mother used to drip in with an eyedropper. Except this one was made of green, not brown, glass, and the dropper looked a little more delicate.

'What is that?'

'Liquid nicotine. Extremely poisonous,' Kaja said candidly. 'I extracted it from e-cigarettes.'

She instilled several drops into the water glass and stirred it with her index finger. The only finger with all its nail polish still intact.

She smiled. 'I switched a year ago, did you know that?'

Mats shook his head, yet it wasn't to her question. 'What are you planning to do?'

Her smile widened. 'But e-cigarettes don't taste like anything. And they can be deadly too.' Kaja closed up the glass vial and shook it.

'I'm not drinking that,' Mats said, but she didn't respond. It was as if he were just an object to her, like some phone recording she'd reached and didn't expect answers and certainly not questions from.

Kaja looked at her watch, sighed and pulled, from the same pocket she'd got the nicotine, a real cigarette along with a lighter.

'I was actually saving this for Berlin, once this was all over, but that's no longer the case.'

She stuck the cigarette in her mouth, lit it and inhaled deeply.

'Ahhh...'

Grey, fog-like smoke filled the Sky Suite when she exhaled. Mats could hardly smell it because of his bloody nose, but the smoke irritated his eyes.

'I've always wanted to do that.' Kaja laughed and quickly took another drag. Her stare turned anxious when she said: 'Oh, man. I should have known. It wasn't supposed to go down like this.'

Mats yanked on his cuffs. 'Kaja, if you're being blackmailed too, if you're somehow involved? You don't have to do this.'

She looked to the window. She seemed only to be speaking to herself now. 'I'm not talking about the plane. I'm talking about you, Dr Krüger.'

'I don't understand.'

She looked him straight in the eyes for the first time. 'We've been over this.'

'Explain it to me anyway, please.'

Kaja leaned towards him. 'It's not the plane that's supposed to fall. It's *you*. You alone.'

Mats heard the truth coming from Kaja's mouth and reacted with all his senses.

The omnipresent hissing of the engines in his ears became louder. The taste of blood in his mouth harsher. He even smelled her smoke now.

'Me? Why me?'

'You were getting really close to finding out, Dr Krüger. I heard what you asked the sky marshal.'

'Trautmann?'

She shrugged. 'That his name? Only the pilots know his real identity. So that we crew can't reveal who he is if taken hostage. All I knew was that a marshal was on this flight and that you were on the list of suspicious passengers because you'd booked so many seats. After the incident with Valentino, the captain instructed me to isolate you up here in the Sky Suite, to keep you as inconspicuous as possible. I never had any contact with the marshal. If you hadn't assaulted him, I never would've known who he was or where he'd positioned himself.'

Mats thought he felt his head becoming heavier. As if these fragments of reality were pressing down on his mind with their leaden weight.

'In any case, Trautmann – or whatever you called him – definitely has nothing to do with Klopstock's company.'

'What about you?'

'I'm only reclaiming some small compensation for what you stole from me, Dr Krüger.'

'Me? What the...' Mats was so dumbstruck he could hardly put words together. 'I treated you, Kaja. I helped you work through the trauma. From being taken hostage as well as from the video coming out later. What gives you any idea I stole anything from you?'

Kaja smiled her disturbing smile again. 'You never treated me. Not then. And not now either. Quite the opposite. You've been trying to destroy me this whole flight.'

'Because I'm being blackmailed. I'm sorry. Please, take these cuffs off.'

He stretched out both hands to her.

'Let me go. We'll settle all of this. It's not too late.'

'Yes, it is. Has been for a long time now. You never did

understand, and you never will.'

'Please, give me the chance to.'

'No. There's no time for that now. Look. The plan was for you to start exhibiting behavioural issues on board this craft, and you've done that repeatedly. You instigated a fight with a flight attendant. You even assaulted a sky marshal. And the whole time, you were trying to manipulate a stewardess psychologically so that she'd make the aeroplane crash.'

'But you don't have a witness to that.'

'Yes I do.' Kaja's lower lip trembled. 'I recorded all our conversations.'

She pulled a tiny mobile phone from her inside pocket. 'Which means you don't have a chance.'

Mats swallowed hard. 'You really think this is enough to convince authorities they need to implement wholesale psychological checks of crew and passengers?'

That will earn Klopstock millions.

Kaja nodded. 'Maybe you didn't get the news in Argentina – in a few weeks the European Parliament will vote on a bill to make checks mandatory. What do you think lawmakers will decide after knowing hundreds of passengers narrowly escaped death today? And that such a scenario can be prevented in future? All because routine tests will block mental time bombs like me and suicidal passengers like you from boarding in the first place.'

Suicidal?

Mats pointed at the water glass with the liquid nicotine. 'I'm supposed to drink this? So it looks like suicide?'

As conclusive evidence of my psychosis. And to eliminate me as a witness.

'That was the plan.'

'That's insane. What did you think would happen? That I'd do this voluntarily?'

'Have you done anything voluntarily yet today, Dr Krüger?'

Nele.

Mats could see her all over again, her eyes bulging, the agony and pain on her face. He instantly heard her screaming in his head.

'Where is my daughter? What have you done with her?'

'I don't know,' Kaja said, without blinking, without looking away, without any kind of tell that she was guilty of a lie.

'Then who does?' Mats asked. 'Who planned all this?'

'That doesn't matter now. Soon no one else is going to care.'

Mats tried but couldn't make rhyme or reason of Kaja's cryptic claims.

'You all think you're going to get away with this? You never will. Someone is going to start wondering why my daughter disappeared on the very same day that I flipped out on board a plane.'

Kaja took another drag of her cigarette, now burned down to a third, and blew smoke right into Mats' face. 'That may be. But then, at some point, the police will find a laptop in your Buenos Aires apartment. With a flight simulator program on it for this very same route you've flown, Dr Krüger. Plus the authorities will discover all those emails between you and Franz Uhlandt.'

Klopstock's driver? was Mats' first thought. If he remembered right, that was the name Feli had figured out earlier.

'A mentally ill vegan who fantasises about taking babies from pregnant women in order to make a statement against industrial milk production. You encouraged him to implement his plan, using your daughter. Provided him with money and cameras.'

'That's not true.'

'According to the information on your computer it is. You're a deranged man, Dr Krüger. You never got over the death of your wife, even emigrated because of it. Your daughter hates you, and you can't bear that Nele will soon start a family while you yourself lost your own.'

'This is insanity!'

'Which is the way the public will see it, yes. You fell victim to insanity. You'd been depressed for years, and lonely, and Nele's pregnancy was the trigger for your suicidal plan to try and take as many people as possible with you when you die. Happy passengers going to see their families. And patients like me, who'd already started the kind of new life that you yourself had been denied, Mats.'

It was the first and last time that she ever called him by his first name.

'It all probably could've been detected with simple blood tests and somewhat expensive psychological testing. I myself would've been exposed as unable to fly in any case. But now...'

She pointed at the glass with the neurotoxin.

'No way!' Mats yanked on his cuffs again. The plastic dug into his wrists.

He pointed at the glass. It seemed the only piece of leverage left, in a game whose rules he still didn't comprehend.

'I won't take one drink of it. Unless you let Nele go, and

I can speak to her immediately. As soon as Nele is safe...'

Kaja stood up. 'Forget it. It's not my call whether your daughter gets free or not. It's up to the vegan to decide. We don't have any control over him. We're just glad he provided us with that photo and audio. Otherwise, he's completely solo. That was at the heart of our plan. No one would end up being able to establish any connection between us and him. You are the only link, Dr Krüger.'

'No connection?' Mats nearly screamed it. 'The man is Klopstock's driver!'

Kaja blinked. 'You found that out? Nice job. But what does that end up proving? Nothing. Because Klopstock has nothing to do with our plan.'

'Come off it.'

'It's true. André doesn't know a thing,' she said, and Mats was about to object when it occurred to him that Kaja had to have at least one other accomplice here on board. And yet it couldn't have been his notorious fellow psychologist. Feli had just seen him in his office today.

'Who was I talking to on the phone the whole time?' he asked Kaja.

Who is the voice?

Here on board.

'Enough questions.'

Kaja pressed her cigarette out on the tabletop with trembling fingers and smiled just as pleasantly as she had at the beginning of this, the most hopeless exchange that Mats had ever conducted in his life.

She took the glass with the liquid nicotine solution in her hand, swirling it like an expensive red wine.

'I'm not drinking it,' Mats declared.

'You said that already.' Kaja smiled, placed the glass to her lips, and emptied it in one gulp.

Mats turned white as chalk.

Next, Kaja opened her phone and kept tapping on a button until it sounded one long beep.

'There. Our conversations are deleted. So much for that,' she said, and her smile had vanished. Only sadness remained in her tired eyes. That unmistakable look of certainty that her life was soon to end.

'Why?' Mats asked.

Whispering. As if in a daze. Again he didn't get an answer.

'I'm on my way to go put an end to all this.'

Mats tried standing up, but his cuffs jerked him back down in his seat.

'What do you mean? Wait, what do you mean "put an end to it"?' he yelled after her. 'I thought the plane wasn't supposed to crash. Right?'

'Yes, that's what I said,' Kaja responded, already standing in the door. 'I should have known better. You were simply too good, Dr Krüger. You opened my eyes. Which, unfortunately, now means that the plan has changed.'

61

Forty-eight minutes left until scheduled landing in Berlin

The snake was back. It had long stayed hidden, somewhere in those well-cloaked dark chambers of his consciousness, keeping warm from his despair, nourished by his nightmares. Yet now it had awoken from its hideous slumber and was reasserting itself with renewed strength.

What was she planning? Did Kaja want to make the plane crash? Was she even capable?

Mats felt the python of fear wrap tighter around his chest with every question. Tighter than the cuffs around his wrists and feet.

What have I done? What have I set in motion?

If it was true that crashing the plane had never been the blackmailer's true goal, then it also made sense that the perpetrator was here on board. And if Nele's fate was completely separate from that of all these people on board, then it was ultimately his fault if a catastrophe were to now happen after all.

'*I should have known better.*' Mats recalled Kaja's last words. There could only be one explanation. She was in on it. She'd known he would try to break her mentally. A fellow conspirator who thought she could play a part in the charade and withstand his attempts at psychological manipulation.

'But you were simply too good, Dr Krüger.'

He had achieved the unexpected and triggered her despite all expectations. Presumably with the video where he'd spotted something that had remained hidden from all involved until this point. And now Kaja really was a living hand grenade whose pin he'd pulled and who at this very moment was seeking out some extremely vulnerable location somewhere on board. Ready to explode there.

'Damn it!'

Mats could hardly get air. The panic throttled his breathing and made the pressure inside his head swell like a diver sinking deeper and deeper into the ocean of his greatest fears. His ears hurt, his eyes teared, and the latter made him recall the last thing that caught his eye.

The cigarette!

On the table.

Kaja had stubbed it out carelessly, leaving a black burn mark on the fine pale wood.

Hurriedly, hands trembling, without any caution. Which was why a nearly invisible thread of smoke was now rising up to the cabin ceiling from the tip of the crumpled butt.

It was still burning!

It burned with only a dull glow, a reminder of its former blaze, little more than a dying echo.

And yet... It was his only chance. Possibly the last chance of his life.

Mats leaned over the table as far as his cuffs let him, but it was hopeless. He wasn't near enough.

The cigarette lay a couple of centimetres from his chin, but it might as well have been a metre since the result was the same: he couldn't get hold of it.

He stretched out his tongue for the smouldering stub, but that was pointless too. Plus trying that only increased the danger that he'd end up extinguishing the cigarette.

Mats looked around.

The glass, the remote, the water bottle – all out of reach.

He was like a man dying of thirst before a soda vending machine. He let his head drop to the table in frustration and screamed out loud. In his despair he'd forgotten about his broken nose. It now felt as if he'd deliberately jammed a screwdriver through his crushed septum.

He struggled to keep his senses and wondered, as he landed back on the side of consciousness from that smouldering ledge of pain-scorched darkness, if he shouldn't have just let himself black out.

And wondered if Nele was feeling the same now.

No, she was guaranteed to be feeling worse. He could only pray that there were no complications with the birth. That someone was caring for her and the baby. But he held out little hope in that regard when he recalled the photo and her scream.

Mats shook his head as if doing so could wipe away the cruel images in his mind. Then he blinked and opened his eyes. It took him a while to notice what had changed.

The cigarette.

On the table.

It had moved. Only a few millimetres, but in the right direction. His head striking the tabletop had shaken it just enough to make a difference.

'Okay, good, okay,' Mats said, filled with a euphoria that actually dulled his pain.

Then he did it once more. Let his head fall again, this time only letting his forehead strike the surface. That alone was still enough to send the pain shooting from his teeth to behind his eyes again. He became nauseous. Yet he was also delighted because the cigarette had again hopped in the direction that could save him. And it was still glowing, which was why he did it again. And again. And again.

Until he felt a lump the size of a plum on his forehead, like he'd grown a third swollen eye.

With an agility he didn't know he had as a non-smoker, he used his tongue to flip the butt about fifty degrees until he could grab the filter end between his lips. Then he sucked on it.

Greedily, like an addict. His eyes kept watering, now from the pain, so he couldn't see if the glow was increasing again, but he could taste it. Next to the iron and mucus in his mouth he suddenly tasted something wood-like, scratching at his throat. He smelled the smoke in the same breath. And now he saw that the gentle thread had become a column. Yet his inner joy didn't last long.

It now had to be proven if this idea he'd formed under fear of death truly was feasible.

Plenty spoke against it.

For one, he could still only use his mouth for placing the burning glow on the right spot.

And it was entirely possible that he wouldn't only singe the plastic of his cuffs. There was also his skin under them, around them.

But he had no choice, and he needed to use the time he

had – no matter how much he had left. Especially now that the fear snake had loosened its grip again somewhat and seemed to have returned to lying in wait on high alert.

Here goes...

Mats raised his wrists, leaned down and pressed the cigarette onto the plastic around his left wrist. He sucked in air, and the unfamiliar smoke in his lungs made him cough. The cigarette slipped and struck his skin, which didn't hurt at first but was then so harsh that he nearly dropped the cigarette from his mouth.

Don't scream or your lips will move, he warned himself and only tried expressing his total anguish with moaning, whimpering. He needed to utter some kind of noise. Burns caused the worst torment on earth. No one endured them silently.

Just like no woman endured a silent birth.

Again Mats couldn't help thinking about Nele and that drawn-out, misery-filled 'Fuuuuuhhh' of hers, and this time the horrible memory motivated him to try once more.

To direct his mouth to his hands, to suck in, to press the glowing butt to the plastic. To suppress the pain, to whimper, to ignore the hissing singe and to keep the stub touching the cuff longer and longer, even though he could already feel the burn hole not just eating through plastic but through his wrist and down to the bone.

'Yeesss!'

He yelled and jerked his head up again, yanking his arms outwards at the same time, and his yell sputtered out in horror when he realised that he still was not free, that his hands were still bound together. Yet he'd lost the butt. It had fallen from his mouth and off the table's edge and onto the floor. Half a metre from his feet, which might as well have been kilometres away.

'Noooo!'

Mats jerked on the cuffs like a man possessed, pulling his hands apart, banging them on the table's edge, heaving his arms apart with all his power and even hitting himself on the chin when the plastic suddenly gave way. At its weakest point, damaged by the heat.

'Yes, yes, yes!'

Mats kept yelling but now from joy and relief.

His hands were free. Now it was on to the glass, which he could shatter and use the shards to undo the rest of the cuffs.

The urge to act surged through him. For the first time he felt confident he could influence this crisis through actions of his own.

Until the in-flight announcement from Kaja Claussen so abruptly destroyed his hopes:

'Attention, this applies to all passengers, pilots, and crew. Remain calm. Do not try anything stupid. If anyone thinks of standing up and tries to overpower me, or if altitude, speed or anything else changes – we'll all die instantly!'

62

'Why?'

Kaja kept screaming this one phrase into her victim's face. The question kept combining, again and again, with the panicked shouts, the wailing, the bawling, the crying and the agitated discussions that had broken out everywhere after her announcement.

'WHY?'

Once Mats freed himself and exited the Sky Suite, Kaja's screaming had shown him the way. Down the steps, to the lobby. He found four people there.

Kaja stood before the entrance door to the first class area, holding a pistol directed at a person squatting on the floor, right under the window in the door. The person was partially blocked by Kaja and cowering so much that Mats couldn't tell from his spot halfway down the stairs whom Kaja was threatening.

To the right of Kaja stood Valentino, his expression earnest, pinched. He held the curtain to the lounge closed, presumably so no passengers could push through from the rear areas of the plane whether from curiosity or to play the hero.

Mats could tell Valentino was trying to tamp down the same fear that everyone else on board must have been feeling, and he wasn't succeeding very well.

'Why did you do that?' Kaja screamed at the person on the floor. She hadn't noticed Mats at all even though she kept checking that the nearby men weren't going to jump her from behind. Though none would've seriously attempted to, not in this situation, not even the sky marshal who'd been trained for this. Kaja must have taken the weapon from him.

Trautmann sat on the circular sofa in the middle of the lobby, his face looking – *like it had melted?*

He had high-degree burns. His skin was fiery red where it wasn't forming hideous white blisters, as if worked over with the coarsest sandpaper.

Or with coffee.

Mats took another step down and on the floor spotted the glass serving pitcher used in business class.

Kaja throwing the freshly brewed, scalding hot liquid in the sky marshal's face explained how she could've overpowered the man, who was at least fifty kilograms heavier, and taken his gun. Which in turn wouldn't have exactly gone unnoticed by the passengers, further explaining why Kaja had made the announcement.

'Water,' Trautmann whispered and held his hands to his scalded face. His eyes had obviously been impaired as well. The sky marshal didn't seem able to see anything or anyone.

Mats returned to watching Kaja, who screamed at the victim kneeling at her feet: 'We've known each other ever since I can remember. You know my secrets, you know everything about me. I thought I could trust you, but it was all just a lie?'

Kaja kicked at the person. The nicotine in her blood still wasn't showing symptoms, which was normal. It could take a half hour for seizures to set in. Mats dared proceed another step down.

'You manipulated me. You manipulated all of us.'

'No,' heard Mats. The female voice was familiar. It belonged to the person curled up on the floor. As if trying to cover something up with her arms and upper body so she could protect it.

'All of you clear out!' Kaja screamed, pivoting rapidly in a circle, aiming the sky marshal's gun. In the process she spotted Mats, and she nodded at him briefly as if she had expected him to free himself somehow.

Those present started moving at once. Valentino, the half-blind Trautmann, and Mats too tried to disappear beyond the curtain. But Kaja held Mats back.

'Not you. You stay here and watch.'

At that moment the baby, which the woman on the floor was trying to protect, began to whimper.

63

'Salina!' Mats blurted.

Kaja shook her head. 'You don't know her. You don't even know her real name. It's not Salina, it's Amelie.'

Mats squinted.

The third girl in their toenail polish gang.

'And her last name is...' Kaja paused as if it all were a quiz show and she the host building the necessary suspense before the big reveal. Then she kicked the red-haired woman on the floor in the side. Not very hard, but enough to make her wince.

'Tell him your last name,' she ordered.

The mother looked up for the first time and, trembling, her face full of fear, stared right at Mats.

He answered for her: 'Klopstock.'

Kaja nodded. 'That's right. The respectable doctor's wife, Frau Amelie Klopstock!' She kicked her again with the tip of her shoe.

'Klopstock's wife.'

'Please,' Amelie pleaded. 'My baby.'

The whimpering had grown louder. Mats saw a tiny little arm trying to break itself free from under its mother's upper body.

'What, you think I'm supposed to have sympathy for you?' Kaja said, aiming the gun at Amelie Klopstock's head. 'For your baby?' She spat in disgust at the lobby carpet. 'You destroyed my life! You filmed that video! Sent it out. I've never had sex since. I'll never have kids, you understand that?' She was screaming. 'So just shut up about your baby!'

Kaja kept shouting but Mats had stopped listening.

His only thought was *the video.*

Amelie was Kaja's friend. She'd filmed the video of her and Peer and sent it out everywhere.

Peer Unsell... Lisping Unsell. The school shooter who'd raped Kaja.

'It was you?' Mats said, stunned.

Kaja told him more of the truth.

'It was her. She destroyed my life. And yours, Dr Krüger. Amelie loved manipulating people. She lured boyfriends with sex. That's how she got Johannes Faber to upload that video and send it to his friends. Isn't that right?'

She pressed the gun to the back of Amelie's head.

'Please, don't,' Amelie pleaded, and Mats frantically tried thinking of some way to defuse the situation. If he only knew the pilot was starting to descend. But they were probably still too far from any airport. So he had to play for time and keep the two women talking as long as possible.

Mats knelt down to Amelie. 'Why did you do it?'

Amelie was trembling even worse from the fear and strain. Kaja answered again:

'It's in her nature. Amelie loves having power over others. And she hates it when she's not the centre of attention. That's why she put out that video. Because she couldn't stand me being honoured as the school hero. Isn't that right?'

'Yes, yes,' Amelie admitted and was now crying louder than her baby.

'The only thing I don't get is why you edited it,' Kaja screamed and kicked her again. 'WHY?'

'We were young. We didn't know what we were doing…' Amelie was trying to talk her way out of it. Mats could hardly understand her.

'Bullshit. You were trying to destroy me one little bit at a time.'

Mats looked at the curtain. It had stopped moving. No one within reach could help him. He was all on his own.

'No, yes. I don't know…' Amelie sobbed, not daring to look up at Kaja. Mats actually believed her. Amelie had likely, without realising it, been acting true to the narcissist's pathological instincts and had wanted to hold off on revealing her special knowledge. She definitely could not have anticipated that she might be able to use the added leverage to control her unstable 'girlfriend' one day.

'I was so stupid,' Kaja said with a sudden calmness to her voice, which only frightened Mats more. 'I actually thought we were working together. But I was just your puppet.'

Just like me, Mats thought. He had volunteered to offer Amelie aka Salina his seat. Triggered by the oldest key stimulus in the world: a desperate mother holding a helpless baby. She had placed the alleged 'weapon' under her own seat. She certainly couldn't have foreseen that he'd ask her to help with the video analysis that ended up revealing her secret. Yet she had still been the mastermind all along.

His next realisation hit him like a slap to the face, one he probably would've seen coming far earlier under less lethal circumstances: *Amelie is the voice!*

She was the one he'd been talking to the whole time, while she was presumably locked away in the toilet or when the baby was sleeping, whether buckled up in the seat or briefly looked after by a flight attendant. Possibly even by Kaja, when the timing was right.

'Stand up!' Kaja now barked at Amelie.

'Please, no.'

'Oh, what's the matter?' Kaja teased. 'You wanted it to look real, didn't you? That's why you showed Krüger the full video. I *really was* supposed to suffer a relapse.'

Kaja glanced at Mats. Her look had turned ice cold.

'Well, you did it, Amelie. It's just bad luck for you that you didn't count on me actually getting hold of a weapon.'

Amelie raised her head. 'Please, help me!' She stretched out a hand to Mats. Raised her upper body. The way she was shielding her baby suddenly created an opening.

Mats reacted automatically. He grabbed the baby by its tiny arm. Pulled it to him, away from its mother. Into his own arms.

'Slut,' he heard Kaja say, then it was over. The recoil nearly jolted the gun out of Kaja's hand.

'Nooo!' Mats shouted, the baby pressed to his chest as he shrunk back from its mother, the shot echoing in his ear.

'Good God,' he groaned and looked to the floor.

Blood seeped like black oil from the bullet hole between Amelie's eyes.

64

'Not another inch, you fucker,' Kaja barked next, and Mats needed a second to comprehend that she meant Valentino instead of him. After the shot he'd reappeared in the entry to business class.

'Clear out or we're all going down.'

Kaja pressed the gun barrel directly to the window pane of the exit door.

'Easy, take it easy,' Mats said, not sure what would happen if Kaja pulled the trigger. In the movies, anyone in the immediate vicinity was sucked out the window from the drastic change in pressure. He had no idea if that held true in reality but didn't want to find out.

He found his way over to Valentino, who stared as if paralysed at the mother shot dead.

'Where are you going?'

'I just want to give him the baby. Please.'

Mats handed Valentino the baby, which had been screaming at the top of its lungs since the bang.

'Get it to safety,' he told Valentino, not even sure if there was a safe spot on board. Then he pulled the curtain shut again and went back to Kaja.

She was sweating; her pupils looked constricted. Signs of an abnormal psychological state, possibly from the poisoning as well. Either way, the situation had changed irrevocably. Kaja had killed. She'd already sunk her teeth in and would do so again, and very soon. Unless someone stopped her. And the only one who was capable on board was him. Her psychiatrist, who knew her mind and her wounds better than anyone on this earth.

He knelt down. Felt for Salina's pulse, knowing it was pointless, but he needed to do something to fathom the horror. A terrible thought hit him: *If Salina was the 'voice', then the only person who knows about Nele's fate is now dead.*

'Where's my daughter?' he said, because he had to ask the question. Even though he was certain that Kaja hadn't lied to him before.

'I really don't know,' she said, and again he believed her.

Mats shut his eyes briefly and collected himself. He stood up.

'It's over,' he said flatly, as much to himself as to Salina's murderer. He pointed at the corpse on the floor. 'This person has no more control over you. You can put away the gun.'

'No.'

'Are you sure?'

He tried making eye contact, but she avoided him.

Kaja sweated heavily, rash spots blemished her pale face, saliva leaked from her mouth. The poison was beginning to wreak havoc inside her, and Mats expected to hear a second shot any moment.

'You still don't get it, do you?' she said to him.

The game was over, no one left to save them. Neither

him or Nele and certainly not Kaja, who'd sentenced herself to death.

The only thing still in his power was preventing an even greater catastrophe.

And it was the only reason why he was even speaking with Kaja and not collapsing in front of her in tears.

'I don't understand all this, not by a long shot, but enough to piece together some of the facts,' he said, as calmly as he could. The world around him had shrunk. The aeroplane and all the people in it didn't exist anymore. It was just Kaja now and him and his words, which found their way out of his mouth as if on their own:

'Amelie is the wife of Dr Klopstock and wanted to create new business from psychological fitness tests like those already being discussed for pilots after the Germanwings attack. My guess is, it has to do with Klopstock's lab and sinfully expensive psychological checks but also blood tests to determine whether any passengers or crew have taken psychotropic drugs. But that required a law, so to get it up and running they were going to need an incident on board an aircraft, just like the one you two caused here today. Amelie Klopstock promised you a huge sum of money for playing along, and you, you felt cheated by the whole world anyway, which was why you wanted to secure at least some of the money in compensation. But now you've seen who actually filmed that video, and you realise that Amelie never considered you an equal partner. Instead, she was controlling you like a puppet from the very start.'

'Bravo!' Kaja imitated applause. 'You covered it. But you know what I don't get? How can one person be so smart and stupid at the same time? Amelie was manipulative. But me, I was, and you've never understood this, Dr Krüger, a thousand times worse. Because I *wanted* it.'

'What?'

'The school shooting.'

Mats nodded. 'Yes, we talked about that. You wanted to take revenge for that video and kill everyone who talked badly about you.'

'No. I'm not talking about the second time. I'm talking about the first.'

'Say again?'

'I planned it together with Peer.'

Mats gasped.

Was Kaja really telling him this?

'I was his girlfriend. I wanted nothing to do with other boys, no matter what the girls in my little gang said. He was my one and all. I wanted to help him show all those fuckers who'd bullied him.'

Of course.

He could've slapped his forehead.

How could I have missed that, in all our therapy sessions?

They were a pair, a team. Partners in crime.

That was why Peer had taken Kaja hostage back then.

It wasn't random. It was completely deliberate.

'But I wasn't able to do it. I wasn't brave enough. I didn't want him killing those girls in the shower too. I wanted him to stop. In the locker room, we had sex one last time. Then we were going to shoot ourselves, together. But I was too much of a coward. So he sent me away.'

'Yet you did come back.'

For one last, intimate goodbye kiss.

Kaja nodded.

'And then that video of my supposed rape got out. Which in reality was consensual. And all those things my schoolmates said? They weren't ripping open old wounds, they were reminding me of how cowardly I was in betraying him. How I got scared and abandoned Peer.'

'So you set off to complete his work, with a second school shooting?'

'To make up for failing. To clear my guilt. Peer was my friend, but I never stood by him. When the others mimicked him, made fun of him, slit his bicycle tyres. I only ever met him in secret, kept him a secret from my little gang. He was just like me. We were soulmates. We'd meet without anyone knowing, listen to the same music, smoke weed and talk about death, and I was starting to realise just how connected we were.'

Mats reached for his nose without realising it, like he often did when trying to focus, and was punished with stinging pain.

At its root, the diagnosis was so simple.

Two shy teenagers, unable to communicate normally, feeling misunderstood. One bullied, the other torn apart inside, both, like so many young people, never finding a release for their emotions. So they planned to make a single loud statement, together. A volcanic eruption from which no one could hide.

Mats realised that he really hadn't understood a thing back then in Kaja's therapy. The whole time he'd believed that her schoolmates' unfair smear campaign, the stinging mockery and shameful abuse from a video supposedly showing her rape, had caused her to experience a post-traumatic embitterment disorder. Yet it was her own twisted secret relationship with Peer Unsell that had damaged her. Her shame for not standing at his side at the end, despite the vows they'd made to one another. A guilt that eats away at a person inside like acid. Mats knew this from his own experience, having been tortured by it himself for years ever since leaving his wife's death bed like a coward.

He swallowed hard, trying to suppress a crippling despair brought about by the hopeless certainty that he no longer knew how to save his daughter. But he also knew that Nele wouldn't have wanted any more people to die on her account. So he kept trying to get through to Kaja somehow.

'So, a year later you went back into school with a loaded weapon, to finish Peer's crime.'

Kaja gave a sad sigh. 'I wanted to collect myself first. Calm before the storm. I went into the bathroom. There I saw this sticker. Mental Health Hotline. Those stupid things were posted all over the school after the first time, and, shit, there I was getting cold feet again.'

'Because you're not a killer,' Mats stated, and Kaja laughed, cynically, glancing at the corpse at her feet.

'I'm not, huh?'

'You don't kill the innocent.'

'No one is innocent. You especially, Dr Krüger. You screwed up everything.'

'With my therapy?'

'By talking me out of it. With your clever, empathetic talk, you took away my most fervent wish. To leave this world with a big, loud bang. I've dreamed of it ever since I can remember.'

'No, you haven't. If you did, you wouldn't have let me discourage you.'

'Just temporarily. Not even you can turn a wolf into a kitten. You can't reverse it, can't re-educate me. Come on, let's go.'

'Where?'

'Where do you think? To the cockpit. How else am I supposed to make this thing crash?'

'You won't be able to get in,' Mats said, recalling another detail from his aviophobia seminar. 'The pilots are locked inside. The door is bulletproof. Not even that gun can open it.'

Kaja gave him a derisive laugh. 'Guess the first thing they changed after that Germanwings pilot's suicide crash? There's now a security code you can use to trip the locking device. So that a pilot can never, ever lock themselves inside again. And I'll give you three guesses as to who knows this code...'

65

'Kaja, please—'

'Let it go. You were able to stop me back when I was crying on that toilet at school. You're not going to again.'

She shoved him towards the cockpit.

'You're right. It is my fault,' Mats said. 'And you know why? Because I didn't give a shit about you.'

She stopped at the locked cockpit door, aiming the pistol right at his chest. Mats could see the keypad next to the peephole that Kaja claimed she could use to open the door.

'All I cared about was my reputation,' he said and kept lying. 'Publicity. "Star Psychiatrist Saves Schoolkids!" That was the headline I wanted.'

Kaja nodded. She was squinting, probably now suffering from impaired vision, a common effect of nicotine poisoning. Her pulse would start to slow next and possibly even cause respiratory paralysis. 'That's exactly what Amelie said.'

Of course she had. She had used the very same lies to lure you in.

'And she was right.' Mats deliberately switched to a disrespectful tone. 'I filled you full of pills, but I didn't care about the truth inside your head. You want to end your life. And it has to be spectacular, because you need to open people's eyes to the fact that our lives are simply not worth living. Right?'

'Exactly.'

I overlooked it.

She had suffered from the usual dark teenage visions. Normally harmless, temporary as they were. A gloomy phase that hit most along with puberty and vanished again. But sometimes the morbid fantasies became firmly entrenched, say, after some traumatic event, such as the death of a relative. Or a friend's suicide. It had been that way with Kaja, and Mats had failed to see it.

'By talking you out of your death wish, I was acting no better than a priest wanting to convert a gay person to straight.'

'Why are you telling me this?' Kaja held the gun tighter, her hand shaking. 'You're only making me madder.'

All the better.

'There's only one single person on board who deserves to die. And that's me.' He lowered his voice. Downright swore to her: 'I used you, Kaja. I didn't listen to you when you were trying to tell me how terrible the world is. Prescribed you meds that repressed your true self.'

Mats fixed his gaze on Kaja. Ready to finally overcome his own worst fear.

'End it,' he pleaded.

He stepped nearer, so close he could have stuck his index finger into the barrel as she raised the gun higher and pointed it directly at his head.

Half a metre away. She couldn't miss from this distance. *All the better.*

She was still saying 'get out of my way' when Mats threw himself at her. He sensed no pain. Just an intense burning sensation, as if Kaja had scalded him with coffee too. A busted loudspeaker droned inside his ears, the shot's echo reverberating like some distorted church bell, its pendulum inside his head striking the top of his skull.

Copper, Mats thought and realised that all those know-it-alls could go screw themselves. It might contain only iron but blood sure as hell did taste like you were sucking on a penny, so any comparison was perfectly apt.

Only the part about eternal blackness wasn't right.

It was more like a grey, with tiny bright spots. The size of pins, a liquid fog seeping out from behind them.

And with the fog came the cold.

And with the cold, nothingness.

66

Eighteen hours later

Once, when Mats was little, his big brother frightened him with a mind game that Mats had never been able to get out of his head his whole life.

'Try to imagine nothingness,' Nils had said as they lay in the meadow along Teufelssee outside Berlin, the lake they used to visit every day on their summer breaks.

'How do I do that?'

'Start by imagining that this lake here, this meadow, and this little shore are not here.'

'Okay.'

'Then imagine that we're not here either. We're gone.'

Next, Mats was supposed to erase Berlin from the map in his imagination, then Germany, and Europe, and finally the whole earth. He was eventually supposed to erase the solar system, the planets, universe and finally all the galaxies from his imagination.

'What do you see now?' his brother had asked innocuously.

'Just a deep, dark nothing.'

'Good. Now imagine that's gone too.'

'How do I do that?'

'Let the nothing shrink, down to a single, tiny dot. Then you make that go away.'

Mats was lying on the meadow and trying so hard to follow his big brother's simple-sounding instructions, but it was futile.

'I can't do it,' he said. Whenever the dot disappeared there still remained a black, endless void that was impossible for him to make go away.

He wasn't able to replace nothingness with nothing.

'You see,' he'd heard his brother say in triumph. 'We aren't able to imagine nothing. Because nothingness is not some endless void but instead the absence of it. Nothingness,' he concluded, 'is a missing hole.'

Back then at Teufelssee, Mats hadn't quite understood what his older and smarter brother was trying to explain to him. But now he was certain that he'd discovered that very place that his brother had told him was unimaginable.

He found himself in that exact focal point, in that missing hole. Surrounded by nothing apart from the absence of any life.

Mats couldn't see. No matter how hard he tried opening his eyes he found all connection to his eyelids lost, just like he'd lost any contact to his muscles, limbs, to his whole body. Speaking, swallowing, gagging – nothing functioned any more.

His sense of touch seemed to be shut off too. Normally a person sensed having clothes on their skin if they thought about it and if they concentrated, they could actually feel them physically. Mats felt nothing at all. No itching, no scratching, no touch, nowhere. It was as if he were drifting naked in a vacuum, incapable of feeling himself anywhere.

Along with the loss of his eyesight and sense of touch, he'd also become mute and deaf. All he heard was his thoughts; not even the sounds of his own body were there anymore, the blood circulating, the intestines working away, his breathing, nothing. Inside him all was painfully still.

Rob a healthy person of one of their senses, went the theory, then the other senses would overcompensate for the loss. The blind heard better, and deaf people could use their eyes to detect the tiniest shifts in feeling on the faces of their fellow humans.

To Mats, who had nothing left to him except his thoughts, the sense of fear appeared to have become the dominant and driving force of his consciousness. He didn't hear how he breathed insatiably, didn't sense the adrenalin surging in him, but he did feel the panic subverting his reasoning.

Where am I? What's happened to me?

His thoughts screamed inside his head, inaudibly loud, deafeningly silent.

Suddenly that all changed.

Mats still saw only nothing, said nothing, felt nothing, but he heard something.

First a humming, similar to an ultrasonic toothbrush. An electric crackling became louder and now reminded him of an artificial cricket, and it was the loveliest sound he could imagine, because it *was* a sound.

Proof that he wasn't falling down that missing hole anymore but was back in contact. In contact with a pleasant, earnest voice that materialised from the humming.

'Herr Dr Krüger? Can you hear me?' said the voice, and Mats attempted to reply. Tried to scream, to pop his eyes open, wave his arms, but he'd already forgotten how to do so.

'I'm very sorry to tell you this, but you've suffered severe damage to your brain stem,' the voice told Mats. The most terrifying of all truths.

Locked in. As a doctor he knew the diagnosis, of course, even if the voice did not come right out and say it. It was never easy for a doctor to let such cruel words cross their lips. Also, because the findings usually resulted from days if not weeks of tests. But Mats was a specialist. He was able to analyse himself, and he recognised that his brain had lost almost all connection to the rest of his being. The plug had been pulled. He was buried alive in his own useless body.

'My name is Dr Martin Roth. I'm the head of the Park Clinic. We once met at a symposium, Dr Krüger. My team of neuroradiologists and surgeons and I are caring for you. You're currently on an artificial respirator, and as a backup measure we've established a brain–computer interface using EEG electrodes.'

Mats nodded, without nodding. In his mind he *saw* those little plates on the shaved areas of his skull, the cables leading from the head to the computers. In his practice he'd all too often seen patients with these severe types of injuries, after a brain stem infarct, for example. The bridge was damaged, the pons – that area between the midbrain and medulla that formed the brain stem of the central nervous system. In some patients, basic communication could only be maintained by monitoring brain waves. Atypical for him was that he could clearly hear everything around him. Most patients with locked-in syndrome could indeed see but not hear anything. With him it was apparently the other way around, and that was more bad news. It meant that, in addition to the brain stem, the occipital area also had to be damaged.

'You're wearing headphones, through which you're hearing my voice. They filter out disruptive external sounds,' he heard Dr Roth say. 'You might not be aware of it, but you can still contract your eyelid muscles, in imitation of a blink. Please try and do so.'

Mats followed Dr Roth's instructions and heard his delight. 'Very good. Let's try a simple discussion. I'll only ask you yes or no questions. Please blink once for yes. Two for no. Do you understand?'

Mats blinked three times and heard Roth laugh.

'You haven't lost your sense of humour. That's outstanding.'

Mats heard a male voice in the background that was vaguely familiar but he couldn't place it.

'We have a visitor I'd like to introduce in a minute,' explained Dr Roth, who was presumably speaking to him over a microphone. 'First, though, I'm sure you want to know what happened to you.'

Mats blinked.

'You were shot. On the aeroplane. The bullet struck you directly in the head. It destroyed the connection between your brain stem and your spinal cord.'

Hearing such a diagnosis Mats would normally have shut his eyes, tried to hold back his tears, maybe scream, at least have trouble swallowing. But not even that was possible for him since he couldn't feel his tongue anymore.

'The police first considered you a homicidal threat, but that's all been resolved.' Dr Roth cleared his throat. 'You're a hero. You rushed the assassin and were able to prevent worst. The only reason the pilots were able to open the cockpit door and disarm the flight attendant was because she was stuck underneath you. The plane landed safely in Berlin. Everyone on board survived.'

The cricket kept chirping, probably just distortion in the transmission from microphone to headphones, and before it got any louder the head physician said, 'All passengers except for the woman who was shot by the perpetrator.'

Amelie Klopstock, Mats thought. His recollection of what happened on that plane was so clear and immediate it was as if he'd just been on board a minute ago. Though the truth was he must have been lying in intensive care for hours if not days.

'You woke up two hours ago,' he heard the doctor say as if reading his thoughts. Maybe he even was. Modern medicine still knew far too little about the syndrome but it had made great strides. After all, it had now become possible to communicate even with locked-in patients who couldn't so much as blink. This however took weeks and months of practice to correctly interpret the scans created as the severely injured person was subjected to extremely long interviews while lying inside an MRI tube.

'Hours after you were admitted, we noticed that we could communicate with you by way of blinking. However, you didn't remember anything. The injury had caused full amnesia. For that reason, we decided on an innovative new method of diagnosis that hasn't been tried before. I requested help from a colleague, Professor Haberland. As you may know, he specialises in using hypnosis. Since your mind is fully functional, and you are awake in the clinical sense, Dr Krüger, we hypnotised you. You may not remember us initiating the procedure, but we're hoping that it ended up working. So that you can relive the flight in your memory, we've had you experience various sensations via the brain interface. We played typical engine noises over your headphones, from take-off and during flight. Your bed is hydraulic and moves with gentle vibrations that simulate aircraft movement. In order to stimulate your sense of smell we placed, directly into your nose, a little stick soaked in room spray.'

Mats recalled the scent of the air conditioning, of the smell of blood – *and the perfume.*

Katharina's perfume!

'The all-decisive question now, Dr Krüger, is: did it work? Can you put yourself back in those last few hours on board the aeroplane with the help of hypnosis? Can you remember now?'

Mats blinked.

'Good, very good. That's fantastic. You're probably asking why we've chosen such an elaborate procedure.'

The missing hole was illuminated by a flash, like someone taking a photo inside his brain – an electrochemical reaction resulting from the slight microphone feedback as Dr Roth said, 'Professor Klopstock will explain everything to you.'

67

'Can he hear me?' asked Dr André Klopstock. Then louder: 'Hello, Mats? My dear colleague.'

Mats blinked.

'Good, that's good. Very good. Oh, man. I'm sorry, so sorry.'

To Mats' amazement, Klopstock didn't sound ingratiating but rather truly shaken. His voice carried no hint of that pomposity Mats had known from him and that people more or less expected from a psychiatrist who liked to see himself in the society gossip columns.

'I'm just heartbroken, and I wish there was some way to make up for this. Even though I myself wasn't directly involved. Which is why I'm speaking with... uh... to you. But I'm not just here to prove my own innocence. I'm fully willing to cooperate with Dr Roth and the authorities, in order to... what was that? Ah, right, fine. I'm sorry.' Mats figured the last part was Dr Roth intervening. The head physician was evidently gesturing at him to hurry it up.

'But there's something you should know before we begin our questioning.'

Questioning?

'I've developed tests for the early detection of certain psychopathological behaviours. I'm steadfastly convinced of their necessity. What's the good of inspecting fluids in carry-ons and not the mental state of passengers and pilots? But we'll leave that for now. This is about Amelie, my ex-wife.

'She was obsessed with the idea of speeding up the approval procedure. You should know that Amelie ran my practice. She had access to all research results, investment plans, and of course patient records. She was actually a photographer and had no training as a doctor's assistant at all. But I hired her because of her knack for organisation. It was only much later, after we were married, that it became clear to me she was pathologically obsessed with details. And was just as brilliant as she was dangerous in the way she manipulated others. For example, I never wanted to have children but suddenly she got pregnant, despite taking the pill.'

Klopstock cleared his throat with embarrassment.

'Amelie always knew just what she had to do, or in this case had to refrain from, in order to get her way. She had a hold over me. For too long I repressed the fact that her compulsion for control stretched back to childhood. She first opened my eyes to it when she presented me with a "business plan" one day.'

Mats heard the quote marks in the way Klopstock stressed the phrase.

'She knew I had a pro bono case, one Franz Uhlandt, an originally harmless but increasingly emotionally disturbed vegan who had the sick fantasy of exposing to humanity how cruel the industrial production of milk was to animals.

And Amelie knew that I was treating your pregnant daughter Nele.'

Nele flashed through Mats' mind. He'd needed to process so many feelings, so much information after waking inside his missing hole that he hadn't thought about Nele until now.

'*Where is she?*' he screamed inside. '*Is she all right?*'

'I thought it was a joke when she asked me if we shouldn't give my patents a little boost. "All we need is one incident," she'd said, but I hadn't taken it seriously. I thought it was her hormones talking, she being pregnant after all, and the birth of our baby would surely bring her back to her senses, you know? Yet her mad fantasies wouldn't quit even after Suza's birth, and I finally separated from Amelie. That was probably my biggest misstep, because then she saw implementing her plan as the way to win me back.'

Klopstock cleared his throat again, yet his voice still sounded hoarse.

'To maintain control, she wanted to be on board the plane herself. Good God, she even took Suza along. Of course Amelie only did that to divert suspicion. To manipulate her environment. Who would suspect anything evil of a breastfeeding mom? And now she's paid for her ludicrous plan with her life. Fortunately just her. Suza's doing well.'

'Doctor...' Mats again heard the head physician's cautioning voice in the background.

'I know, I know, Dr Roth. I'm getting to the point. But it's essential that Dr Krüger knows the context. How else is he supposed to separate the relevant details from the unimportant ones?'

Klopstock's voice was growing louder.

'For you to understand things, which is what you'll need to do for us to prevent even worse from happening...'

EVEN worse?

'My wife went to school with Kaja and had kept in loose contact with her over the years. In her manipulative way, Amelie managed to convince Kaja that she was being mistreated by you, Mats. That she was at least entitled to compensation. Money. A lot of money. She made it clear to Kaja that her life was messed up, but also that people like us made a mint off the psychological suffering of their patients.

'She used this argument to win Kaja over. To do her crime. And she had an easy time of it with Uhlandt, who'd long dreamed of showing people, using a real living object, what it meant for a pregnant mother to have her baby taken from her. She provided him with money and a camera.'

Mats suddenly had the horrible feeling of needing to scratch himself inside. Klopstock's words were like itching powder inside his mind.

'These aren't all the facts – much of it I'm only guessing at or piecing together from the information that I do have. Frau Claussen unfortunately can't be questioned. She died shortly after landing from the effects of nicotine poisoning. And, there is one other thing I have to get off my chest, that you need to know, before—'

Before what???

'I'm innocent from a legal point of view, but not morally. None of this would've happened without my involvement. Because when I treated Nele, I was the one who'd convinced her to get back in touch with you, Mats. To restore the family bonds.

'My wife must've read about it in my session notes. I even wrote down your flight number when your daughter told me about it. Amelie must have then given it to Kaja Claussen.'

Mats' itch was getting worse. If he could only scream at Klopstock to get to the point.

'As bad as it is, I cannot help but admit some respect for my dead wife in her madness. She never had to resort to any physical violence herself. It was all about proper timing and manipulating people. Her speciality. You could even say she came up with a brilliant psychological plan that was, at its core, distinctly feminine. She influenced Kaja and you only with words, Mats. And in Franz Uhlandt she had a stranger to get his hands dirty, one with a completely different motive than hers. Which was why any connection between the two crimes wouldn't have been easy to prove, especially since you, Mats, were supposed to end up paying with your life...'

Before Mats could tell whether he'd heard Klopstock crying he detected the voice of Dr Roth again, who said in a far more straightforward yet urgent way: 'Good, now that you know the background, this brings us to the crucial question, Dr Krüger: where is your daughter?'

No!

Mats knew this question was coming and yet was praying he wouldn't have to hear it. Now it was out there, and the darkness all around him opened its hideous maw, threatening to devour him once again.

Oh, God, so you never found her?

Mats' mind spun, that missing hole inside him becoming a vortex. Then he thought: *Good Lord, the baby!*

It must have been born after this long.

Or... *it had died.*

This one word droned so loudly in Mats' thoughts that Dr Roth was hardly able to reach him with his next question: 'Did you learn of anything at all on board that aeroplane, heard, seen or otherwise found out, that might tell us Nele's current whereabouts?'

68

Dr Roth

'Was that a blink?'

Roth nodded at Klopstock. Of course it was, unmistakably. The electrodes on Dr Mats Krüger's eyelashes had recorded it. The jump on the monitor above the bed showed it.

Roth stood next to the bed in the intensive care unit holding a silvery-grey pencil microphone and watched as the patient's eyeballs moved under his closed eyelids like disorientated beetles.

Krüger's face was completely bandaged except for his eyes and mouth. He looked like some mummified alien with the black earphones, breathing tube in his mouth and little plates wired to his skull. Drainage was maintaining a sufficient avoidance of pressure at the locations where Kaja's bullet had entered and exited, but the swelling could not be arrested for long and the patient would eventually lose consciousness. Fortunately, he wasn't feeling any pain.

Hopefully.

The research on patients with locked-in syndrome was still in its infancy. They knew far too little about serious brain damage. Still, it had been recognised that those affected were quite fully aware and could be put into a trance by means of acoustic indicators. To his knowledge, though, Dr Krüger was the first patient on whom they'd used hypnotic regression to restore memory.

Whether it was successful or not would soon be clear.

Roth grabbed his mobile phone, pressed the speed dial for his office and asked them why the police weren't here yet. It had already been twenty minutes since he'd informed Detective Hirsch that Krüger had 'woken' from his trance.

The same detective who, when Krüger was admitted yesterday, had made a fool of himself by insisting on interrogating the 'suspect'.

'The detective's coming from across town,' Roth's assistant told him. 'Might take a little longer.'

Roth thanked her, hung up and decided not to wait. He'd continue questioning his patient on his own.

'I can imagine what you're thinking, Dr Krüger. Too much time has passed, and with kidnapping cases the chances of finding a victim alive decreases by the hour.'

Roth was deliberately not mincing words. It was crucial that his patient ignore his own terrible fate and focus only on his daughter.

'On your phone we found the torture photo the kidnapper made of your daughter. The official search for Nele hasn't produced any leads so far.

'Until a while ago, we didn't know the connection between events on board the plane and a possible kidnapping. We only became aware of this from statements made by Professor Klopstock, who volunteered his help after his wife was identified. He told us everything he knows. Now you're our only witness. We're not sparing any effort or expense in questioning you because we want to save your daughter. Do you understand?'

Roth was pleased to see a blink.

'Good. I'm now going to try using yes/no questions to feel my way towards what you experienced and anything that might help us searching for your daughter. Okay?'

Mats signalled agreement with another blink, and Roth squeezed his patient's hand even though the man couldn't feel it anymore. Such an emotional form of contact had become an unconscious habit for the head physician of the Park Clinic. He viewed himself as not only a man of words and pills but also one of humane sympathy.

Roth began with the most direct and important question: 'Do you know where your daughter is?'

Mats blinked. To Roth's amazement, he didn't only do it once or twice – he did it six times in a row.

'What's he doing?' Klopstock asked.

Roth had no idea and first waited to see whether Krüger resumed blinking after a longer pause.

When nothing happened, he asked his patient as loudly and clearly as possible: 'Did you just blink six times on purpose?'

Mats blinked once.

So, yes.

Then he blinked five times and paused again before twitching his eyelids twelve times.

'Wait, give us a little time, please,' Roth requested and reached for a clipboard at the end of the bed.

'Morse code?' Klopstock asked.

'No, the blinking doesn't have the cadence for that.'

Roth made some hurried notes, verified his suspicions by

counting with his fingers, and finally felt he'd solved the mystery.

'Are they letters?'

He stared at Krüger's eyes.

'The alphabet. Are you going through the alphabet?'

A weak, but visible twitch.

'Yes!' Klopstock said in excitement behind him.

Roth, no less thrilled, asked Mats to start from the beginning.

He blinked six times again.

F

Then one less.

E

'Twelve,' Klopstock counted out loud and Roth wrote:

L

Krüger's blinking finally ended with a nine count.

I

'Who is Feli?' Dr Roth asked Klopstock.

'Felicitas Heilmann. A colleague.'

Roth turned off the microphone. 'A friend of Dr Krüger, you mean?'

Klopstock nodded. 'Yesterday she visited me at my practice and told me that Nele was in trouble. And that

Mats was on an aeroplane flying from Buenos Aires to Berlin. That was the moment I first put two and two together. I knew that Amelie was on that plane with Suza, supposedly coming back from vacation. So when Feli came to me at the clinic on Ku'damm, I got this bad feeling that Amelie actually might've put her plan in motion.'

Roth lowered the clipboard, astounded. 'And you didn't say anything?' He bristled. 'Why didn't you go to the police immediately with this information instead of reporting it only after this tragedy already occurred on board?'

Roth's verbal onslaught had riled Klopstock somewhat and he launched a counterattack: 'So what was I supposed to tell the police? *"Hey, listen, one of my patients might have been kidnapped? Her father might be causing a disaster? My wife might be pulling the strings on board?"*'

He shook his head.

'All I had was conjecture. And the fact that Dr Krüger was preferring to act on his own initiative instead of informing the authorities told me that I shouldn't attempt anything that might endanger Nele's life, no, not on mere suspicion.'

Roth made a disparaging wave of his hand, unable to suppress his anger. 'I don't believe a word you're saying, Dr Klopstock. You wanted that incident,' he stated frankly.

'No.'

'Or you at the least wanted to save your skin. Not to be connected at all if possible. If your wife hadn't died, you probably never would've reported this and offered your help. You're only doing this now to clear your name.'

Klopstock bristled, angry now too. 'That's not true. I

even gave Felicitas Heilmann a tip when she came to see me. I had my assistant give her Uhlandt's contact info, who no one's been able to locate as you know.'

'I still don't understand why you never told me about Dr Heilmann.'

'Why should I have? Fine, she was looking for Nele, but that's something we're all doing if I'm not mistaken.'

Roth had stopped listening to his excuses. He stepped over to the intensive care window facing the park, with his phone to his ear.

It was a sunny fall day, the visitors and patients strolling along the leaf-lined avenue or chatting on one of the park benches. No one out there seemed to have even the slightest idea of the suffering and misery residing just a few metres away inside these clinic walls.

Roth could now hear the police detective he'd just called, road noise in the background. 'Hirsch? It's Dr Roth, Park Clinic.'

'I'll be there any second.'

'Good. One question first: has the name Felicitas Heilmann come up in your investigation?'

'No, should it?'

'The patient just gave us a lead.'

'Okay. Hold on...'

Roth heard the line go silent, and after a short while the detective came back on. He was either asking around or was checking case files using his phone.

'Felicitas Heilmann, forty-two years old, registered psychiatrist from Prenzlauer Berg?' Hirsch asked.

'Has to be her.'

'That's odd.'

Roth switched the phone from one ear to the other. 'What is?'

'We hadn't seen any connection until now. But her partner has reported her missing.'

'Come again?'

The head physician exchanged a glance with Klopstock, who made no secret of the fact that he was trying to listen in.

'They were supposed to get married yesterday, but she left him standing at the altar.'

'That cannot be coincidence.'

Hirsch sounded like he was biting into something and now spoke with his mouth full: 'Way I see it too. I mean, left at the altar, that's not exactly a priority for us. But along with this here… shit.'

'What?'

'Heilmann's fiancé had given us his wife's last mobile phone location. You won't believe it.'

Hirsch sounded like he was speeding up, the road noise louder.

'Where?' Roth asked. And felt a chill like he was freezing on the inside as soon as the detective told him Feli's last location:

'That former East German meat processing plant. Right near the old dairy.'

69

Hirsch

'Should start charging admission,' grumbled the wheezing, short-winded security guard who barely fit in his blue-grey uniform. Not to mention the M&V Security vehicle from which he'd just squeezed out of with a tortured look on his face.

He counted out the matching key for the padlock on his absurdly large key ring and opened it for Chief Detective Hirsch and the two uniformed officers assisting him in searching for Felicitas Heilmann. A man with the face of a choirboy and an even younger-looking woman, both fresh from police academy – which was what they assigned you in Berlin when you launched a missing person search on the spur of the moment. In the movies, a black-masked SWAT team armed to the teeth crashed down the door with a battering ram. In reality, you trekked through smelling cow stalls with a panting Homer Simpson double and two greenhorn cops in tow.

'Third time already in twenty-four hours that someone's been interested in this dump,' complained the security guard, who introduced himself as Helmuth Müller. He was having a tough time keeping up with the chief detective.

Geez, I practically break the scales myself, but this guy could wear a hula hoop for a belt, Hirsch thought as he turned to the security guard.

'Who all was here before?'

Müller waddled up to him like a penguin.

'First it was students, trying to film a porno here yesterday without permission. Then the groom looking for his runaway bride, and now you.'

Hirsch gave his two uniformed officers the signal to split up. The girl was to search the front, the boy in the rear part of the big barn. He'd meanwhile inspect this gated enclosure towards the rear that the security guard had just led him to.

'A porno?' he asked, eyeing the camera tripod and secretion-smeared stretcher.

'At least that's what they said. I kicked them out right away, of course.'

Of course.

Hirsch pointed at the tripod and stretcher. 'And you just left this stuff here like this?'

The security guard scratched at his double chin and snorted. 'Why not? I mean, there's so much trash lying around here anyway, and at some point they'll just tear the old plant down. Keep wondering why they even still have me play Mister Watchman here.'

Hirsch examined the smeared plastic surface of the stretcher and studied an impression left on the dirty slatted flooring next to it. It looked as if a crate had recently been standing here.

'How did it go with Janek Strauss?' Hirsch asked.

'Who?'

'The groom, searching for his bride.'

'Oh, right, him.' The security guard scratched again. 'Didn't know that was his name. Man, did he make a fuss. Didn't let him in, though. I mean, it's forbidden. He didn't have any warrant or that kind of thing.'

'Affidavit,' Hirsh corrected.

'Come again?'

'It's called a search warrant affidavit. Which he never could've had as a civilian. You're sure he didn't try convincing you with some other sort of legal paper?' Hirsch rubbed his thumb and forefinger together to make it clear.

'Hey, I'm an upstanding citizen.'

'Sure,' Hirsch muttered under his breath, 'and Trump's a feminist.'

'What did you say?'

Hirsch shook his head and at the same time heard the boy cop shouting through the barn from a distance. 'Detective, sir, you'll probably want to take a look at this.'

Hirsch left the stalls area for the aisle that the animals and feeding carts used to be driven down and made his way over to his colleague.

The cop stood in the most remote part of the barn, about fifty metres from the entrance. He pointed to a staircase leading down.

'Find anything?'

'Afraid so, yes. But you're not going to like it.'

Hirsch borrowed the security guard's flashlight and climbed down the grated steps behind his colleague, into the musty smell.

Hirsch heard the security guard behind him saying, 'Over on the other side, at the entrance where that chick…

er, where your other officer's searching, there's another way into the basement,' but the detective wasn't interested for now.

'Look,' the boy cop said but hadn't needed to.

Hirsch had already spotted what had caught his attention.

'Not like I'm blind,' he muttered and shined light on the wooden slab on the floor. It had been covering up the abyss that now gaped before him.

Hirsch stepped to the edge and shined light, into a type of pit.

Good Lord...

He held a hand to his mouth. The boy cop gasped too though they couldn't make out anything in too much detail. They could only guess.

The beam from both their flashlights first found a piece of fabric soaked red, then the bloody parts of the motionless body.

'*Damn it, shit,*' Hirsch thought, then he said it out loud, and eventually the detective spoke the truth, of which there had been little doubt: 'We're too late.'

70

Mats

They were able to simply turn it on and off.

The missing hole. It got larger and darker and colder when they robbed Mats of the only sense he had left. As soon as the microphone went off and the earphones stopped transmitting, it was as if he were in a never-ending freefall, a nightmare that kept exceeding itself.

As a child, he could never get one particular scary fairy tale scene out of his five-year-old head – one where a prince had been walled in alive. Mats had imagined dark, rough clinker bricks forming an impenetrable wall, inside which he was damned to an eternal darkness. He never could've imagined that the invisible, intangible walls of his own body would create an even more horrific dungeon.

'Hello, Dr Krüger?'

The head physician's voice was the loveliest sound he could imagine. Every sound that penetrated the darkness and thwarted his freefall was a gift.

'Can you hear me?'

He blinked, and Roth told him thanks. His voice sounded different somehow than before. More tense. Like someone who's trying not to say what's really on their chest.

'*Where is Nele?*' Mats shouted into the eternity of his prison, inaudibly loud. Of course he got no answer.

'We still don't have any news from the police,' Dr Roth said, and it sounded like a lie.

Were they trying to spare him?

'We've currently been condemned to wait...' Mats heard Dr Roth take a heavy breath, then he added: 'But perhaps we could use the time we have and something might occur to you that could help the investigators with their search.'

What search are you talking about? The one for Nele – or for her murderer?

Mats wanted to flail about, bite, kick and so much more that he'd probably never be able to do again. He knew Roth was hiding something from him. He didn't need to see him standing by the bed with his face so clearly ridden with guilt.

'Please, Dr Krüger, I know how terrible this whole situation must be for you. But we're grasping at straws here, and the police are requesting that I ask you one more time.'

Mats tumbled inside his own universe, rotating sideways like a lumbering comet. He was certain that Roth was keeping something from him so that he didn't fully and forever withdraw inside himself. And since he still harboured the silent hope that Nele could be alive – provided that Roth didn't utter that most horrible of realities – he decided to continue playing along and answer the question the head physician had just posed to him: 'Dr Krüger, please think. Did you notice anything else suspicious on the aeroplane that could help us in the search for your daughter?'

Mats thought about it. Then he blinked.

Once.

71

Livio

He wasn't exactly sure what the hell he was doing way out here, but he couldn't just sit at home in front of the TV and act as if he hadn't seen anything.

Though he wasn't even sure if he had seen *anything*. Yesterday. When he drove back to that old meat processing plant to check on Feli. An ivory-coloured cab with its plates removed leaving an abandoned industrial area – sure, that was pretty odd.

But maybe the driver was only dropping off a delivery or was buying drugs or looking to dump some trash. There were hundreds of possibilities. The thing was, Feli had said that the guy she was looking for was acting as Klopstock's driver and that they were to keep an eye out for a cab on the grounds of that former meat plant. And the fact that the same guy had then moseyed out here to the boonies forty kilometres north of Berlin only to stop at yet another industrial wasteland here in the middle of nowhere, it definitely did not make things any less mysterious.

The thing was, Livio hadn't been able to spot anything that suspicious after he'd followed the cab at a safe distance.

The cab driver hadn't opened his trunk and pulled out a corpse or anything like that, nor had Livio heard screams or seen anyone fighting. Quite the opposite. The driver didn't even get out.

The guy had simply sat there for an hour and kept facing out the whole time, and at some point it was all getting too stupid for Livio.

Everything will be all right, he'd thought, put it into reverse and had driven back home.

That was yesterday.

And today I'm even more nuts.

He could not get his thoughts about Feli and a possibly mentally ill and unpredictable cab driver out of his head, especially since the lady doctor still hadn't answered her phone.

It had to be turned off.

But on the day of her wedding, as well as the day after?

No, Livio just couldn't believe that she'd simply wanted her honeymoon rest – no amount of self-delusion was going to calm his gut feeling.

What if the driver had noticed him yesterday? He wasn't exactly an expert in shadowing people, and maybe what he thought was a safe distance hadn't been far enough and he'd looked conspicuous?

For a moment he'd actually toyed with the idea of calling the police, but that wasn't the smartest move for someone the cops were already out to get on account of his record. Feli herself had told him not to repeatedly, *and, who knows, maybe I'm only seeing ghosts, and everything's just hunky dory?*

Then again, *no.* It didn't feel that way.

This afternoon, after that voice inside his head gave him no peace and wouldn't stop telling him that something was fishy, he had made his way back out here, the whole long way up to Overhavel country. And he was hardly that surprised the cab was still parked in front of that barn.

He'd been sure of it all along, basically. His gut feeling had never let him down.

Something was really screwed up here.

The cab itself didn't appear to have moved a bit since yesterday. And the driver wasn't at the wheel anymore, of course.

He was now on the move. Slowly, but deliberately.

From his hiding place behind the old water tanker, Livio watched the lanky and longhaired loser student step out of a construction trailer and shuffle across the muddy yard until he disappeared inside a grey and weathered clinker-brick building. Holding a plastic case in one hand and a camera in the other.

What the hell was he up to?

Livio strained to see from his spot but still couldn't get a look inside the building when the cab driver opened the door.

He saw neither Felicitas nor Nele.

But if he wasn't mistaken, he thought he'd just heard one of the two screaming for their life.

72

Mats

Mats blinked.

'Yes? You did notice something?'

He blinked again.

'Okay, okay.' The microphone rustled, but Dr Roth stayed silent. The doctor was obviously searching for the best way to proceed with the yes/no questions. Mats tried making it easier for him by continually blinking.

Dr Roth initially asked him what was wrong, not understanding what Mats wanted to tell him. But he finally just asked: 'You want me to count along with you?'

Mats signalled yes to him.

'Okay, understood. Then once more from the beginning please.'

Mats blinked forty-seven times in a row.

It again took a while for Dr Roth to find the right question for getting at the truth:

'Forty-seven can't be a letter, so, a number?'

Mats blinked once.

'A number in a document you had on you?'

Mats negated this question with two blinks, as well as

one about an address or part of a telephone number.

'You mean a seat? Row 47?'

He could practically hear Roth laugh when he confirmed his guess.

'Okay, in row 47 there was something suspicious. A passenger?'

Mats blinked once.

'Which seat exactly? Please blink once for A, two for B, and so on.'

Mats blinked six times.

'47F? The window seat. Wait one moment...'

It crackled, and again Mats plunged into that numb nothingness of his mental universe. The fact that they could simply switch him on or off inside that missing hole magnified his horror all over again.

After what felt like an hour yet could've lasted a year or only ten seconds, he again heard the cricket chirping. Then Dr Roth said, sounding somewhat confused, 'I was just talking with one of the investigators. He says you booked four seats on the flight. One of the them was 47F.'

Without a yes/no question, Mats was doomed to inaction.

'So, what I meant to say was: were you sitting in seat 47F?'

Mats blinked twice, signalling no.

'Someone else had taken your seat?'

Mats blinked once.

'A man?'

Mats answered yes again, and to the next question: 'Could you describe him if it were possible for you? Did he have any distinguishing features?'

Subsequently, Roth only asked questions that Mats had to say no to.

No, he didn't know the name, and it wasn't a face he would recognise, no special features like tattoos, piercings, scars, birthmarks. He also wouldn't be able to identify him by his voice, posture, hair colour or clothing.

Finally, Roth asked the all-important question:

'Is it his smell?'

Mats blinked once.

'That man had an unmistakable smell?'

He confirmed again.

Again there was a pause, again the microphone was briefly switched off, and again he plunged down that bottomless pit of the missing hole, until he heard Dr Roth say: 'We triggered you using only a few olfactory stimuli, Dr Krüger. As I said before, it was the air conditioning, so, room spray, and some women's perfume.'

Mats blinked once.

'The perfume? The man in seat 47 you alerted us to, he smelled like your daughter's perfume?'

Mats blinked twice.

'So it isn't that?'

Ah, shit. Mats felt like he was in some twisted game of blind man's bluff where all those hiding had to wear the blindfold instead of the one searching. And, what was worse, until the end of his now only very short life.

'I'll try again. The man smelled like perfume?'

A single blink.

'But not Nele's perfume?'

Again Mats affirmed it, and Dr Roth apparently resorted to thinking out loud.

'But we only exposed you to this one perfume. There was no other. If you're now telling me that you smelled a different woman's perfume, then...'

... you made a mistake and put the wrong one under my nose by accident. Nice job, Sherlock.

All of a sudden Mats felt infinitely weary, but it was a different weariness than the one he'd known before. It was all-encompassing, deeper, combined with an unspeakable sadness. He now realised that there was a completely logical explanation why he had such a real and nearly hallucinatory perception of his wife during his trance and it threatened to destroy whatever will to live he had left.

They'd triggered him using the wrong scent. He had no other info that could help Nele, whose death Dr Roth was most likely keeping a secret. So why was Roth still torturing him with more senseless questions?

'Was it the perfume of a person that you know?'

Of course it was!

'A person who's played a significant role in your life?'

Mats blinked once again.

'Kaja Claussen?'

No.

'Felicitas Heilmann?'

'Your wife...'

Mats now grasped that the police would never find the person who did it. But that meant little to him now. Everything on earth had been taken from him: his wife, his daughter, his own life. And nothing was ever going to bring any of it back to him.

'Was it your wife's perfume?'

Mats did Dr Roth this one last favour. After Mats blinked

once, the man sounded beside himself from excitement.

Yes. Katharina's favourite scent.

Mats heard Dr Roth ask someone else in the room a question, possibly a doctor or a nurse: 'Who did we get the perfume from? Who gave it to us?'

Then nothing existed again and no one but him alone, lost in the screaming silence of his thoughts.

73

Franz

He could have cried just seeing the satellite image on Google Maps. To be now standing at the very spot was an extremely sad experience of a whole different magnitude. Franz got nauseous just thinking of all the sorrow and misery this site had seen and experienced.

Franz was convinced that every serious injustice left behind a gravitational imprint in its surroundings. Here, in the decommissioned calf fattening plant in Liebenwalde, he threatened to break under the force of this imprint.

A factory of horrors, built to fatten small calves for the slaughter while, day after day, automated suction pumps robbed their mothers' inflamed udders of the milk intended for their children.

Though the suffering had ended here long ago, it still paralysed him, for he knew it was still being reproduced hundreds of thousands of times across Germany.

He shuffled across the desolate yard heading for the cold storage warehouse. He was still only able to make slow progress here in Liebenwalde. He had suddenly felt so wiped out after arriving yesterday that he'd just sat in the car for an hour and done nothing at all. He'd been so exhausted he even fell asleep for a few minutes – until the sound of a car driving away woke him up.

Luckily he'd unscrewed his licence plates. His taxi parked outside the barn could've caught the attention of that unsuspecting car that had driven by yesterday, since he was guessing that not too many people got lost around these parts.

If he'd had any idea how much trouble those nosy types back in Berlin would've brought him he damn well could've taken off long ago. First that security guard, then the doctor lady. But it didn't matter. He'd always had a plan B up his sleeve, after all, and now it finally seemed to be working.

Franz opened the aluminium door retrofitted to the former cold storage building and could already hear the screaming from here.

'Help! Help...'

Good thing there was no living soul for kilometres. The screaming fell silent as he stepped into the cold storage room, one of two massive steel walk-in refrigerators inside this building. Larger than a double garage and not working any more of course apart from the inside light that he kept on the whole time because he was scared the old neon tubes would never turn on again if he turned them off. As a precaution, he'd left the heavy door cracked open and held it there by a brick, worried it might shut airtight.

Franz set down his yellow plastic case and turned on the camera. Nele tried breaking free from her restraints at once.

'Where is she? Where did you take her?'

She was beside herself with rage and now full of energy. Completely different than yesterday when he'd pulled her out of the pit semiconscious with that hardware-store winch and carried her over here.

Franz had laid straw in the walk-in fridge and dragged in a metal bed frame without a mattress. On it lay the object of his demonstration, now bound to it with handcuffs. But only her left arm; she could move everything else freely. Franz didn't see the need for any other constraints as long he kept his distance from her.

'My baby! Where is she?'

Nele tried standing up taking the bed on her arm with her but wasn't able to move it an inch before dropping to her knees. In the white nightgown he'd pulled over her, barefoot and hair clotted with dirt, she looked like some hysterical mental patient.

'That's good. That's real good,' Franz said and, crying now, held the camera to the struggling mother. 'This is exactly what I'm talking about. See how it feels, Nele?'

'Where is she? Where is my child?' she screamed at him.

'This is the exact question every mammal asks when we rip their babies from them after birth. Every cow who's separated from her calf, all so that we can stuff ourselves full of cheese, chocolate, yogurt and everything else that makes us fat and sick.'

'YOU are the one who's sick,' she shouted so violently that her spit struck him.

He nodded. 'That is the exact pain that I need. Anyone who sees this will not be able to close their eyes to it. Here.'

Franz pushed the yellow plastic case over to her, using his foot.

'What's in there?'

'A breast pump.' Franz pointed at her chest. 'It's not an

electric one, unfortunately, but it will serve its purpose,' he said and wiped away more tears with his sleeve. *Oh, yes*, he certainly did understand her fear and her suffering and her sorrow, but sometimes you had to do what was wrong in order to bring about what was right. What revolution had ever been successful without a fight? What war concluded without violence?

'You know what's going to happen to you when they find you?' Nele said, crying now as well.

'They'll only find me when I want them to,' Franz replied and aimed the camera again.

In the process he sensed a slight draft on his sweaty neck. He turned around and all he heard was: 'Don't be so sure!'

Then a brick came hurtling down on him, its edge slamming into his forehead and splitting his skull.

74

Nele

Nele first saw Franz drop the camera and then collapse next to her, the blood streaming off him. He uttered no sound, not even a stifled groan as he struck the metal floor with his face without trying to break his fall whatsoever.

The splintering sound of his skull cracking and nose breaking reminded her of her most horrible moment down in the pit. It was that first time she was sure she was being rescued and the darkness above had brightened a little because someone had removed that wooden cover.

Someone who had destroyed all her hopes with a single phrase. 'Just die,' he said before covering over her dungeon again.

The exact same person who had now returned to betray her yet again.

'David,' Nele wanted to yell, the name of her ex-boyfriend, but her mouth couldn't get out much more than a broken whisper since the fear was cutting off all her air.

'Livio,' he corrected her, smiling. 'I'm now going by my real name again. Not in the mood for cheap tricks anymore. David Kupferfeld has fulfilled his duties.'

He tossed the brick down next to Franz dead on the floor, wiped the dirt off his gloves on his jeans, and looked around the cold storage walk-in.

'Why?' she screamed at him.

'You still don't know? You infected me, you slut.' He was trembling with rage, the veins of both temples throbbing. It wasn't enough for you to get knocked up with some brat by me. I now have to spend my life in that clinic in Wedding, just like you. HIV-positive. It's all your fault.'

Another bout of rage hit him. He grabbed Franz's body by the collar, hauled it up and pulled it towards Nele.

'So this was your big plan?' she said, stunned. She couldn't believe how easily he'd turned from a violence-prone stalker into an actual murderer. 'All because I infected you? All because you didn't want to support your baby?'

'Don't give me that.' He pulled Franz along another half metre or so. 'I had nothing to do with this lunatic, that's for sure. But he is a gift from God. Your just punishment.'

Saliva gathered in the corners of his mouth as he talked.

'When you kicked me out, all I wanted to do was piss you off somehow. So I distributed a few "presents" around your apartment.'

Nele remembered those razor blades between the cushions.

'But then, when I got my diagnosis, I wanted to flatten you just like those tyres I slashed.'

And as dead as that rat you left in that basket outside my door.

'But I didn't have any plan. In contrast to this nutjob here. Man, you really are good at being a pain in men's asses. Got no clue why he was so pissed at you, but I'm good with whatever it is he's doing to you here.'

'Why did you come back?'

'Because I was worried this psycho wouldn't be able to go through with it. And, lo and behold, it's just as I feared: here you are, still alive. Speaking of, where's Feli?'

'Who?'

He dropped the corpse about half a metre from Nele bound to the bed frame.

'Felicitas Heilmann. That doctor who was looking for you.'

'You leave her alone!'

'Says who? You?' Livio shook his head. 'Don't worry. I did my standard routine, reeling her in. The old "charming-scammer-awakens-protective-instincts" number works every time on you chicks.' He grinned filthily. 'But I wasn't looking to get into her pants. Just wanted her to lead me to you. And now I need for her to keep her trap shut. So where is she?'

Nele's stomach tightened up. All at once, she felt a deep sorrow inside her. The fact that she was so alone and abandoned and lost had never been made so clear to her.

'Do what you're gonna do with me, Livio. Hit me like you used to, you hothead piece of shit. I'm not going to betray the one person who helped me.'

'Helped you how?'

Livio picked up the brick he used to kill Franz. Nele started talking faster, horrified of sharing her kidnapper's fate.

'Franz hurt her really badly with an iron rod, but she was still able to help me with the delivery. There was some problem with the umbilical cord. Without her, I wouldn't have made it. Feli took care of me.'

Livio kept two arm's lengths away from her. The brick switched from one glove to the other.

'You didn't tell her about me, did you? She know who I am?'

No, dumbshit. You think we had time for a nice chat? Nele thought, furious, but she also knew what Livio was actually trying to find out – if Feli would somehow be able to testify that he had found Nele down in the hole and left her in the lurch.

That he was a murderer exploiting another person's crimes for his own goals.

So Nele lied. 'Yes. I told Feli everything about you. She knows who you are. If you kill me now, the police will know who it was, and you'll be sitting behind bars your whole life.'

Livio recoiled a second, then he roared with laughter. 'You're lying. I know you too well.'

Still snickering, he pulled Franz back up, grabbing him by his long hair this time, then held him under his arms and shoved him at Nele on the metal bed.

She was buried under the weight of her dead kidnapper. She writhed in disgust, shoved the lifeless body off the bed.

'You want it to look like it was Franz?' she screamed once she was free, now stained with the blood of her kidnapper. She wiped at her face like mad with her one free hand but only ended up smearing it all over. 'You seriously believe you'll get away with this? The father of the child is the first one they always suspect.'

Livio shook his head and pointed at the camera on the

floor. 'There's a video of the guy tormenting you. And there's not a single thing linking me and this nutjob.' He laughed again, cynically. 'Yes, I do think I'll get away with it.'

Livio threw the brick down next to Franz's corpse on the floor. Far enough from Nele that she couldn't get at it. But near enough to suggest to investigators that she'd killed her kidnapper in self-defence when he was careless enough to get too close to her.

The only question is, what's Livio going to do with me? Nele thought in panic. *Does he aim to kill me? Or simply leave me again?*

She glanced towards the door, and couldn't help but smile.

'Besides, I was extremely cooperative,' Livio said, though she was hardly listening to him now. 'Plus, you told your gynaecologist I was the father before we had broken up. Oh, I got a call today from a nurse at the Park Clinic. Your dad's lying in a coma there.'

'What?' He had her full attention again. 'What did you just say?'

'They're trying to communicate with him somehow and they asked me about your perfume.'

My father's lying in a coma?

'What happened?'

Livio didn't answer her, or had at least misunderstood the question, since all he said was: 'He's supposed to be dying. So I thought to myself, your old man definitely won't want to give up the ghost knowing about his slut daughter sick with AIDS. I told them it was Shangril, that gross scent you keep in your bathroom in memory of your mother. Remember that time you made me smell it? Like I cared what your mother smelled like alive. Anyway, in the end it was just too good. They don't make Shangril anymore, but I was courteous enough to tell them about a remainder shop in Friedrichshain.'

Nele closed her eyes. After all the pain she'd had to suffer over the last few hours, both physically and mentally, after all that had already strained and torn at her thoughts, the idea that her father was also about to die was now pushing her beyond the point of suffering.

'You made a big mistake,' was all she was able to say. Quietly, calmly, like someone having an awkward yet wholly civilised discussion.

'With the perfume?' Livio asked.

'No, with the brick.'

'I'm wearing gloves. There's no fingerprints on it.'

'That's not what I mean. Franz was using it as a doorstopper.'

She watched Livio look over at the exit. Saw how his eyes widened, how they nearly fell out of their sockets as he realised what she'd already realised a little while ago. The door to the cold storage walk-in had closed all the way. And locked shut in doing so.

Livio whipped around and reached the door in two quick strides and patted at the aluminium panel.

'You might as well spare the effort,' Nele said and bent down with all the strength she had left. Stretching her free arm towards the corpse.

Livio meanwhile searched in vain for some kind of handle or opener. But the door only had a keyhole.

'We're trapped. And it's in an airtight prison, sealed off,' Nele said, although she wasn't so sure. But after all the fear that she'd had to endure, it felt good to turn the tables and make Livio start panicking.

'No. Nooo. It can't be,' he shouted and kicked at the door like a madman.

Nele meanwhile found what she was after, and pulled her hand back out of Franz's anorak.

Right then Livio turned her way. She froze where she was.

'What you got there?' he said.

She clenched up the fingers of her tied-up hand.

'Is that a key?' her ex guessed, and she shook her head none too convincingly.

'All right, fine,' she said. 'The psycho had a key on him.'

Livio came at her laughing crazily, and Nele slid back away from him on the bed, as best as she could.

'Give it to me.'

Livio punched her in the stomach, bent down to her. She groaned, yet didn't give in. He tried bending back her clamped fingers, and she didn't last long with all his strength.

'What's this?' he asked in surprise as she finally showed him what was inside her palm.

'Chewing gum,' she said, telling the truth.

Franz had some in his jacket. Nele had grabbed it with her free right hand and switched it to her left.

'No key?' Livio said, pale with despair.

'Nope,' Nele said, exhausted, but ready for anything.

'No key, we're going to die in here together.'

Then Nele slashed half his eyeball and down his cheek and shredded his carotid artery, all using the carpet knife she'd also found in her kidnapper's pocket.

75

Dr Roth
Three hours later

It was his first time, and he was gravely worried that it would end in tragedy.

Although he'd been involved in solving many criminal cases, Roth had never visited a crime scene. Once he'd even flown with officers to the Côte d'Azur to help solve a case, but all he did was lead the police to a missing person and never got to inspect a crime scene. And nothing like a corpse, which he feared today.

'Both vehicles identified,' said Detective Hirsch next to him. 'The taxi at the barn is registered to Franz Uhlandt, our suspect. The Renault behind the water tank belongs to Livio Kress.'

They stood alongside the already searched and secured construction trailer in the muddy yard of a former calf fattening facility in Liebenwalde, waiting for the SWAT team to report in over the radio.

Three heavily armed officers in black gear had just disappeared inside a battered old clinker-brick building.

'Soyuz?' Hirsch asked the team leader over his walkie-talkie.

'Building secure,' the man answered promptly. 'Now opening the cold storage walk-ins.'

'Hats off to you. I wouldn't have predicted this,' Hirsch openly admitted to Roth. 'Looks like your hocus pocus did get us somewhere.'

He waved at Roth to follow him, and they walked up to the brick building.

'Hypnotherapy isn't hocus pocus,' Roth countered. 'If we hadn't used regression, the patient wouldn't have been able to remember any of the things that happened to him on the plane.'

'Right, right. I know that and I have a ton of respect for your work, doctor. Though, just between us, I do think it's a little weird when people start barking all at once or forget how to count like I've seen in those hypnosis shows. But, with a coma patient? Amazing.'

Roth rolled his eyes and sighed. They now stood at the entrance to the building with the walk-ins.

'Medical hypnosis has nothing to do with any carnival fakery. And Dr Krüger isn't lying in a coma. He's locked in, so awake, and very easily put into a trance by means of sounds and voices.'

Hirsch laughed. 'And in the process it occurred to him that we should be searching for his daughter here in the middle of nowhere?'

Roth followed him into a tiled outer room. He heard a cutting torch somewhere in the distance.

'He made it clear to us that we had tried to trigger him with a perfume that someone had mistakenly told us was his daughter's favourite scent. That someone was none other than Nele Krüger's ex-boyfriend, the probable father of her child—'

'... and we weren't sure why he told us the wrong perfume, so we tracked his mobile phone here to his car because he hadn't called us back; I know, I know, heard it already—' Hirsch grabbed Roth firmly but not unkindly by the arm, preventing him from proceeding any further for the moment. 'Look, I'm not going to fool you. I hate these kinds of ops. The chances don't ever look very good when—'

Hirsch's walkie-talkie crackled. The cutting torch was silent.

'Detective?'

They were so close they could hear the team leader in person as well as over the speaker.

'What?' Hirsch said and ran out of the outer area and around the corner.

Roth followed him and saw the three officers standing with their weapons lowered before the welded-open steel door to an enormous walk-in.

'Good God,' said Hirsch, the first to reach the site.

'How long did they have air in here?' asked one of the three SWAT team men, but no one answered.

'Don't touch anything,' Roth heard as he tried glancing past the men and inside the room.

All that he saw was red and blood. And red. And more blood.

The most awful sight was her face, smeared so glossily, as if Nele had dipped her head in a blood-filed bathtub and then lain herself down to rest forever with eyes closed.

Together with the other two corpses, one with a bashed-in skull, the other with its throat slit open, the three presented a still life of horror.

Roth retched, lost control of his stomach and probably would've thrown up if there hadn't been that flash. The white flash distracted him so much that he even forgot his nausea.

The white flash... of Nele's eyes.

'She's alive,' he heard someone say behind him, and it was only later, when he was finally inside the walk-in, when he'd been kneeling next to Nele and feeling for her faint pulse, all while several of the men screamed at him for contaminating the crime scene, that he became aware that it was he himself who kept repeating the two words.

'She's alive.'

Over and over again, until Nele opened her mouth too, unable to scream, so weak and half-asphyxiated after so many hours using up nearly all the oxygen inside this chamber. Yet Roth didn't even need to hear what she was saying. He could read it on her lips, and even if they hadn't been moving, he would've been able to read her thoughts. A mother could only have one single thought in this situation.

'Where is my baby?' she asked him, and somewhere, far, far away, in another world outside this chamber of horrors, an officer was shouting for Detective Hirsch and saying: 'Oh, God. Come on, get back here. You have to see this for yourself!'

76

Nele
Two days later

Winter had arrived. There could be no doubt about it. Up here in the former smoking room of Park Clinic, now used as a patient lounge, the harbingers were already clear to see. The floor-to-ceiling panorama windows of the main building's fifth floor offered a view far above the grounds of this facility that ten years ago had still been strictly a mental hospital but had now, under the guidance of its unconventional chief physician, grown into a comprehensive and highly renowned private hospital.

The oaks' and lindens' leaf-deprived branches bowed in the wind. The lawn that a week before the patients and their loved ones were still using for one last soak of the fall sun was now looking grey and hard. You could easily imagine it covered by the snow that would soon fall from the dirty grey blanket of clouds and release a constant drizzle.

Nele got a chill thinking about what it would've been like getting kidnapped in this crappy cold and wet weather.

She then got a chill thinking about all that she had been spared. Thanks to the woman who was sitting across from her in a wheelchair and warming her hands with a coffee. Two scoops of sugar, but no milk.

Neither one of them was going to be drinking milk anytime soon.

'You really doing okay?' Nele asked, and Feli nodded. Her head was still bandaged, no wonder considering the wounds she had thanks to Franz. The blow from the iron pipe hadn't been especially hard, according to the doctors, presumably not with any intention to kill, but it had still led to a severe concussion and a fracture on the top of the skull. When the police officers had found the doctor in that pit in the decommissioned meat plant, their first thought was that she was dead.

And Feli presumably would have died down there where Franz left her if Hirsch and his team hadn't discovered her just in time.

'Everyone's talking about what a marvel you are.' Nele smiled and grabbed Feli's hand. 'No regular midwife could've pulled off such a miracle with injuries like that.'

Feli smiled, and just like Nele's her gaze wandered over to the Maxi-Cosi car seat holding the little baby munching on its pacifier in peace. With big eyes opened a tiny crack, and a blissful angelic smile on its dozing face.

'Without you, we would've died down there.'

'You mean without your father,' Feli corrected her, gently.

In truth, both deserved the honour. Franz had frisked Feli and found a doctor's ID in her pocket. When she confirmed his question of whether she could act as Nele's midwife, he had lowered her down into the pit using the winch despite her severe head wound. Down there, among the filth, the stench and the tight confines, the doctor had performed a superhuman feat.

Feli attempted to play it down. 'All I did was try and remember that nursing internship I had in gynaecology.'

If she hadn't solved the problem of the umbilical cord with some bold handiwork, mother and child would've likely died together in agonising pain. And if her father hadn't solved the mystery involving Livio, they never would've identified their location using his phone signal. And never found the calf fattening facility in Liebenwalde.

'Have you decided on a name?' Feli asked, prying her eyes off the infant.

'Viktoria,' Nele said, and they both had to laugh.

'The goddess of victory,' Feli said. 'That fits.'

'Sure does.'

They had found Viktoria in a calf pen past another walk-in refrigerator. Somewhat chilly and thirsty, but alive and kicking and otherwise unscathed. Franz actually had, true to the logic of his madness, never wanted to kill the baby but only wanted to keep it separated from its mother. Whether Viktoria had suffered any long-lasting damage, and especially whether she'd got infected during her now quite dramatic and bloody birth from Nele, couldn't be determined at this time and would be clarified within six weeks at the earliest. But that was beside the point considering the fact that she had already survived what was guaranteed to be the hardest test of her life. HIV was not a death sentence any more. That Viktoria was alive was all that mattered now to Nele.

Again Nele thanked Feli. 'You're my hero.'

'I'm an idiot,' the doctor replied, but smiled. 'As a psychiatrist, I probably should've recognised that something wasn't right with Livio.'

Nele scrunched up her nose. 'Believe me, I'm the first to admit that a person can fall for his charms. Me, I even fell *in love* with his wild and reckless ways.'

'But you were never taught to recognise the narcissist behind the facade. I haven't been able to get over missing that.'

Feli pulled her phone from the dressing gown that all patients wore here in the clinic, and placed it on the table.

'Yesterday, after I could think again clearly for the first time, I called that pharmacist in your building. On my request, they went through all the surveillance videos again.'

'And?'

'On the same day of your kidnapping, when your father sent me to your home? He'd got inside your apartment.'

'Livio?' Nele was confused.

'Yes. You left the door open in your rush after your water broke, which was the way I got in too. He came in and looked around, and I must have surprised him.'

Feli showed Nele her left hand, and at first Nele wasn't sure what she meant. Feli explained: 'He heard me talking on the phone with Mats about your kidnapping. Once I was in the bathroom, he turned off the lights and smashed my fingers in the door so that he could take off. On the tape you can see him running out of your building right before me.'

'But, what was he doing at my place?'

Feli leaned forwards and placed her other arm on the table as well. They now held both of each other's hands.

'A narcissist can't get over rejection. He stalked you after your breakup, Nele. Later he probably wanted to exact revenge for being infected and for the baby, which he saw as an imposition. The police are assuming he was also responsible for slashing the tyres on your street. He only did the other ones so it wouldn't look so suspicious.'

Feli's revelation made Nele remember that razor blade between her cushions. *Your blood kills!* Livio had apparently placed them there right before she had the locks changed because of that scare with the rat basket.

Way too late.

Rats, car tyres, razor blades, revenge.

It all sounded logical. There was just one thing Nele couldn't figure out.

'How did the two of you end up searching for me together?'

Feli nodded. 'He cleverly manipulated me. Makes me so mad. I should've recognised it.'

The psychiatrist leaned back a little without letting go of Nele's hands. 'First, Livio hears in your apartment that you're being kidnapped. He wants to know more. He follows me to Klopstock and manages to reel me in using sleight of hand.'

'He stole your phone.'

'Exactly right. And then lets himself get caught like he's trying to sell it.'

Nele gently drew her fingers away and stood. 'Oh, man, I can see it exactly, how he set it all up. In the beginning I ran around after him like some love-crazed teen. And those sleight-of-hand tricks were how he made his living.'

Feli still looked sad. 'At the very latest, I should've become more suspicious when we were in that old dairy and split up. I checked the front basement area, he checked the back. When we finally parted ways upstairs, he looked at me in such a funny way. But I had just slipped while searching around and had got all dirty. I wasn't able to interpret that wariness in his eyes. Now I know that he was worried I'd realise he'd discovered you. And then he was suddenly in such a hurry to leave me alone there. Damn it. I shouldn't have called Mats – I should've called the police right away.'

'No, you did everything right.'

Nele sat down again and reached for Feli's hand. She touched the doctor's engagement ring in doing so. Silver filigree topped with a half carat.

'Do you have a new date?' Nele asked cautiously.

Feli blinked and looked towards the window. It was only 4 p.m. but already much dimmer, and the streetlamps in the park were starting to come on.

'Janek is the opposite of what I look for,' she said quietly. 'He is not wild, not chaotic, not unpredictable.'

She turned her head back to Nele. 'But the thing I've searched for my whole life, it keeps trying to wreck me.'

Nele swallowed and wiped an incipient tear from the corner of her eye with her index finger.

'You're telling me.' She gave Feli a sad smile. She too had always been on the hunt for a certain prey and it had only ever punished her. Livio wasn't the first who'd hit her – who'd needed to dominate. Though he was the first who'd wanted her dead and in the process had even, always the freeloader, tried to exploit the crimes of a certain fanatical animal rights activist.

The two women said nothing for a while, just holding

each other's hands and listening to the soft creaking of the patient fridge and the gurgle of the coffee maker next to the door.

Finally Nele mustered the courage and said: 'You know, my father always told me that falling in love happens automatically. You're powerless against this sudden, all-encompassing feeling that strikes you like lightning. "Falling in love is random," he always said. But, love itself...' Nele took a brief pause, in which the last of the park lights came on, bathing nature in a sulphurous yellow light. 'Love is a decision.'

Feli nodded, but Nele wasn't certain she was following.

'There's no partner that fits a person one hundred per cent. Maybe it's only seventy – or eighty. And there will always be people who fulfil their significant others twenty to thirty per cent. The question is: do you stick to your decision anyhow, or do you break it off with every new challenge and keep on looking?'

'You have a smart father,' Feli said, and Nele thought she saw her face darken a little. Maybe she was recalling the day that Mats had gone away.

'So?' Nele asked, stroking Feli's engagement ring again. 'What about Janek? Have you decided?'

Feli took a deep breath. 'He did. Janek still wants to marry me. Despite everything. But I...' She pulled her hand back. 'I have to think about it. I'm still not so sure.'

Feli reached for her coffee, which had surely gone cold in the meantime, and made a hand gesture like she was shooing a fly. 'But, there's something you need to do now.'

Nele felt a lump swelling in her throat and stood up, still a little unsteady on her legs. She had been lying too long.

Her muscles were flabby.

'You're right. I should hurry.'

She picked up her car seat with a sleeping Viktoria, thanked Feli once more for everything, then she left the visitor's lounge and started out on the hardest journey of her life.

Epilogue

Mats

While Mats fell down that missing hole into eternal nothingness, where black was the brightest of all colours, there remained only one thought he held onto. An observation, one that couldn't halt his plunge but might just impede his dizzying spin. And this thought was of a one-euro coin that kept landing on the very same side, again and again. Always on the side with the eagle, the one Mats had bet on. And it was ten nonillion times in a row. Ten thousand octillion.

A one with thirty-one zeros.

That was how slim the odds were that God did not exist.

God. Always the last hope of dying atheists, thought Mats.

But it was the mathematicians and natural scientists – and non-believing theologians – who'd drawn up the following calculation: the fact that the universe exists at all is mathematically as probable as the hypothetical case of a person tossing an unaltered, completely normal coin into the air ten nonillion times and this coin always falling invariably on the same side. Only one tiny deviation, a hundred thousandth of a second after the Big Bang, and the world would not exist. Not even that nothingness Mats was now falling through.

Meaning, the idea that there was a God behind it all was far more plausible scientifically than betting on that quintillion coincidence.

As Mats unsuccessfully attempted to visualise the number with thirty-one zeros, he heard a very quiet and familiar voice from far, far away. He couldn't understand what she was saying. But he could *see* the words. They formed a long, purple shimmering chain, a polar light that his mind could reach out to. Using the power of his thoughts, he held on tight to the chain and stopped his fall. At the same time the voice became louder, and Mats now believed he had finally found salvation. He thought he had died. He couldn't explain why he was hearing Nele otherwise. Her soft, beautiful voice, completely without hatred or reproach. So gentle and loving.

'Daddy, do you hear me?' she asked.

And he blinked, just like he'd learned from Dr Roth.

'I brought you something,' Nele said and then gave him a gift that illuminated his innermost darkness like a spotlight. It was a scent that drove out all that had dominated his being over the last days and hours: fear, spiritual pain, darkness. He was still inside the missing hole, but the scent brightened it with feelings he'd believed forgotten: hope, assurance, love.

'This is Viktoria,' Nele said, and he eagerly breathed in the baby scent of the little bundle of life that she must have placed upon his chest.

'I love you, Daddy,' he heard her say. 'Thank you for saving me.'

She cried, just as he cried inside, and he blinked without knowing how he could let her understand that he had been such an idiot, that he'd done everything wrong and never should've left her, but that now all was well because she and the baby were alive.

That's all that counts.

'I have something else for you,' he heard Nele say, still crying. Another octave sadder.

And then all truly was bright.

As if someone had pulled a mental curtain to the side and switched on a light.

Mats felt his tears well in his eyes, blinded by the light that he not only saw but felt too.

He blinked, but not like he had been doing when he'd attempted to control his eyelids with his mind without affecting his ability to see. He really was blinking. And he *could* see!

The missing hole did not exist anymore. He had his body back instead.

Mats, slowly adjusting to the light, took a look around. The sonorous, sleep-inducing sounds had already revealed it to him, but now he could see it with his own eyes: he was back on board the plane. Back in the Sky Suite.

He saw the cream-coloured leather chair, the windows with the blinds open, a daytime flight in brilliantly beautiful weather high above a blanket of cumulus clouds.

He removed the straw hat he wore on his head, and turned it in his hands. The very notion that he himself had been that sleeping man he'd seen in seat 47F during his trance, it made him smile.

The mind works in strange ways.

He slowly walked across the thick carpet, touching the precious wood covering the cabin walls.

He walked past the bathroom towards the bedroom, its door cracked halfway open. Warm, soft light streamed into the hallway from the slight opening.

The scent that had propelled him back on board grew more intense.

He opened the door.

'There you are,' said the most beautiful woman in the world. She lay on the bed and smiled at him as if he, the greatest love of her life, had been away far, far too long.

'Katharina?' Mats asked, fearing she could disappear again.

She nodded and patted the covers next to her.

'Come here.'

He sucked in air through his nose. Smelled his wife's perfume, which Nele must have brought him, and lay down next to her.

'I'm sorry,' he said and began to cry.

Katharina reached for his hand, rested her head against his and smiled. 'I know,' she said.

Then she looked up to him, and he neared her, cautiously, just as they had done with that very first kiss they had given each other in that dimly lit bar in Steglitz and knew that they were meant for each other. And the light grew brighter, and the aeroplane, the cabin walls, the bed and all around them dissolved until there was only the air and the blanket of clouds below them, until this too vanished, leaving only what truly counted.

Forever.

Comments and Acknowledgements

First let me make one thing clear before I get hate mail: I have nothing against vegans. Nothing could be further from the truth. I admire people who are capable of accomplishing what I myself can only manage one day a week. I too would like to completely forgo animal products, except I lack the willpower. I can even understand the motives driving Franz, whose depictions of the modern milk production process were unfortunately not made up in the least. Though of course I have no sympathy for the methods he uses in wanting to change the situation.

And let me anticipate another question, one I was often asked during my research: no, I don't suffer from a fear of flying. *Concerns about flying* might be a better way of putting it. I don't break out in a sweat upon take-off, but I can certainly imagine far more reasonable things than having myself launched thousands of metres above ground in a tube speeding over a thousand kilometres per hour through ice-cold air masses. Like Mats Krüger, I simply don't think that humans are made for it. And after landing I often wish I could just plop down on the tarmac cross-legged like an Native American and wait for my soul that

– unlike my body – wasn't able to keep up even remotely that fast.

Of course I know that more people die yearly from swallowing parts of ballpoint pens than in a whole decade of aeroplane crashes. Yet such sober statistics don't ever pacify me that easily, especially when I start considering just how many of those unlucky ballpoint pen victims might've been gnawing on their writing utensils during in-flight turbulence... but, whatever.

Even though I don't have to deal with panic attacks myself, I still sympathise with all those people whose hearts start racing well before we've left the tarmac. Such as the young woman who grabbed the hand of the man sitting next to her right before taking off from Munich for Berlin and said to the stranger: 'I don't know you, but would you please squeeze my hand? Before I start screaming.'

I managed to catch this conversation because I was sitting right on the other side of the very man the woman had chosen for emotional support. The poor guy was looking a little overwhelmed, so he tried defusing the situation with a joke. It started with: 'A Bavarian, a Swabian and a Berliner are sitting in a plane...' (It really did happen, I swear.)

I never did get to hear how the joke ended because the lady started to cry, and in that moment it must've become all too clear to her hand holder that it wasn't such a wise idea trying to tell an aeroplane joke to someone with aviophobia.

No, that was not the situation that gave birth to this novel. Unlike usual, I can't point to a concrete cause for why I took on the subject. At readings, people always ask me how I find my ideas. I always try explaining somehow, but the undeniable truth is: the ideas find me, and it's usually after I've started writing. I might discover the inspiration for a subject in real life. Yet my characters only start coming alive once I'm at the computer working. And I often feel less like the one creating their experiences than like an observer who's frequently just as surprised at how the story unfolds. Which is also why I don't have much choice in the stories I want to tell.

Sometimes I get emails asking: 'Sebastian, don't you ever want to write something besides thrillers?'

When every publisher rejected my first-ever manuscript on the grounds that a psychological thriller from Germany would have no chance on the market, I thought to myself: 'Well, look at that – what I was writing was a psychological thriller.'

I also found it pretty odd that psychological thrillers weren't something I read much back then. I'd never given much thought to the genre, preferring to just write the kind of story I myself would like to read – and was hoping that I wouldn't end up being the only one.

Recently I often get asked how long a book takes me and how I manage to write 'so much'.

In June of 2017, I posted a little about that on Facebook:

Each of my books is different. I don't write series or serials with recurring main characters but rather individual stories that are always self-contained. This increases the chances of not repeating myself and falling into the same pattern. But there is also the danger of disappointing readers who'd like to see a sequel in the style of such and such.

As a reader myself, I used to always think that the reason I didn't like a book from a certain author was because the person wrote too much. That the author didn't take enough time. Until I too became an author and had to learn something about myself: my impression of the writer's profession and their daily work was completely false.

I thought a thriller took years of mental groundwork, during which time it was best if I retreated to some lonely island and pondered, a lot, until I'd finally gathered together all those ideas for bringing the characters and plot to life. This may be a good formula for some of my fellow writers. For me, though, a story simply doesn't arise solely through contemplation. The ideas, twists and aha-moments come to me almost exclusively while writing. So I have to write to be creative.

This has always been the case. Yet earlier, at the beginning of my career, hardly anyone had noticed that I'd actually published four thrillers in just under two years (*Die Therapie*, *Das Amokspiel*, *Das Kind*, and *Der Seelenbrecher*).

Today I'm sometimes told that I should return to how I started and 'take more time'. The fact was I had to write far, far more obsessively back then because I still had a regular day job on the radio at the time and was only able to work on my ideas on weekends, on vacation and after work.

Today, all thanks to you, my readers, I have much more time and can concentrate exclusively on the writing for months. Unlike many of my colleagues, some of whom also publish every year despite working full-time as translators, teachers or in a bank. I highly admire this creative energy and discipline of theirs, which often spans many years.

I also had to learn that being an author is not a conventional job where I can set my own hours. By the same token, I can't just say to myself: 'Sebastian, today you're writing a comedy.' The idea finds the author and determines how it's executed, not the other way around.

It sounds esoteric, but many fellow writers have confirmed this to me. We authors often have no idea exactly where we get our ideas from. All we know is that there's something inside of us, an urge that forces us to stay at our desks.

Writing books isn't a made-to-order product but rather an act of self-realisation. I feel very fortunate to be able to sit down at my desk every day, just like a musician who has to play music every day and an athlete who has to get out on the field every day. And, yes, I admit it: I'm a little manic in this regard. When I'm 'in the zone', I write every day, including on my birthday and Christmas.

The formula 'more time = better book' is certainly not wrong when it comes to the care required for carrying out research and for revising the first draft. But, apart from the fact that I practically suffer from writer's block compared to the admirable output and range of some other authors (Markus Heitz, Martin Walser, Stephen King), there does exist evidence to the contrary. I recently had to wait over five years for a new book by one of my favourite thriller authors who'd previously published annually – and was left a bit disappointed.

By the way: I have to set my own deadlines apart from the publisher because otherwise I would never deliver. I'm never completely satisfied with any of my books, and if I hadn't had a deadline back in 2006 I'd still be sitting there today working away on my first one, *Die Therapie*

Roland Emmerich once said that a story was never finished. All you can do is let it go. Keeping that in mind, I hope to be able to send many more books your way, even if two books per year will probably remain the exception in future.

I can't promise that these thrillers will suit your taste or even compare to your favourite story so far. If they do, then it's more fluke than anything, because I'm trying not to repeat myself. (Which I just did, see above ☺).

What I can solemnly and faithfully promise you, though, is that each of my stories comes from the heart, and always with my great expectation that I'm reaching yours as well.

So I keep on writing, on until that point when someone breaks down the scenery, claps their hands and says: 'My dear Herr Fitzek, the experiment is now over. Over these last eleven years we've let you believe that you're a writer. How does it feel now to learn that the truth is you're just another patient at the Park Clinic?'

Until then, I'm always happy to receive your messages inside my cell, at the following address:

fitzek@sebastianfitzek.de

★ ★ ★

So, after thanking you, the most important people in an author's life, I'll now work through the rest before they get cranky with me again. From Droemer Knaur publishing house, they include: first, the boss of it all, Hans-Peter Übleis, and his wonderful team – Josef Röckl, Bernhard Fetsch, Steffen Haselbach, Katharina Ilgen, Monika Neudeck, Bettina Halstrick, Beate Riedel, Hanna Pfaffenwimmer, Sibylle Dietzel, Ellen Heidenreich, Daniela Meyer, Greta Frank and Helmut Henkensiefken. I have to mention Beate, Ellen, Daniela and Helmut in particular, since they've outdone themselves once again in marketing, production and cover design (in my opinion).

My editor Regine Weisbrod should be entitled to a stress allowance for her efforts on this manuscript because she actually does suffer from a fear of flying. It didn't stop her from meticulously breaking down each sentence like an Airbus during maintenance. The same for Carolin Graehl, my other invaluable editor. You two manage to keep me on course again and again, motivate me to fly higher, and save me from any crash landings.

Marc Haberland (a good friend of mine, who only let me mention his last name for the first time in *Seelenbrecher*) visited one of those aviophobia seminars talked about in this book because of his fear of flying. He provided me with so much interesting and useful info that I could barely process it all. For example there's the fact that most people's claustrophobic horror starts at boarding when they have to walk down that narrow tentacle-like airlock connecting the gate to the plane. (At which point things always get jammed up and you're asking yourself how many people can actually fit inside this people-silencer before it starts buckling.) This is the reason why some of these giant fingers have windows or are made entirely of Plexiglas.

Marc also gave me the tip that you should tighten all your muscles just before take-off. A conscious and controlled whole-body cramp apparently tricks the brain, which can't concentrate on several abnormal circumstances at the same time. A more sophisticated version of this trick called 'Jacobson's progressive muscle relaxation' is recommended for anxiety disorders in general. You might want to try it out when needed – it should definitely work better than an airline crash joke from the passenger next to you.

By the way, Marc's seminar ended with an incident that once again proves that life itself writes the most incredible and unlikely stories. On their graduation flight, the plane entered a state of such heavy turbulence that not only the seminar participants but even the most hard-boiled passengers began to scream. The pilot admitted afterwards that he'd rarely experienced anything that severe in his career. Marc said that his 'worst comes to worst' experience nevertheless prevented him from claiming the money-back guarantee. But he was probably the exception among seminar participants.

★ ★ ★

As always, I wasn't looking to write non-fiction. Yet many details that did make it into the novel are true. The issue of the safest versus the most unsafe seat on the plane is a matter of dispute, and a lot of research has been carried out, with the overwhelming assessment that the rear seats have the highest chances of survival. And yes, there was indeed a crash test in which the first seven rows were completely destroyed and seat 7A was ripped from the plane. Even the incredible incident involving Juliane Koepcke actually happened. Compulsory smartphone users like me are not particularly enthusiastic about the news that some airlines let you surf the net and make phone calls with your phones. That final oasis of peace is now gone. And, of course, psychological tests for crew and pilots have advanced beyond the discussion stage, along with more extensive testing.

Yet I also do not describe in any fully precise way how the main characters in this book could have actually caused a plane to crash, of course, just as I also define things vaguely on purpose when it comes to suicide methods. I want to entertain, not create instructions.

Speaking of research: unlike for my novel *Passenger 23*, where I had to spend months searching for a ship captain not afraid of appearing to speak ill of the cruise industry, I had no problem finding a knowledgeable adviser for this story. My old schoolfriend Marc Peus shared his experiences as a pilot with me and read all relevant passages. So if you're about to board a plane in Europe and a Captain Peus welcomes you, then you can relax and enjoy the flight, because this guy is the best! (Or you can head up to the front and hit him over the head with the book if you didn't like it. Then you'll be arrested, and I'll have one less critic!)

I would also like to thank Captain Frank Hellberg, the

managing director and owner of Air Service Berlin, who has advised me for *Amok*, *Abgeschnitten* and other books – and whom I forgot to invite to the *Noah* premiere as a reward. I apologised to him for that, regrettably, because it was only then that he even noticed. It won't happen again – my apology, that is.

I would like to thank my manager, Manuela Raschke, and would like to make an urgent request: Take a vacation for once! Everybody says you work way too much, Manu. And I really can do without your excellent, untiring and super-professional support for a while. Say, a day or two. Christmas and New Year's Eve. That's when your mother Barbara can step in, whom I shouldn't forget here any more than your husband Kalle. I'm thanking you for your help, but also for understanding that working with a psychological thriller author brings certain peculiarities along with it – which my wonderful PR agent Sabrina Rabow has unfortunately forbidden me to talk about. Seriously, though: Sabrina, you deserve my deepest thanks for your advice, your support and years of loyalty.

My list of indispensable people continues with my favourite mother-in-law Petra, who, like Jörn 'Stolli' Stollmann, Markus Meier and Thomas Zorbach, sees to such obsolete media as the internet while this cutting-edge early adopter is still using the fax machine.

I would like to thank my favourite Bavarian, Franz Xaver Riebel, who once again served as literary taste-tester. And my friends Arno Müller, Thomas Koschwitz, Jochen Trus,

Stephan Schmitter, Michael Treutler, Simon Jäger and Ender Thiele.

By mentioning the name of *this next man* I'm only making his life harder, since statistically speaking every other German has an idea for a novel. And Roman Hocke is the best man for finding a publisher, (hey, he even placed me...) supported at his literary agency AVA International by Claudia von Hornstein, Gudrun Strutzenberger, Cornelia Petersen-Laux, Lisa Blenninger and Markus Michalek.

Every now and then at a reading someone asks if they can take a photo with me. Usually there's a man standing in the background looking like someone just stole his schnitzel: this is my true friend and tour manager Christian Meyer from C&M Sicherheit, with whom I've been travelling so long that many people consider us to be an old couple. Which we are, by the way.

Dear Sabine, I hope I was able to incorporate all your medical notes. Along with my brother Clemens, my sister-in-law is one of my regular medical advisers. I wanted to thank both of them by giving them a cruise vacation. I then wrote *Passenger 23*, just in time for them to accept the gift.

Of course, as always, I would like to thank all the booksellers, librarians and their staff.
  The success of internet retailers can never be rolled back. And it would be highly cynical of me to condemn them, since I'm a beneficiary of them like many other authors. In fact, my career wouldn't have been possible without the

internet because my first book was not readily available on physical bookstore shelves back in 2006. And yet I urge you to support your local bookstore. There are countless reasons for this, such as the fact that desolate inner cities do no one any good. Let me mention just one more thing:

If you like an author so much that you want to meet him or her in person at a reading, where do you think this will happen? On the internet, or in a bookshop?

Please don't misunderstand – I do not believe in demonising large online merchants. You don't have to radically alter your shopping habits. You'll be doing your part simply by visiting, every so often, the spot where books feel most comfortable: next to their own fellow species on a well-organised shelf in the knowledgeable and accommodating local bookstore of your choice. But don't be alarmed if I also happen to be there.

Thank you for your time as always!
Lots of love, *auf Wiederlesen* ('till the next read')
Yours truly,
Sebastian Fitzek
Berlin, feels like April though it's already 6 July 2017

PS: The best and favourite one gets saved for last:

A reader recently asked me how my wife could sleep calmly next to 'someone like me'. The thing is, my wife's the one who watches *Hostel* or *Saw* for relaxation and who'll always nab first prize for the bloodiest costume in any Halloween contest in Berlin. Thank you, Sandra, for being both so unconventional and loving that you put up with me without resorting to weapons. Most of the time, anyway.

About the Author

SEBASTIAN FITZEK is one of Europe's most successful authors of psychological thrillers. His books have sold 12 million copies, been translated into more than thirty-six languages and are the basis for international cinema and theatre adaptations. Sebastian Fitzek was the first German author to be awarded the European Prize for Criminal Literature. He lives with his family in Berlin.

About the Translator

STEVE ANDERSON is a writer and translator. He writes novels, narrative non-fiction, short stories and screenplays, as well as translating from German to English. He lives in Portland, Oregon with his wife.